A HARVEST OF THORNS

"Through his broad, intelligent research and insightful writing, Addison prods the conscience, trumpeting justice while acknowledging that the cost of a globalized society is incalculably higher than the price of a T-shirt."

—*PUBLISHERS WEEKLY*, STARRED REVIEW

"The shocking prologue in Addison's latest starts the book off with a bang and sets the tone nicely. This should appeal to fans of meaty whodunit stories; it's also compelling, captivating, and moderately paced."

—RT *BOOK REVIEWS*

"This exposé of the underbelly of the international fashion industry is disturbing, moving, and thoroughly engrossing."

—PHILLIP MARGOLIN, *NEW YORK TIMES* BESTSELLING AUTHOR OF *VIOLENT CRIMES*

"This a poignant and engrossing description of the manner in which men and women from the poorest countries on the globe are pressed into working for slave wages to manufacture soft goods to be sold in the most affluent countries such as North America and Western Europe. Corban Addison will hold you spellbound with his elegant prose from his first word to his last. A statement he placed in the mouth of one of his leading characters could have been uttered by the author speaking of himself: 'He told me to go to law school to learn how the world works, and then to go into journalism to change it.'"

—WILBUR SMITH, BESTSELLING AUTHOR

"A must read book which uncovers what lies behind what we wear every single day. I promise that you will never be able to look at your clothes the same way again."

—LIVIA FIRTH, OXFAM GLOBAL AMBASSADOR, UN LEADER OF CHANGE, FOUNDER OF ECO AGE LTD.

THE TEARS OF DARK WATER

"Beautifully written, *The Tears of Dark Water* spins an intricate tale, involving hostage taking on the high seas. This novel has love, romance, guilt, and suspense all in one story. Corban Addison is a truly gifted storyteller, and *The Tears of Dark Water* will stay with you long after you've read the last page. *The Tears of Dark Water* is pure gold!"

—LIS WIEHL, FOX NEWS LEGAL ANALYST
AND *NEW YORK TIMES* BESTSELLING AUTHOR

"This is great storytelling. A riveting story of modern-day piracy, a clash of cultures [and] people's lives torn apart."

—BOOKSELLERS NEW ZEALAND

"Read [*The Tears of Dark Water*] for entertainment, and you will find yourself pondering the machinations of the world's largest democracy, and who really wields the power."

—*CAPE TIMES*, SOUTH AFRICA

A WALK ACROSS THE SUN

"Since my first novel was released over twenty years ago, I have been presented with many opportunities to endorse the works of other authors hoping to find a publisher. I have always declined, until now. Corban Addison has written a novel that is beautiful in its story and also important in its message. *A Walk Across the Sun* deserves a wide audience. And I strongly suspect that Mr. Addison will be heard from again and again."

—JOHN GRISHAM

"In his debut novel, lawyer Addison uncovers the labyrinthine underside of human trafficking in this dazzling transcontinental story about the power of conviction, the bonds of family, and the tenacity of love . . . The novel successfully explicates the magnitude of the human trafficking business, the complexities of international legalities, and the impact of the Internet's role in this horrifying underworld."

—*PUBLISHERS WEEKLY* ON *A
WALK ACROSS THE SUN*

THE GARDEN OF BURNING SAND

"A hauntingly good read. *The Garden of Burning Sand* is a powerful and moving novel . . . This one's an absolute must-read."

—*RT Book Reviews*, 4¹/₂ stars, Top Pick!

"In dealing bluntly with crucial issues such as rape, AIDS, superstition, and poverty, [Addison] effectively touches the consciousness of his readers."

—*Booklist* on *The Garden of Burning Sand* (Stephanie Zvirin)

A HARVEST OF THORNS

A NOVEL

CORBAN ADDISON

THOMAS NELSON
Since 1798

© 2017 by Regulus Books, LLC.

All rights reserved. No portion of this book may be reproduced, stored in a retrieval system, or transmitted in any form or by any means—electronic, mechanical, photocopy, recording, scanning, or other—except for brief quotations in critical reviews or articles, without the prior written permission of the publisher.

Published in Nashville, Tennessee, by Thomas Nelson. Thomas Nelson is a registered trademark of HarperCollins Christian Publishing, Inc.

Published in association with Creative Trust Literary Group (www.creativetrust.com) and Baror International (www.barorint.com).

Interior design: Mallory Collins

Thomas Nelson titles may be purchased in bulk for educational, business, fund-raising, or sales promotional use. For information, please e-mail SpecialMarkets@ThomasNelson.com.

Publisher's Note: This novel is a work of fiction. Names, characters, places, and incidents are either products of the author's imagination or used fictitiously. All characters are fictional, and any similarity to people living or dead is purely coincidental.

ISBN: 978-0-7180-4229-5 (trade paper)

Library of Congress Cataloging-in-Publication Data

Names: Addison, Corban, 1979- author.
Title: A harvest of thorns: a novel / Corban Addison.
Description: Nashville, Tennessee: Thomas Nelson, [2016]
Identifiers: LCCN 2016027881 | ISBN 9780718042387 (hard cover: alk. paper)
Subjects: LCSH: Secrets--Fiction. | Journalists--Fiction.
Classification: LCC PS3601.D465 H37 2016 | DDC 813/.6--dc23 LC record available at https://lccn.loc.gov/2016027881

Printed in the United States of America

17 18 19 20 21 LSC 5 4 3 2 1

For the women of Tazreen,
whose stories will never leave me.

On behalf of a forgetful world,
let me say I am sorry.

What is done in our name must not remain invisible to us.
We are responsible for all the workers who make our goods.
—Yvon Chouinard, Founder of Patagonia, Inc.

Bangladesh

November 2013

MILLENNIUM FASHIONS FACTORY

DHAKA, BANGLADESH

NOVEMBER 4, 2013

8:53 P.M.

The sparks danced like fireflies in the semidarkness of the storeroom. They emerged from the wall outlet in a shower of white-gold radiance, casting a flickering glow across the concrete slab beneath them. The sounds they made, the snapping and crackling of suddenly electrified air, were drowned out by the rattling of three generators across the room, whose whirling magnetic coils were straining to satisfy the demand of hundreds of lightbulbs and ceiling fans and sewing machines on the floors above.

The cause was elementary, as the investigators from Dhaka would later discover—an aging circuit, copper wire exposed through melted sheathing, a worn-out breaker box, a peak load the factory's designers had never anticipated, and the gentle, inexorable persuasion of time. A short, the investigators would say. A common fault in a building so poorly maintained.

But what happened next was far from commonplace. The fire that started to burn in sacks of cotton jute—the leftover cuttings of T-shirts, sweatpants, and children's apparel destined for Chittagong piers and American closets—would sweep farther and faster than any fire before it.

This fire would ignite the world.

MILLENNIUM FASHIONS FACTORY

FIVE FLOORS ABOVE

Nasima's hands moved swiftly over the fabric before her, wasting neither motion nor strength. Her fingers joined textured labels to stretchy waistbands and fed them through her plain machine with a pianist's precision, her foot caressing the pedal in time—on, stitch, off, rest, on, stitch, off, rest. After she completed each piece, she swept it aside for a helper to deliver to packaging, then took another set of pants and Piccola labels from the hands of her fourteen-year-old sister, Sonia.

Nasima and Sonia were the fastest finishing team at Millennium, a relentless symbiosis of diligence and productivity. They communicated with looks and gestures, seldom with words. Their bond was a matter of blood and history. At the age of ten, Nasima had attended Sonia's birth. She had been the first in her family to witness the crowning of Sonia's head, the first to look into her sister's dark eyes, brown as river-fed soil. She had bathed Sonia, and changed her, and soothed her, and raised her like a surrogate, not because their mother, Joya, lacked devotion, but because she had four rowdy sons and a job on the sewing line that sequestered her from dawn to dark every day but Friday.

The Hassan family had come to Dhaka from Kalma, their native village, when Nasima was a toddler, after the great cyclone of 1991 washed away their fields and reshaped the land beneath their feet. The bustling city had offered them refuge and the chance of employment in garment factories springing up everywhere in the suburbs, fueled by the frenzy of globalization. Joya had started at Millennium as a helper, but with training, determination, and patience, she had worked her way up to sample sewing operator in the pattern room—a specialist in charge of translating designs conveyed by the clothing brands into samples that won contracts and set the standard for everyone else.

Nasima had followed her mother into the factory as soon as Sonia was old enough to attend school. Sonia had joined them when she was thirteen, though her employment documents recorded her age as fifteen, the legal minimum in Bangladesh. The hours were brutal, the influx of overseas orders relentless, and the wages subsistence level and often paid late. But it was honest work, steady work, and with three of them collecting paychecks, the money had multiplied, allowing the boys to stay in school. It was Joya's hope—and Ashik's, her rickshaw-driving husband—that their eldest son would be the first in the family to attend college. Nasima's dream was simpler. She wanted to get married and have children of her own.

"*Ēṭā ki?*" Sonia asked in Bengali. "What is that?"

The question caught Nasima off guard. She pulled her fingers back from the plunging needle just in time. "What is what?"

Then Nasima heard it—the sound of shouting carrying over the clatter of machines and the whirring of fans. She looked around to see if anyone else had noticed. There were two hundred sewing stations in the cavernous room, four lines of fifty, each with an operator and a helper, along with ten supervisors and four line chiefs. Most of the workers were on task. A few, however, were glancing about with concern.

"Get back to work," barked her supervisor. "No delays. The order must go out tonight."

Nasima gave her sister a reassuring look and slid another waistband and label into the machine. The pants were bright red and sized to fit a girl about six years old. How much would the child's parents pay in America? Five dollars? Ten? Fifteen? It was a guessing game she sometimes played to break the monotony. The fabric was nice. Twelve, she guessed. At her current wage of forty-two cents an hour, Nasima had to work four days to earn such a sum, but she felt no bitterness. Nor did she wonder—as she had when she was younger—how Americans could afford such luxuries. The West had grown rich, while much of the world remained poor. The ways of Allah were mysterious. It was not for her to question them.

Minutes passed. Piece after piece went through the machine. Nasima fought to maintain concentration, but the distant shouting did not subside. More operators looked up from their work, searching for an explanation. Supervisors began to stomp about, chastising the laggards for their indolence, but the ranks of the curious swelled. Finally, the line chiefs intervened. They marched brusquely up and down the lines, issuing orders and threats. Nasima hunched over her machine and picked up her pace. The supervisors were harmless. They had no power to hire or fire. The line chiefs, however, could dismiss workers at whim.

Then came the first explosion.

Nasima heard it and felt it simultaneously—a rumbling like thunder rising from deep inside the building. The floor trembled. The walls shuddered. The lights flickered and swayed. Workers cried out as the sound reached a throaty pitch and then died away. The fire alarm began to ring. Nasima sat transfixed, clutching the pants she had just finished. In a glance she saw Sonia's fright and the fright of the workers around her. She turned toward the nearest line chief and saw him shouting into a radio. The worry in his eyes convinced her to move.

She stood up and took her sister's hand, walking briskly toward the central stairwell—the only way out of the factory. Her supervisor shouted at her to sit down, but she ignored him. Other workers left their stations, stepping over piles of fabric in their quest for the exit. They made it halfway to the stairs before one of the line chiefs placed his body in front of the door. He waved his arms wildly and yelled over the bleating of the alarm.

"Go back to your stations! Your work is not done! If you leave, you will be fired!"

Nasima hesitated, as did the rest of the workers. The crowd stewed about in confusion.

"Why is the alarm still going off?" a male sewing operator shouted.

"A generator malfunctioned!" the line chief yelled. "It is a mistake! Go back to your—"

He was interrupted by the second explosion. It was louder and more violent than the first and rocked the factory to its foundations. As the building quaked, Nasima's stomach twisted with dread. She pulled Sonia toward her, certain the factory was about to collapse. But the floor did not give way. Instead, the lights went out.

The workers began to scream. A great wave of bodies pressed against Nasima and Sonia, jostling them toward the now invisible door. Hands shoved. Elbows flew. One collided with Nasima's forehead. Stars swam in her vision. She clutched Sonia's hand and dragged her away from the crowd. It was there that she caught her first whiff of smoke. It was pungent, revolting. She coughed and turned back toward the stairwell. As her eyes adjusted to the dimness, she saw a mass of moving shadows and heard hysterical shouts.

"Open the door!"

"Get out of the way!"

At last, Nasima saw a wedge of rose-gray light along the doorframe. The crowd swarmed toward the opening, and Nasima and Sonia followed. For a few beats in time they made progress. Then the crowd stopped. The workers at the rear shouted in anger and dismay.

"*Go! Move! Get to the door!*"

Suddenly, a new kind of scream erupted from the crowd. It was more like a shriek, really, a crystalline expression of terror. The shrieks coalesced around a single word.

"*Fire!*"

The workers backed away from the door, then pirouetted and began to stampede. Nasima yanked Sonia out of their path, her mind spinning. The factory had no fire escape. The only extinguishers were on the first and second floors. The stairwell was blocked. In a moment of terrible clarity, she knew the windows were their only hope.

She pulled Sonia toward the outer wall of the room, covering her mouth to ward off the acrid smoke. The windows were not glassed in, but they were enclosed by iron bars and webbed netting—the owner's attempt to prevent workers from stealing clothing by throwing it down to friends on the ground. The only way out was to sever the netting and dislodge the bars.

Sonia began to cough. Nasima pulled her into a crouch and told her to cover her mouth with her arm. It was then that she remembered the pants in her hands. "Use this as a mask!" she cried, pulling Sonia's head toward her. She placed the crotch of the pants over her sister's nose and mouth and cinched the legs behind her head. "Lie down!" she ordered. "The air is better!"

Nasima glanced toward the stairwell and saw an orange glow beneath the door. She covered her mouth with her headscarf and peeked over the windowsill toward the cinderblock dwellings where her family and most of the workers lived. On evenings when the neighborhood had power, lamps illumined windows and bulbs lit footpaths. But the power was out. All light had vanished from the night.

Her eyes began to burn from the smoke. She coughed once, twice, then dropped to her knees, retching until her chest ached. At last, the paroxysm passed. She lay down beside Sonia, struggling to make out the contours of her sister's face.

"I'm afraid," Sonia said, her voice barely audible above the chaos of screams and pulsing of the alarm. "What are we going to do?"

Before Nasima could respond, someone kicked her in the head. She cried out in pain, but the man made no attempt to apologize. Instead, he yelled, "The bars are not secure! Help me!"

In the shadows behind him, Nasima saw the outline of a table. She ordered Sonia not move and rolled into a sitting position, breathing through the fabric of her scarf. She blinked her eyes rapidly, disregarding the sting of smoke, and took hold of a table leg. She helped the man pull the table toward the window. When it was flush with the sill, he climbed onto it, drew a knife from his pocket, and attacked the netting with all of his strength.

Nasima lay down again and placed a hand on Sonia's shoulder. "It's going to be okay," she said despite the doubt in her gut. "The fire service is coming."

Even as she spoke, Nasima knew it was a false hope. The closest fire station was half an hour away, and the lanes around the factory were too narrow for large trucks. The firefighters would find a way to get their hoses through. But they would almost certainly be too late.

By the time the netting fell to the ground, the temperature in the room had passed the point of discomfort. Sweat coated Nasima's skin, and her backside prickled from the heat. For the first time since the explosions, she thought of her mother two floors below them. Was she still alive? She *had* to be alive.

Suddenly, she saw the man's face in front of her. "Help me lift the table!" he shouted. "We need to dislodge the bars!"

Nasima blinked away burning tears. Behind the man stood a cluster of human shadows. They helped her to her feet, and together they picked up the table and threw it against the bars. The iron groaned, and mortar fell away into the night.

"Again!" the man commanded.

On the second try, all but one of the bars came loose. The man levered himself onto the windowsill and wrested iron from crumbling mortar, tossing it into the dark. He turned toward them for an instant, but Nasima couldn't see his face.

Then he jumped.

Nasima stared at the empty window in shock. It was not as if the thought had never occurred to her, but the sheer brutality of watching it happen shook her to the core. Five floors. Sixty feet to the ground. A fall like that was suicide.

But the man was not alone. Two women climbed onto the sill and leapt into the abyss.

Madness! Nasima thought, glancing at Sonia. There had to be another way.

She looked into the smoke-filled gloom of the factory. There were hundreds of unfinished pants at the sewing stations. If she could make a rope long enough to halve the distance to the ground, she and Sonia could survive the drop.

She crouched beside her sister and asked, "Are you okay?"

Sonia coughed once, then nodded.

"Stay here. I'll just be a minute."

Nasima crawled slowly across the floor, keeping her mouth low to the ground. When she reached the nearest sewing line, she gathered an armful of pants and returned to the window. She tied legs together one by one, tugging at them fiercely until she detected no slippage. She didn't know if the pants could bear the weight of a body, but she knew her knots would hold.

While she worked, more workers jumped from windows all around. She heard their screams as they faded into silence. She felt the waves of heat coming from the stairwell. Smoke billowed around her, choking her with stench and soot. Her lungs burned and her eyes ran with tears. Still, she pressed on.

Five pants became eight, then twelve. By the time she reached fifteen, she could no longer keep her eyes open. Her mind was slipping gears. She wanted nothing more than to sleep. But something in her resisted. Something made her rise up one last time.

She nudged Sonia. "Come, *Khamjana*," she said, using her sister's nickname—hummingbird. "It's time for us to go."

She helped Sonia to her feet and held her protectively. At the age of fourteen, Sonia still had the diminutive build of a preadolescent girl. She had been born six weeks prematurely, and her growth had never caught up with her peers. In the schoolyard and among her brothers, her slight stature had brought her much shame. Now, though, it was a gift.

They stood before the window, the night beckoning from beyond. Those who would jump had already jumped. The rest were shadows on the floor, some groaning, others still. Nasima looped the makeshift rope around a table leg and tied it securely. Then she threw the remainder out the window. She placed her forehead against her sister's and spoke words that belied her fear.

"You can do this. You must climb down and then drop to the ground. The rope will hold, but you must be quick. There is no time to waste."

"It's too far," Sonia replied weakly. "I can't."

Nasima looked into the dark wells of her sister's eyes and her heart began to break. It came to her that she might never see Sonia again. "You *can*," she said emphatically. "You *must*." She forced the rope into Sonia's hands and nudged her toward the window. "Go now."

Sonia hesitated a moment longer, then swung her legs over the sill, one after the other. She clutched the rope tightly and began to slide down.

Nasima leaned over the sill, willing the rope to hold. In the darkness, she could see only the crown of Sonia's head. *It's like the day of her birth*, she thought. *Please, God, let her live.*

In the seconds that followed, Nasima banished from her mind the death throes of the factory—the moans of asphyxiating workers, the numbing ring of the alarm, the roaring of the inferno. She heard only the sound of Sonia's toes scuffing the wall as she descended.

Scrape . . . Scratch . . . Scratch . . . Scrape.

"Keep going," Nasima urged, fighting for breath. "You're almost there."

Then, in a terrifying instant, the rope gave way.

Nasima cried out in horror. She stared into the void and shouted Sonia's name, but no reply came. She sank to the floor, her grief a blade buried to the hilt at the center of her heart. She sat paralyzed for uncounted seconds.

Then she opened her eyes and saw the flames.

The fire was no longer in the stairwell. It had spread to the floor. Scattered fabric went up like tinder. Oxygen raced in through open windows and fanned the flames until they rose up to the ceiling. The heat was unbearable. It was impossible to breathe. Nasima turned back toward the window, her twenty-four years of life resolving in a single thought—a quote from the Quran.

"*Kullu nafsin zaikatul maut.*" "Every soul shall taste death."

She climbed onto the windowsill, the blaze at her back. The choice before her was simple. If she stayed, she would burn, and her family would have nothing to bury. If she jumped, she would die, but her father and brothers would find her and put her to rest with Sonia. She mouthed a prayer, asking Allah to welcome her on the Day of Judgment.

Then she stepped off the ledge.

PART ONE

Cameron

November 2013

CHAPTER ONE

The desk was a statement of pride, a great slab of black walnut from the Berkshire Hills of Cameron's native Massachusetts, ten feet wide and four feet deep and burnished to a red-brown shine. Upon it stood the usual accoutrements of a corporate executive: a widescreen iMac, a stainless steel desk lamp, a multiline phone, a container for writing implements—and a few more personal pieces: a baseball signed by the Boston Red Sox after the 2004 World Series, a Montegrappa fountain pen, and a glass globe his wife, Olivia, had bought in Prague. The rest of the vast surface was uncluttered, like the office that surrounded it, its only other furnishings a leather executive chair, a walnut file cabinet, a laser printer and scanner, and a pair of colonial-era wingback chairs arranged on the far side of the desk.

Cameron stood beside the floor-to-ceiling window, eating salad from a bowl before the draft minutes from a recent board meeting called him back to work. His office, located on the top floor of Presto's global headquarters, was a perquisite of his position as senior vice president and general counsel. It was also a gift from Vance Lawson, the company's CEO and Cameron's best friend. Steps away from Vance's corner suite, Cameron's office faced east across the Potomac and overlooked the most famous skyline in DC—the Lincoln Memorial, the Washington Monument, and Capitol Hill. In the evening when the building was quiet and Cameron was working late, the otherworldly glow of the monuments offered him a measure of solace. But in the forge of the workday, with two hundred fifty in-house lawyers to manage, five board committees and a dozen senior executives to advise, the view was just part of the background.

He turned his head and saw a ghost of himself in the glass—the arrow-shaped nose and sturdy chin, the moustache and thoughtful eyes, as dark as his ebony complexion. He was the only African American in the C-suite and one of only eleven black executives in the building, despite the diversity initiative Vance had instituted in his first week as CEO. But Cameron had never allowed his minority status—or the occasional discomfort it engendered—to affect his performance. He had grown up in a world of white privilege and learned early on to master its rules of success. While his skin was one of the first things people noticed, it wasn't what they remembered. They remembered his eyes and his mind, the sterling clarity of his judgment.

"Cam, will you come in here, please?" It was Vance on the speakerphone, his voice uncharacteristically grave. "We've got a problem."

Cameron put down his lunch and walked next door, tossing a wave to Eve, Vance's secretary, before entering the CEO's office through double doors. The corner suite was twice the size of Cameron's office and was laid out like a drawing room with artwork on the walls, two sitting areas, a wet bar and liquor cabinet, and an array of flat-screen televisions. The desk was almost an afterthought. Vance preferred to work standing up, conferencing with his team, or on the couch, documents spread out on the coffee table. It was the way he had been when Cameron met him at Harvard Business School, the way he had been for thirty years.

"What's going on?" Cameron asked, taken aback by the distress on Vance's face.

His friend was standing in front of the televisions, his lake-blue eyes moving from one screen to the next. There were four TVs, each tuned to a different news station. Ordinarily, their coverage was diverse, but occasionally, when a story was big enough, they became a refracting chamber, drawing light from a single source, as they were doing now.

The source was a burning building.

"It's a factory in Dhaka," Vance said as CNN zoomed in on flames shooting out of an upper-story window. "They'll show it again . . . There." He stabbed a finger at the screen. "I don't know who took it, but it's going to go viral. The whole world is going to see it."

In the frame was a photograph of a young Bangladeshi girl lying in the dirt, one arm splayed out at her side. The factory was behind her, engulfed in flame. There was blood on her forehead and a mask over her face. No, not a mask—a pair of child's pants. Cameron looked closer. The pants had a silver label. The photographer had caught it cleanly. At the center of the label was the letter *P*. It was the logo of Piccola—one of Presto's apparel brands.

Cameron's jaw fell in silent alarm. After three decades of dueling and deal making in the Beltway swamp, he had developed the carapace of a crocodile and a monk's sense of poise. The picture, however, left him wordless, thought-deprived. But only for a moment. Then the poise returned, along with the instinct for self-preservation.

The iPhone was in his pocket—his digital leash. He called Presto's senior vice president of communications. "Kristin, we need you in Vance's office. Now."

"Coming," she replied.

His next call went to the legal department, compliance section. "Declan, there's been an incident at an apparel factory in Bangladesh. I need you to find out if it's one of ours." Cameron saw the words at the bottom of the BBC feed. "It's called Millennium Fashions."

When Declan came back with the answer, Cameron spoke to Vance. "The factory is on our Red List. We deauthorized it six months ago because of safety concerns."

Vance's eyes flashed. "Then what the hell are our pants doing on that girl's face?"

"I don't know," Cameron replied, struggling to remain calm.

A moment later, Kristin Raymond appeared at their side. Sharp, sassy, and supremely qualified, she had a master's degree in communications from Columbia and an extensive résumé in both network and cable news. Cameron briefed her in three sentences.

"We need to get out ahead of this," she said. She took out her phone and called her secretary. "Leslie, assemble the critical incident team in the fourteenth-floor conference room. Put all calls through to my mobile. No one talks to anyone on the outside except me." She hung up and turned to Vance. "We need a company-wide lockdown. All information needs to go through my team. Cam can draft the e-mail, but it should come from your account."

"I'm already typing," Cameron said, his thumbs flying across his iPhone's touch screen. "Short and sweet. Circle the wagons. No breaches." He read the message out loud for them to hear, then hit Send. "I copied Eve."

"We'll get it done," Vance said, walking toward the door. "Kristin, keep me posted."

Cameron turned back to the televisions, acid churning in his stomach. It was a nightmare scenario. Only three days ago, Presto had released an abysmal third-quarter earnings statement—eleven points below estimate. The spring and summer buying seasons had been soft. Store traffic was anemic, and online had barely seen a bump. Analysts were speculating about Presto's viability. And Class-A shareholders who had never been denied a dividend were wetting their pants. To appease investors and pundits alike, Presto needed a near miraculous fourth-quarter rebound. Ads were already running across the country fueling the holiday frenzy. Black Friday promotions would be historic. On Vance's orders, Presto had bet the house on the compulsive spending of festive consumers. If they didn't contain the damage from the fire quickly, heads would start to roll, and those in the C-suite would be first in line.

"I'm heading downstairs," Kristin said. "I'll start drafting an investor memo, but I don't think we should put out a statement until we see how bad this is going to get. It's still nighttime over there. We have no idea what we're going to see when the sun rises."

"Stay positive," Cam said, feeling just the opposite.

"I'll get out my ruby slippers," Kristin quipped, breezing out of the room.

Vance returned a moment later and wandered over to the window. Cameron followed him, knowing he would speak when he was ready. Outside, the November day was golden, the forests on Theodore Roosevelt Island flecked with color.

"This could eviscerate our market cap," Vance said, his voice whisper-quiet. "Our customers could bolt. God knows how many options they have."

"We shouldn't overreact," Cameron countered softly. "We have a solid foundation, and consumers have a short memory. If it comes to it, we can do what BP did—hire a PR firm and do a glossy ad campaign. 'People First.' It's always been the core of our business."

"It's a good idea," Vance said. "But it's not enough. I want answers from Bangladesh." He took a ponderous breath. "That girl is Annalee's age."

Cameron nodded, understanding. Gifted with limitless advantage, a magnetic charisma, and an indefatigable will, Vance had only failed at one thing—family. He was an inveterate philanderer. His exploits were Solomonic. Not even Cameron knew the whole of it, but it was his job—first as Vance's attorney, now as his general counsel—to keep the women distant and quiet.

Vance had only been married once, an ill-fated experiment with a French super-model that had imploded after two years. But the union had produced a child, Annalee, now thirteen and living with her mother in Paris. She was the love of Vance's life, and also his greatest wound.

"I want this to be top priority," Vance said. "Bring the Risk Committee up to speed, but don't involve the full board. When the time comes, we'll go to them together. Paper the file. Make this about liability and keep it confidential. I want to know how this happened. And I want to know what we can do to prevent it from happening again."

Cameron took a long, slow breath. "I'd like to know that too. But there's a risk to asking questions. We don't know what we're going to find."

"It doesn't matter," Vance said with a shake of his head. "You've said it more times than I can count—integrity is essential to performance. Someone needs to take responsibility for this."

Cameron stood in silence, vaguely disquieted by the exchange. In the corner office, there were moments when deliberation was more valuable than decisiveness. For Vance, however, patience had never been a virtue. Eventually Cameron asked, "What's the time frame?"

"Whatever it takes. The same goes for resources."

Despite his reservations, Cameron gave his friend a cautious smile. "Consider it done."

CHAPTER TWO

The story of Presto was a legend in American business. Like Romulus and Remus, the myth had its twins—the husband-and-wife team of Hank and Dee Dee Carter—and a birthplace in the Roman countryside. On a visit to Italy in 1962, the Carters had discovered that commerce in the villages was both communal and centralized. Shops were arranged around piazzas where friends met and musicians played. It was shopping made easy. Everything in one place. But the dance of buying and selling was more than materialistic. It was organic, personal, and enjoyable.

Upon their return to the United States, the Carters had a conversation that reshaped the world of retail—or so went the legend. Hank was an entrepreneur with half a dozen variety stores in his portfolio. At fifty-five, he was ready for a new challenge. Dee Dee, too, was in transition, her children all married and starting lives of their own. Over pasta—could it have been anything else?—the couple charted a new course. They would bring Italy to America in a novel kind of store, an "omnishop," as Hank christened it. Its departments would be organized around a plaza that, while enclosed by a roof, would feature greenery, benches, and sunlight. They would call it Presto, after the Italian word and the magician's invocation. But their motto was quintessentially American: "Everything you need at the snap of your fingers."

In an era of profound social transformation, when department stores were old news but shopping malls were still on the horizon, Americans greeted the first Presto omnishop—opened in Fairfax, Virginia, in 1963—as a vision of the future. They flocked to its resplendent displays and kaleidoscopic wares and lingered to eat ice cream in the plaza. In 1965, Hank opened three more stores. When they succeeded wildly, he became more ambitious. Over the next ten years, he launched thirty-eight stores in twelve states. By the time he died in 1984, Presto had grown to one hundred stores in thirty-two states. But it was still a family-owned enterprise with only two shareholders—Hank and Dee Dee. They had resisted the gilded promise of Wall Street because they had no interest in building a corporation. They cared about community. Their goal was to give Americans access to quality goods at an affordable price, and to donate a portion of their earnings to charity. "Invest in people," Hank often said, "and people will return the favor."

It was all in the company handbook, hand-delivered to new hires on their first day. Cameron had received his from Vance, along with a flippant "Read this. Inspiring stuff." In truth, it was more hagiography than history. Hank Carter was not a saint. He had driven countless Main Street retailers out of business. But this much was true: Hank never wanted his company to become the behemoth his son, Bobby, created after his death—with two thousand five hundred stores across America, three hundred fifty thousand employees in thirty-three countries, and annual revenues over one hundred billion dollars.

Cameron opened the black file folder on his desk and slid the memo he had just written into it. Beneath the memo were e-mails from Vance and Blake Conrad, chairman of the board's Risk Committee, formally requesting an inquiry into the fire. The documents were critical to preserving the confidentiality of the investigation. As long as Cameron was rendering legal advice, not business advice, all of his communications within the company were privileged. Yet the distinction between the two was notoriously shifty. It was his job to make sure that anything that went into the "Black File"—board's eyes only—stayed there.

He donned his suit jacket, stored the folder in his filing cabinet, and locked the drawer with a key only he and Blake Conrad possessed. Then he headed toward the door, briefcase in hand. Behind him, the shadows of dusk stretched across the rooftops of Washington, and lights winked on in buildings and monuments.

In the hallway, he spoke to his secretary, Linda. "I'm headed to the conference room. Please forward all calls to Anderson."

He walked briskly down the hallway, past the wood-paneled executive lounge with its Pellegrino-stocked refrigerator and Italian Nespresso machine, past framed portraits of Hank, Dee Dee, and Bobby Carter and the two CEOs who had succeeded them—Rick Mason and Vance Lawson—and entered the C-suite conference room, the site of executive strategy sessions and meetings of the board. The room had three predominant features: a black granite table with twelve high-backed chairs, a wall of windows, and a massive flat-screen television. Two people were seated at the table—Declan Mays, director of global compliance, and Manny Singh, Presto's director of sourcing for South Asia.

Cameron dropped his briefcase in front of them and then switched on the TV, tuning in to CNN. "This is what millions of Americans are going to be watching tonight," he said just as the network cut from Wolf Blitzer's face to live footage of the Presto Tower. "As you can see, we are the lead story. It's our job to find out why."

He took a seat and turned up the volume. Blitzer was in front of the camera again, introducing Karen Hwang, assistant director of the Global Alliance for Worker Rights in San Francisco, and Beatrice Walker, a spokeswoman for the US Chamber of Commerce.

"Karen," said Blitzer, "let's start with you. Seven months ago, the collapse at Rana Plaza claimed the lives of more than eleven hundred Bangladeshi garment workers. Now a garment factory in Bangladesh is on fire. We've seen gruesome footage of bodies on the ground, including a photo of a young girl that everybody's talking about. We don't have a lot of details yet, but I have to ask: Why are factory disasters like this continuing to happen?"

"Unfortunately, Wolf," said Hwang, "this tragedy was entirely preventable. The global market for consumer goods—clothing, toys, electronics, et cetera—is fueled by a system of labor that is, in many cases, as exploitative as the sweatshops that existed in this country at the time of the Triangle Shirtwaist Factory fire a century ago. The primary driver of this exploitation is economic. Corporations like Presto thrive in environments where labor protections don't exist. They go wherever they can get the lowest possible price."

"That's quite an indictment," Blitzer said. "Beatrice, you represent the business community. What's your response?"

"Despite Ms. Hwang's unflattering portrayal," Walker replied, "US companies care deeply about worker rights. Many of our members participate in initiatives like the Fair Labor Association that monitor factory compliance with international labor standards. After the disaster at Rana Plaza, apparel brands in North America and Europe formed the Alliance and the Accord, which are currently inspecting all registered factories in Bangladesh. The brands have pledged millions of dollars toward improvements. This fire is a terrible tragedy. Our hearts go out to the victims and their families. But to lay the blame at the feet of American business is offensive."

Cameron hit the Mute button. "Obviously Ms. Hwang has a twisted conception of what we do every day, but she's far from alone. That's why this inquiry is so important. Declan, when we spoke earlier, you said we moved Millennium Fashions to our Red List six months ago. Do you have the last factory audit report?"

"Right here," Declan replied, pushing a stack of paper across the table. Born in Dublin and raised in New York, Mays had the tenacity of a bulldog and a star-studded CV—economics at Cornell and Oxford, law at Georgetown, and a decade in practice as a compliance specialist at Cameron's old law firm, Slade & Barrett. He was the first person Cameron had hired after moving to Presto. When it came to ferreting out the truth, no one was more effective.

After scanning the audit report, Cameron could barely contain his indignation. "Three fire extinguishers for a thousand workers. Exposed wiring. Aging breaker box. Generators in a storeroom of flammables. How did we ever authorize this factory in the first place?"

"We didn't know how bad it was," Declan said, his voice laced with disquiet. "The audit company we used before was compromised."

"You mean corrupt."

"We couldn't prove it, but we think so. The new audit company is more expensive but beyond reproach. As soon as we got their findings, we put Millennium on the Red List."

"And you communicated that to our sourcing folks in Dhaka?"

Declan nodded. "We informed them immediately."

Cameron tossed the report on the table. "So here's the fifty-million-dollar question—and I mean that literally. The negative publicity alone is going to cost us that much in sales. What were our pants doing at Millennium last night? Manny, tell me about the order."

Singh folded his hands. "It's nothing unusual," he replied. "A hundred and twenty thousand pieces. Six-week turnaround time. Our supplier is Rahmani Apparel—one of the best in Bangladesh. The shipment is due at the harbor in Chittagong in three days."

Cameron stared at Manny until the sourcing executive began to fidget. A veteran of the retail industry and the direct hire of Rebecca Sinclair, Presto's senior vice president of sourcing, Singh was incontrovertibly competent but accustomed to deference. It was the mien of his department. Sourcing was Presto's skunk works. As long as each new product line appeared in stores at the price point set by the costing analysts, no one looked behind the veil.

Cameron opened his briefcase and took out the picture of the girl, which he had printed on photo paper. He slid it toward Manny. "Take a good look at her. We don't know if she's dead or alive. What we know is that she's wearing our pants—*kids'* pants, mind you—like a mask. Are you telling me our clothes were not at Millennium?"

Singh looked suddenly nervous. "I'm not saying that. I can't explain it."

"You were responsible for the placement of the order, were you not?"

"Our Dhaka office chose the supplier. It was Rahmani Apparel. I signed off on it."

Cameron nodded. "At last, a semblance of transparency. Keep going. Connect the dots. Did Rahmani subcontract the order to Millennium?"

Singh shrugged. "I don't know. It's four in the morning over there."

Cameron allowed his displeasure to show. "You can't be serious. A factory is burning, people are dying, our company is getting trashed in the international press, and you're concerned about somebody's sleep? Get them out of bed."

Singh looked at Cameron in astonishment. "Now?"

Cameron shook his head, exasperated. "No, tomorrow. You can use the phone over there. Or you can go back to your office. Just get me an answer."

Singh leaped to his feet. "I'll be back in a few," he said, then disappeared out the door.

"That was pleasant," Cameron said evenly, retrieving the photograph without looking at the girl's bloodstained face. He couldn't handle the despair it evoked in him, not in the midst of a crisis. A year and a half he had trained his mind to forget. But Olivia was always there, lying beside him in the darkness of the roadway, her lips unmoving, concealing the scream that never came. *Let her go*, he commanded himself. *You can't change what happened.*

He turned back to Declan. "You know how these things work. Explain it to me."

"You said it yourself," Declan answered. "Rahmani subcontracted to Millennium. Or they subcontracted to another factory that subcontracted to Millennium. It's hard to turn around a large order in six weeks. Rahmani might not have had capacity for it. Or maybe they ran into delays. Manufacturing is dynamic. We don't see most of it."

.

"But Rahmani signed our Code of Conduct," Cameron objected. "All subcontracting has to be approved by us or they're in breach."

Declan leaned forward in his chair. "Without Manny here, I'll be frank. As long as our supplier gets the shipment to the port in Chittagong on time, nobody in sourcing really cares how it gets done. The Code of Conduct is window dressing."

Cameron's studied calm began to slip. "Why have I never heard this before?"

"Because I can't prove it," Declan said simply.

Cameron took a moment to think. The Code of Conduct was an addendum attached to Presto's supplier contracts—all twenty-two thousand of them around the world—that set forth requirements relating to factory safety, worker rights, environmental protection, corruption, and financial integrity. Every retail company had one, but Presto's was more thorough than most. Cameron had written it himself. Occasionally, suppliers were found in breach. That was why Presto conducted factory audits twice a year—to enforce compliance. But the notion that Presto's own sourcing team treated the code dismissively left him profoundly unsettled.

"Has a supplier ever ignored the Red List before?" he asked.

Declan cleared his throat. "I've heard rumors, but again, I have no proof."

Cameron turned toward the television and watched as firefighters shot streams of water into the conflagration. Against his better judgment, he pictured the girl again, imagined her terror as she chose gravity over flames. He knew what fear felt like on the meridian between life and death. For a vanishing moment, he was there again with Olivia as shadows and metal twisted around them. He closed his eyes and banished the memory.

"So what you're telling me is that Millennium is not alone," he said. "There are other high-risk factories out there making our products without our knowledge."

Declan looked at him gravely. "I don't know how many, but yes."

Manny reappeared at the door, a line of sweat on his brow. "I spoke to our office director in Dhaka. He was horrified. He told me the order is with Rahmani, not Millennium. He promised to look into it right away."

Cameron looked Singh in the eye, thinking, *Why am I not reassured?* An idea came to him then. It was highly unconventional, but the situation was dire. "I'm starting to believe he may need some additional motivation."

Manny regarded him in confusion. "What do you mean?"

When Cameron made the decision, he knew it was right. "Go home and get packed, both of you. We leave for Bangladesh in the morning."

CHAPTER THREE

THE GANGPLANK MARINA

WASHINGTON, DC

NOVEMBER 6, 2013

6:17 A.M.

Candlelight flickered on the tablecloth, diamonds danced on her fingers, but Cameron saw only dismay in Olivia's eyes. His phone was in his hands, the screen bright with Vance's words, anxiety and apology etched upon the dreamscape of his memory. "Just got off the phone with Red. Ravenswood acquired a 4.9% stake right before close. Confirms the rumors. Getting crisis team together at 8. Need you there. Sorry for the timing. Tell Olivia I'll make it up to her." Cameron didn't want to go, but Vance's orders were clear. He suggested to Olivia that she stay through the weekend and take the train home. But he knew she wouldn't do it. She didn't want to spend her birthday alone. *It's time*, he heard her whisper, later on. He felt her skin beneath the covers, her warmth all around him. He hated the thought of leaving. He wanted to stay with her forever. But she insisted. *It's time to go*, she whispered again, a touch louder. *Cameron—*

His eyes shot open in the darkness, and he breathed to steady his racing heart. For an instant he thought he was back in their old apartment, hearing Grayson, one of Olivia's Russian Blue cats, scratching at his post. But then he realized it was water sloshing beneath the hull of his sailboat. The apartment was gone—he'd sold it almost a year ago. Grayson and his sister, Bella, were with his parents in Boston. He was living on the *Breakwater*, his custom-built yacht, the only artifact from his previous life that didn't feel haunted. Olivia had never enjoyed sailing. It was Vance who went with him in search of blue water.

He looked at his watch and climbed out of bed. After a quick shower, he ate a bowl of granola in the galley, dressed in a navy suit and red tie, and then grabbed his suitcase and went topside, locking the companionway door behind him. He had never quite gotten used to it, living at the marina. It felt transitory, impermanent, but that was the way of things now. Olivia had been his polestar. When she died, his world had spun like a gyre and never stopped.

He left a note for the harbormaster and drove his Lincoln sedan out of the lot. He made it to Reagan airport in eight minutes. The Gulfstream G550 was waiting for him on the tarmac, bronzed by the sunrise. Declan Mays and Manny Singh met him in the hangar and walked with him to the plane. Inside the oak-paneled cabin, they took seats on leather chairs near to the flat-screen television. The flight attendant, Bridget, offered them coffee or espresso. Cameron ordered a cappuccino, along with sparking water, and then tuned the television to CNN.

The fire was again the lead story. Daylight in Bangladesh had brought with it footage of the burned-out factory and the lifeless bodies that surrounded it. But there were no new close-ups—nothing like the picture of the girl. According to reporters on the ground, the factory owner had barred the gates after the fire-fighters brought the blaze under control. With limited information, death toll estimates were ranging wildly.

"Anything new from Dhaka?" Cameron asked Manny as the plane began to taxi.

The sourcing executive gave him an impervious look. "Nothing yet."

Cameron turned to Declan. "Do you have the supplier list?"

"Here," Declan replied, handing him an expandable folder.

Inside was a printout showing every Bangladeshi factory that Presto had ever authorized to make clothes for its three brands—Piccola, its kids' line; Burano, its adult and activewear line; and Porto Bari, its premium line of business and resort wear. The list contained over twelve hundred suppliers and was organized into five categories in order of preference—Gold, Silver, Green, Yellow, and Red. Only a few were Gold and Silver; the majority were Green and Yellow.

Cameron flipped to the Red List at the back. The criteria for banning a factory were stringent. The transgressions had to be egregious—either a threat to the life or health of workers or a serious infraction that remained uncorrected after a second audit. He was surprised to find more than ninety companies on the list. Almost all were small outfits, with fewer than 300 workers. Millennium was an outlier with 942.

"Prepare for takeoff, folks," said the captain over the intercom.

Cameron sat back in his chair as the Gulfstream accelerated down the runway. It took flight gracefully and banked east toward the rising sun. As soon as they left DC airspace, the pilot slowed their ascent, allowing Bridget to prepare breakfast. Cameron returned to the supplier list, scanning the columns of data—names of managers, physical addresses, years in business, number of lines and capacities, audit history, and style specialty. Most of the factories on the Red List made "basic" clothing—T-shirts, polo shirts, shorts, and pants. And most, Cameron noticed, had been added in the past six months, likely the result of the new auditing firm.

"Mr. Alexander?" Bridget said, holding a tray of scrambled eggs, bratwurst, and croissants. "Would you like me to put this on the table?"

"That's fine," he said distractedly. An idea was taking shape in his head. He flipped backward in the report and found Rahmani Apparel. His suspicions were confirmed.

"Line capacity," he said, looking at Declan, then Manny. "We know how many pieces every factory can make each month. Correct?"

"Of course," Manny replied. "It's critical to our decision making. We not only know their capacity, we get daily updates about how it's being allocated."

"And if memory serves," Cameron went on, "our policy is to book no more than 30 to 40 percent of a factory's capacity, even with our best suppliers."

Manny nodded. "Sometimes we push the limit, but I've never gone higher than forty."

"Then explain this to me," Cameron said. "Rahmani has a monthly capacity of one hundred fifty thousand pieces. The Piccola order required them to make that amount in six weeks. Unless we booked two-thirds of their capacity, they *had* to get help from someone else."

Manny answered deliberately. "With large orders, we anticipate subcontracting. But we expect our suppliers to handle it properly, with all the necessary permissions, including ours."

"What other permissions are there?"

Manny glanced at the table where Bridget had placed their trays. "Can we continue this over breakfast? Our food is getting cold."

Irritated, Cameron almost rejoined, *You can eat when I'm finished with you.* Instead, he nodded politely and moved the conversation to the table.

After a few bites, Manny answered his question. "There are four thousand factories registered with the Bangladesh Garment Manufacturers and Exporters Association, or BGMEA. Many more are unregistered, but we don't work with them. When a registered factory subcontracts to another registered factory, the BGMEA issues a license, signed by both factories. We require our suppliers to provide us a copy of that license for every subcontract."

Cameron ate a slice of bratwurst. "So if Rahmani subcontracted our order to Millennium, they had to get a license. That means there's a record of it somewhere."

"Not necessarily," Declan quipped, even as Manny said, "Yes."

Cameron pointed at Declan. "You first."

"Manny is technically correct," Declan said, "but this is Bangladesh. A lot of suppliers don't have the patience for formalities. Here's an illustration. Our supplier falls behind on an order. He doesn't want us to know because it will reflect poorly on him, and we might not give him our next order. So he calls a friend with extra capacity and does a deal over the phone. The friend sends a truck for the materials and returns the finished garments. Or the friend might call another friend—a *third* factory—and send part of the order—say, the finishing work—to him. Our supplier doesn't know about the third factory, and we don't know about any of it."

Cameron set his fork down, his stomach puckering. *What am I walking into?* "Manny," he said quietly. "Tell me this isn't the core of our business."

"It isn't," Manny replied, a little too quickly. "Look, informal subcontracting happens. But we monitor our suppliers carefully. There isn't room for orders to fall through the cracks."

Declan shook his head. "I have a fifteen-year-old daughter. What she does and what she tells me afterward are often worlds apart. Our suppliers are the same. They're in a cutthroat business. They do what they have to do to make a buck, and they tell us what we want to hear."

"You don't know what you're talking about," Manny shot back. "You get their audit reports twice a year. We get e-mails from them every morning."

Declan smiled in a subtle way. "I have back channels. I know more than you think."

Manny stared at his plate, his dark eyes smoldering. Cameron watched him, feeling little sympathy. The people at the pinnacle of Presto's sourcing apparatus were paid handsomely, for they were the rainmakers, the beating heart at the profit center of the firm. As long as they did their job, Cameron had no qualm with it. But this kind of lapse was inexcusable.

And it was only the beginning. He was certain of it.

CHAPTER FOUR

SHAHJALAL INTERNATIONAL AIRPORT

DHAKA, BANGLADESH

NOVEMBER 7, 2013

10:18 A.M.

The sky over Dhaka was washed out like parchment, the horizon soot-stained as if singed by flame. Cameron looked out the window as the Gulfstream made its final approach. The city was at once dense and sprawling, a vast concatenation of buildings heaped upon one another between rivers brown with silt and streets clogged with vehicles and pedestrians. They landed with barely a bump and taxied to a remote spot on the tarmac. Two SUVs were waiting for them—one marked with the name of the airport authority and the other an unmarked black Mercedes. The copilot lowered the steps and admitted a customs official who stamped their passports, issued them visas, and welcomed them to the People's Republic of Bangladesh.

Cameron stifled a yawn and collected his briefcase. They had been in transit for sixteen and a half hours. He had slept off and on and taken anti–jet lag pills, trying to adjust to the new time zone in advance. But the shock was inevitable. It was midnight in DC. Here the sun was at its zenith. He felt as if his brain had been tumbled in a washing machine.

He moved toward the exit and descended the steps into the sweltering heat, Manny and Declan at his heels. The moist tropical air surrounded him like water, and his first breath came out like a cough. A Bangladeshi man in a business suit stood beside the rear door of the Mercedes. He gave Cameron a vigorous handshake.

"Welcome, Mr. Alexander. I am Shelim Madani, director of the Dhaka office." He opened the door and gestured to the leather interior of the vehicle. "Please, it is cooler inside."

After they climbed in, Shelim took the wheel and tore across the tarmac at a fierce clip, rounding an aircraft hangar and merging onto a side road.

"The Radisson Blu is not far," Shelim said, his accent blending the lilt of Bengali with something starchier—perhaps a bit of Britain. "You can check in, and then we can talk in the Business Class Lounge. It's very private."

Cameron shook his head. "I want to go to our office."

"There are reporters there," Shelim objected gently. "No one goes in or out without being questioned. Also, traffic is bad in the city. It would take us at least an hour to get there."

As soon as he said it, they ran into congestion at the airport roundabout. Cameron gazed out the window at the deadlock of cars, trucks, buses, and rickshaws all measuring progress in inches. The honking was deafening. "How far away is the Rahmani Apparel factory?"

Shelim glanced over his shoulder in confusion. "Rahmani?"

"Our supplier for the Piccola pants."

Shelim's voice took on a perceptible edge. "It would be two hours by car or twenty minutes by helicopter. But I would need to make arrangements."

Cameron watched Shelim's face carefully. "Does the hotel have a landing pad?"

Shelim tightened his grip on the wheel. "There is a field nearby."

"Excellent," Cameron said. "Summon the chopper. We'll eat while we wait."

They ordered room service in Cameron's suite and took seats in the living area. Apart from the bleating of horns on the street and the faint odor of something burning seeping through the seal around the window, they could have been in any city in the world. The "business bubble," Cameron called it whenever he found himself wishing for a more authentic cultural experience. Today, however, he didn't care. He was here for answers, nothing more.

"Tell me how the Millennium order came about," he said to Shelim.

The office director glanced at Manny Singh. "We placed it in late August, but there was a modification at the last minute. Our designers in Hong Kong were not satisfied with Rahmani's sample. The factory asked for an extension, but we could not grant it. The pants are part of our holiday collection. Rahmani agreed and made adjustments to its line schedule."

Cameron scribbled on his notepad. "You cut the turnaround time by half. That's a lot of pressure to put on a supplier."

"They are used to it," Shelim said with a shrug. "Changes happen regularly."

"I looked at the data. Rahmani didn't have capacity to fulfill the order themselves. They had to subcontract part of it."

Shelim nodded. "They sent sixty thousand pieces to Freedom 71. I authorized it."

"Was that by e-mail?"

Shelim shook his head. "We do business on the phone."

"I assume you have a record of the license from the BGMEA?"

"The license is on file."

Cameron took a moment to think of his next question. Internal interviews were a delicate dance—neither adversarial nor friendly. His instinct as a lawyer was to treat them like a deposition, but unless an employee was accused of wrongdoing, that was a mistake. He had to massage the truth out of Shelim, convince him that it was in his interest to be transparent.

"When was the last time you spoke with Rahmani? Before the fire, I mean."

Shelim glanced up at the ceiling. "I called the general manager on Sunday. He confirmed with his production manager that the order was on schedule."

"Did you have a conversation like that with the other factory—Freedom 71?"

Shelim shook his head. "Rahmani is our contractor. I deal only with them."

"What about quality control?"

As soon as Cameron spoke the words, he knew he had touched a nerve. Shelim blinked and looked down at the floor, then turned to Manny as if searching for cover. The sequence happened in less than a second, but Cameron missed none of it. Years ago, when he was a junior partner at Slade & Barrett looking for a way to distinguish himself, he had taken lessons from a deception expert. In time, most people had become an open book to him.

When Shelim replied, his words were measured. "There is an inspection before the order ships to the port. My quality-control people handle that."

There's something you're not telling me, Cameron thought. "What happens if the order fails the inspection?"

"We open random boxes," Shelim explained. "If we find too many issues, we can reject the whole lot. But Rahmani is a Gold supplier. We've never had problems with them."

"I take it you do the same with subcontracting factories?"

Again, Shelim's eyes shifted ever so briefly to Manny. "We inspect everything. Our suppliers ship only the highest-quality merchandise."

Another deflection, Cameron thought. He considered asking a follow-up question but decided to reserve it until he spoke with Rahmani. "Let's talk about Millennium. They're banned from our supplier list, but somehow they received a portion of our order. Who sent it to them?"

Shelim tensed visibly. "I don't know. Rahmani doesn't know. It is a mystery."

That much was clearly a lie. "Have you spoken to Freedom 71 since the fire?"

"No," Shelim said, rubbing his hands together. "Only Rahmani."

Cameron gave the office director an incredulous look. "You didn't think it would be valuable to find out if they subcontracted the order to Millennium?"

"Rahmani is our contractor," Shelim repeated. "They spoke to Freedom 71. No one knows how the order found its way to Millennium."

In his younger days, Cameron might have allowed his rage to slip, but he held his feelings in check. "What about the apparel association? Did you ask them whether Rahmani or Freedom 71 had obtained a license to subcontract to Millennium?"

Shelim's eyes widened a fraction. "I did not. I trust Rahmani."

Or you want them to cover for you, Cameron thought. Just then, he heard a knock at the door. Declan opened it, and a male attendant wheeled in lunch on silver trays.

"Is the helicopter on its way?" Cameron asked Shelim.

The office director glanced at his wristwatch. "It will be here in twenty minutes."

"Good," Cameron said. "We'll see if your faith in Rahmani is merited."

CHAPTER FIVE

RAHMANI APPAREL, LTD.

NARAYANGANJ DISTRICT, DHAKA, BANGLADESH

NOVEMBER 7, 2013

2:01 P.M.

Even from the height of five hundred feet, the Rahmani factory was immense. There were at least a dozen buildings scattered around the grounds, three of which were as cavernous as airport hangars. The roads were all paved and marked with centerlines. There were trees in abundance and park-like spaces with lush grass, footpaths, and benches. The largest building, connected by skybridges to its two smaller cousins, had a tower encased in blue glass with a helipad on the roof. And off to the side was an indigo-colored pool, churning like a vat of butter.

"Is that a water treatment facility?" Cameron asked Shelim over the whir of the blades. It was widely acknowledged in the industry—but not so widely publicized—that the production of textiles was one of the most prolific sources of water pollution in the world.

Shelim nodded. "It's state of the art. After they wash their jeans, the water is scrubbed and then recycled. Only a quarter of it goes back into the river."

When the helicopter settled onto the landing area, an aircrewman escorted Cameron and his entourage across the sunbaked helipad to a stairwell that led to a conference room lined with windows. Two Bangladeshi men dressed in European suits were waiting for them.

"Mr. Alexander," said the older one, a heavyset man with graying hair and penetrating eyes. "I am Habib Khan, owner of Rahmani Apparel. This is Khaled Chowdhury, my GM. I hope your flight was comfortable."

After the obligatory pleasantries, they sat down at a round table. A young woman entered the room with a tray with teacups and sugar cookies.

"*Cha*," Habib explained as the woman distributed the snacks. "In India, it is chai."

Cameron took a sip of the tea, and it nearly scalded his tongue.

"Ah," Habib said with a smile, "you must allow it to cool a bit." Then in an instant, his mercurial eyes grew sad. "We are all deeply troubled by the tragedy unfolding at the Millennium Fashions factory. We are especially troubled because it appears that part of the order you entrusted to us was diverted there without our knowledge. We have spoken to our subcontractor, Freedom 71, and they have yet to provide us with a satisfactory explanation. I can assure you that if we do not receive one, we will cease doing business with them."

Cameron folded his hands on the table and returned Habib's gaze. In only a handful of minutes, he had already made a number of critical observations about the owner. He was a man in control of his emotions, which made him a formidable adversary. But he wasn't immune to the involuntary movements of face and body that revealed hidden wells of deception. Cameron had caught one of them when he spoke the word *Millennium*. It was a small thing, but it was there—a shrug of the shoulder. And it gave Cameron all the confidence he needed.

"You're lying to me," he said simply and watched Habib's facade crumble. The owner broke eye contact with Cameron and glanced at Khaled, struggling to recover his poise.

"Mr. Alexander," he said, "our relationship with Presto goes back two decades. We have never missed an order. We have invested millions in updating our facilities to keep your business. Your accusation is . . . *unprecedented*."

In a glance, Cameron saw Declan's intensity, Shelim's discomfort, and Manny's bewilderment. "That may be," he replied, keeping his face impassive. "But the only thing that matters right now is the truth. The clock is ticking."

Habib stared back at him, and his mouth began to twitch.

Cameron counted to ten, then stood abruptly. "That's fine. I'll go to the apparel association and pull all the licenses they've issued to you in the past six months. Then I'll find someone from Millennium—someone who's still alive—to talk to me about our order history. When all is said and done, I doubt Presto will order from you again."

"No." Habib's objection came out almost like a bark. He found his footing quickly. "That will not be necessary. Perhaps—if you are not in a hurry—I could give you a tour of the factory. I know Khaled and Shelim have business to discuss. The others can stay with them."

Cameron made a show of pondering this, but he had already made his decision. He glanced at Shelim again and saw the lines of apprehension on his forehead. "I'd like that," he said and followed Habib out the door.

❄

The Rahmani factory was a paragon of efficiency, as intelligently managed as it was maintained. The sewing floors were spotless, brightly lit, and well ventilated. The stations were neither cramped nor cluttered with stray fabric. The workers—mostly young women—were focused on their tasks, their supervisors strolling among them, doling out instructions. A few sewing operators looked up when Cameron and Habib walked past, but only briefly.

"The last pieces of your order," Habib said, holding up a pair of nearly finished Piccola pants. "They will be packaged tonight and shipped tomorrow to the port."

Cameron took the pants in his hands and rubbed the spandex fabric between his thumb and forefinger, imagining mothers across America dressing their six-year-olds in them for Christmas. *Of all the things to die for*, he thought.

After the sewing areas, Habib led him across the cutting floor, a vast open space with tables piled high with bolts of fabric. Around the perimeter of each table, eight workers—all young men—smoothed out wrinkles in the fabric with combs while cutters guided saws along cardboard patterns, creating one hundred pieces at a time.

"As you can see, safety is a top priority," Habib explained, pointing out a shiny fire extinguisher beside a marked exit door. "This building was built in accordance with the highest international standards. What happened at Millennium and Rana Plaza will never happen here."

Next, Habib showed Cameron the printing floor, where an array of machines deposited ink on T-shirts—three primary colors blended together into images and words. Then came the embroidery floor, where workers were stitching floral patterns onto children's dresses using machines that resembled the control panels on the starship *Enterprise*.

Eventually they entered a glass-enclosed room with a table and chairs and a large display of finished garments on hangers, illumined by halogen bulbs. A sign on the door read PRESTO.

"This is where your quality-control people conduct inspections," Habib said. "They will be here tonight and tomorrow to check the Piccola shipment." He gestured to a chair. "Please, sit down. I will tell you what you want to know."

Cameron took a seat and calmly folded his hands on the table, waiting for Habib to make the next move. The owner sat down too, shifting his weight to get comfortable. Beneath the dazzling lights, Habib's eyes were limpid, his forehead dotted with perspiration.

"I have no wish to deceive you," Habib began. "But your question presents me with a dilemma. We used to be a profitable company. Now we are struggling. The water treatment facility you saw on the flight in? That was funded by my real estate ventures. Our competitors abroad are undercutting us. Many factories in China are vertically integrated, their lead times down to thirty days. Vietnam has better technology. Indonesia and Cambodia have cheaper labor. Buyers—including your people at Presto—are demanding lower prices and faster turnarounds, or they will go elsewhere. We have no choice but to agree and then find a way to deliver."

Habib adjusted himself again. "When I received your last-minute changes, I got help from Freedom 71. But they ran into problems and had to cancel half the shipment. I had two weeks to make thirty thousand pieces and no capacity in my lines. So I did what I have done for years. I called Millennium. They told me they could do it for a very reasonable price. I did not ask how. I have never asked how. Now I am beginning to see. Before I sent the materials along, I made another call—to Shelim. I explained the situation and told him Millennium could finish the order. He made only one request—that I deliver the pants to the port on time."

Cameron sat perfectly still, listening to the sounds of the factory filtering through the glass. He thought of Vance at his desk fielding frantic calls from investors, Kristin Raymond in the war room fending off press inquiries, and traders at the New York Stock Exchange taking sell orders for Presto stock. The company's share price had tumbled 12 percent in two days. It was not in free fall, but it would be if the media ever learned what Habib had just said.

"Millennium is no longer on our authorized list of suppliers," Cameron said slowly.

"That is why I called Shelim," Habib replied, his breathing laborious now. "Otherwise I would have gone straight to the BGMEA for the license."

"Has our office ever given you permission to ignore the Red List before?"

Habib blinked, his face awash with guilt. "Shelim is a good man. He has a family. I do not wish to make trouble for him."

"Shelim is not your concern. I need an answer."

At last Habib nodded. "The Red List does not matter. Only 98 percent on-time delivery."

Cameron touched his wedding ring, drawing strength from the cool metal on his skin, the band without beginning or end, unbroken despite Olivia's death. His eyes bored into Habib. "In the past six months, how many of our orders have you subcontracted to Millennium?"

Habib swallowed visibly. "I don't know the dates. But there have been others."

When Cameron heard the owner's words, he came within a hairsbreadth of revealing the shock that twisted his gut. Presto had eleven hundred authorized apparel suppliers in Bangladesh. If Shelim had given Habib carte blanche to keep the orders flowing, he had almost certainly done the same for other suppliers. It was a compliance breach of staggering proportions. Yet the fire and the media spotlight bound Cameron's hands. He could neither terminate Rahmani Apparel nor relieve Shelim of his duties. For the time being, at least, he needed to keep them close and quiet.

"This practice ends today," he said. "I hope that goes without saying."

The owner nodded again, this time vigorously.

Cameron stood up and walked to the display case, running his hand along the rack. Rahmani's wares ranged from Burano T-shirts and athletic shorts to Porto Bari winter dresses and tops. The designs were unexceptional, but the workmanship and fabrics were two or three cuts above what other discounters offered.

He turned around and saw Habib watching him intently. "I have another question. When you subcontract part of an order, how is quality control handled?"

"That depends," Habib replied. "When we have time, we bring all the pieces from the order together so your people can do an inspection here. When time is short, they inspect the pieces at the subcontracting factory."

Cameron felt suddenly queasy. The executive in him did not want to know the answer to the next question, but the lawyer had to ask. "With the pants you sent to Millennium, did any of our people ever visit that factory?"

Habib held out his hands as if the truth were self-evident. "I spoke to Millennium the afternoon before the fire. Your people were there."

CHAPTER SIX

IZUMI RESTAURANT

DHAKA, BANGLADESH

NOVEMBER 7, 2013

8:15 P.M.

The sushi was a knockout, as elegant in form and delicate in flavor as anything Cameron had tasted in the United States. Shelim had suggested the place. It was called Izumi, in the Gulshan neighborhood of Dhaka, within sight of Presto's office but far enough away to avoid the media blitzkrieg. Cameron had witnessed the circus from behind the tinted windows of the Mercedes SUV. Television vans were still encamped outside the entrance, reporters congregating on sidewalks, skulking in vehicles, and swarming like pack wolves when anyone appeared at the front door. Their questions and accusations had so rattled the staff that Shelim had shuttered the building until further notice, ordering everyone to work from home.

The office director was the only other person dining with Cameron. They were seated in a quiet corner of the restaurant, where no one could eavesdrop on their conversation. Between them stood a wooden table, an accent candle, glasses of water—not wine, as it was against Bangladeshi law—and plates decorated by the chef with rainbow-colored works of gastronomic art. It felt strange, almost profane, to ambush a man at such an establishment. But that was exactly what Cameron intended to do.

After his visit to the Rahmani factory, he had dispatched Manny Singh and Declan Mays to an evening of personal revelry—whatever it was that they did with an expense account in a foreign country—and invited Shelim to a meal, pretending to be interested in developing a deeper understanding of the local sourcing process. In truth, he had lied to everyone. Manny and Declan thought that Habib had confessed to subcontracting to Millennium without permission and that Cameron had granted him forbearance, reasoning that the damage was done and the shipment was too important to delay. Cameron had spun the deception deftly, leaving Declan stewing in indignation and giving Manny cause for secret relief that the inquiry would go no further. Declan would forgive him as soon as he learned the truth, but Manny needed to remain in the dark. Cameron had a hunch that the rot in the sourcing system went deeper than Shelim.

"Habib is running an impressive operation," Cameron said, squeezing a piece of maguro tuna between his chopsticks. "It's no wonder Rahmani is a Gold supplier."

"He is one of our most trusted allies in Bangladesh," Shelim replied. "But I am concerned about the way he handled this order. It is not like him to ignore protocol."

Cameron regarded Shelim in the soft light, weighing whether to name his prevarication openly or lure him into a trap. "I found that peculiar too. He told me that you are the sort of buyer who understands the pressures he faces. He said you've always been accommodating."

Shelim's eyes darted to the table, then refocused on Cameron. He crafted his response with care. "Our interests are aligned. If our suppliers do not produce in the time frame and at the price points we require, we miss our targets, and our customers suffer."

You don't give a damn about our customers, Cameron mused. *But I bet the targets keep you awake at night.* "It must be difficult to keep everyone happy. I imagine many of your suppliers are not accustomed to Western production standards. The cultural gap is wide."

Shelim laughed and relaxed a bit. "That is an understatement. We are required to—how do you say?—play both sides of the fence. But in the end, we hold all the cards. Without our orders, our suppliers cannot stay in business."

Cameron took a moment to savor his sashimi. Then he said, "Is it true that your sourcing benchmark is 98 percent on-time delivery? That is an extra-ordinarily thin margin."

"Yes," Shelim affirmed, dropping his guard further. "It is the same for all Presto suppliers across the world."

Cameron smiled thinly. "But it isn't just our suppliers that have to meet that standard. It is my understanding that your office's performance is judged on that basis. That must be a great burden for you to carry."

Shelim looked nonplussed, his chopsticks hovering in midair. "It is not a burden. It is our job. If we fail to deliver, our customers have nothing to buy."

Cameron tilted his head inquisitively. "Have you ever been to one of our stores?"

Shelim's eyes narrowed a touch. He clearly had no idea where Cameron was taking the conversation. "I have not. But I have always wanted to visit one."

Cameron nodded, his expression nonchalant. "The biggest is two hundred thousand square feet. More than a hundred thousand items on the shelves. A bonanza of consumerism."

Shelim stared back at him, his brow furrowed.

"If Rahmani had missed its delivery deadline," Cameron went on, "our customers never would have noticed. They have more choices than they know what to do with."

Shelim set his chopsticks down. "I'm not sure what you are saying."

Cameron took another casual bite. "What I'm saying is this: The 98 percent target is not for our customers. It is for our *investors*. It is about earnings, profits, market share, stock price—all of the things that we executives worry about. And our worry at headquarters becomes your worry here, and your worry becomes our suppliers' worry. So all of us do what we have to do to keep everyone happy."

Shelim's gaze fell to the table. He was smart enough to know that a blow was coming, but he couldn't see it to defend himself.

"The thing is," Cameron continued, "no one is happy right now. Our investors are unhappy. Our customers are unhappy. My senior executive team is unhappy. Because people died making our clothes. Because our pants are being plastered all over the world—on televisions, computers, mobile devices—in a photograph that will live in infamy."

Cameron took a breath, and Shelim began to squirm. "So now the discussion has turned from profits to losses, from trading on our positive brand image and generating historic fourth-quarter sales, to piecing together the shards of our corporate dignity and shoring up investor confidence before our market cap falls off a cliff. I have to tell you, it's not pretty."

"It is a disaster for all of us," Shelim said, his voice starting to crack. "What Habib did is inexcusable. If you would like, I will cancel all Rahmani orders, terminate the relationship."

Cameron shook his head slowly. "That would do no good. As I said, the damage is done. What we need now is not recrimination but reform." He paused, the boom in his hands. "I need to know why you authorized Habib to subcontract to Millennium in contravention of the Red List, not just this time, but multiple times. Before you answer, beware. Your job is on the line."

In an instant, Shelim's fear became a palpable thing. He sat totally still, eyes locked with Cameron, as if his body were imprisoned in a block of ice. "I didn't do it on my own authority," he said in a voice just above a whisper.

And there it was, a morsel of the purest truth. "Go on," Cameron said gently.

Shelim hesitated at the water's edge, the Rubicon lapping against his toes. Cameron watched as he struggled, weighing the compromise and the consequences that would follow. But he really had no choice. Survival required betrayal.

"Manny," he rasped at last.

For a moment, Cameron felt the thrill of vindication. Then the moment passed, and vindication turned into anger. "What did he tell you?"

Shelim fingered his napkin. "He told me not to worry, to do whatever it took to ensure the orders reached the port on time."

"When?" Cameron pressed.

"When the new Red List was published, after the last round of audits," Shelim said. "We were in Bangkok at a sourcing meeting. I expressed concern that some of the banned factories were critical subcontracting partners. He told me the people in compliance didn't understand our business. He said they were no better than the regulators."

Cameron folded his hands in his lap, his expression unflappable despite his fury. He was well acquainted with the enmity between sourcing and compliance. But in his experience, the contest had always remained a gentleman's game, a cold war of wits and politesse, not open defiance of company policy.

"How many red-listed factories have you used in the past six months?" he inquired.

Shelim hung his head. "I don't know."

"Take a guess."

"A dozen, maybe. Habib is unusual. Most owners ask only once, if at all."

Cameron looked down at his plate, saw the tender flesh of the maguro shimmering in the light of the dining room. *Olivia would have loved this place*, he thought, allowing a moment for his emotions to find expression. His wife had been a connoisseur of sushi, as much for the artistry as the delicacy. *If only she could see me now, the way I'm about to defile it.*

"Habib tells me you have a wife and three children," he said to Shelim. The office manager nodded, afraid.

"You are fortunate. Tonight many husbands in this city will go to sleep without their wives, many fathers without their daughters. They are the reason we have compliance, the reason we have regulators. Death is a one-way street. Once someone is gone, we don't get them back."

Shelim continued to nod, like a bobbing head ornament on a dashboard.

"Do you know who sent me here?" Cameron asked, and Shelim's nodding turned to head wagging. "Vance Lawson. On his authority, I could fire you right now. But I'm not going to do that. I'm going to give you a second chance."

Shelim's back straightened, his eyebrows arching in astonishment.

"When we leave here tonight, you are going to contact every owner who asked you for permission to use a red-listed factory and order them to desist. Then you are going to write a letter to all of our suppliers in Bangladesh, re-iterating the standards in the Code of Conduct and the penalties for infraction. Lastly, you are going to say nothing about any of this to Manny or anyone in the sourcing department who might inquire about my visit. What we have discussed tonight stays between us. Or I *will* fire you. Is that clear?"

"Abundantly," Shelim said, letting out the breath he was holding. "Thank you so much, Mr. Alexander. I'm so sorry—"

"Save it," Cameron interjected. "No one cares."

Shelim gulped, chastened.

"I'm only interested in two things. That you do exactly as I said. And that you go home tonight, look your family in the eye, and make them feel as lucky as you are right now."

With that, Cameron raised his hand and asked for the check.

PART TWO

Joshua

February 2015

CHAPTER ONE

OLD EBBITT GRILL

WASHINGTON, DC

FEBRUARY 11, 2015

9:12 P.M.

Even at nine o'clock on a Wednesday evening, the restaurant was bustling. Waiters scurrying. Glasses clinking. Bartenders pouring. Gaiety erupting. And conversations—the central currency of this supremely political town—drawing heads down and faces together, translating ideas into speech, aspirations into asks, in an endless quest for an angle, a vote, a promotion, or that most liquid of Washington assets—a favor. Josh loved it, the multidimensional poker game of personality and power. For fifteen years, he had been a regular at the table, here at Old Ebbitt, a century-old, mahogany-and-brass eatery steps away from the White House, and at places like it in Tokyo, Rio de Janeiro, and London. He had mastered its nuances, cultivated quid pro quos, and built an enviable reputation as an international journalist, netting him two Pulitzer Prizes and a book that hit number one on the *New York Times* bestseller list. But all of that was gone now. A single error in judgment had laid waste a lifetime of achievement. His colleagues at the *Washington Post* were colleagues no longer.

"Joshua Griswold," said Tony Sharif, slipping into the green velvet booth across from Josh and draping his arm across the top. "It's been too long."

Josh shook his head. "I know it. Half the people in here are strangers."

Tony's face—a mélange of his Indian father and Anglo-American mother—remained impassive, but his eyes were alive with humor. "You're getting old. I see gray in your beard."

Josh gave a sarcastic laugh. "That's purgatory for you. I feel like the Old Man of the Mountain. One day you're a fixture. Everybody wants a picture. Then the earth moves, you disappear, and no one remembers what you looked like."

Tony grinned ironically. "Could be worse. Nobody ever wanted a picture with me."

"You should ditch the news and try Bollywood," Josh jested. "With a mug like that, you could be the next Shah Rukh Khan."

Tony put out his hand, and Josh clasped it. "It's good to see you again, my friend."

"That makes two of you," Josh said.

Tony raised an eyebrow. "Who's the competition?"

"Reggie, the homeless guy at my old apartment building."

Tony shook his head, and his eyes grew thoughtful. "It's a shame what they did to you. The stories you wrote are some of the best in American journalism. The thing with Maria, it could have been any of us. She deceived a lot of people. It doesn't change your reporting."

She didn't mean to deceive anyone, Josh thought. *She did what she had to do.* But he couldn't say that. Not even to Tony Sharif, the man who had been at his side when shrapnel from an exploding IED sliced through their Humvee in Sadr City and buried itself in Josh's thigh. Tony was the closest thing he had to a brother. But Tony would never understand Maria. She was a riddle in the flesh. Even Josh didn't understand her, and he had spent years trying.

"Don't sweat it," Josh said. "Shit happens. It's what makes our world go round."

"I'll drink to that," Tony replied, raising his bottle of Sam Adams. "To shit. May it survive long enough for me to earn a pension and for you to get back on your feet."

"Cheers," Josh said, taking a sip of Heineken, his beer of choice not so much for its flavor as for its ubiquity across the globe.

"So you're in town again," Tony said. "That means you're working. What's the story?"

"Corporate malfeasance," Josh replied. "Apparel supply chains. A body count. The underside of American business."

Tony's face lit up. "Sexy. Who's the target?"

Josh lowered his voice. "Presto."

Tony leaned back against the booth, clearly intrigued. "The Millennium fire. We reported on that, you know. A lot of people did. That photo was like

Napalm Girl in Vietnam. But this time the girl in the picture disappeared. We couldn't track her down."

Josh nodded but didn't reply, allowing Tony to interpret his silence.

"Wait a minute," Tony said. "You have a source." He let out a grunt, then began to grumble. "You've got to be kidding me. You found someone willing to talk."

It was the response Josh had expected. For five years, Tony had been the *Post*'s bureau chief in India. Last year he had taken a senior editorial position in Washington, but his network in South Asia remained as far-reaching as the Ganges. Josh was intruding upon his territory.

"I've got to hand it to you," Tony went on, struggling to be generous. "My guys would have given anything to keep that story alive." For a moment, he looked like he was going to probe, but then he didn't. "So what can I do for you? You obviously got further than we did."

The corners of Josh's mouth turned upward. He still found it hard to believe. The e-mail had arrived in his in-box two days ago, its provenance untraceable. *I have information about the Millennium fire*, it read. *It relates to Presto Omnishops Corporation.* Hours later, when the rest of DC was asleep, Josh had met a man at the Lincoln Memorial who gave him the names of workers and factories in three countries, including the name of the girl in the photograph. The man had divulged nothing of his motives, but his seniority inside Presto was beyond question, as was his charge: he wanted Josh to make Presto pay.

"This thing dropped into my lap," Josh said. "That's all I can say. But I need your help. I need to find a fixer in Dhaka with high-level contacts in the apparel industry."

Tony spoke without hesitation. "Rana Jalil. Except he's in Los Angeles these days."

Josh gave him a confused look, and Tony clarified, "Rana's a mutt like me. His father owns one of the oldest garment companies in Bangladesh. His mother is Bangladeshi, but she was born in California. He has a law degree from UCLA. Dhaka's his backyard. He helped us cover the Rana Plaza disaster. He's an ace, and 100 percent trustworthy."

Josh took another swig of beer. "What's he doing in LA?"

Tony chuckled. "Shining a light into the dark hole of American fast fashion."

Josh made no attempt to disguise his ignorance. "Explain."

"You know those teenybopper stores in the mall, the ones that dress their mannequins like hookers and make you want to keep Lily under lock and key?"

Josh nodded. Lily was his eight-year-old daughter and the light of his life. He was an absentee father, but not completely derelict.

"A lot of the clothes they peddle are made in sweatshops in LA. The fashion companies know about it, but they don't give a rat's ass. So long as they keep feeding American teens a fad a week, they see it as the cost of doing business. Rana freelances with a public interest group called La Alternativa Legal, or 'LA Legal.' They represent the workers in court. California has a labor law that gives them firepower against the brands. I don't really understand it. But I know he's nailing them to the wall."

"I'll take him," Josh said. "Can you make the introduction?"

Tony whipped a smartphone out of his jeans and started typing. "He'll be tickled. The great Joshua Griswold. He might even give you a discount since you're out of work at the moment." After he transmitted the message, he got the waiter's attention and ordered another round of drinks. Then he stared at his watch intently. "I'll give him one minute, then I call."

"What?" Josh didn't know anyone that quick on the draw.

"Wait. Ha! There he is." Tony held out his wrist and showed Josh his smart-watch. On the screen was a text from Rana. "He's thrilled, as promised."

Josh shook his head, marveling at the speed of new media. "I owe you one."

Tony's eyes sparkled, his lips askew in a beer-tinged smile. "You owe me nothing. I want this as much as you do. You break this story, I mean really break it, and I'll see what I can do about getting your job back."

CHAPTER TWO

The place was too empty to call home. It wasn't the fault of the condominium. Located in a steel-and-brick hipster retreat steps away from the urban oasis of Charlottesville's pedestrian mall, it had hardwood floors, fashionable details, and a walkout terrace with a striking view of Brown's Mountain in the direction of the Blue Ridge. The vacancy was the vice of the occupant. Josh had never really moved in—and never wanted to.

He had lived there six months, since the previous August when Madison, his wife of sixteen years, had evicted him from his real home, a renovated farmhouse in the horse country of Keswick. He had taken almost nothing with him, except some books from the library, half of his closet, his computer equipment, and a framed map of the world festooned with red pins, one for every place he'd been. The mattress on the floor and the desk by the window he had bought from a student on Craigslist. The clothes that didn't need to be hung he kept in a suitcase.

It was the rootlessness that bothered him, not the address on his letter box. He had been a nomad his entire professional life, gallivanting from story to story, hot spot to hot spot. But he'd always had a port of call, and his wife waiting for him when the plane landed. Madison had grounded him, kept the lights on and the sheets warm. Then Lily had come along—dear, sweet, precious Lily—and given

47

home a whole new meaning. The apartment was provisional. It had to be. He couldn't stand the thought that the separation might become permanent.

It was twenty minutes before noon on Friday, two days after his meeting with Tony at Old Ebbitt Grill, and he was up to his neck in research, reading every legal case he could find in which foreign workers had sued a multinational corporation for abuses suffered outside the United States. It was heady stuff, and outside his wheelhouse. He hadn't given thought to the nuances of the law since his days at Harvard Law School, before he took a reporting job at the *Post*. But his training was coming back to him, as his source had promised him it would.

His iPhone vibrated—a text from Madison. "Don't forget Lily."

"I'm on it," he replied. "Leaving in a few."

He put the phone down and returned to *Doe v. Wal-Mart Stores*—a far-reaching but ultimately unsuccessful lawsuit brought by workers in five countries to hold the world's largest retailer accountable for labor abuses committed by its foreign suppliers.

A minute later, his iPhone vibrated again. *What now?* he wondered. Madison's obsession with punctuality—a consequence of her type A personality and work as a lawyer—rankled him to no end. He preferred to live on the edge, squeezing every last drop from the clock. He glanced at the phone and inhaled sharply. The text wasn't from his wife. It was from Maria.

"I send you e-mail. Please read. *Beijinhos*. M"

He shook his head almost unconsciously. A thousand times he had considered blocking her number and changing his e-mail, but his heart had never permitted it. It wasn't Maria he was worried about. It was her girls—by last count thirty-two of them, all teenagers rescued from penury and prostitution in Vidigal, a drug-infested *favela* in Rio de Janeiro just down the beach from the glittering wealth of Ipanema. *I can't deal with her now*, he decided. *Lily is waiting*.

He collected his keys and leather jacket from the kitchen counter and left his apartment. In the parking garage, he slid behind the wheel of his white BMW convertible—his single concession to vanity after his book, *The End of Childhood*, topped the *Times* list—and sped out of the lot. Traffic was heavier with the approach of the lunch hour, but he had grown up driving in DC and had a cabbie's sense for shortcuts.

He made it to St. Anne's a minute shy of noon. Perched atop a grassy knoll outside the city, the prep school was one of the crown jewels of Charlottesville's educational establishment. Lily met him at the entrance, hands buried in the pockets of her pink puffer coat. He reached across the console and opened the door for her.

"Hey, sweetie," he said with a grin as big as hers. "Hop in. It's cold out there."

When she was seated, backpack between her legs, he kissed her on the forehead and took a long look at her. She was a willowy girl of eight years, with Madison's chestnut-brown hair and chocolate eyes and Josh's upturned nose and infectious smile. Her face was a bit fleshy around the edges—a consequence of the steroid dexamethasone, or Dex, as they called it, that she had taken since her diagnosis—but she was beautiful, radiantly so, and he was smitten.

"How was school?" he asked, accelerating down the road beneath the gunmetal sky.

"I made something for you in art class," she said, her fairylike voice as articulate as a young adult. She rummaged in her backpack and removed a painting of green mountains and a black horse with a man at the reins wearing breeches, boots, and a riding helmet.

"Is that me?" he asked mirthfully as he merged onto the bypass again. "I still haven't had a chance to wear the outfit you got me at Christmas."

"Mommy says it's supposed to be pretty tomorrow," Lily replied, always the optimist. "We could go riding. Tommy misses you."

"And I miss Tommy," Josh lied, picturing the quarter horse and barely suppressing a laugh. *I doubt Tommy would shed a tear if I got run over by a bus.*

It was one of the great ironies of his life—his daughter's love affair with horses. He was a city boy through and through, a denizen of skyscrapers and sidewalks and sounding horns, more alive in a crowded bar than in the sunshine of a Virginia meadow. Madison, on the other hand, had been born in the saddle on Painted Hill Farm, a two-hundred-acre homestead that had been in her family since Reconstruction. It was impossible not to admire the place. It was as idyllic as a storybook. But the horses were a scourge. Tommy, an otherwise placid gelding, had once tried to buck him. In Lily's mind, however, they were made for each other.

Fifteen minutes later, they pulled into the parking lot at the University of Virginia Medical Center. As always when they reached the hospital, Lily fell silent. She was in the long-term maintenance phase of treatment for acute lymphoblastic leukemia—a curable form of the illness, but still a grave threat. Gone were the early days of blood transfusions, PICC lines, and intensive chemotherapy. Her hair had grown back to the length it had been before falling out in clumps. But her monthly clinic visit meant another round of Dex, another round of moodiness, hunger, and suppressed creativity. She hated the steroid—they all did. But there was no getting around it.

They walked together hand in hand into the Children's Hospital and took the elevator up to the pediatric oncology department. The outpatient facility had the bright, airy feel of a candy store, with walls the color of lollipops, waiting rooms suffused with natural light, and play areas with toys for the patients and their siblings.

"Hi, Lily," said an African American nurse, standing with her clipboard beside the check-in desk. "Hi, Josh. You can come on back."

"Cherise!" Lily cried, skipping across the floor and giving the nurse a hug.

Cherise led them to an intake room and checked Lily's vitals. Then she took them to an infusion room with a window overlooking the city. There, she conducted a physical exam, drew Lily's blood, and administered an injection of the chemotherapy drug Vincristine.

As Cherise and Lily went through the motions, Josh examined the artwork beside Lily's chair. It was a painted glass mosaic of a girl and a tree with a bird hovering above them. He squinted his eyes and tried to identify the tiny shapes that formed the girl's body—a rain cloud, a telescope, a shark, a cowboy boot, the planet Saturn. For ten minutes, he managed to ignore the e-mail waiting in his in-box. Eventually, however, his restless mind returned to it.

He knew what Maria wanted. It was a devil's bargain, the only way out to deny his conscience. He could recriminate all day about the choices he had made—the way he'd gotten too close, asked her too many personal questions, and allowed the answers to affect him, to turn his attraction into affection and affection into a centaur of love and lust; the way he'd extended his research trips to Rio to spend time with her, not just at Casa da Amizade, where her girls lived, but over dinner and on walks along the sand; the way he'd escorted her to her flat after a meal at Zuka, ostensibly for her safety but knowing full well it was more than that; and the way, once they were intimate, that he had carried on the deception, his heart a divided thing, loving Maria in São Paulo and Madison almost five thousand miles away. But the past was gone. The present was the problem. Maria's girls had nowhere else to go.

He took out his iPhone and saw her name in the message header: Maria Teresa de Santiago. "A Brazilian Mother Teresa" he had called her in his first dispatch for the *Post* about Casa da Amizade, or Friendship House. A child of Vidigal, Maria had escaped the slum only to return in adulthood and adopt a houseful of children as her own.

He opened the message. "Joshua," she had written, "please, we must talk. Your gift at Christmas is gone. We cannot pay the bills. No one helps us. All donors are gone, even the church. You only can understand. You promise me to help. Please help my girls."

Josh put the phone away and massaged his face. Suddenly he had a splitting headache.

"Daddy," he heard Lily say, as if from a distance. "Are you okay?"

He looked up and nodded, watched Cherise pump the last of the Vincristine into Lily's vein. *How unfair is this world*, he thought, mustering a smile despite the ache.

The rest of the appointment was a blur. He greeted Dr. Holiday when she appeared, even interacted with her, but his focus was shot, his thoughts in another place, wandering the haunted lanes of Vidigal, smelling the stink of rubbish, staring into the hollow eyes of drug addicts and street kids advertising their bodies for sale. He was there as he was before the celebrity and scandal, as an orphan abandoned on the steps of the National Cathedral, as the protégé of an adoptive father destined for the Carter White House and a mother who served the homeless, as a scribbler whose power was in his pen. It was in Vidigal where he had first conceived of *Rio Real*, the feature that had won him his first Pulitzer. And it was Vidigal to which he had returned with *The End of Childhood*. How could he forsake it now?

When the visit was over, Josh took Lily's hand and led her back to the car. On the drive downtown, she was quiet, pensive.

"You're somewhere else," she said perceptively. "Like Mommy always says."

"I'm sorry," he replied, his guilt increasing. "I'm just thinking."

"About what?"

He shook his head. "Nothing."

She crossed her small arms in protest. "You mean I wouldn't understand."

He tried to think of something to say. "I have some decisions to make. I want to do the right thing, but I'm not always sure what that is."

"Like when you're going to make up with Mommy and come home?"

Her words ran him through. "Yes."

"You should hurry," Lily went on. "She isn't happy."

Josh winced. "How do you know?"

"I just do," she said and looked out the window again.

Before long, Josh drove through Court Square, past the Albemarle County Courthouse where Thomas Jefferson, James Madison, and James Monroe had

once practiced law, and pulled to the curb in front of the stately brick building that housed the Center for Justice in Action, or CJA. Founded in 1986 by
Madison's father, Lewis Ames, CJA was one of the most prominent nonprofit
legal organizations in the South. A scion of the Virginia bar, Lewis was a lawyer-
statesman with a professor's intellect and the courtly manner of a squire. He had
argued five cases before the US Supreme Court and won all of them. For years,
he had enticed Madison to leave the global law firm that allowed her to play hop-
scotch with Josh around the world in order to do "the real business of justice," as
he put it. When the *Post* transferred Josh back to DC, she acceded. Six years on,
she was CJA's chief litigation counsel.

Madison was waiting for them on the sidewalk, her lithe equestrian's
body swaddled in a gray day coat and blue scarf that complemented her long
brown hair.

"Come riding tomorrow," Lily said, giving Josh a hug. "Mommy won't mind."

Josh glanced at his wife and saw her indecision. "I wish I could," he replied,
kissing Lily on the cheek. "But I have to go on a trip. I'll be back soon. We'll do
it then."

Lily stepped back and sighed, and Josh felt the lash of her dejection. He
took the whip from her silent eyes and turned it upon himself. How many times
would he walk away? It was a question that had no answer until Madison decided
to forgive him—if she decided to forgive him. He thought of Maria's e-mail and
flogged himself harder.

"Run inside," Madison told Lily. "Grandpa's got something for you."

"Bye, Daddy," Lily said with a wave.

"Bye, sweetie," he replied, watching her go. Then he stood up and faced
his wife.

She was a strong woman, even imperious when she wanted to be, but she
bore in her heart all the self-doubt of a perfectionist and had never quite recon-
ciled the conflict. As soon as Lily disappeared, the strain began to show around
her eyes.

"So you're going away," she said, burrowing her hands into her coat.
"How long?"

He scuffed his toe on the ground. "I don't know. Could be a couple weeks.
Maybe more."

"Is it a story?"

"Not exactly. It's hard to explain. I'll tell you about it later." He paused, feeling the sting of the winter wind. "I'm sorry to do this to you—to Lily."

"It's already done," she said matter-of-factly. "This is the fallout."

He bit his lip hard enough to notice. *I miss you*, he thought, but he couldn't bring himself to say it. "I'll keep in touch."

She turned away as if to leave, but a thought brought her up short. "Bring something home for her," she said, looking at him again. "You owe her that much."

"No," he said, "I owe her more."

CHAPTER THREE

There was something about the light in Southern California, the way it embraced the world, as if the sun and sky were lovers, and the earth the bed beneath them. It was February in Los Angeles, but there were no coats in sight. There were cyclists on the highway, runners working up a sweat, even a few sun worshippers soaking up rays on the beach. It was a photographer's paradise—the bronze hills graced with the green of rain-fed grass, the indigo ocean cradled by golden sand, the sky a patchless quilt of cornflowers.

Josh had the top down on his rental convertible—a muscle-bound Mustang that made him feel like a kid again. He was on the Pacific Coast Highway, following its serpentine arcs through Santa Monica and Pacific Palisades, the drizzling damp of the DC winter barely a memory in the mirror. His lips curled upward beneath his aviator shades, the warm wind tousling his curly hair. It was almost enough to make him forget the sorrow he had left behind. But not quite.

He pulled into the lot at Gladstones restaurant, locked his luggage in the trunk, and left his keys with the valet. The place was a shrine to the sea, its umbrella-covered tables separated from the shore by a thin pane of glass. Rana Jalil was already there, having claimed a table at the edge of the deck that afforded a little privacy. He was dressed like a man on holiday—linen pants, calfskin flip-flops, and an untucked shirt that revealed a wedge of ebony chest hair. He greeted Josh with an easy grin and a loose handshake.

"You picked a fine day," he said, the trace of a Bengali accent beneath his words. "It rained all last week. It's good for the drought, but I much prefer sunshine."

A waiter appeared at their side as soon as Josh sat down.

"What are you drinking?" Josh asked, glancing at the menu.

"Perrier," Rana replied. When Josh gave him an odd look, he explained, "I'm Muslim even in LA, but you get what you want. I hear they serve a mean vodka martini."

"I'll try it," he told the waiter.

When they were alone, Josh sat back and watched the waves roll in off the ocean. He was weary from travel. He had been in transit for eleven hours. But he rested only a moment before reaching for something germane. "So you sue the clothing brands," he began. "Tell me how you do it."

"California makes it easy," Rana replied. "Under the law, the brands are guarantors of a worker's wages. If the factory doesn't pay—which they often don't—the workers come to us, and we go to the labor commissioner. The brands usually settle. The factories are harder to nail. They just close up shop, create a new corporation, and reopen down the street."

"Do you ever take the brands to court?" Josh asked.

"We'd love nothing more," Rana said, "but we've never been able to find plaintiffs. Think about it. You're an immigrant without a green card working the only job you can find to feed your kids—in a sweatshop, sewing clothes, being ripped off, probably abused. We offer you compensation now or the possibility of systemic impact in three years, with the real possibility your case will get kicked out of court and you'll end up with nothing."

The waiter delivered their drinks, and Josh took a sip of his martini. "What if I told you I could find you plaintiffs? But you'll have to work with another organization."

Rana pushed his sunglasses onto his forehead, giving Josh a glimpse into his eyes. They were fairer than Josh expected—somewhere between hazel and topaz. "You want to bring a lawsuit?" he inquired, openly intrigued. "I figured you were after a story."

Josh nodded, recalling his own surprise when his source told him what to do with the names. "I have my reasons," he said.

"Who's the collaborator?" Rana asked.

"CJA. Lewis Ames." Josh spoke the words with confidence, though neither Madison nor her father knew anything about it—yet.

A smile spread across Rana's face. "A family connection." When Josh didn't reply, he began to nod. "Where are the plaintiffs?"

"Bangladesh. Malaysia. Jordan."

Rana's intrigue turned into fascination. "An *international* case."

"Against a global retailer. One of America's favorite companies." Josh took a breath, then spoke the word in sotto voce. "Presto."

"I'm riveted," Rana admitted. "But I'm also dubious. Now that the Supreme Court has gutted the Alien Tort Statute, all we have left is the federal trafficking act and a quagmire of foreign and state law claims. The trafficking act is good, but to prove liability, we'd not only have to show forced labor in the factories, we'd have to show that Presto knew or should have known that they were benefiting from it. That's a hell of a high bar, especially with a defendant as powerful as Presto. Global corporations don't just play to win. They play for keeps."

Josh shrugged. "Does that mean you're out? Or are you willing to roll the dice?"

Rana grinned and picked up a menu. "I bet you're famished. Everything's good here."

"So you're in then."

"I'm in," Rana said. "Tell me your plan."

CHAPTER FOUR

Even in his glory days as a reporter, Josh hadn't traveled like this. It was ironic that he could afford it now, after everything that had happened. When his father had been at the *Post*, in the heyday of newsprint, foreign correspondents lived like ambassadors, flying first class, dining at the best restaurants, and leasing flats in expat neighborhoods. Then the Internet arrived, shattering the old ad-and-subscription business model and sending newspaper executives into a frenzy of budget cutting and buyouts. By the time Josh took an overseas post in Tokyo, his expense account looked more like a piggy bank. He'd thought his per diem might get an epinephrine shot after he won his first Pulitzer, but he was wrong. Even in London, when he was deputy bureau chief, his travel budget was so lean that he had usually skipped lunch.

All that had changed, virtually overnight, when he hit the speaking circuit with *The End of Childhood*. His hosts—mostly foundations and universities— treated him like a dignitary, reimbursing his expenses without a glance. At first the red-carpet treatment came as a shock, but over time he grew accustomed to it, as if the music would never stop. And it might not have, had it not been for the Brazilian paper *O Globo* and the story it broke about Maria and Catarina, one of her girls. These days Josh couldn't afford to fly business class, especially not with Rana in tow. But old habits died hard. He had booked them at the Westin, Dhaka's flagship hotel.

He stood at the window and looked out at the city fifteen floors down. Nestled between finger lakes, the neighborhood of Gulshan was a concrete jungle of glittering high-rises, decrepit warehouses, and half-built buildings filigreed with rebar. A chorus of horns drifted up from below. Even at ten in the morning, the traffic was nearly impassable.

Josh's iPhone vibrated. It was a text from Rana—"Anis is here. The meeting is set."

"Coming," Josh typed back and grabbed his backpack off the bed.

After an elevator ride to the lobby—an exotic mélange of marble, wood, and club lighting—he met Rana outside the revolving door. His driver, Anis, was waiting for them on the street beside a vintage burgundy Toyota Corolla. Before they could reach him, however, a swarm of beggars descended on Josh. Barely clothed children, skin caked with dirt, made hunger signs with their hands. Careworn women in saris and headscarves clucked at him. And men, old and young, jostled him, touching his forearms and shoulders.

"English," said an elderly man in a skullcap. "You English. Need help. No job."

"I'm sorry," Josh replied, gently making a path with his arms. "I can't help you."

He hated saying it, hated the pretense, the lie. He could buy the man food. He could buy all of them food. But it wouldn't change their circumstances. He'd seen it a thousand times. Poverty like this was crushing and sometimes criminal, orchestrated by begging rings.

He followed Rana into the Corolla. "How far to the Millennium factory?" he asked Anis, trying not to think about the palms on his window, hands pawing at the door.

"Two hours," the driver said, then grinned widely. "I will make it less."

✦

In most places in the world, the rules of the road left margins for error—the space between lanes, the delay between red and green lights, speed limits that encouraged caution and care. On the streets of Dhaka, there were neither rules nor restraint. Anis used his horn more frequently than his brake pedal, and slowed only to avoid an imminent collision—an occasion that repeated itself with stomach-churning regularity. Judging by the scars on every vehicle in sight, collisions were inevitable. Indeed, on the drive to Ashulia, an industrial district north of the city, Josh witnessed a truck burning on the side of the road, a bus sideswiping a car in the quest to turn a corner, and a motorcyclist ditching his bike to avoid a street vendor. Anis, however, didn't seem to notice.

After an hour of demolition derby, they left the teeming city and crossed the floodplain of the Turag River, its banks littered with brick factories. Before long, Anis turned off the road and took them into a warren of dirt lanes thronged with shops and stalls. Here the traffic was mostly pedestrian—women buying vegetables and cloth, men browsing for cell phones, young children scampering about. A few paused to stare at Josh. Most paid them no heed.

"Millennium is there," Anis grunted, pointing out the windshield.

The factory rose up before them like an elephant resting on his haunches, its mottled concrete walls draining light from the sky. Josh had watched footage of the fire, seen columns of flames shooting out the windows, the building's innards completely ablaze. Fifteen months later, the only visible remnants of the holocaust were halos of soot around broken glass and twisted iron bars. The place had the forlorn look of abandonment.

Anis pulled the Corolla to the side of the road, allowing a middle-aged man to join them in the front seat. He shook Rana's hand over his shoulder and gave Josh a thin smile. He and Rana exchanged a few words in Bengali. Then Rana translated for Josh.

"This is Mohammad," Rana explained. "He is a labor activist. He was able to arrange interviews with some of the survivors."

Josh was immediately curious. "Tony Sharif said his people couldn't get them to talk."

Again, Rana and Mohammad chatted in Bengali. Then Rana said, "That was the owner's doing. He promised to pay the workers' medical expenses if they kept quiet. By the time they figured out he was lying, the media was gone."

"What happened to him?" Josh asked.

"He went to jail for a little while," Rana said. "But his friends in the government bailed him out. Now he's asking them for a loan to reopen the factory."

Josh grimaced. "Did the survivors get any compensation?"

Rana shook his head. "The BGMEA—that's the Bangladesh Garment Manufacturers and Exporters Association—gave them a little money, but not nearly enough to cover their hospital bills. The brands ran for the hills. All of them said the same thing: 'Our clothes weren't supposed to be there.' Even Presto didn't pay a dime."

Anis parked in an alleyway beside a medicine stand, and Mohammad led them to the factory gates on foot. The lanes here were narrow and badly rutted. A cluster of young men sauntered by, their eyes fixed on Josh. Mohammad spoke a string of sharp words in Bengali, but the posse didn't disperse. Instead, the men lit cigarettes and lingered in the shadows nearby.

"We should go," Rana said, looking unsettled. "The owner doesn't like attention."

He took Josh by the arm and guided him quickly down a footpath between cinderblock dwellings, Mohammad in the lead and Anis behind them. At six foot three, Josh had to duck his head to avoid clothes drying on lines and shuffle his feet to avoid sandals scattered around doorways. A few heads peeked out of windows, but no one spoke. The footpath led to another, and that one intersected with a third. Soon, Josh lost all sense of direction in the maze, his only landmarks sky and earth and Mohammad's red shirt.

At last, the labor activist slowed and knocked on a doorframe. The curtain parted and a young woman invited them in, covering her head with a scarf. Her home was a single room with a bed, a dresser, a kitchenette, and an old-fashioned Singer sewing machine. The unfinished concrete walls were decorated with newspaper clippings. On the bed sat three other women and a man, all in their twenties, and two children, a girl and a boy about six or seven.

"This is Ishana," Rana said, translating for Mohammad and gesturing toward their host. "She worked at Millennium. They all did, except for the children."

Ishana placed a plastic chair on the floor in front of the bed and pointed at Josh.

"She wants you to sit down," Rana explained.

Josh glanced around the cramped space. "Where will she sit?"

Before Rana could answer, Ishana wedged herself between the women on the mattress.

"Please," Rana said, gesturing with his hand. "You are her guest."

To Josh, the honor felt wrong in every way, but he accepted it out of respect. He took a seat and retrieved his notebook from his backpack. Rana squatted beside him, and Anis and Mohammad stood outside the door. Rana made introductions in Bengali, and then Ishana began to speak. While Josh waited for the translation, he studied the woman. Her face was a kind of contradiction—round and cherubic, yet fraught with sorrow. Her hands were small, her fingers and wrists free of jewelry. Beyond her dress and headscarf, her only adornment was a nose stud.

"She's twenty-eight years old," Rana began. "She worked on the fourth floor. The day of the fire was her daughter's birthday, but she couldn't leave because of the last-minute order. Around nine o'clock they heard shouting, then two explosions. The lights went out. The stairwell was blocked. The fire came quickly."

Rana listened awhile longer, then went on. "Some men broke a window and made space between the bars. The woman beside her tried to jump, but the bars stopped her. Ishana felt something dripping on her. She thought it was water, but it was blood. She was terrified, but she knew she had to jump. When she was on the sill, someone bumped into her and she fell sideways. She would have died if she had hit the ground directly. Instead, she fell through a roof, and it cushioned the impact. It was hours before her uncle found her."

Josh closed his eyes, the horror of it washing over him. He saw her standing on the ledge, the growl of flames behind her, saw her shadow falling through the air, heard the shriek of metal as the roof gave way, then the thump of her body landing on the cold floor of someone's home.

Before long, Rana spoke again. "She woke up twelve days later in a trauma center. Her back was broken. The pain was unbearable. Eventually she was discharged, but her back never healed. She doesn't have money for treatment. She is in pain and exhausted. Her husband—who is the man on the bed behind her— worked in the cutting room. When he jumped, a piece of metal pierced his skull. He has terrible headaches now, two or three a day. Neither of them can work. They asked a charity for money to help with treatment. But the charity only gave them a sewing machine." Rana pointed at the Singer. "Unfortunately, she is in too much pain to use it. They have no money for rent. The landlord is about to evict them. They don't know what to do."

Josh stared at the floor, his eyes welling with tears. His first instinct—as always in moments like this—was to drive his fist through a wall and then shake it at the heavens. But he didn't do that. He absorbed the anger, buried it down deep with all the stories that had shattered his heart. He had a library of them now, tales of war and rape, beatings and stonings, even a crucifixion. But Ishana's story was among the worst. His second instinct was to embrace her, but he suppressed that too. She was Muslim; he was a man. It would only aggravate her pain.

He looked back at her and wiped his eyes. "Please tell her . . . ," he began, searching for words that would matter. "Please tell her I'm sorry. It's an awful thing they suffered."

Rana interpreted, his voice almost a whisper now, and Ishana nodded.

Josh waited a moment, then spoke the first two names his source had given him. "I'm looking for a man, Ashik Hassan. He has a daughter named Sonia." Josh took out his iPhone and showed Ishana the photo of Sonia from the night of the fire.

Ishana glanced at the screen, and her eyes fell to the floor. When she spoke, her tone was laced with pain. "She knew them," Rana translated. "Ashik and his wife, Joya, lived close by. They had six children—four boys and two girls. Joya died in the fire, as did their other daughter, Nasima. Sonia was badly injured. The hospital bills were too much. Ashik couldn't afford to stay in Dhaka. He took Sonia and his sons back to his village."

"Does she know where they went?" Josh asked gently.

"Kalma," Rana said. "It's on the Padma River south of here."

Josh nodded and thought back to the stories he had read from the media's coverage of the fire. "The last order Millennium handled was the Piccola pants. Does she remember making any other clothes for Presto around that time?"

When Ishana heard the question, her eyes brightened and she spoke with surprising animation. Josh watched Rana's face as he listened, saw his brows arch, his eyelids expand, and knew that they had stumbled upon something significant.

"You're not going to believe this, but Presto was one of their biggest buyers," Rana said. "Millennium was making clothes for them up to the time of the fire."

"*What?*" Josh was thunderstruck. "She's certain of this?"

"She saw the labels. Piccola, Burano, Porto Bari, all of the company's lines." Suddenly Ishana spoke again. "There's more," Rana continued. "On the day of the fire, Presto's quality-control people were in the factory."

A shiver coursed down Josh's spine. He remembered something then, from the night he met his source at the Lincoln Memorial. There had been a moment when the man let down his guard, and Josh saw a trace of grief in his eyes. Now Josh was beginning to understand. The story Presto had delivered to the world, a story about authorized suppliers and color-coded lists and the company's unwavering commitment to worker safety, was not merely a half-truth packaged for public consumption.

It was a bald-faced lie.

CHAPTER FIVE

The road to the village of Kalma, fifty kilometers south of Dhaka, was less a highway than a dirt track worn down by thousands of vehicles and runoff from the monsoon rains that fell in the summertime, replenishing the Himalayan snowpack and making the rivers of Bangladesh run swollen into the sea. The land between the rivers was flat and verdant, with wild grass, leafy trees, and cultivated fields. Josh was in the backseat of Anis's battered Corolla, struggling to tap out an e-mail to Lily on his iPhone between bumps in the road. She had sent him a message the night before, updating him about school and her friends and, of course, the horses. Priscilla, one of the mares, had equine distemper, which meant she had to be quarantined and treated with penicillin. Josh found the dramas of stable management about as interesting as the *Internal Revenue Code*, but for Lily's sake, he forced himself to care.

"How much longer?" he asked Rana, who was in the front passenger seat.

Rana chatted with Anis. "Ten minutes," he replied. "We're close."

"Thank God," Josh said, putting the finishing touches on his message.

On the Internet, the trip to Kalma had looked like a pleasant jaunt—ninety minutes at most. But the wizards at Google seemed blithely unaware of Dhaka's insane congestion. The traffic anaconda had snared them at the hotel, throttled them for two hours, and only released them south of the bridge at the Buriganga River. They had been in transit since eight a.m.

After sending the e-mail, Josh looked out the window and watched as they approached the village. He saw low-slung buildings in the distance shaded by trees and surrounded by fields of waist-high jute. There were pedestrians on the roadway, men riding bicycles and women carrying babies in slings. Anis slowed behind two hand-pulled carts piled high with sacks of rice. He honked twice, and the carts made space for him to pass on the shoulder.

Soon they drove into a square with thatched-roof stalls and squat houses with stick fences. Some of the dwellings were constructed of mud bricks. Others were made of logs lashed together and enclosed by sheet metal.

"Wait here," Rana said. "I'll get directions."

He climbed out of the car and struck up a conversation with an old man resting languidly outside a fruit stall. "They live down by the river," he said when he returned. "Ashik has a new wife. The oldest boy has a job in Dhaka. The others live here."

On the far side of the square, they followed a cart path through groves of trees and planted fields. Everywhere, children were at play—swinging from limbs, splashing in a pond, chasing each other in a game of tag. It was a Saturday, and school was not in session.

At the end of the road, they came upon a trio of mud huts standing beneath a date palm tree. A scrawny goat and three lean chickens were wandering about, nibbling at clumps of grass. Behind the huts, Josh saw the sparkle of water. A wispy girl was seated on a plastic chair outside the doorway of the center hut. Her eyes were open, but her body was motionless, as if frozen in time. *Is that Sonia?* Josh thought. In the photo, the girl's features had been obscured. But she was the right age, and her face had a similar shape.

Rana left the vehicle and approached the girl, greeting her in Bengali. The girl didn't reply. A woman in her thirties appeared in the doorway, clad in a sari and headscarf. After listening to Rana, she spoke a few words and set out on foot toward the river.

"Ashik and his sons are fishing," Rana said. "She will fetch them."

Josh climbed out and waited with Rana beneath the date palm. A few minutes later, the woman returned with a wiry man and three teenage boys, all reed-thin with clothes that hung like drapes from skeletal limbs. The man approached them warily, looking at them through eyes stained pink by the tropical sun. While Rana made the introductions, the man sized them up. His face was gaunt, his skin stretched taut over bone. At last, he welcomed them with handshakes.

"*Salaam*," he said. "My name, Ashik." He pointed at the boys. "These, my son."

Ashik spoke to the woman in Bengali and led them into the center hut. They took seats on a rug between the rough-hewed frames of two beds while the woman busied herself preparing the midday meal on a mud stove. The hut had no electricity. Its interior was illuminated only by daylight filtering through the doorway and a window on the opposite wall.

"He's invited us to lunch," Rana told Josh. "It will be ready soon."

"*Dhonnobad*," Josh said, putting his hands together, palms flat, and bowing his head slightly in a sign of respect. "That is kind of you."

Ashik returned the gesture, then said something to his youngest son who was standing just outside the door. The boy disappeared for a moment, then returned with the girl, guiding her to the rug and speaking gently into her left ear. She sat down cross-legged, hands in her lap, and stared blankly at the wall. The boy sat next to her, regarding Josh with open curiosity.

"This is Sonia," Rana said, translating for Ashik. "Her head was injured in the fall. She is mostly blind, and she can hear out of only one ear. She can still speak, but not well. Conversation is exhausting to her. She will need to lie down soon."

Josh looked into the girl's vacant eyes. She was a beautiful child with a graceful ovate face, a pixie nose, caramel-colored skin, and bone-straight hair. In a different world, she would have had her pick of suitors. Now her body was a prison, her mind bound in chains.

"How old is she?" he asked.

Rana spoke to Ashik, then shook his head. "She's fifteen now, but she started working at Millennium when she was thirteen. The manager falsified her papers."

Josh made a note in his notepad. "I'll try to keep my questions brief. I'd like to know what she was working on when the fire broke out."

Rana translated for Ashik, and Ashik spoke to his son. The boy leaned close to Sonia and murmured the question in her good ear. The girl didn't seem to register that he had spoken. For a poignant moment, Josh worried that the impact from the fall had wiped her memory clean. But then her lips parted and a word escaped.

"Piccola."

Josh struggled to suppress a smile. If she could remember, she could testify. The conditions would have to be right. They would need experts to convince the court that she retained capacity despite her injuries. But once the procedural hurdles were cleared, she would make a spectacular witness—the kind that would haunt a juror's dreams.

"Where was she located on the sewing line?"

This time Sonia's response came quicker. "She and her sister, Nasima, were in the finishing section," Rana translated. "They sewed on the labels."

"What does she remember about the fire?" Josh asked.

After listening to her brother, the girl spoke for at least a minute, possibly two. The effort left her winded. She leaned her head on her brother's shoulder as Rana interpreted.

"She remembers loud noises and shouting. The lights flickered and then went dark. They found a window and lay down on the floor. The smoke was thick. Nasima made a mask out of pants to help her breathe. She remembers the heat, and the screams of workers jumping from windows. Nasima tied pants together into a rope and told her to climb down. She was terrified, but she went. She remembers falling. Then nothing."

Josh nodded and scribbled on his pad for a while, allowing Sonia to bear up under her pain. It was a lesson he had learned from Maria after his first interview at Casa da Amizade. *The hardest stories are like the people who tell them*, she had said when his questions made one of her girls cry. *You have to give them room to breathe.* He had lived by that creed ever since, training himself to be patient and putting the human before the headline. It had won him the trust of people the rest of the media couldn't reach.

At last, when Sonia's eyelids grew heavy and he was afraid he was about to lose her, Josh leaned forward again. "Can she tell me anything else about Nasima?"

When she heard her sister's name, Sonia lifted her head and blinked away sleep. Her reply came out in a whisper.

"Nasima called her *Khamjana*—hummingbird," Rana said. "She misses her very much."

Josh took a breath, sensing he had pushed the girl as far as he could. "Please tell her she is very courageous. She can rest now."

Rana passed along the message, and the boy helped Sonia to one of the beds. She curled up on the mattress and closed her eyes. As soon as she was situated, Ashik gathered the older boys on the rug. After a moment, his wife placed a tray in their midst and knelt beside it, serving steaming *cha* in mugs. While they sipped their tea, she brought them plates piled high with rice, curried potatoes, and boiled fish. Finally, she passed around a basket of flatbread.

"River fish," Ashik said proudly. "Fresh."

They ate until they were satisfied. Afterward, Ashik's wife fixed a plate for herself and took it outside. The boys sat quietly, watching Josh, until Ashik sent them away.

Josh collected his notepad and spoke to Rana. "I'd like to know what he saw that night."

Ashik listened to the translation, then turned toward the doorway and stared out at the yard. In time, his gaze shifted and his memories began to emerge. Josh examined his face and saw the strain in the wrinkles around his eyes, heard the tremor of anguish in his tone, and beneath it the darker notes of shame and guilt. He understood Ashik's burden better than most. He was a man damned to live every day in the presence of his own powerlessness, a father who saw his child suffering but could do nothing to save her.

Rana gave voice to Ashik's story. "He was home with his sons when he heard the first explosion. They went outside and looked at the factory. The power was out in the area, and it was the only building that still had electricity. After the second explosion, he saw the flames. He called the fire department and went to the factory gates. But the guards were only letting workers out. No one could get in. He heard screams and saw shadows falling. He didn't realize until later that his daughters were among them."

Rana looked at the floor, and Josh saw tears in his eyes. "The fire trucks took a long time to get there. By then it was too late. They forced the gates open, and a few people managed to get in. They found Sonia near the entrance. Nasima was beside her. The people took pictures, but then the firefighters closed the gates. Later that night, ambulances came. One of them took Sonia away. Ashik went with her. She was at the trauma center for two weeks. Then she was moved to a hospital. A month after the fire, they sent her home. But Ashik had no one to take care of her. He couldn't support the family driving a rickshaw. He had to move back to the village. His new wife is a distant cousin. His uncle arranged it. This is his uncle's land. Ashik helps him fish."

Josh met Ashik's eyes and nodded compassionately. "I have a few more questions. Did any of the brands that made clothing at Millennium ever contact him after the fire?"

"Some people came a few months later," Rana said eventually. "They said they were from the US. He told them everything. He thought they were with the media, but he never heard from them again. Now he doesn't know. That's why he was suspicious when we showed up."

Josh was immediately curious. "Does he remember anything else about them?"

"There were two men and a woman," Rana explained. "One of them was a translator."

Josh pictured his source at the Lincoln Memorial and wondered if he'd sent them.

"Go ahead and tell him about the lawsuit," Josh said, "but downplay the money part. I don't want him thinking about dollar signs. Just the possibility of justice."

Rana nodded and began to elucidate their proposition. Meanwhile, Josh watched Ashik's wife sweeping the dirt outside the hut. He imagined the man's sons casting their nets into the river, hoping to snare a catch to sell at the market. It was a hardscrabble existence. Whatever chance the family had to escape poverty had burned in the Millennium inferno. Yet the three-trillion-dollar global apparel machine continued to hum, minting money for the brands.

Rana interrupted his thoughts. "He wants to know if Presto can make trouble for him, and for his eldest son in Dhaka. I told him no, but he wants to hear it from you."

Josh spoke candidly, holding nothing back. "They've already made all the trouble they can. It's you who can make trouble for them."

When the man understood, he spoke a burst of words, staring at Rana.

"He's willing to fight," Rana said, excitement buoying his voice. "He doesn't care if they give him money. He wants the world to know his family's story."

Josh bowed his head, honored by the man's courage. He smiled grimly. "I can promise him that. The world will hear."

Malaysia

February 2008

KLIA EKSPRES TRAIN

KUALA LUMPUR, MALAYSIA

FEBRUARY 12, 2008

6:55 A.M.

The clouds of sunrise were like a wedding dress draped over the earth, red silk piled upon gold, weaving new patterns in layers and folds. Jashel saw her reflection in the glass, saw Farzana smile at him, dimples cleaving her cheeks, her lips spread in a gracious arc, showing the gap between her front teeth. She was everywhere around him now, on the teeming streets of Dhaka, in the waiting room at the agency, on the plane, in airport terminals, even in the line at passport control. Every time he saw a purple headscarf veiling dark tresses, he remembered her, pined for her, wished the world were different, that his father were still alive, that his family were secure, and that he had married her in the New Year as he had planned.

But it was not to be. Allah had spoken. The planet had turned. The cable had snapped, the crane had canted, and the concrete blocks had fallen thirty meters from the sky, crushing his father into the ground. It was a death as shocking as it was untimely. In an instant, Jashel's destiny changed. His father had no savings. He had poured all of his earnings into the land and the house and the animals in the village of Matiranga where his family lived. Jashel was the first of eight children. He was twenty now, a graduate of primary school but not secondary. At the age of fourteen, he had left the classroom and followed his father to Chittagong to build factories and apartments for the elite. His earnings had paid for the education of his siblings, but the amount was not enough to support the family. With his father gone, he knew only one way to keep the land in his mother's possession. He had to find work abroad.

Jashel looked out the window as the train glided toward Kuala Lumpur, saw the sun peek out from behind the clouds, brightening the city skyline. He thought back to the day he welcomed Mr. Amin into his mother's home and took a new path into the future. Mr. Amin was from Dhaka, but he was well known in the village. He was a recruiter for an outsourcing agency that placed able-bodied Bangladeshis from the rural areas in employment overseas—construction and housekeeping in the Middle East, electronics in Southeast Asia, and apparel in a dozen countries between Jordan and Vietnam. Although the contract was written in English—a language Jashel did not speak—Mr. Amin had scrawled the key terms in Bengali.

The factory was Rightaway Garments, the country Malaysia. The length of the contract was three years. The agency would obtain all the necessary documents—the most important being Jashel's passport, work permit, and airline ticket—and cover the levies and fees, including the cost of a physical exam. The agency's counterpart in Kuala Lumpur would house him in a dormitory and manage his employment. His basic pay would be eight hundred Malaysian ringgits per month—about two hundred ten dollars—for eight hours a day, six days a week, plus time and a half for overtime. In exchange, Mr. Amin's agency would charge a onetime fee of two hundred thousand taka—roughly twenty-five hundred dollars.

The recruitment fee had nearly scuttled the deal. Jashel's family had no way to cover it, short of selling their land. But Mr. Amin had been ready with an alternative. He told Jashel that most of his recruits required loans to pay the fee. His agency collaborated with a lender who offered financing at a reasonable interest rate, so long as the debt was secured by property.

"In garments, you will work overtime," the recruiter explained, scratching out figures on a pad. "That will raise your monthly pay to one thousand ringgit. At that rate, you can repay the loan in eighteen months while still remitting ten thousand taka to your family per month. After that, you will be able to remit twenty thousand taka per month. A good deal, no?"

Though the numbers were indeed attractive, Jashel had not made his decision hastily. He took the matter under advisement, seeking counsel from other families whose relatives had sought greener pastures outside Bangladesh. While no one in Matiranga had migrated to Malaysia, their stories were generally the same. The labor was grueling and the hours long, but the pay was far better than anything in Dhaka or Chittagong, at least for unskilled workers.

A week later, Jashel signed the contract and promissory note, and his mother executed a mortgage on her land. After that, he paid a visit to Farzana. He found her washing clothes along the banks of the river with her younger sisters, her raven hair uncovered and tied behind her in a bun. She stood up when he approached, clasping her hands behind her back. He kept an appropriate distance out of respect for the traditions and for her honor as a virgin.

"I have to go," he said in Bengali, looking deep into her eyes. "I am sorry."

She nodded stoically, but her bottom lip began to quiver. "How long will you be gone?"

"Three years, perhaps six," he answered, struggling to hold his emotions in check. "Your father will find you another husband."

A tear escaped from her eye. "Tell him that yourself."

"You would wait for me?" Jashel asked, hardly able to believe it.

She looked out at the river twisting away into the distance. "I will wait, but only if you promise to come home."

They stood in silence for long seconds, the water flowing lazily behind them, in no hurry to reach the sea. How badly he longed to take her into his arms, to stroke her hair and kiss the sorrow from her cheeks. He had been dreaming of holding her since they were children. But the time had not yet come.

"I will come home," he said.

He left her there with a plainspoken good-bye and walked back to the village, her face emblazoned upon his heart. He loved her like his own. Of that much he was sure. But the future he had no way to predict. He didn't know what awaited him in Malaysia, or how the years would change him. He had no idea when he would return to the village, or if Farzana would be there, watching for him when he did.

The train pulled into KL Sentral station and the doors slid open with a quiet *whoosh*, allowing the passengers to disembark. Jashel stood up and took his suitcase—a beat-up Samsonite rollaboard—off the rack. He shouldered his backpack and trailed the rest of the group onto the platform. There were six other Bangladeshis with him, all from Mr. Amin's agency, all destined for Rightaway Garments. Only one of them spoke passable English, but his reading skills were rudimentary. They stood in a huddle, observing the other passengers make their way toward an escalator with signs posted above it in languages none of them understood.

Jashel pointed at the escalator. "*Ye upaya*," he said, at once confident and nervous. "That is the way." The others nodded in unison, grateful to have direction.

Following the path of the crowd, Jashel led them up to the bustling terminal and scanned the floor for the escort Mr. Amin had promised them. The scene was overwhelming—the swirl of travelers, the chatter of languages, the bright lights and digital screens and faces in a hundred shades of color—but it was no longer novel to him. Dhaka had given him a glimpse of the wider world. He was a quick study and unafraid of new experiences. He knew how to adjust.

"*Assalamu alaykum*," said a gray-haired man with glasses.

Jashel shook the man's hand. "*Wa alaykum assalam*."

"I am Foysol," the man said in Bengali, surveying the group. "My agency works with Mr. Amin. Good. All of you are here. Come along. Our transport is waiting."

They walked together through the throng and left the terminal for the sidewalk. A van was standing at the curb, its sliding door open.

"We will go to the factory first and process your paperwork," said Foysol. "Then you will have a day of training on the machines. After that, I will take you to your dormitory."

The young men piled into the vehicle and Foysol climbed behind the wheel, driving them out of the station. Since his departure from the village, Jashel had tried to picture Kuala Lumpur by conjuring photographs from old textbooks. But the sprawling metropolis he saw through the windows rendered all of his musings vain. There were towers everywhere, glistening in the sun. There were giant bridges and manicured parks and grand buildings and sweeping motorways with expensive cars that stayed in their lanes and honked only occasionally. The streets were immaculate, the pace of life rushed but orderly.

It wasn't long, however, before he realized that the city had many faces. Outside the commercial district, the skyline flattened out, the glamor retreated, and a vast urban landscape stretched toward the horizon, its buildings and roads and shops and residences neither majestic nor tidy. In a way, Jashel was relieved. In another way, he was disappointed. But he had little time to think about it. His destination had arrived.

Before the van stood a metal gate with a large printed sign—RIGHTAWAY GARMENTS. The guards waved the van through, and Foysol found a parking spot alongside a handful of other vehicles. He turned off the ignition and swiveled around in his seat.

"Now that we are here, I will take your passports for safekeeping. I will do the same with your work permits. I will return them to you when the time is right."

Jashel clutched his backpack, feeling a vague sense of foreboding. Mr. Amin had said nothing about relinquishing his passport and work permit. In fact, the agent had advised him to keep the documents with him at all times in case a police officer or immigration official ever questioned his legal status. He watched the others reach into their bags and hand over their passports. Foysol collected them in a bundle, binding them together with a rubber band.

Jashel shook his head forcefully. "The documents are mine. I will keep them safe."

As soon as he spoke the words, Foysol's expression hardened. "You are a guest of Malaysia. And you are my guest. You will follow my rules or your stay will be difficult." He extended his hand, palm open. "Now, give me your passport."

Jashel's heart began to race, but still he refused.

Foysol glowered at him. "Let me tell you what will happen if you do not obey. I will report to immigration that you arrived with HIV. They will revoke your work permit. The factory will disown you, and your contract will be void. I will then hand you over to the immigration police, and they will take you to a detention facility where you will rot until you are deported, either because your family bought an airline ticket, or because the government finally decided to get rid of you." Again, Foysol put out his hand. "Your passport, please."

The blood drained from Jashel's face. If Rightaway Garments voided his contract, not only would he forfeit the chance to send money home to his family—and, in time, to Farzana—but the lender from whom he had borrowed two hundred thousand taka would call the note and foreclose on his family's property, leaving them destitute. His brothers were fourteen and twelve, his sisters between seventeen and five. If he were detained as a criminal, they would be forced to beg—or worse. And when the time came for his deportation, he would return home an outcast. Farzana's father would call off the betrothal. No outsourcing agency would ever speak to him again. His only option would be to return to construction, no matter how poor the pay.

At that moment, Jashel realized that Foysol held his fate like a parrot in a cage. If he sang the agent's tune, Foysol would watch over him. If he disobeyed, Foysol would ruin him. He slipped a trembling hand into his backpack and withdrew his passport, handing it over to the agent. Foysol opened it and examined Jashel's picture. He grinned malevolently.

"You're smarter than you look, Jashel Sayed Parveen. Let's hope you stay that way."

PART THREE

Cameron

November 2013–January 2014

CHAPTER ONE

The bullhorns were still audible two hundred and fifty feet off the ground. The height dampened their effect, as did the glass, but the strident chanting and squawk-like sirens were impossible to ignore. Cameron stood at his window looking down at the protestors outside the tower's entrance. There were at least fifty of them huddled together against a stiff wind blowing off the Potomac. Their numbers were down from two hundred a week ago, but the demonstration was still large enough to merit the attention of the police. The mob was waving placards, most of them homemade. They were calling for Presto's head.

Cameron regarded the slogans with amusement. They were juvenile things, some warmed-over relics of the Occupy movement, others sophomoric interpretations of Marx and Lenin—"Capitalist Pigs," "We Are the 99%," "Wall Street Is Evil," "Our Kids Want Clothes Made in the USA," "Justice for Workers," "Corporations Oppress the Poor," and other such pabulum. But one sign pierced him with its appeal. "Tell Us the Truth!!! End the Cover-up!!!" Though the exclamation marks were gauche, the accusation was accurate. But the truth was something Presto could never tell.

It had been nearly fourteen days since his return from Bangladesh, but he had slept less than sixty hours—many of them on the sofa in Vance's office. In the late evenings after the emergency meetings adjourned, and the phone grew quiet, and Vance and Kristin Raymond and the rest of the C-suite ran out of questions, he searched for a metaphor to describe the madness. A bullet train with no stops. A rock skipping across water. A death march. On the long flight home, he had formulated a plan to widen the investigation. But it was predicated upon assumptions that had floundered as soon as the Gulfstream landed at Reagan—that Vance would give the investigation top priority; that Anderson, Cameron's deputy general counsel, could handle the battalion of advice-seekers with minimal oversight; that Blake Conrad would run interference with the board, giving Cameron space to ferret out the causes behind the crisis.

But events had overtaken all of them. Right now, with Presto's share price down 18 percent—25 at the nadir—online sales more sluggish than they had been in three years, and Black Friday only a week away, no one gave a damn about the *why*. Only the *what* mattered. What written reassurances would prevent a sell-off among nervous investors? What Facebook and Twitter messaging would tranquilize the piranhas on social media? What TV ads would keep consumers spending without making Presto appear callous? What charity campaigns would salvage the company's reputation as a family-friendly retailer? What disclosures would temper the media's insatiable curiosity? The cascade of practicalities was endless, and all of it—for reasons Cameron hadn't quite discovered—seemed to require his attention.

It was flattering in a way. He had never seen executives so deferential to a lawyer. But his body was starting to rebel against the pace. His eyes were perpetually bloodshot. His memory was slipping. He was having heart palpitations. If Olivia were still alive, she would have intervened. But she was gone, and he was responsible.

He went to his desk and picked up the phone. "Linda, I need half an hour with no interruptions. Please get Blake on the line, and have Declan in my office when I'm finished."

"Certainly, sir," Linda replied. Cameron heard a couple of clicks, then a pause, then Linda's voice again. "Mr. Alexander, please hold for Mr. Conrad."

While he was waiting, Cameron rehearsed the high points of his proposal. Blake was a managing partner at Preston Conrad—a K Street law firm with an outsize reputation. A graduate of Yale and Yale Law School, Blake had learned the art of lobbying from his father, a former US congressman. Now he was one of the most sought-after favor-brokers in DC. At Cameron's behest, he had joined Presto's board and taken the helm of the Risk Committee.

"Cameron," Blake said, coming on the line. "What can I do for you?"

"We have a situation," Cameron replied. "I need a backstop."

"Should I make notes?" Blake asked.

"No, it's just preliminary. It's not ready for the board."

"Go ahead then."

Cameron swiveled around and looked out at the Washington Monument, its white spire blanketed by gray clouds. "I made some discoveries in Bangladesh. The Millennium factory was on our Red List, but our Dhaka office authorized the order anyway. Apparently some of our sourcing people think that on-time delivery is more important than our Code of Conduct. This order was not an exception. There have been others. How many I'm not sure."

Blake took a slow breath. "Who else knows about this?"

"I was able to contain it. Our supplier confessed to me in confidence, as did our office director in Bangladesh. I swore them to secrecy by promising to take no action against them. They assured me it would never happen again. Beyond that, you're the first."

Blake cleared his throat. "My people have been monitoring the media. The jackals are starting to tire of the story. They'll go away as long as we don't give them another carcass."

Cameron listened to the faint chorus of amplified voices wafting up from below. The protesters had taken up a new chant. "Tell us the truth! Tell us the truth!" They were persistent. He had to give them that. But they had lives to live, jobs to attend, holiday shopping to do. They, too, would soon go away, sublimating their anger into seasonal good cheer.

"Nothing's going to leak," he said. "But that isn't what worries me. I'm concerned about the next time. In the best case, our problems are limited to South Asia. But there's a chance that the infection may be company-wide."

"You really think your sourcing people are going off the reservation?"

"That's not the way they see it. They see supply-chain metrics, sales targets, and growth calculations. They think they're doing us a favor."

"While at the same time helping themselves," Blake said. "What are you proposing?"

"I want to bring someone in from the outside, someone who can look behind the Red List and tell me how compromised we are. I'll get Declan involved, but I'll keep everyone else in the dark—even Vance, for now. He has other things to worry about."

Blake was silent for a long moment. "I have great respect for you, Cameron.

If you think this is necessary to protect Presto, I'll support you with the board. Just keep me in the loop."

Cameron let out the breath he was holding. "Much obliged. I'll be in touch."

Seconds after the call ended, he heard a knock at the door. His secretary's efficiency was legendary. "Come in," he said, and Declan made his entrance, closing the door behind him. Cameron waved his hand at the wingback chairs. "Make yourself comfortable."

Declan examined him closely. "How are you doing? Are you getting any sleep?"

"Not enough," Cameron said brusquely. "Sit down."

When Declan situated himself, Cameron spoke with gravitas. "Everything we're about to discuss is confidential. I just got off the phone with Blake Conrad. He cleared it. No one else can know. Not your ex-wife, not your secretary, not your mistress."

"I don't have a mistress," Declan demurred earnestly.

If only Vance were as prudent, Cameron thought. "I need you to set up a meeting with Kent Salazar of Atlas Risk Consulting. He's in New York, but I want to meet him here. Reserve the private room at the Capital Grille. It'll be just you, me, Kent, and whoever he brings along."

Declan made a note on his phone. "What's the nature of the meeting?"

"The Red List. We're going to find out how often it's being ignored."

Declan sat up straighter. "There's something you're not telling me."

"There is, but now is not the time. After you set things up with Kent, I want you to create an encrypted folder on your hard drive and use it to store everything about Atlas. That includes the note you're writing right now. I want you to gather all the electronic documents you have about our red-listed suppliers and put them in that folder—all audit reports, all correspondence with our offices and buying agents, and all internal memoranda, anything that relates to our rationale for delisting suppliers. Assuming Atlas wants the job, you're going to give the folder to them. And then we're going to go hunting."

Declan's green eyes brightened. Cameron could see the wheels in his Oxford-educated brain turning. "You want information beyond Bangladesh?"

"I want the entire Red List."

Declan gave him a piercing look. "Rahmani Apparel didn't act on its own, did it?"

Cameron shook his head. "That was a ruse. I'm sorry, but it was necessary."

Declan processed this at light speed. "You mean Manny—"

"I don't mean anything," Cameron interjected. "Not yet."

He heard his iPhone vibrate. The name on the screen sucked the air out of his lungs. Iris Alexander. His mother. He glanced at his watch. He had eight minutes before a briefing with Kristin's PR team. His blood pressure reached new heights.

"We'll talk more later," he told Declan. "For now, set up the meeting and aggregate the files. And use the confidential channel for e-mail. This stays completely dark."

"Got it," Declan said, disappearing through the door.

Cameron answered the call just before his mother disconnected. "Mom? How are you?"

As soon as she spoke, he knew something was amiss. It was the catch in her voice, usually so steady and sure. "I've seen better days. But that's par for the course at my age."

Cameron went to the window again, his heart twisted in knots. "What's going on?"

His mother's composure broke. "They found another tumor," she said, sniffing away tears. "It's malignant."

Cameron closed his eyes, the weight of dread settling upon his shoulders. It was the worst of all his fears coming at the worst of all moments. He and his mother had always been close. When he was a child, she had been a shield to his father's steel, her winsomeness and empathy exceeded only by her wisdom and faith in his goodness. In his adulthood, she had become his oracle, his conscience, and his confessor. And in the aftermath of the car accident, when his only wish had been to climb into the casket beside Olivia, his mother's voice had pulled him back from the abyss, persuading him to forgive himself, at least enough to live again.

The cancer had appeared without warning in February, striking her in that most private of spaces—her uterus. It was stage two, her oncologist said and recommended surgery and then radiation. The hysterectomy was successful, and the disease retreated, vanishing from her bloodstream. As the months passed, her doctors grew more hopeful, as did her family. But if Cameron had learned anything about life, he knew it was a fickle thing—that every beginning had an end, every gain a requisite loss, every feeling and experience and wonder and gift a moment when it would all just slip away.

"I'm so sorry, Mom," he managed. "What is Dr. Radcliffe saying?"

"I'm going in for more tests. But the tumor is in my liver. The cancer is spreading."

"Does that mean chemo?"

"Probably," she said. "We'll know more next week."

Cameron touched the windowpane with his fingertips. "How is Dad?"

"He's not worried. You know your father."

Cameron nodded silently. The optimism of Cornelius Benjamin Alexander, civil rights luminary and legendary Harvard Law professor, was a force of nature. His platitudes on the subject were legion. *Doubt is the nemesis of progress,* he was fond of saying. *No great achievement can rest on such a foundation.* His students loved him for it—most of them, at least. Those more inclined to skepticism locked horns with him in debate until he subdued them with brilliant rhetoric and an encyclopedic command of history. But there was a category of disbelievers for whom Ben reserved his scorn: those who saw the world as a matrix of risk to be managed and avoided. People like Cameron.

"Are you still coming for Thanksgiving?" Iris asked hopefully.

Cameron tried to sound positive. "Of course. I already have my train ticket."

He heard a knock at the door and looked down at his watch. *Damn,* he thought, feeling irritated and guilty at the same time. Kristin's briefing was in three minutes. "I'm so sorry, Mom," he said. "I have to go. I'll be there next week. Call me with any news."

"I'm glad I caught you," she said. "It's good to hear your voice."

"I love you much," he told her and searched for something to cheer her up. He found it in the unlikeliest of places. "Dad's right. Keep your chin up."

"I love you too," she said.

CHAPTER TWO

The restaurant was quiet even for a Monday, but Cameron wasn't surprised—Thanksgiving was only three days away. Congress was already in recess, its members long gone, sipping mai tais with their wives—or paramours—in the Bahamas or Grand Cayman, and its staffers and aides burning the midnight oil with the rest of Washington's apparatchik class before fleeing the city until the second of December. Cameron scanned the candlelit dining room for familiar faces but didn't recognize anyone, which was a relief. In DC, people had a way of talking and name-dropping that spread word of liaisons like chemical accelerant.

Cameron followed the maître d' to the Fabric Room, a private space decorated with floral wallpaper, wall sconces, and a gilt-framed painting of the American West. He saw Kent Salazar, the principal of Atlas Consulting, sitting at the table with attractive fortysomething woman, her blonde hair pulled back in a twist. Kent introduced her as Victoria Brost, his chief of research. After greeting them, Cameron summoned the waiter and ordered champagne.

"I hope you'll forgive the indulgence," he said, taking a seat between Declan and Victoria, "but the last restaurant I was in couldn't serve alcohol."

Salazar's eyes glinted with humor. "Was that in Bangladesh?"

Cameron didn't blink. "A fair presumption, but I can't confirm or deny it."

He watched as Salazar reacted to this, saw the way his eyes narrowed and his shoulders stiffened, as if he was mildly offended, the way he sat back a touch, his mind seeking a reason for Cameron's parry. It was a test delivered on the fly, a way to gauge Salazar's tolerance for dissimulation. He was a truth-teller, Cameron decided, and smiled coyly, restating his answer.

"I was in Dhaka meeting with an office director who told me lies."

In an instant Salazar relaxed. "Welcome to my world. Lies are everywhere in global supply chains. The important question isn't whether your people are telling them, but who they're deceiving. The most dangerous lies are the ones you allow yourself to believe."

Cameron was intrigued. "Give me an example."

Salazar responded instinctively. "You think your supply chain is free of slavery."

Cameron stared at him incredulously. He couldn't recall the last time he had been caught so completely off guard. *Slavery* was an explosive word in any setting. But to an African American descended on his mother's side from a band of Guinean tribesmen who survived the Middle Passage only to greet the whip on a Louisiana plantation, and on his father's side from one of the first Africans forced to labor in the New World, it nearly wrecked his poise.

"If that's a lie I tell myself," he replied slowly, "it's one of omission."

Salazar tilted his head. "We shield ourselves from the truth by pretending not to see."

Cameron was about to reply when he heard the sudden *pop* of a champagne cork. He took a flute glass from the waiter and sipped it, looking over the menu even though he knew most of it by heart. His mind was abuzz with follow-up questions, but he decided to set them aside. If they were relevant, he would ask them later.

After everyone ordered and the waiter disappeared again, he began. "As you can imagine, this is a difficult moment for our company. It's the biggest shopping week of the year, and our sales are lethargic. Our stock price is at a four-year low. We have activists demonstrating on our doorstep. And the media has yet to let go of the story. The fire exposed us at the worst moment."

"It wasn't the fire," Salazar said. "It was the girl in the photograph."

Cameron met his eyes. "Unfortunately for us, that photo is only the beginning. I've been in the corporate world a long time. I know how to manage risk. But in the last three weeks, I've heard things I never expected, things that go way beyond my ability to control. That makes me nervous. Presto pays me to spot cliffardice and greed. He pictured his mother, the cancer spreading through her theiph nodes, infecting her blood. He knew what she would say, what she had vays said. *Your heart is good, Cameron. Follow it.* He thought of the girl lying en the dirt in front of Millennium, and Olivia slumped against the car door, her byes closed, never to see again. *It's time*, he heard her say from beyond the grave.

ι   "I'm serious," he said suddenly, looking at Declan and seeing his eyes sparkling.

"Excellent," Salazar replied, raising his glass. "Now let's talk about how we do it."

CHAPTER THREE

When Cameron walked into the corner office two days later, he found Vance stretched out on the couch, shoes off, feet on the coffee table, a glass of bourbon in hand. In the distance, the lights of Washington twinkled and glowed. It had been a murderous day for both of them, a dawn-to-dark rush to the witching hour of Thanksgiving. But now, minutes before midnight, it was over, all threats deflected, all blazes under control—at least for the time it would take Presto's legion of antagonists to carve a turkey, play nice with their in-laws, stuff their faces, and stampede the aisles of their favorite stores. It was a bleak vision of the holiday, Cameron knew, but after a day like this, he felt little generosity. What he needed was a drink.

The bottle of Pappy Van Winkle's Family Reserve 20 Year was on the coffee table, a tumbler beside it. Vance poured generously and passed along the glass.

"To escaping the gauntlet with only cuts and bruises," he said, raising a toast.

"Cheers," Cameron replied and took a swig of the burgundy liquid. For most of his adult life he had disliked whiskey. But on his first day as general counsel, Vance had introduced him to Pappy, and in the years since it had become a tradition between them to chase away the most hellish workdays with the world's finest bourbon.

"He's in the Canaries with his daughter," Cameron answered, maintaining his calm. "He hasn't seen her in a year."

"Ah," said Ben, a bit off balance. But he recovered quickly. "I saw the footage from Bangladesh. A terrible tragedy, but predictable, given the way corporations operate these days. You know, I had a thought. If Vance gave away one year of his salary—not his stock options, just his paycheck—he could take care of every person who was injured in that fire for years. But I can't imagine that thought has ever crossed his mind."

Cameron's skin was thick, but the accusation stung. He glanced at his mother and saw the wound in her eyes. "Dad," he said evenly. "I don't want to fight."

"Neither do I," Ben rejoined. "This isn't personal. This is about that beast of a company you work for. Their clothes go up in smoke in a sweatshop, hundreds of people die—people who happen to be brown and poor—and for the next three weeks we're bombarded with ads in which middle-class white people are praising all the good Presto is doing in their communities and shopaholics are hyperventilating about the deals they're going to get after waiting for Black Friday like it's the Second Coming. Tell me the whole thing isn't sick, and I'll be quiet."

Cameron sat motionless, his fist clenched around the napkin in his lap. He knew his father was baiting him. "Leave it, Dad. This isn't the time."

But Ben was far from finished. "What do you mean? You're here. Do you want me to call your secretary and schedule an appointment? I want you to tell me something, Cameron. I know the boy I raised. He was a gentle boy, a sweet boy, with one of the most finely tuned moral compasses I have ever seen. He stood up for the powerless. He defended the weak. I don't believe that boy is gone. He's sitting right here in front of me, in a man's body. I just want to know how he lives with himself when the company he works for is reaping colossal profits from the abuse of the powerless and the weak. Please, enlighten me. I'd like to know."

Cameron rubbed his temples, feeling a migraine coming on. The dagger had plunged deep, down to the roots of his identity, raising doubts he had wrestled with since his twenties, since he had heeded the advice of his maternal grandfather to get an MBA as well as a law degree, since he had met Vance and developed a taste for the perquisites of privilege. There was truth in what his father said. But there was also bias. If his father had a blind spot, it was his hatred of the very engine of production by which wealth was created, not just for the rich, but for everyone from the top to the bottom of the economic totem pole.

"We're not a perfect company," Cameron admitted, offering Ben an olive branch. "When we make mistakes, we pay for them." As soon as the words left his lips, he saw the trap he had laid for himself. His mind scrambled for a way to backtrack, but there was no way out.

Ben's rebuttal came swiftly. "How much has Presto paid for this mistake, other than the temporary nosedive in sales? Is Presto going to create a fund for the victims? What about the children who lost their parents? Will Presto pay for their education? And that girl in the photo they keep showing, do you even know her name?" Ben shook his head like a judge delivering a sentence. "Of course you don't. You've run like rats from the light. You've done it for your investors, because that's the nature of capitalism. You've done it for yourselves, because we're all self-seeking. But it doesn't make it any less repugnant."

"Enough!" The cry came from Iris. Cameron turned and saw his mother's face stained with tears. "This is a festival of gratitude, and I will not have it polluted with bitterness." She took Cameron's hand. "We are a family. We are not perfect, but we know how to love."

Cameron glanced at his sisters and saw them nod in agreement.

"I have an idea to reclaim the evening," Iris continued, an undercurrent of reproach in her voice. "We're all going to say three things we're thankful for. I'll start. I'm thankful for my children and grandchildren. You mean the world to me. I'm thankful for my husband, even though right now a part of me would like to kick his teeth in." Subdued laughter rippled around the table. "Ben, you're an honorable man—most of the time. We've had many good years together. I hope there will be more." Her voice began to break. "Third, I'm thankful for time. I don't know how much longer I'm going to get, but I plan to make the most of it. I've lived a good life, better than any woman could ask. When my time comes, I want to go peacefully with all of you by my side. Promise me that." She wiped her cheek. "Promise me."

All eyes were on her, not one of them dry. Even Ben was blinking away tears.

"I promise," Cameron said and heard the chorus of echoes fill the room.

Ben took a ponderous breath, his countenance filled with remorse. "I'm sorry," he said heavily. "To all of you. My remarks were unbecoming of a holiday. I should have held my tongue." He met Cameron's eyes and held them. "Please forgive me."

No one spoke. Everyone looked at Cameron as he returned his father's gaze. He couldn't remember the last time Ben had apologized for anything. His motives were as plain as they were pragmatic. Still, in the catalog of Cameron's memory, it was an astonishing event. He hesitated, allowing Ben to stew a bit in his penitence, and then he reached deep, found the tip of the blade, and prized it loose. The pain didn't relent, but he threw the dagger down anyway.

"I forgive you, Dad," he said. For now at least.

Then he squeezed his mother's hand.

CHAPTER FOUR

PRESTO TOWER, 16TH FLOOR

ARLINGTON, VIRGINIA

JANUARY 22, 2014

10:02 A.M.

Two months later, after the swirl of the holidays faded into the long winter grind, Cameron sat at his desk reading the first draft of a letter Vance had written to Presto's preferred stockholders, celebrating the company's end-of-year rebound. Presto was just days away from releasing its fourth-quarter earnings statement, which in a near-miraculous turn showed the strongest sales in three years. The Black Friday bonanza had saved them, as had the image-oriented ad campaign that was still airing on stations around the country. Cameron made a few changes to the letter, then reached for the speakerphone, thinking to discuss them with Vance. Before he pressed the button, his iPhone vibrated. He glanced at the screen and saw Kent Salazar's name. Immediately his mood soured. Until now, the Atlas consultant had limited his communications to e-mail. That he was calling meant that something had happened.

"Do you have a minute?" Kent said when Cameron answered.

"How bad is it?" Cameron asked, turning away from his computer and looking out at the clouds huddled low and close over the Capitol. Four inches of snow had fallen the night before, blanketing streets and rooftops and brightening the stubble of winter grass on the National Mall.

"A clear-cut case of forced labor," Salazar replied, his voice lagging as it circled half the globe. "And I'm afraid it's only the tip of the iceberg."

Cameron winced but took the news in stride. Salazar and his team of researchers were in Malaysia conducting unannounced audits of Presto's largest garment suppliers. It was part of a strategy Cameron and Salazar had hashed out over dinner at the Capital Grille. With a supply chain as sprawling as Presto's, a complete investigation of illegal activity would have required a battalion of researchers over a number of years. Since Atlas had only six months, they had decided to focus on two countries—Malaysia and Jordan—that had widespread corruption and substantiated reports of forced labor. In addition, Atlas had agreed to conduct spot audits of select Red List suppliers outside South Asia to determine whether the rot in Presto's sourcing system extended beyond Manny Singh. Also, after his father's chastisement at Thanksgiving, Cameron had asked Salazar to search discreetly for the girl in the photograph. He didn't know what he would do if they found her, but he wanted to keep all options on the table.

"Go on," Cameron said.

"A worker at Rightaway Garments opened up to us in an interview. He was duped by a manpower agency in Bangladesh and by their affiliate here in Kuala Lumpur. The fees were so onerous that the kid worked for three years before he made a dime."

Cameron shook his head. "Tell me the factory's not on the Red List."

"Nope. It's green. We looked at the audit history for the past five years. All of the reports were filed on time, and the auditors' language was complimentary. No issues whatsoever. We did our interviews randomly. It was obvious that the workers had been coached, but we read between the lines. Most of them were probably trafficked. If your audit company followed Declan's protocol, they should have seen something."

"Have you talked to them?" Cameron inquired.

"No," Salazar said. "I thought it would be more effective if you did."

Cameron scrolled through his calendar. The board's Strategy and Finance Committee had a meeting at the end of the week that he could join via telephone. He had a raft of real estate deals and employee contracts to approve by Monday, but Anderson, his deputy general counsel, could handle them in his absence. His Thursday-morning call with his mother—a weekly occurrence since her relapse—could be rescheduled. Everything else could wait until his return.

"I'll get there as soon as I can," he said and then called Reagan airport and requisitioned the Gulfstream.

✵

Twenty-six hours and twelve time zones later, Cameron woke with a start. The phone was ringing. He jerked his head toward the nightstand while his jet-lagged brain struggled to catch up. For an instant, he didn't know where he was. Then he saw the scalloped steel of the Petronas Towers out the window, and a flurry of thoughts struck him at once. Kuala Lumpur. The Mandarin Oriental. He had a meeting with Kent in . . . He glanced at the clock. *Shit!*

He grabbed the phone. "Yes?"

"Mr. Alexander, I'm calling from guest services. A Mr. Salazar is here to see you."

"Send him up in ten minutes," Cameron replied and hung up.

He dressed in a rush, throwing on the suit he wore on the plane and summoning Declan, who had also fallen asleep. When the knock came at the door, he let all of them in—Declan, Salazar, Victoria Brost, and a middle-aged Chinese American man whom Salazar introduced as Peter Fung, Atlas's director of field research in Asia. They took seats in the living room.

"We have a meeting with the auditing company at noon, so we'll need to make this quick," Cameron said. "What's the latest?" he asked Salazar.

"Our informant at Rightaway Garments is Jashel Sayed Parveen," Salazar replied. "After I spoke with you, we met with him again—at the dormitory furnished by his outsourcing agent. He's been at Rightaway long enough to know how Mayang handles audits. The picture he painted isn't pretty. Mayang sends only one inspector—always the same man. He comes and goes in three hours. He spends most of that time in the office. Then he does a cursory walk-through and interviews two workers selected by Rightaway's general manager in the GM's office with the GM present. At the end, the man always leaves with an envelope in his briefcase. Jashel doesn't know what's in it, but he's seen the man take it from the GM."

Cameron felt like muttering an expletive. On the flight over, he had read Presto's factory auditor contract three times. The prohibitions against bribery and corner cutting were written in boldface type. Yet they were just words on paper. Enforcement was the problem. The closest oversight authority was Kanya Nguyen, Presto's compliance director in Bangkok. Apart from her occasional visits to Malaysia, Mayang operated entirely independent of supervision.

"What's the relationship between the factory and the outsourcing agent?"

Peter Fung spoke up. "To protect Jashel, we haven't asked. But it's probably fluid. The agent is Foysol Rashid. He's Bangladeshi, but he's been working in Malaysia for fifteen years. His agency is a shadow company. They're a dime a dozen here. They serve as a bridge between outsourcing agencies abroad and factories looking for cheap foreign labor. I'm working on getting more about him. But from what I've heard, he's a shady operator."

This just keeps getting better, Cameron thought. "How many workers does he represent?"

"Jashel told us there are others, but he doesn't know how many," Fung replied.

"I want to know where Rightaway gets its employees," Cameron said, revealing a hint of his mounting impatience. "If they deal with outsourcing agents, they need to be transparent."

Fung traded a glance with Salazar and looked suddenly nervous. "We'd like that too. But our hands are tied. Nothing in your supplier contract requires that kind of disclosure."

Cameron winced. Fung was right. The contract was silent on that point. He looked at Declan, who was writing furiously on his notepad. "We need to draft an addendum."

"I'm on it," Declan replied.

Cameron gave Fung a penetrating look. "Dare I ask where the Malaysian government stands in all of this? Don't they have immigration controls?"

Fung's laugh came out like a bark. "That's being charitable. The Malaysians are where the Colombians were with drugs in the 1980s. Weak and riddled with complicity."

When Cameron didn't reply, Fung elaborated. "Thanks to the Asian boom, Malaysia is now a middle-income country. As incomes have risen, the manufacturing sector has taken a hit. Malaysians don't want to work in factories anymore, but the government doesn't want the sector to die. So they've bent over backward to bring in foreign labor from countries further down on the global poverty index. That's where outsourcing agents come in. They do all the recruitment work for the factories and jump through all the bureaucratic hoops, but they don't charge the factories a fee. They charge it to the workers, and the workers usually pay by taking on debt. The debt, more than anything else, traps them in bonded labor. The government is well aware of this. For years, the US State Department has chastised Malaysia in its *Trafficking in Persons Report*. But the government has done little to regulate the agents and protect the workers. If anything, they've exacerbated the problem by legalizing total outsourcing, where the agent, not the factory, holds the work permit. That kind of outsourcing is a petri dish for forced labor."

"It sounds to me like we need to get the hell out of Malaysia," Cameron grumbled.

"And go where?" Fung rejoined, allowing the question to dangle in the air. "Half the countries that make clothes for Presto have child labor or forced labor—not in every factory, but in enough to make it a statistically significant issue. And the other countries you source from aren't much cleaner. Take Cambodia, for instance. It has one of the strongest labor laws in the region. It's also the site of the International Labour Organization's first Better Factories initiative. There's no evidence of forced or child labor, but there are sweatshops galore, crackdowns on unions, terminations for worker pregnancy or illness, and other forms of exploitation. The ILO does what it can, but the government's enforcement record is abysmal."

For a moment, Cameron stared out the window at the smog-tinged skyline of Kuala Lumpur. A memory came to him from the day of the Millennium fire. He saw Vance again, standing at the window in his office, demanding answers. He heard his own voice counseling reason and caution. *There's a risk to asking questions. We don't know what we're going to find.* At the time, he wouldn't have called himself prescient, just prudential. Now his heart was a divided thing. The risk manager in him wanted to run from the danger. But another part of him couldn't look away. *I know the boy I raised*, he heard his father saying. *I don't believe that boy is gone . . . I just want to know how he lives with himself . . .*

He blinked, forcing his mind back to the present. "What are you telling me?"

This time it was Kent Salazar who responded. "You asked us for the truth, Cameron. This is the truth. There's a reason companies like yours do all their sourcing in the developing world. It's because cheap labor is plentiful and workplace regulations are largely unenforced. You could reduce your lead times by making clothes in the United States. But then you'd have to deal with the Department of Labor and OSHA and the federal minimum wage and labor unions. That would increase your costs and cut into your profits, unless, of course, you raised prices, in which case you'd give your competitors an edge. Nobody wants to admit it, but the push to manufacture overseas was a calculated end run around all the labor protections that American workers gained a hundred years ago. Malaysia may look like a banana republic when it comes to outsourcing agents. But you're not going to avoid the plague if you cut and run. What you need is a vaccine."

When Salazar fell silent, Cameron's head was wobbling like a top. In less than a minute, the Atlas consultant had indicted not just Presto but the entire American retail economy in colluding with labor abusers, corrupt governments, and human traffickers. It was hard to assail his logic, but Cameron didn't have time to process it. He had back-to-back meetings with the president of Mayang and then with Kanya Nguyen, who was flying in from Thailand.

"This vaccine," Cameron said, "am I right that it involves exposing corrupt auditors?"

Salazar glanced at his watch. "Your lunch meeting. I got carried away."

"Go back to Rightaway. Ask the questions our auditors didn't. I want to know what the owner says about the outsourcing agents he works with. If he doesn't want to talk to you, then tell him he can talk to me."

Salazar nodded. "I'll reach out to him this afternoon."

"Declan," Cameron continued, "get room service on the line. I want a banquet on the table in half an hour. If we're going to fire the bastards, we might as well do it in style."

Everyone in the living room grinned. "With pleasure, sir," Declan said.

CHAPTER FIVE

MAISON FRANÇAISE

KUALA LUMPUR, MALAYSIA

JANUARY 24, 2014

6:02 P.M.

In a feat of uncanny legerdemain, the restaurant Declan's secretary had selected for their meeting with Kanya Nguyen had the look of a manor house in Provence, notwithstanding the skyscrapers that towered around it and the throb of city life just down the street. The décor was refreshingly spare, the walls and tables bright white, the floor and exposed beams walnut brown. The paned windows were expansive. There were fans turning on the ceiling and a pool out back, surrounded by a patio with trees and vines. Cameron and Declan met Kanya in the lobby and followed the hostess to a table in the second-floor dining room. The tables around them were empty, and so they would stay. Declan's secretary had booked all of them.

"Do you drink wine, Ms. Nguyen?" Cameron asked when they were seated.

"Of course," she replied, offering him a deferential smile. "But, please, call me Kanya."

She was petite, not an inch taller than five feet, and looked about twenty-five, though according to Declan, she was a decade older. She had the figure of a dancer, slender as a reed, and the symmetrical face and flawless complexion of a model. But it wasn't her beauty that impressed Cameron. It was her quiet intensity and cultivated intelligence. There were layers beneath the surface of her, an interior world rich with variegated life. He had discerned this after only ten minutes in her presence, and he was certain his assessment was correct. It was the same trait he had seen in Olivia when they first talked on the lawn at Harvard Law School.

"Their selection is good," he said. He signaled the waiter and ordered a bottle of Chablis. Then he turned to business. "When was the last time you were in Malaysia, Kanya?"

It was a gentle opening, even solicitous, given what he now knew about the extent of Presto's compliance failures in the region. On the drive from the hotel, he had contemplated the opposite approach—a blunt entrée designed to catch her in a lie. But then he met her and saw his wife under the surface of her skin. In honor of Olivia, he decided to treat her kindly.

"It was last July," she replied, her English softly accented.

Cameron regarded her candidly. "And the time before that?"

Discomfort swam in her eyes. "The year before, also in July."

"And what did you do on those visits?"

She brought her hands together and twisted a ring on her little finger. "I spoke to our auditing company, Mayang. I observed two factory inspections and spoke to the owners and a few workers. I didn't have time for more."

"Did you come alone, or with staff?"

"I brought my assistant," she said. "That is all our office could spare."

The waiter appeared and poured Cameron a taste of the wine. He swirled it around in his glass and sipped it delicately. "Exceptional." He gestured with his hand, and the waiter poured all three glasses, promising to return after they looked at the menu.

"Tell me about the Bangkok office," Cameron said. "Declan says you have responsibility for three countries—Thailand, Malaysia, and Indonesia—and over seven hundred factories."

Kanya nodded. "It's just under eight hundred, mostly in Thailand and Indonesia."

"How many people work for you?"

She glanced down at the table and twisted her ring again. "There are four of us. There were five until six months ago, but my deputy resigned."

"Wait a minute," Declan interjected, his alarm palpable. "I get quarterly reports from your office director, Aran Wattana. He says there are ten people in compliance."

Kanya's lips spread into a wry smile. "I suppose if you count the people in legal, IT, and HR who work with us on a regular basis."

Cameron felt a clench of disgust. Once again, the rot was in the roots. "Your deputy," he said, homing in, "why haven't you replaced him?"

Kanya looked suddenly anxious. "I've held interviews. But Mr. Wattana believes that none of the candidates are qualified."

"What do *you* believe?" Cameron asked softly.

When Kanya hesitated, he perceived the truth as clearly as if she had written it down on a napkin. He saw it in the tension that compressed the muscles in her cheeks and neck, in the way her breathing shortened and her pulse appeared in the artery below her jawline, in the way her eyes searched his face just as he was searching hers. He felt suddenly exposed. Her vulnerability was disarming, as was her beauty. In another life, he might have allowed the emotions to linger and turned them into a request—for a drink, after hours, in a place where they could talk as people, not as colleagues. It struck him then, in a way he never could have anticipated, how lonely he was, how starved of companionship. But the timing was wrong, and the relationship so imbalanced that nothing could even the scales. In an instant, he locked down his heart and cleansed his mind of distraction. He had a job to do.

"Kanya," he said, "I need you to be honest with me. I've discovered certain *anomalies* in our apparel supply chain. I'm trying to find out why. If you tell me what you know, I assure you that no harm will come to you. Declan? Tell her."

"He's a man of his word," Declan affirmed.

Kanya vacillated another moment. Then her expression hardened. "All right. I only interview qualified candidates. And I *should* have ten on my staff. We should be making quarterly trips to Malaysia. Better yet, we should have an office here. It's impossible to provide adequate oversight from Bangkok."

Again, Cameron found himself stirred. "What would you say if I told you that our auditors have been taking bribes from factory owners?"

She grimaced. "I would say it is inevitable. You get what you pay for. Mayang's fees are notoriously low. Malaysia is rife with corruption. There's a link between the two. I didn't want to hire them. Mr. Wattana did."

Cameron smiled. "Then you will be pleased to know that their contract has been revoked. I spoke to the owner today. He tried to lie to me."

Kanya's face radiated surprise. "Who will take over for them?"

Cameron held out his hands. "Whoever you choose. Aran Wattana will not stand in your way. But I need to understand something. Presto's compliance budget is robust. Vance Lawson is on our side. Whatever my compliance people need, they get, so long as they can justify it. What is Wattana's game? Why is he not spending the money?"

"Oh, he's spending it," Kanya replied acerbically. "Just not on compliance."

The waiter appeared again, but Cameron waved him away. "Where is the money going?"

"It's going to the sourcing staff. Mr. Wattana gives them perks when they get suppliers to drop their prices. The most effective sourcing associates fly business class and stay in five-star hotels. Their last team review took place at a resort in Phuket. Our last review took place in the office over lunch."

Cameron's fingers curled around the edge of the table. It was offensive enough that Presto's sourcing managers had ignored the Red List. But it was immoral to deliberately underfund factory oversight in order to finance junkets for people whose objective was to squeeze every last millimeter of margin out of Presto's suppliers—thus tempting those same suppliers to violate the law and Presto's Code of Conduct to cut their own costs.

"Okay," he said. "Complete the picture for me. What does Wattana get out of it?"

It was Declan who answered. "He gets a stellar performance review from corporate. I've been worried about the incentives for some time, but until now I've never had proof of abuse. Our offices are rated on four metrics—quality control, on-time delivery, gross margin, and cost containment. Office directors manage their own budget, which means that if they want to, they can take funds from a cost center like compliance and deploy them in creative ways to drive margin on the goods they're sourcing. I bet if I got Wattana's performance ratings from HR, I'd find that he's been getting top marks across the board."

"Mr. Mays is right," Kanya said quietly. "For the past five years, we've been the highest-rated office in the world. We are the darlings of Presto's sourcing department. The incentives to shirk compliance are built into the system."

Cameron took a breath, overwhelmed by the dimensions of the shit pile he'd stepped into. The day was coming when he and Rebecca Sinclair, Presto's sourcing VP, were going to have a talk, and Vance was going to hear about it, and the system was going to change. But some things needed to happen before he could confront her.

"Where are you staying tonight?" he asked Kanya.

"At the DoubleTree," she replied.

Cameron shook his head. "Not anymore. You're staying at the Mandarin

Oriental with us. Wattana is flying in tomorrow. He and I are going to sort a few things out. I don't care how beloved he is. He's stealing money from my people, and I won't stand for it. Prepare yourself for a budget boost. Hire the best auditing company in Malaysia, and tell them they have one job more than any other. They need to find out how our suppliers are getting foreign workers, and how those workers are being treated when they get here. I'm probably not telling you anything you don't know, but right now, in this city, there are people making our clothes who are not free to leave. That's a form of slavery, and I want it to stop. You can help make that happen."

To Cameron's astonishment, he saw Kanya's eyes moisten. "Thank you," she said, imbuing her voice with the utmost sincerity.

"It's nothing," he replied.

"No," she insisted. "It's not nothing. I've seen them with my own eyes. They come from so many places hoping for a better life. But when they get here, they find that it's all a lie. Awhile ago, I gave up hope that I could do anything about it. Now I see that I can."

In an instant, the flutter of pheromones in Cameron's stomach turned into a full-fledged rush of adrenaline. For precious seconds, he allowed himself to imagine what it would be like to take off his coat, loosen his tie and shoelaces, and relax in the presence of a woman again, *this* woman, to laugh at a joke unencumbered by its professional implications, to seduce her with wit and kindness, to feel the touch of her fingertips on his skin, to watch her let her hair down and fiddle with the zipper on her dress, and to throw back the sheets and chase her into the embrace of ecstasy. Then the moment passed, and the fantasy slipped away.

"You're welcome," he said, smiling at her in the most genuine way. "Now let's have a look at the menu. I don't know about you, but I'm ravenous."

PART FOUR

Joshua

March 2015

CHAPTER ONE

THE INTERCONTINENTAL HOTEL

KUALA LUMPUR, MALAYSIA

MARCH 3, 2015

9:50 P.M.

The night was cloudless and clear, but the stars were nowhere to be seen. The humidity was a swamp in the equatorial sky, and the lights of the Malaysian capital were everywhere bright. Josh saw them from his room, perched like a bird at the level of the surrounding rooftops, the Petronas Towers in the distance gleaming like emerald-crusted fingers. He was in yet another hotel in yet another country, a new stamp on his passport, two thousand airline miles closer to the watershed mark of one million. Rana was behind him on the couch, a burner phone plastered to one ear, a fixer on the line, ironing out the details of a meet.

"Who's your contact?" Rana was saying. "Is he trustworthy? . . . How many workers are there? . . . Where are they staying? . . . Are there any guards? . . . What about the outsourcing agent? . . . We can go tonight, but we need to be sure it's safe . . ."

Josh's iPhone vibrated in his pocket. He pulled it out and glanced at the screen. Of all the times! He took a breath and counted the cost. Then he caught Rana's eye. "I'll be right back," he said and walked to the bathroom, locking the door behind him.

He read Maria's text again. "Joshua, where are you? It has been three weeks, and I hear nothing. Please do not forget us. We have no one else."

He wavered in indecision. He knew if he opened this door, it would not be easy to close. He thought of Madison and remembered the way her tears had shined in the light of the foyer when she confronted him with the *O Globo* story. He had known what was coming, but he hadn't been prepared for the way her rejection would level him.

"Is it true?" she had asked, holding up the page like an indictment.

The guilt in his eyes was his judgment.

"How could you?" she whispered. "After all I gave up." She shook her head, daggers in her eyes. "All those times you were in Rio, you were with *her*, weren't you? You were banging her while I was slaving away at a job I hated so you could follow your dream."

"It wasn't like that."

"Shut up," she cried. "I hate you. I *hate* you!" She crumpled to her knees and buried her face in her hands. "Go away. I don't want you here. Leave me alone."

Now Josh closed his eyes and felt the despair as if for the first time. He pictured Lily's face, recalled her words. *Come home . . . She isn't happy.* He wanted that more than anything—to find a way back into Madison's good graces. He had a chance with this investigation, the lawsuit he and Rana were building, to prove to her that neither his success nor his sins had fully corrupted him, that he was still the man she had fallen for in law school, the rabble-rouser with an uncompromising compassion for the poor. But therein lay the snare. His compassion was also his downfall. Maria was not exaggerating. He was all she had left.

He found her number in his contacts and placed the call.

"Joshua!" she said, sounding relieved yet desperate.

He hesitated, and the silence dragged.

"Are you there?" she asked. "Is it you, Joshua?"

"Hello, Maria," he said at last.

"Ah, thank God! It is you."

"I thought I was clear. This can't go on."

She was quiet for a moment, her breathing audible above the static on the line. "I know," she admitted. "But this is not about us. This is about my girls. I have tried everything. I went to all the donors. I spoke to the bishop. I even went to Alejandro. No one would help me." Her voice trailed off, and she started to cry. "Your last gift was kind. But it was not enough."

Josh tried to steel himself, cursing the way her suffering so easily moved him. But he might as well have tried to hold up the sky. It was her comment about Alejandro that pierced his defenses. Alejandro Varela was her erstwhile benefactor and lover, a real estate magnate who had rescued her from the horrors of her childhood, educated her, and inducted her into Brazilian society. It was his seed money that had planted Casa da Amizade, his largesse that had floated her through the early years, and his financial collapse that had sent her back to the streets and into the beds of strange men to care for her girls.

Then Josh had come along and written her story in the *Post*—a story of poverty and prosperity set against the backdrop of Brazil's economic boom. When the Pulitzer committee handed him journalism's highest honor, everything had changed for her. The world had opened its hand and fed her. *The End of Childhood* had elevated her further, turning her into a household name in global philanthropy. Until *O Globo* started digging around in her rubbish bin and found Catarina, and convinced her to talk about Maria's darkest days. And then the glittering cathedral had come crashing down, and the world had abandoned her. That she had gone back to Alejandro meant that she was beyond all humiliation. If Josh turned her down, he knew where she would end up—back in the nightclubs in Copacabana, trolling for johns to keep the lights on. And she would not be alone. A fresh-faced girl from the Casa, another Catarina, would be with her.

"I'll send you some more money," he said quietly. "I'll wire it tonight."

"Thank you," Maria said softly. "You are a good man."

Josh conjured his wife's face. What was goodness when fidelity and generosity were at odds? "I have one condition."

"Yes?"

"Keep your girls away from the bars."

Though she was on the other side of the world, he saw her shaking her head. "I will never take them back. You have my promise."

"Good-bye, Maria," he said.

✻

When Josh returned to the living room, Rana was standing by the window, looking out at the night. He turned around and read the dismay on Josh's face. "Everything okay?"

"Yeah," Josh said, trying to sound convincing. "Don't worry about it."

For a moment, Rana did look worried. Then he decided to let it go. "The meeting is set," he said. "We're going to the workers' dormitory. You ready?"

Josh nodded and grabbed his backpack off the bed, following Rana out the door. "What part of the city?" he asked when they stepped into the elevator.

"Cheras," Rana replied. "It's south of here. But first we have to pick up

Ajmal's friend." He shook his head. "The kid is incredible—one of the sharpest fixers I've ever seen."

The kid was Ajmal Alam, and he was a living paradox. He was Bangladeshi, but he knew Kuala Lumpur like he had grown up there. He was barely out of university, yet he spoke with the sagacity of a much older man. And his list of friends in the apparel industry was second to none. In less than twenty-four hours, he had made contact with workers at Rightaway Garments, the Malaysian factory Josh's source had named at the Lincoln Memorial, and convinced them to talk. The workers knew Jashel Sayed Parveen.

Leaving the elevator, Josh and Rana crossed the hotel lobby and exited through glass doors, making their way down a stone-paved roundabout to the noisy street. After only seconds, the humid, tropical air, still over eighty degrees Fahrenheit, swelled inside Josh's lungs and began to prickle the skin beneath his shirt. The sensation took him back to Rio de Janeiro in the early days, when he was a fledgling correspondent searching for a story that would make him a name like his father's, a byline that would signal to the world that truth was about to be served. *I was a fool*, he thought with a half smile. *But the world was my oyster. Now I'm wiser and trapped inside the shell.* He shook his head and watched Rana make another call.

"We're on the street," Rana said. "Do you see us?"

A moment later, a beige sedan pulled to the curb, and Ajmal jumped out. He was taller than Josh expected and stockier, with the distinctive features of South Asia—deep-set eyes, close-cropped hair, and carefully trimmed beard. But his self-confidence and rapid-fire speech were like that of a hundred other cosmopolitan millennials Josh had encountered in his travels.

"I've read all your work," he said as Josh settled into the passenger seat and Rana climbed into the back. "Your book is a masterpiece."

"Thanks," Josh replied, no longer impressed by praise.

Ajmal floored the accelerator and pulled into traffic. "I have a question, though. If you wanted to be a journalist, why'd you go to law school?"

"It's what my father did," Josh said.

Ajmal swerved around a bus and made a sudden turn down a side street. "Your father was Jimmy Carter's press secretary, right?"

"*Deputy* press secretary," Josh corrected. *The kid reads Wikipedia and thinks he knows my family.* "But, yes, he was in the White House. He told me to go to law school to learn how the world works, then go into journalism to change it."

Ajmal bobbed his head so vigorously that Josh worried that he had more caffeine than plasma in his bloodstream. "I like that a lot."

"So tell me about Rightaway," Josh said. "What kind of factory is it?"

"Midsize," Ajmal replied as they whizzed by a mosque. "About a thousand workers, mostly migrants from Cambodia, Indonesia, and Bangladesh. They make sports apparel for the export market. That's pretty much all Malaysia has left after the Multi-Fibre Arrangement."

Josh nodded. The MFA was a quota system adopted by the United States and Europe in the 1970s to govern garment imports from overseas. Designed to insulate the Western textile industries from third world competition, the MFA had the unintended consequence of offering small countries like Malaysia the chance to compete with large countries like China and India. It also fueled the globalization of the industry, leading manufacturers in countries with maxed-out quotas to partner with underutilized countries to keep the orders flowing. When the world, acting through the World Trade Organization, finally retired the MFA in 2004, buyers and brands went on a global quest for greater margins. They found more efficient production in China, Thailand, and Vietnam, faster turnaround times in Mexico and Latin America, and rock-bottom labor costs in the Philippines, the Maldives, and Madagascar. In middle-income countries like Malaysia, the garment sectors adapted but shrank dramatically in size.

"Who are Rightaway's buyers?" Josh asked.

"All the big Western brands," Ajmal replied. "The only exception is Presto. Rightaway used to make for them, but they don't anymore. I don't know why."

A few minutes later, Ajmal stopped outside a Chinese restaurant in a neighborhood of low-rise apartments and commercial buildings. A diminutive Bangladeshi man with a moustache and glasses stood on the sidewalk waiting for them. He climbed into the backseat with Rana.

"This is Sarwar," Ajmal said, throwing the sedan into a U-turn. "He's from Dhaka, but he's been in KL ten years. He knows everyone at Rightaway. He's been trying to form a union for some time, but the owner isn't in favor, naturally. The guy usually retaliates by sending the pro-union workers away and replacing them with others who don't complain."

Ajmal drove for a while longer, navigating Kuala Lumpur's arterial network of freeways before taking an exit ramp into an area dominated by dimly lit storefronts and rambling factories.

"Welcome to Cheras," he said. "Garments are all around, though the signs don't show it. Many are shells for subsidiary factories that employ undocumented migrant workers."

"Is Rightaway a subsidiary?" Josh inquired.

Ajmal shook his head. "It's one of the model factories—where the brands send buyers and auditors to make sure everything is A-OK in the supply chain. But Rightaway shares orders with the subsidiaries. The subsidiaries are the lean, mean, human-abusing machines."

Like Millennium in Dhaka, Josh thought. "What do the brands think of them?"

Ajmal laughed under his breath. "The brands pretend they don't know. But they do."

Soon, Ajmal pulled the car into a dingy alleyway littered with trash. He drove for twenty feet, then stopped in a courtyard surrounded by unmarked buildings and lit by a single lamp, its halo barely five yards wide.

A group of men emerged from the shadow of a stairwell and walked toward the car. Ajmal and Sarwar climbed out, and the men formed an arc around them and lit cigarettes. One of them offered Ajmal a drag, which he took. Then he returned to the car.

"We're set. They're going to take us to the dormitory."

Josh looked at Rana and saw the question in his eyes. They were in a sketchy quarter of an unfamiliar Asian megacity ninety minutes shy of midnight—not a great place for Americans to make the acquaintance of strangers. "What does your gut tell you?" he asked Rana.

Rana hesitated, then said, "I think we should trust him."

Josh shrugged. "Works for me."

They left the car and followed the men into the darkness, stepping around discarded bottles and cans. Somewhere nearby a dog barked, its voice echoing off the walls. Josh kept his hands free and his senses on high alert, scanning the surroundings for danger. The men led them through a breezeway between buildings. Josh tripped over something and almost lost his footing, but he couldn't make out anything on the ground.

"How much farther?" he asked Ajmal.

Ajmal repeated the question in Bengali, and one of the men grunted a reply. "It's just up ahead," Ajmal said, showing no hint of concern.

On the far side of the breezeway stood another courtyard with scattered trash and a lamp emitting grainy light. Around the courtyard they walked, the buildings on all sides as dark as the sky. At last, the men showed them to a stairwell and pointed upward.

"The dormitory is upstairs," Ajmal said. "They're going to stand guard."

The men stood in a huddle at the base of the steps and watched them pass.

Josh took the stairs two at a time and joined Ajmal, Sarwar, and Rana on the landing. Before them lay an open-air hallway with doors on one side and a railing on the other. The shapes of men were leaning over the railing, their faces limned by the reddish glow of cigarettes.

Ajmal said a few words in Bengali, and one of the shapes opened a door, allowing light to spill into the hallway. All at once, color returned to the world and the shapes turned into young Bangladeshis. Beyond the door was a room with bunk beds and cabinets along the wall, a kitchen area with a stove, and a small washroom. There were men lounging on the bunks, paging through magazines, and chatting in soft tones. When they saw Sarwar, they greeted him with broad smiles and gathered round, sitting cross-legged on the floor.

Ajmal left his sandals at the door and sat on a mattress, gesturing for Josh and Rana to do the same. While Sarwar spoke to the men, Josh studied them. There were thirteen of them, between the ages of twenty and thirty. Some were dressed in T-shirts and jeans, others in gym shorts, their chests bare. But all of them wore the same expression of unaffected curiosity.

When Sarwar deferred to Ajmal, he spoke briefly, then passed the baton to Josh. "They will answer your questions as long as you say nothing to Rightaway or publicize their names."

"That's not a problem," Josh said. He turned to Rana. "You speak the language. Why don't you find out what they know about Jashel?"

Rana nodded and began to ask questions in Bengali. The men replied without resistance, speaking in turn and occasionally correcting one another. As the minutes passed, Josh watched Rana carefully and listened to the timbre of his voice. He saw his friend's intrigue turn into indignation. Eventually Rana filled him in.

"Jashel came to Rightaway in 2008. A number of these men were with him. An agency in Dhaka made the arrangements, but a local outsourcing agent named Foysol took over when they arrived. He handles everything for them—documents, accommodations, transportation, work permits, and medical care. The factory pays Foysol, then he pays them. When they got here, they found out that the agency in Dhaka had lied to them. The wage was three hundred ringgits less a month, there was no escalator for overtime, and there were many hidden fees and deductions. Most of them worked three years before they were able to send money to their families."

Josh shook his head in disgust. "That's forced labor."

"Yeah, but it gets worse. Their contracts are with Foysol, not Rightaway.

They didn't know this when they signed, but the documents were written in English, which none of them can read. Foysol has their passports and work permits. He has complete control over their lives, and he uses it. A year after they got here, one of them got sick and couldn't work. Foysol canceled his permit and reported him to the police for deportation. They never saw the guy again."

Which means his entire family paid the price, Josh thought bitterly. "So where's Jashel?"

"He was here until a year ago. Then one day Foysol showed up at the factory and took him away. They don't know what happened to him, but they're worried Foysol turned him over to immigration. Jashel was an outspoken critic of Foysol's agency. He couldn't wait for his second contract to expire so he could go home to his family. He has a lady in Bangladesh—Farzana. He was saving money to marry her."

Josh gritted his teeth, allowing his anger to show. "Ask them if they recall anything unusual around the time that Jashel disappeared. Did he do anything that might invite reprisal?"

Rana translated the question for the men while Josh surveyed their faces. Most of their expressions remained blank, but Josh saw a flash of recognition in the eyes of a heavyset young man in the back. His gaze fell to the floor, and he began to rub his hands together. Josh waited, hoping the man would volunteer what he knew, but the man stayed silent.

Josh pointed him out to Rana. "He's hiding something."

When Rana called him out, the young man shook his head forcefully.

"Tell him he can talk to us now or later," Josh said, locking eyes with the young man. "But we're not going to leave him alone until he helps us."

After another exchange, Rana said, "His name is Enam. He knows how Jashel got into trouble, but he's afraid you will talk to the factory or to Foysol."

Josh nodded, understanding. "Tell him that nothing he says in this room will get back to Rightaway or anyone else in Malaysia. I'm a journalist. I protect my sources."

Enam pondered this, his face fraught with tension. At last he began to speak.

Rana listened intently and interpreted. "About this time last year, some auditors came to the factory unannounced. They were American, like you. They had conversations with many workers. Jashel was one of them. Enam was another. He knew what to say. His manager had told them how to handle auditors. But Jashel didn't follow instructions. The auditors came here to speak to him a second time. It was after work, late in the evening. The others were in the court-yard smoking, but Enam was in the washroom. He overheard the conversation."

"Let me guess," Josh said. "Jashel told them the truth." When Rana nodded, Josh asked, "Did Enam tell anyone about what he heard?"

As soon as Rana translated the question, Josh knew the answer. He saw it in the guilt that flashed across Enam's face, in the way he clasped his hands together as if trying to reassure himself that he had done nothing wrong. It took him a little while to gather the courage to speak. But the words came eventually, and when they did, Rana took a sharp breath.

"Somehow Foysol found out about the audit," Rana said. "He took Enam and Jashel aside and asked them about the interview. Enam was scared. He told Foysol everything."

Josh felt the mood in the room change, saw the way the other men looked at Enam, the judgment that darkened their eyes. His instinct, too, was to con-demn Enam. But he understood the context. As much as their circumstances had bequeathed these men a sense of brotherhood, their camaraderie was paper-thin. They were living on the edges of the law in a foreign land under the control of a man who held their destiny in his hands. When Foysol came to him, Enam fingered Jashel because he wanted to survive. Almost anyone would have done the same.

He had one last question for the men. "Do they know who sent the auditors?"

Rana smiled grimly. "They came from Presto."

CHAPTER TWO

The mall was a monument to Asia's rise. The shine and sparkle were every-where—in the open-air cafés with fountains and lush vegetation, in the bling-filled jewelers' cases and rainbow-colored displays, in the Harrods-style gloss and gleam of foodstuffs in the grocery, in the glam fashion of British India, in the European sports cars parked in the entry hall, even in the glass exterior itself, tinted tourmaline like a tropical ocean. A bird could fly from the tony enclave of Bangsar to Jashel's old dormitory in Cheras in about eight miles, but the sociological distance, the gulf carved by money and education and privilege, was almost infinite.

Josh was sitting with Rana in the rainforest-like courtyard when Ajmal walked up, his eyes wide, as if running on double voltage. "Foysol is on his way. He was tied up in traffic."

Josh patted the compact digital receiver on the table. "The reception is excellent. I heard you like you were next to me. I even heard Foysol's voice on the phone. How's the wire?"

"I barely feel it," Ajmal said, touching his pink dress shirt just above the spot where the transmitter was taped to his chest. "It's smaller than the ones I usually wear."

The meeting with Foysol had come together after two days of meticulous planning. Armed with the agent's name, Ajmal had tapped his contacts for information about Foysol's company and the factories with which he did business, and put in requests with friends in the government to determine Jashel's immigration status and the validity of his work permit. Within thirty-six hours, they had learned that Foysol was a man with multiple masks, supplying Bangladeshi workers to top-tier factories like Rightaway and to shady subsidiaries. They had also learned that Jashel was still in Malaysia, at least according to the country's passport records, but that his work permit had expired a year ago, which meant that he was now a member of Malaysia's pariah class of undocumented workers, hunted for sport by RELA, the country's volunteer corps of anti-migrant vigilantes, and subject to the threat of detention and deportation.

"Undocumented migrants live in a fraternity of fear," Ajmal had explained. "We'll never find out where he is unless we talk to Foysol."

So they had devised a scheme and set up a sting, buying the recording equipment, inventing a backstory, and convincing Foysol that Ajmal was a labor broker who represented garment factories looking to acquire workers on the cheap, under the radar of the authorities. Foysol had made no promises and divulged nothing incriminatory, but he had agreed to the meeting on the condition that Ajmal would pay for lunch.

The fixer's phone trilled in his hand. "The taxi just dropped him off," Ajmal said, typing a reply with his thumbs. "I'll see you guys later."

As Josh and Rana watched, he strolled leisurely across the courtyard and stopped outside the entrance to the café. "He could have picked a less ostentatious outfit," Josh quipped, putting earbuds in his ears. "He looks like a flamingo on Savile Row."

"People notice flamingos," Rana replied, inserting a second set of earbuds so he could interpret for Josh anything spoken in Bengali. "Twenty bucks says Foysol does the same."

The outsourcing agent appeared two minutes later, dressed in a khaki suit, a blue shirt, and polished loafers. *Touché*, Josh thought, listening to the men greet each other. Rana translated in real time, speaking in an undertone that only Josh could hear.

Ajmal led Foysol to a table that offered Josh and Rana a clear view of the conversation. The men sat down and looked at the menus. Then a waiter appeared and took their orders.

"You're new to me," Foysol said, "but your references are impressive."

"I take care of my clients," Ajmal replied.

The references had been the trickiest part of the planning. The factories Ajmal had delivered to the agent were real, but the phone numbers had led to burner phones operated by lawyers at Kebaikan, a human rights agency that Ajmal assisted with investigations. If Foysol had looked behind the numbers, the facade would have fallen apart. But Ajmal hadn't given him time. The meet had been set only six hours ago.

"So tell me what your clients are seeking," Foysol said. "I supply many things."

"Skill is not important," Ajmal replied. "My clients make only basic items. What matters is cost—and control. My clients don't have time for paperwork."

They paused while the waiter delivered them juices with straws. Then Foysol spoke again. "Management is easy. I offer complete outsourcing. Your clients will only have to train the workers, oversee their work, and pay me their wages. I will do the rest. Cost, however, is more difficult. There is the minimum wage."

Ajmal sipped his drink. "My clients were more comfortable under the old system. They don't like the way the government has kowtowed to labor activists."

"I share their opinion," Foysol said cagily, "but I don't make the law."

Ajmal lowered his voice. "But what if other laws had already been broken, not by you or me, but by the workers? Would the minimum wage apply then?"

Foysol stirred his drink, saying nothing for seconds. Then he glanced around the café and answered in an even softer tone. "There is a class of workers I sometimes meet, migrants who have certain . . . *troubles*. Their terms are more flexible."

"Do you manage these workers?" Ajmal asked.

"It is complicated. But, yes, I offer the same services."

"My clients will need your assurance that if problems arise they will not be implicated."

Foysol nodded. "There will be no problems. I make all the necessary arrangements."

Bribes, Josh thought as he listened to Rana's translation.

"I will need to inspect them for health issues," Ajmal said. "I have a doctor I use."

Foysol replied testily, "That will not be necessary. My workers come with guarantees."

"My clients insist," Ajmal rejoined. "But don't worry. The doctor is reliable. Are these workers accessible? I'm happy to compensate you for your time."

Again, Foysol fell silent, weighing the cost of further disclosure. At last, he said, "I think I may be able to accommodate you. How soon is this doctor available?"

Ajmal pondered this. "Friday is his day off, but for me he will do it. Is it far away?"

Foysol shook his head. "For five hundred ringgits, I can take you there now."

"Done," Ajmal said. "I will make the call."

Half an hour later, Josh sat in the back of his rented Toyota SUV, Rana in the driver's seat, peering through tinted windows at a pair of ramshackle bungalows in a forgotten corner of Kuala Lumpur. According to Google, they were in Petaling Jaya, a concatenation of working-class neighborhoods on the urban center's western flank, but to Josh the place looked more like a village slum. The buildings were in various stages of disrepair and smashed together in a haphazard assemblage that seemed almost, but not quite, random.

For the majority of the drive, Rana had followed Foysol's taxi with ease, first to collect Dr. Tareq Hussain—a Bangladeshi physician and one of Ajmal's many acquaintances—and afterward through the streets of Petaling Jaya. But then, without warning, the taxi had taken a sudden turn and vanished down an alley that emptied into a rabbit warren of dirt lanes. If not for the dust kicked up by the taxi's tires, they might have lost it. But Rana followed the cloud, and they found the SUV again after it pulled to a stop.

"I'm glad you're driving," Josh said as Rana maneuvered into the shade of a tree about forty yards away. "Right now, every eye on the street would be staring at me."

In fact, the street was largely deserted, apart from a few stray dogs and pedestrians. But Josh had visited enough slums to know that faces lurked behind every window and nothing passed without the notice of someone. He turned on the digital receiver and inserted his earbuds, handing Rana the second pair. Then he watched as Foysol led Ajmal and Dr. Hussain toward a passageway between buildings gone to seed, their stucco dingy with grime.

"The entrance is this way," Foysol said and Rana translated.

Dr. Hussain seemed to hesitate, but Ajmal cajoled him with a look and he walked ahead gamely. A moment later, all three of them disappeared from view.

Josh heard a door creak open, then footsteps and Ajmal's breathing.

"Bring everyone upstairs," Foysol barked, and Josh heard scuffling and the sounds of incoherent speech. "If people are asleep, wake them up."

"How many live here?" Ajmal asked, his voice betraying a hint of repulsion.

"Today there are twenty-nine," Foysol replied. "Tomorrow, it might be more."

"How do you find them?" Ajmal inquired.

"They come to me," Foysol replied. "As long as they are compliant, I take care of them."

Bullshit, Josh thought angrily.

He heard more noises, breathing, people moving, chairs scraping, words spoken in undertones, then Ajmal's voice again. "How many are available?"

"As many as your clients need," Foysol said. "They have jobs in other factories, but the arrangements are negotiable."

After a brief pause, Foysol addressed the group. "This is Dr. Hussain. He needs to check your vitals and draw blood. I may have new employment for you."

Dr. Hussain spoke up. "I will see you each in private. It will only take a moment."

As the men murmured, Ajmal and Foysol chatted about business. Josh was so focused on the conversation that he didn't see the man in a black T-shirt walking up behind the SUV—not until the man's face was pressed against his window, his eyes squinting to see through the glaze. Josh turned around quickly and saw three more men approaching from the rear.

"We need to get out of here," he said.

Rana turned the ignition and threw the SUV into reverse, backing away from the man in the black T-shirt. The man snarled and started after them. As Rana accelerated, the men behind them scattered. A road opened up on the left. Josh pointed it out with a shout, and Rana slammed on the brakes, shifted into drive, and took the turn. Dogs barked and people stared as they shot past, but Rana managed to stay in the crowded lane without inflicting damage.

As the danger retreated, Josh remembered Ajmal and Dr. Hussain. The earbuds were still in his ears, but the receiver was broadcasting only static. The transmitter was well beyond range. His first thought was the loss of recording capabilities. His second was concern for their safety.

"Did you hear anything more before the signal went out?" Josh asked.

Rana yanked the wheel hard to the right and threw the SUV back onto the main road, then pulled to the shoulder. "It was all garbled. I wasn't paying attention."

Josh took out his iPhone. "Should we text him?"

Rana shook his head. "We should let it play out."

"It could be awhile."

Rana grimaced. "Let's just hope they find something."

Josh watched traffic and counted minutes. An hour passed without word, then another. Slowly, the blazing sun climbed down from the sky, turning gold then orange in the haze. Josh snacked on a granola bar and shared a piece of it with Rana. In between bits of conversation, he killed time by writing Lily and reading news stories on his iPhone.

Finally, a few minutes after seven, Josh's phone vibrated in his hand.

The text was from Ajmal. "Where are you? I'm back at the mall."

Josh breathed a sigh of relief. He told Rana and then typed, "We had a problem with bystanders. Did you find Jashel?"

"He was there," Ajmal replied. "Dr. Hussain spoke to him."

"Does Foysol suspect anything?"

"No. I told him I'd call when we get test results."

"Good. We'll come to you and discuss next steps."

Rana met Josh's eyes, his expression grave. "We're going to have to get Jashel out. That's the only way we can talk to him. But if we do it, we can't send him back."

Josh nodded, the weight of decision like a yoke on his shoulders. He grappled with the moral and existential consequences of action, his professional instinct locked in combat with his conscience and commitment to the cause. The rule of noninterference was nowhere in the journalists' Code of Ethics, but it was a line reporters tried never to cross. To tell the story was impact enough. To step into the story was to compromise neutrality. But that rule didn't apply to legal investigations. Nor did it make any sense in the rest of human experience. Jashel needed their help even more than they needed his. There was no good reason to step back now.

"I'm in," Josh said, feeling an anticipatory rush. "How do we make it work?"

CHAPTER THREE

The building looked like any other in Cheras, a warehouse with windows, the glass mostly covered by signage promoting dozens of businesses, none of which had anything to do with the garment factory that lay behind the walls. Class 5 Fashions was a textbook subsidiary venture, operating with hand-me-down machines from other, more reputable factories, skating on the thinnest of regulatory ice kept solid by payoffs to the police, and surviving on subcontracted orders from suppliers like Rightaway who denied its existence—and that of its off-the-books brethren—when asked by the clothing brands.

Even Ajmal never would have found it without help from Jashel. But now, six days later, the fixer knew everything there was to know about the factory. Now he was friends with the general manager, Faruq, who had confided that the owner was a miser and didn't pay him half enough. Now he was on a first-name basis with the guards who watched the factory's doors. They had been fortunate to get a break, but fortune was like glass; as Publilius said, the brighter the glitter, the more easily broken. In Josh's mind, Jashel was the brightest of all possible glitter. They needed him on the witness stand. But to get him in a courtroom, they needed him free.

The stratagem they had planned was brilliant but brittle, with no margin for error. Rana had spun the cover story, and Ajmal had sold it to his new buddy,

Faruq. In a Muslim country like Malaysia, everyone wanted the blessing of God, especially those trying to climb the socioeconomic ladder. As Faruq had told it, his parsimonious boss had drawn up plans for a house on a nearby island, but he didn't have the money to begin construction. Enter Ajmal, the man whose network extended to the farthest reaches of the God-fearing world, or so he said.

He knew an imam from Afghanistan who had devoted his life to *dawa*—preaching and conversion. The imam spoke only Pashto and Arabic, but he had an acolyte who spoke many languages. If the factory owner wanted to meet the imam and solicit his blessing, Ajmal could arrange it. But there was a catch. The imam would not come if he couldn't speak to the workers. Faruq was delighted by the idea, as was the owner. They invited the imam and his acolyte to the factory during the workers' lunch break, which the owner agreed to extend so the imam could deliver private blessings.

What made the plan brittle was Josh, who had to play the cleric. Rana would never be questioned as the acolyte. Josh, however, was an American whose Pashto was limited to a few phrases he had picked up on a trip to Kabul a decade ago. Of course, no one in the factory spoke the language either. But he couldn't just repeat the same words without raising suspicion. Nor could he speak English with a South Asian accent. Thankfully, he had a backup language. He would speak Brazilian Portuguese, making his words incomprehensible to all. He and Rana would pretend to understand each other, even when they didn't, but Rana would be in control of the conversation, which was just as well, for he knew the Quran.

The greatest hurdle was Josh's appearance. Thus Rana's use of Afghanistan in the cover story. Contrary to the Western stereotype, many Afghans had fair complexions, and some even had blue eyes. Josh's beard was the lynchpin. While many Muslim men wore no facial hair, neither he nor Rana had ever seen a clean-shaven imam. It was fortuitous, therefore, that he had been growing out his stubble—a lesson from his days in Iraq.

By the time he arrived at the factory, he fit the part. His clerical robes were long and white. His *taqiyah*, or skullcap, was embroidered with indigenous designs. And his feet were shod in Peshawari chappals acquired from a shop in Little Pakistan. In his hands he held a gently worn copy of the Quran. Rana had given him a crash course in the most famous suras in case Josh needed to establish credibility. But the burden of the ruse rested squarely on Rana.

"Are you ready for this?" Ajmal asked.

Josh felt the butterflies raging in his gut. *"Estou pronto."*

Rana clapped him on the shoulder. "Let's do it."

After Ajmal unlatched the trunk, they stepped out of the car and crossed the sidewalk, following a lane that snaked between buildings. The air was stiflingly hot and thick with humidity. Within seconds, Josh began to perspire. In a minute, he was sweating profusely. Yet he maintained a leisurely gait, walking like a man who kept God's time, not his own.

The door to the factory stood at the end of the lane. Ajmal knocked twice and the door swung open. The guards greeted Ajmal with toothy grins and honored Josh with a bow and a self-effacing *"Assalamu alaykum."* He returned the greeting and nodded serenely, trailing in their wake as they showed him the way to the sewing floor.

The factory was filthy, poorly lit, and jammed with rattling machines. Half of the light sockets didn't have bulbs. Paint was peeling from the walls. Water stains mottled the ceiling. The temperature in the room was at least eighty degrees. The fans around the perimeter were powerless against the heat. And the stations were packed so close together that Josh could barely see the floor beyond the harried bodies of workers and piles of half-finished clothing.

The workers were multiethnic, but all of them were young—somewhere in their twenties—and all were wearing the same dead-eyed expression of exhaustion as they raced to keep up the pace. Josh watched their hands as they fed the machines. Their movements were almost hypnotic, as if they were automatons, their brains engaged only by habit. He struggled to keep his expression beatific despite the revulsion rising in him. *Like slaves on a plantation*, he thought. *It's the pushing system all over again, but retooled for the modern age.*

The guards led them along the wall of the sewing floor to a pair of offices overflowing with paperwork. In one of the offices, two men were chatting over tea. When they saw Josh, they stood up and welcomed him warmly, and then offered him and Rana their seats.

Josh sat down and began to speak in Portuguese, affecting an air of authority that the owner and Faruq met with complete deference. Communicating in a tongue unknown to them liberated Josh in a way he hadn't anticipated. It allowed him to give voice to his rage. He called the men names, swore at them with his most colorful invectives, even threatened them with divine judgment, though he was a lapsed Catholic and, in moments of doubt, an agnostic.

He stopped after a while and allowed Rana to "interpret." They had devised a script of sorts with three acts: introductions, public preaching, and private counsel. As planned, Rana spoke to the owner and general manager in English, their common language. Rana, it turned out, had a talent for the confidence game, and spun webs of drivel and deceit with unwavering earnestness. He praised the men for their "efficient operation" and "exceptional piety." He asked about their attendance at Friday prayers. He encouraged them not to neglect zakat—charity for the poor. He reminded them to fast during Ramadan. He exhorted them to make the hajj—the pilgrimage to Mecca. And he promised to pray for the success of their business.

The men nodded along as if mesmerized. When Rana fell silent, they showered Josh with praise for his "generous gift" to their "humble community." Purely out of spite, Josh let loose with another string of Portuguese curses, all the while maintaining the most sublime calm. In other circumstances, he would have fallen out of his chair laughing. But the cartoonishness of the owner and manager did nothing to diminish the human suffering beyond the window.

"The imam is telling you that he would like to address the workers now," said Rana, not missing a beat. "They are the children of Allah and in need of instruction."

The owner stood and gestured toward the door. "Of course, of course," he said, his English sharpened by his ancestral Mandarin. "This way. Faruq, signal lunch."

They left the office and split up, the GM heading in one direction and the owner leading Josh and his retinue in the other. Seconds later, Josh heard a vibrato sound, more alarm than bell. The workers looked up from their stations in confusion, many of them glancing at the clock on the wall. It was four minutes shy of the designated break time.

When the mechanical clatter died down, the owner held up his hands and spoke loudly over the fans. "Today is a special day. We have an honored guest, Imam Mehtar. He is a servant of God, and he has come to teach us wisdom. Listen to him."

The owner stepped aside and allowed Josh to take the floor. Josh looked out over the sea of faces. He saw the sheen of sweat on skin, the stares leaden with fatigue, the lines of misery stitched into every brow. For a disturbing moment, he felt the unfairness of his fraud. All of them had families in the lands from which they came. None had migrated to Malaysia knowing what awaited them. All were in need of rescue. But he had come for only one of them.

Josh's heart started to palpitate, and his hands began to tremble. He nearly lost his composure. But a face in the crowd saved him. The young man was sitting on the fringes of the room, a third of the way down. His features were angular, his cheekbones prominent, and his dark hair tousled, almost wind-blown. But it was his eyes that gave him away. Josh had studied them many times after getting a picture from the Rightaway workers. They were eyes that confronted the world without flinching.

It was Jashel.

Josh took a breath to steady himself, then he began to speak in Portuguese. He had no idea why, but the words that came to him were words he had never spoken to anyone except Madison. They were the unedited story of his life—the shadow that hung over his childhood, the bewilderment he felt when he realized he didn't look like his parents, the shame he carried from the day he learned that his birth mother hadn't wanted him, the haunting sense of inferiority that had driven him to push past every limit, to defeat the privileged at their own game, and, finally, the guilt that displaced the shame, the mistake he made in believing he could love two women intimately without being forced to choose, the seeds of pain and perplexity he sowed in his daughter's heart, and the anger he lived with because he had no way to fix it.

Eventually he grew weary of the confessional and stopped speaking. He heard Rana take the cue and deliver the message they had agreed upon in English and Bengali, but his thoughts were miles and years away. He was with Madison again, at Harvard amid the red-gold leaves of autumn, listening to her wit in the classroom, watching her walk down the aisle at the old stone chapel in Charlottesville, seeing her spread her wings and grow into a woman in Tokyo, São Paulo, and London, and then standing at her bedside on that joyous day in 2007 when she gave birth to Lily. He realized then, as never before, that he had to make things right with her. He wasn't just here to save Jashel. He was here to save himself.

When Rana finished, he informed the owner that Imam Mehtar would select five workers to bless. To avoid impropriety, Josh chose only men. Jashel was the third. The young man's expression didn't change when Josh pointed him out. He just stood quietly and followed along.

Rana suggested that they use the meeting room near the factory entrance. The owner agreed and escorted them there. Josh smiled and spoke another sentence in Portuguese.

"The imam is concerned that you are hungry," Rana explained. "He says there is no need for you to wait while he gives his blessings."

The owner bowed his head in gratitude, then left them alone.

Ajmal brought in the workers one by one. Josh and Rana talked with each of them briefly, asking about their families and encouraging them in their piety. Then they sent them back to the factory floor. Jashel was the last of them. He took a seat across from Josh, folded his arms, and stared at them unblinking. Josh felt a tremor of apprehension. If Jashel didn't believe their story, or if he panicked in the face of danger, the deception would fall apart.

Josh examined the young man through veiled eyes as Rana spoke in Bengali. He told Jashel who they were and recounted their visit to the dormitory. Then he outlined their plan to reunite him with his family. Jashel remained impassive until he heard Farzana's name. It was then that his eyes went soft, his lips parted, and he spoke a few words.

"He'll do it," Rana said.

"Tell him we'll handle the guards," Josh replied. "But he has to make it look real."

Rana nodded curtly. "He understands."

Josh stood and went to the door, Rana and Jashel beside him. He took the handle and swung it open, allowing Jashel to stumble out holding his stomach. Rana followed, one hand on Jashel's back. He and Ajmal traded a glance even as the guards stepped forward, their faces contorted by disgust. Rana waved them away and directed Jashel to the washroom next door.

As soon as Jashel was safely in the washroom, Rana turned to the guards and added his apologies to Ajmal's. The guards weren't mollified and kept looking at the washroom door until Josh approached them and spoke a question in Portuguese, stretching out his arms in welcome. He gestured to the meeting room and beckoned them with his hand.

"The imam apologizes too," Rana said in English. "He says you have a hard job and wonders if you would like a blessing before he departs."

The guards pondered this, clearly torn between personal desire and professional duty. It was then that Ajmal spoke the coup de grâce.

"You should go," he told the men. "It would be rude to decline the imam's invitation. I will watch the door. When the boy is finished retching, I will send him back to the floor."

At last the guards conceded and followed Josh and Rana into the meeting room. As he began to counsel the men, Josh imagined the rest—Ajmal's knock, the dance of doors as Jashel slipped out of the washroom, then out of the factory, his flight down the alley and across the sidewalk to Ajmal's sedan, and, finally, his climb into the trunk, his body curling into the fetal position in the compact space, his hand pulling the lid down until it locked in place.

It was a grave risk that they had asked him to take. The trunk was in the direct sunlight. If they didn't come quickly, he would suffocate. But Jashel would do it, Josh was sure. As he lay down in the heat, he would picture Farzana's face, remember the timbre of her voice, and play her name over and over again in his mind. As the memories multiplied, they would take hold of his imagination. And he would begin to believe what only hours before had seemed impossible.

There was a chance—a real chance—that he was going home.

CHAPTER FOUR

The look on Foysol's face was grim, the antithesis of his bonny appearance. In front of him on the café table was another juice, but he hadn't taken a sip. He was staring at Ajmal, his eyes hooded by mistrust and something darker—loathing. It was quite a change from a moment before. He had been almost joyful when he sat down, no doubt counting the ringgits he would make supplying his stable of undocumented workers to Ajmal's "clients." But then Ajmal had said Jashel's name, and the agent had frozen, glass in hand, the straw inches from his mouth.

Thirty feet away at the courtyard table, Josh couldn't help but smile.

"Where is he?" Foysol finally asked in Bengali, his voice barely above a whisper.

"Somewhere safe," Ajmal replied. As before, the fixer was wearing a wire, and Josh and Rana were listening and recording the conversation.

The agent's nose began to twitch. "What do you want?"

"It's very simple, really," Ajmal said reasonably. "We want his passport back. We also want every other passport and work permit you have in your possession, along with a list of the factories where all of your workers have been placed."

Foysol couldn't conceal his shock. "What you request is not possible. I am responsible for over one hundred workers."

Ajmal didn't budge. Instead, he fished a compact digital recorder from his jacket pocket and pressed Play. Foysol spoke through the speakers: "*There is a class of workers I sometimes meet, migrants who have certain . . . troubles. Their terms are more flexible.*"

Ajmal stopped the recording. "I have the entire conversation on file. What I ask is not only possible; you will make it happen today."

In an instant, Foysol's shock mutated into fear. "Who are you?"

"That doesn't matter. All that matters is what I can do to you. This is how it will be. You will give me the documents along with the factory list. You will then have twelve hours to leave Malaysia. After that, we will turn everything over to my contact, a senior officer in the Criminal Investigation Division, and he will see to it that your workers are repatriated to their home countries or placed with another agent who will not swindle them."

Foysol's eyes began to dart around.

"And don't think of trying to escape. The officer is watching you right now."

Foysol's head swiveled left and right until he caught sight of Rana staring at him across the courtyard. The agent blanched. "Who is the other man?" he asked softly.

"A member of the American FBI," replied Ajmal. "This is an international investigation."

The agent's hands began to shake. "I will do as you ask."

Ajmal smiled, clearly enjoying himself. "I thought so."

❀

Three hours later, Josh slipped his magnetized key card into the slot reader and opened the door to his room at the InterContinental Hotel. Jashel was sitting in the chaise lounge by the window, exactly where Josh had left him. If he had moved at all during the afternoon, he had done so without a trace. The space was immaculate, the refrigerator and minibar untouched. Rana and Ajmal entered the room behind Josh. Rana threw a duffel bag on the bed and rummaged through it, handing Josh a green passport bearing the seal of Bangladesh.

"I believe this is yours," Josh said, passing it along to Jashel.

The young man opened the cover and stared at his picture. The abuse he had suffered in the past six years had taken its toll. He looked much older now than he did in the photograph. He shook his head slowly, fixing his gaze on Josh. "Thank you," he said, using the only English phrase he probably knew. The gratitude in his eyes, however, was rich enough to fill volumes.

"Ask him if he called Farzana," Josh said, glancing at the burner phone on the table.

When Rana translated the question, Jashel's weary face brightened a bit. He nodded eagerly and spoke a waterfall of words in Bengali.

"He reached her an hour ago," Rana explained. "It was the first time they had spoken in over a year. She was afraid he had died, but she didn't give up hope."

Foysol got off too lightly, Josh thought. *He should be in jail for the next twenty years.*

It was a scandal, but it was necessary. After debating the matter ad nauseam the night before, Josh and Rana had decided to let Foysol go. It was the only way they could guarantee the protection of his workers, especially those, like Jashel, whose work permits had expired. The police were the problem. Neither Ajmal nor his friends at Kebaikan knew an officer who was above reproach. Had he been taken into custody, Foysol would have made arrangements for his case to disappear. Meanwhile, Jashel and the other undocumented workers would have been arrested, detained, and quite possibly abused. With the police out of the picture and Kebaikan in control, the workers were safe as long as they remained in the country. As soon as the lawyers straightened things out with the government, Jashel could return to his family.

Josh sat on the edge of the bed, and Rana and Ajmal pulled up chairs. It was time to take the next step. "Tell him I'm excited for him. But before he goes home, we need to talk."

Rana translated, and Jashel replied. "Go ahead," Rana said.

"It is not an accident that we came for you," Josh began. "I received your name from a source. I knew where to find you. I am a journalist. My friend here is a lawyer. We're looking to hold someone accountable for what you and others have suffered. There are many people who are responsible—the agency who lied to you in Dhaka; Foysol; Rightaway; and Class 5. But there are others who benefited from your exploitation. They are the companies whose clothes you made. We want to take one of those companies to court—Presto. At Rightaway, you knew them as the owners of the Burano brand."

When Rana interpreted, Jashel wagged his head in agreement. He spoke again, and Rana engaged him in Bengali. Their exchange lasted for almost a minute before Rana turned back to Josh, his face aglow with excitement.

"Whoever your source is," Rana said, "he just gave us the golden ticket. Jashel made clothes for Burano almost every day for five years. Foysol was a friend of the factory owner. Jashel saw them have many conversations. He also saw Presto's auditors come to the factory. He watched them take bribes. He told this to the men who came from Presto a year ago. They said he wouldn't get in trouble for speaking to them. But he did. Foysol made sure of it."

Josh met Jashel's eyes. "You can do something about that. If you let us, we'll take you and Farzana to America and you can tell your story."

Jashel didn't require more than a moment to think. He presented his decision in the form of a bargain. Rana translated: "If you get him home, he will do all you ask."

Josh smiled and extended his hand. "You have yourself a deal."

Jordan

March 2014

SUN STAR ENTERPRISES

CYBER CITY, HABAKA, JORDAN

MARCH 1, 2014

2:30 P.M.

The heater was rattling again, but at least it was running. There had been times during the winter when it malfunctioned and days had passed before one of the factory maintenance men found time to fix it. Those nights had seemed interminably long. The cold was so deep that Alya's breath crystallized in vapor, and she shivered uncontrollably. Sleep was impossible, even after a twelve-hour shift on the sewing floor. Beyond her blanket, her only defense against the chill was the companionship of her "sisters," Nina and Bipasha—like her, guest workers from Bangladesh. They shared Alya's bunk, curling into spoons beside each other and using their hands and feet to create friction on skin until, at last, the night faded and the alarm clock sounded, and the dawn broke over another workday.

The winter was one of many things Alya had not expected when she arrived in Jordan more than a year ago. She had pictured the Middle East as a waterless expanse of sand and heat, the antithesis of the green forests and flowing rivers that surrounded her childhood village in southwest Bangladesh. Jordan surprised her with its hills and valleys and trees and grass, and with the cycle of its seasons—cold and hot, rainy and parched. In her dormitory in Cyber City, just south of the Syrian border, she had watched snow fall for the first time. She had also seen the land boiling beneath the summer sun, the heat billowing like steam from a pot.

Jordan was an alien place, but Alya had precious little time to think about it. Sun Star was not paying her to ponder the strangeness of her fate. It was paying her to sew garments together piece by piece, order by order, creating shirts and shorts and pants and dresses to be wrapped in plastic, boxed up, and shipped on pallets to America. Alya knew less about the United States than she did about Jordan, except for the glimpses she had seen on the TV in her dormitory. But it didn't matter where the clothes were going. All that mattered was her plain machine, and the products it made, and the orders they generated, and the wages she received at the end of each month, wages that finally, after a year of repaying her recruitment loan, were substantial enough to provide a meaningful remittance to her mother and siblings in Bangladesh.

Work was the stitching that held Alya's days together. Work that began at seven in the morning and didn't end until seven in the evening—often later when the production schedule jammed up, or a buyer made a last-minute change. She didn't waste time considering the past and the misfortune that had brought her here. Neither did she spend her energies considering the future. When she was a girl, she had dreamed. These days, she did not. She was eighteen years old and a master sewing machine operator. As long as Sun Star chose to renew her contract, she would send money home to her family.

But there was a problem with her plan. She had put off thinking about it for as long as she could, reassuring herself that the suffering she had endured was curse enough and that God in his mercy would not burden her with more. But it had been two months and she had seen no blood. The timing was right and also terribly wrong. She recalled the wetness she had felt when Siraj forced himself on her the last time, the way it had hurt a bit less than the time before. As much as it frightened her to admit it, she could no longer deny what in her heart she knew to be true.

She was pregnant.

When the numbers on the clock turned from 5:59 to 6:00, the alarm bleated with sudden urgency, and Alya swung her legs out of bed. She waited in line to use the toilet, then dressed quickly in a long-sleeve shirt and jeans and wrapped her body in a green hijab and headscarf. Her nine sisters did the same, dancing around the room in a flurry of elbows and knees, yet without a curt word or a collision. Breakfast was a communal affair. The attached kitchen was cramped and the food bland to her taste, but it satisfied her hunger and for that she was grateful.

At twenty minutes before seven, she heard a knock. Seconds later, the door swung open, and Mr. Abbadi, one of the maintenance men, greeted them with the same stern expression he always wore. "Come," he said. He didn't speak Bengali, and none of the young women spoke Arabic. So they communicated in Pidgin English supplemented by hand gestures.

Alya and her sisters followed Mr. Abbadi out of the dormitory and down the path to the factory. Other workers joined them, and their group swelled into a crowd. The walk was no more than a hundred meters, but Alya cherished it. Apart from a supervised trip to the market on Fridays, the trip back and forth to the factory was the only time she got to spend outdoors. She looked toward the east and saw the sun rising above the rooftops of Cyber City. As its light suffused her eyes and its heat warmed her skin, she knew she could work another day, even with a child growing inside of her, even with a production manager who had raped her seventeen times, even with an owner who had deported two other women Siraj had impregnated. For Alya, it was all a matter of perspective. Her mother and siblings needed her. She would live for them.

As he always did, Siraj met the workers at the factory door and watched them stroll past on their way to the sewing floor. He was a compact man, short and barrel-chested, with a square jaw dimpled at the center, a mess of curly hair, and a moustache and goatee that he kept perfectly trimmed. His ancestry was Indian, not Bangladeshi, but he was from Kolkata and spoke Bengali. When Alya reached the door, she turned away, afraid to meet his eyes. Every time she looked at him, his face became a mirror reminding her of all the wicked things she had done to please him.

She walked quickly down the line and greeted her helper, Rohema, with a thin smile. Most of the workers at Sun Star were from Bangladesh, but a few were Indian, from West Bengal. The pieces were already at her station. The factory was in the middle of fulfilling a large order of men's dress shirts for Porto Bari. She knew from conversations she had overheard between Siraj and his general manager that Porto Bari was owned by an American company called Presto. But the buyer meant nothing to her. Only the clothes mattered.

Alya and Rohema started working as soon as Alya was situated. Her job was to fasten the sleeves to the body. She knew the pattern by heart. The motions came to her without thought, the fruit of endless practice. As she moved her hands and feet, controlling fabric and pedal, time passed like the current of a great river, carrying everyone in the factory downstream.

Before she knew it, the lunch bell rang. The workers streamed to the cafeteria, scarfed down servings of South Asian rice, dal, and flatbread—a concession by the Egyptian owner to prevent grumbling during the workday—and returned to their stations. Alya picked up another shirt body, the sleeve pinned and ready to be stitched. She didn't notice Siraj approaching until he spoke to her. She was so startled that she nearly dropped the shirt. It took all her mental fortitude to turn around calmly and look at him.

"Your work is excellent," he said in Bengali, examining one of her finished pieces.

"Thank you," she replied, her eyes shifting from his face to the floor and back again.

"I would like your help with something," he went on. "Rohema can manage in your absence. It will not take long."

Alya shuddered as chills raged along her spine. Her mouth went slack and her breathing grew shallow. She nodded obediently and stood up, making room for Rohema to take her place at the machine. The helper's skills were rudimentary, but Siraj knew that Alya would correct any lapses in quality, even if it meant she had to skip her afternoon break to fulfill her quota. He was intent upon only one thing—the flesh beneath her clothes.

Siraj strolled casually toward the product room with Alya on his heels. The room was located on the periphery of the floor. Unlike his office, it had no windows. Once the door was closed and locked, no one could see or hear what was happening, not unless Alya cried out. But she had trained herself to stay quiet, to do exactly what he asked without complaint, and to move toward the conclusion as swiftly as possible. The brevity of his pleasure was her only consolation. She would be back in her seat in ten minutes.

When they reached the product room, he stepped aside and allowed her to enter ahead of him. Then he drew the door closed and twisted the lock. He turned to her, and his lips spread into a boyish grin. This was the part Alya found most confusing. He didn't look at her like a predator. He looked at her like he was in love with her. He sauntered up to her and murmured poetry in her ear while he undressed her. It was as if somewhere in the dark recesses of his mind he truly believed she was his, and he was hers, and this bestial act was about romance and not rape.

She gripped the edge of the table at the center of the room, digging her fingernails into the surface until she felt the wood give way. She let him do it. She gratified him. But she wasn't there. She was back in her village on the banks of the Sela River, collecting the fish her brothers had caught. The last great wilderness in Bangladesh beckoned from across the river, tinting the horizon green and calling her heart to remember. When she was small, her father told her stories of the tigers that roamed the mangrove forests, animals more noble than any king. They were the heritage of her people, the pride of her land. Although history had not been kind to the Bengalis, the tigers were theirs. Nothing could take them away, not if she kept them alive in her soul.

The forest was the place she went and stayed, as Siraj finished his business and adjusted his clothes. She covered herself again and wiped away her tears. She despised Siraj for what he had taken from her. But her hatred was pointless. It could not feed her family. If this was the price she had to pay to meet their needs, she would do it, and she would do it again. That was the power she had over Siraj—the power to meet each sunrise with purpose. But that purpose now had a question mark beside it.

What would happen to her when he found out about the baby?

PART FIVE

Cameron

April–June 2014

CHAPTER ONE

THE GANGPLANK MARINA

WASHINGTON, DC

APRIL 7, 2014

5:48 A.M.

The road was dark beneath the starless Virginia sky. Cameron had the high beams on, cutting through the gloom, but the glow of tarmac and trees only seemed to accentuate the emptiness of the landscape. He didn't want to be there, speeding through the night, the bags he had packed for a celebratory weekend stuffed hastily in the trunk, the warmth of the bed and Olivia's embrace only a memory now. He saw her in the bathtub again, waiting for him. He remembered the feel of her wet skin on his, even as he struggled to keep his tired eyes from shutting. He felt anger growling in his gut, anger at the circumstances, anger at Ravenswood, anger at Vance.

He had planned the birthday getaway for months, told everyone in the C-suite about it, even marked it on Vance's calendar. But still he had been interrupted. There was blame to go around. That Ravenswood, an activist investment fund, had acquired a 4.9 percent stake in Presto just before the market closed on Friday signaled that the fund was making a move. They had yet to issue demands, but Cameron knew what they were after. The annual meeting of the shareholders was less than two months away. They were taking aim at the board, looking to open up a seat or two, which would give them leverage over the hiring and firing of Presto's officers. They were gunning for Vance. They wanted to put a kid from Silicon Valley in the corner office to usher "the Presto dinosaur into the digital

age," as Ravenswood's president had put it. Cameron understood why Vance
was apoplectic. But there was little the critical incident team could do over the
weekend that wouldn't appear desperate. Hands had to be held, investors courted,
defenses mounted, and the board appeased, but all of that could wait until Monday
morning.

He glanced at Olivia in the passenger seat. She was dozing, her head against
the window, her chin supported by her hand. He wanted so much to stop the
SUV and sleep until his alertness returned. The clouds of weariness were all
around him now, swimming in his vision, fogging his brain, softening his grip
on the wheel. He thought about cracking the window and cooling his face with
cold air, but he didn't want to disturb her. He had already ruined her birthday.
He owed her so much, more than he could ever repay. Why was she still with
him after all the sacrifices he had asked her to make? She said she understood.
She was a lawyer too, a partner at his old firm. But did she really? Was there a
part of her that wished she could walk away?

Cameron yawned, then swatted at the air and yawned again. He gave serious
thought to stopping, but he didn't have time. They were just twenty minutes
from the interstate, with its bright lights and wide lanes and the promise of home
only miles away. A hot shower and a triple espresso were waiting for him there.
He could make it . . . could make it . . . could . . . make . . . it . . .

He didn't know when it happened, or how. All he knew was that the world
was suddenly black and spinning, and his body was spinning with it, pummeled
relentlessly by surfaces he couldn't see. The air was filled with the screams of
metal assaulted by asphalt. If Olivia cried out, he didn't hear it. Her voice was
lost in the terror of the night.

And then, in a shocking moment, it was over, and everything was silent,
and he was upside down, and his knees were throbbing, and pain was shooting
through his neck, and he was reaching out for her and mumbling her name, but
she wasn't responding. Her head was hanging listlessly, her hands splayed out on
the crumpled ceiling. He was weeping and wailing her name, crying out as if by
the sheer force of his passion he could summon her back from the dead.

The next thing he knew he was hearing the sirens in the distance. But they
didn't sound right. The wail wasn't shrill; it was soft, like the ringtone of his
phone. In an instant, his eyes opened, and he realized it was all a dream—or,
more precisely, a memory. He hadn't recalled it so vividly since a year ago April,
on the eve of the first anniversary. He sat up in the darkness, his veins shot
through with ice. His phone was on the shelf above him, trilling mindlessly.

He glanced at the clock and saw it wasn't yet six. Who the hell was calling him now?

He let the call go to voice mail and fought to bring his emotions under control. The guilt was like a python around his heart. He embraced and resisted it at the same time. It was useless. Olivia was gone, her grave on a hillside across the District. He should have died with her, or in her place. But that wasn't the way of the universe. Life was a roulette wheel with rare glimpses of something more—what some called fate and others called Providence. But not everything was a matter of chance. This moment was his. It was all he would ever be able to claim.

He took the phone off the shelf and saw Kent Salazar's name. The consultant's voice mail was curt and devoid of detail. Cameron left his bed and went into the galley of the sailboat, starting the espresso machine—one of the few items from the old apartment that he had kept. He looked out the wide portholes at the lights of the harbor. Dawn was half an hour away, but he couldn't go back to sleep. When the coffee was ready, he took his mug to the wraparound booth and sat down, sipping it quietly and inhaling the steam.

After a moment, he placed the call.

"Cameron," Salazar said, his words clipped by the long-distance transmission, "I know it's early over there, but we have a situation that can't wait."

Cameron took a breath and ordered his thoughts. After canvassing Presto's suppliers in Malaysia for evidence of human trafficking and corruption, the Atlas team had moved on to the Middle East. They had been in Jordan for over a month, visiting factories, talking to workers, and developing better intelligence about the conditions on the ground. After sixteen years of doing business in Jordan, not one of Presto's suppliers had been demoted to the Red List. It was highly suspicious, but so far the news from Salazar had been ambivalent—nothing glaring, but nothing particularly troubling either.

"I'm awake now," Cameron said. "What's going on?"

As Salazar passed along the details, Cameron's heart sank into a different quicksand. The truth was far worse than he could have imagined. He drained his coffee and went to his closet, retrieving his suitcase. He put the call on speaker and packed as he listened.

When Salazar wrapped up, he gave his orders tersely. "Keep them happy until I get there. I'll do whatever they want, so long as they don't go public. We can't have another PR debacle."

"That's what I thought you'd say," Salazar replied.

Cameron terminated the call and rang the general aviation terminal at

Reagan airport, making the necessary arrangements. Then he called Declan. His compliance chief answered with a grumble that sounded like "Hello." In the background, Cameron heard a woman mutter, "God, it's early. Who is it?" Cameron recognized the voice. It was Victoria Brost, the Atlas researcher, home on a furlough. He smiled despite himself. Declan hadn't dated anyone in three years, not since his wife ran off with her fitness instructor.

"Time to get up," Cameron said. "We have a plane to catch."

After a pause, Declan's mind caught up. "Jordan?"

"I'll tell you when I see you. Oh, and bring Victoria. She might be useful."

"Uh, right," Declan said, sounding embarrassed. "We're moving now."

After hanging up, Cameron ate a quick breakfast, dressed in his most intimidating suit and tie, and took his luggage topside, locking the companionway door behind him. He left a note for the harbormaster and sped out of the parking lot. Traffic was starting to pick up in advance of the workday. Still, he made it to the airport in ten minutes.

Bridget, the flight attendant, greeted him in the lounge with coffee, which he accepted gratefully. Declan and Victoria arrived a few minutes later, suited up and dragging rollaboards. Cameron grinned when he saw Victoria blushing beneath her makeup.

"I'm happy for you," he said, putting her at ease. "But we have work to do."

"This way, sir," Bridget said and led them out to the flight line.

The pilot greeted them beside the aircraft and ushered them aboard just as the morning sun peeked over the horizon and flooded the cabin with light. They took seats in the conference area at the rear of the plane and strapped themselves in, looking out the window as the plane began to taxi. Cameron waited to start his briefing until the wheels left the ground.

"We're this close to another media disaster," he said, holding his thumb and forefinger a hairsbreadth apart. "But we got lucky. Kent found out about it before the media did. There's an activist group in Jordan called Al-Karama— 'dignity' in Arabic. For about a year, they've been investigating garment factories in Cyber City near the Syrian border. One of those factories is Sun Star Enterprises—our biggest Jordanian supplier. Three weeks ago, they had a breakthrough. A worker opened up. The following week he disappeared. Al-Karama thinks the factory sent him back to Bangladesh. Here's the punch line: the production manager at Sun Star, Siraj Ahmed, is a sexual predator. He's been assaulting female workers for years. He picks the pretty ones, rapes them until he gets tired of them, and then moves on. If they get pregnant, the owner deports them. All of the workers know about it. But they've been afraid to speak. Until now."

"Sun Star is on our Gold List," Declan said, his eyes bright with fury.

Cameron nodded. "It gets worse. Al-Karama's director, a woman named Ghada Azizi, reached out to our Dubai office last Monday. Ms. Azizi is smart. She knows the media can create a firestorm, but they have no power on the ground. She was hoping we would take action—"

"I haven't heard anything about this," Declan interjected.

"Precisely," Cameron said. "Neither has Ms. Azizi. She called Dubai on Wednesday, and then again on Thursday, asking for our office director, Hosni Shaaban. The receptionist assured her that he was in the office, but he hasn't called her back. She was planning to take the story to the BBC, but Kent intervened. His team was at Sun Star last week doing interviews. One of the workers told them about Al-Karama. Kent reached out to Ms. Azizi, and she told him the story."

Declan shook his head angrily. "Dubai is an information laundry. They whitewash everything. It's not just Jordan either. It's Pakistan, Mauritius, Madagascar. I've talked to Hosni Shaaban myself about the lack of detail in their audit reports. He says the reason we don't see problems is that they don't exist. He's a snake-oil salesman."

"He's not alone," said Victoria. "Other companies have seen the same thing in the Middle East. Some people over there consider a polite lie better than an impolite truth."

Cameron grunted. "Before this is over, we're going to recondition them. But we have to tread lightly. The involvement of Al-Karama creates additional risk. Our messaging needs to be clear. Sexual assault is a violation of our Code of Conduct. By allowing it, Sun Star is in breach. We're not going to tell them how to run their business, but we're going to read them the contractual riot act."

"What about Shaaban?" Declan asked.

Cameron gave him a devilish smile. "Leave that part to me."

CHAPTER TWO

THE INTERCONTINENTAL HOTEL

AMMAN, JORDAN

APRIL 8, 2014

9:08 A.M.

The seven hills of Amman were as white as Arabian sand beneath the spotless blue sky. The austerity of the scene drew Cameron in, even as the glare of the sun made him squint behind the windows. He was seated in an alcove in the Club Floor Lounge of the InterContinental Hotel, the remnants of his breakfast on the table in front of him. It was morning in Jordan, but his body was certain it was still night. He felt at once lethargic and agitated, his mind alternating between spurts of activity and flats of calm. Declan was across from him, sipping his third cup of coffee, his eyes bleary and unfocused. Victoria and Kent Salazar were making conversation in the sitting area next to them, waiting for a text from Atlas's Middle East research chief who was in the lobby anticipating the arrival of Ghada Azizi. By Cameron's watch, she was eight minutes late.

"There he is," Kent finally said. "They're coming up."

Before long, Atlas's research chief appeared on the far side of the lounge, with Ghada Azizi behind him. The Al-Karama director was a diminutive woman, but her frame belied the intensity of her presence. Cameron noticed it right away— the purpose in her gait, the clarity in her eyes, the stalwart set of her jawline. She was younger than he was, but not much.

When she reached the alcove, she put out her hand. "Mr. Alexander," she said in polished English fringed with the guttural accents of Arabic. "Welcome to Jordan."

Cameron stood and smiled genuinely. "Ms. Azizi, thank you for coming. Please, have a seat. Would you like something to eat or drink?"

She shook her head abruptly, mincing no words. "I'm here for one reason—to convince your company to act. If that is not your intention, tell me now and I will contact the media."

Cameron gestured to the seat beside him. "Please, sit. I'm not your adversary. I'm very interested in what you have to say."

The humility of his entrée seemed to disarm her. She sat down beside the window and crossed her legs. "Your office in Dubai is a disgrace."

Cameron softened his tone further. "I apologize for the way you were treated. It's something I intend to address. You know the authority I carry. My promises are not empty. But your findings are more important to me. How can I help you?"

Ghada shifted in her seat, taken aback by Cameron's solicitousness. "Sun Star Enterprises," she said, a touch friendlier. "It is one of Jordan's flagship factories, and you are their largest customer. They look like a model operation. If you go there, you will see it. Everything is new and shiny and neat. The workers look content. The owner, Hamad Basara, is a gentleman. But I know my Shakespeare. That same disguise is used by the devil himself."

Cameron arched his eyebrows. He had never been impressed by hyperbole. It was a lesson his father had drummed into him as a boy. *When you overstate your case, you blunt it. Your words should be precise, like the edge of a knife.* But Ghada didn't seem like the sort of person to waste her breath. Her tongue was razor sharp, as were her eyes.

"You have my attention," he said. "Tell me what's under the surface."

She laid it out for him. Siraj. The young women he fancied, some of them teenagers with passports that falsified their age. One in particular: Alya Begum, a girl from Bangladesh who could have been a movie star. The product room. The pregnancies—four of them, by Al-Karama's count. The deportations and devastated lives. All presided over by Hamad Basara. All permitted by irresponsible and sometimes crooked auditors. All perpetuated by buyers like Presto who placed order after order despite reports from the media about human rights abuses in Jordanian factories. Sun Star wasn't the first, or even the worst, offender. Nor would it be the last—unless something changed.

As Cameron listened to her, he curled his fingers into a fist and imagined taking Siraj by the hair and hurling him off the roof of the hotel. He had never been a brawler. It was his father's influence—brain over brawn. But the thought of a manager forcing himself on teenage girls in a factory making Presto's clothing made him wish he could settle the score.

"Have you told this to anyone other than my people?" he asked.

"No," Ghada said. "We did our investigation covertly. Going public is a last resort. We approached your company because Hamad Basara cares about one thing—his buyers. And Presto is responsible for about 60 percent of his capacity, from what we can tell—"

"Sixty percent?" Declan interjected. "Are you sure?"

Ghada looked at him in irritation. "That's what the workers tell us."

Cameron gave Declan a knowing look. Dubai had a lot of explaining to do.

"As I was saying," Ghada went on, clearing her throat, "Hamad cares only about his buyers. The police are in his pocket. The media is irrelevant. As long as he keeps getting business, Siraj will keep raping girls."

Cameron gave a thin smile. "That is going to end today. The only question is whether you'd like to see it."

✸

The caravan of three Mercedes SUVs pulled into the parking lot at Sun Star five hours later. Everyone from the gate guards to the workers in the loading bay to passersby on the street stopped and stared. Cameron emerged from the middle vehicle with Ghada Azizi. Salazar climbed out of the lead vehicle with Victoria and Declan, and the rest of Atlas's in-country research team joined them from the rear. The coterie wasn't essential to Cameron's mission. He could have come alone. But multiplicity projected power. An emperor was never without his aides. And on this day, in this place, Cameron reigned supreme.

Hamad Basara, the owner, met them on the stoop in front of the office entrance. He gave Cameron a megawatt smile and pumped his hand heartily, assuring him that it was Sun Star's highest honor to welcome such an "esteemed visitor." But the sand dollar size of his eyes and the shiftiness of his gaze betrayed the depth of his apprehension.

He escorted them swiftly to a conference room where an assistant offered them coffee and biscuits. Then one by one he brought in his managers to offer greetings. Through it all, Cameron maintained an expression of absolute boredom, even when Siraj himself appeared and delivered an obsequious tribute to Presto's "top-class style and loyalty." Finally, when the last well-wisher had departed, he told the owner he wanted to speak with him in private.

Hamad inclined his head. "Certainly. My office is quite comfortable."

Cameron shook his head. "I'd like to see the product room."

In an instant, Hamad's jaw went limp and his eyes filled with fear. He was so shocked, in fact, that seconds passed before he managed to stammer out, "Of course." Cameron kept his expression tightly controlled, but inside he felt more gratification than he had in years on the job.

The owner showed him to the sewing floor while delivering a monologue that sounded like a marketing brochure. Cameron ignored him and surveyed the factory. Ghada's description had been spot-on. The floor was swept and de-cluttered, the paint on the walls bright and fresh. Even the noise was noticeably lower than it had been at Rahmani Apparel in Bangladesh. It was no wonder the auditors had been complacent.

"As you wished," Hamad said, holding out his hand toward a door at the end of a long hallway. "This is our product room."

"Just a minute," Cameron said. He took out his iPhone, touched the screen a few times, then put it away. "My apologies. A text from the office."

As soon as they entered the room, Hamad revived his monologue, parading item after item before Cameron in a kind of fashion show on hangers. Cameron paid almost no attention. He walked slowly around the room, playing out his imagination like a kite string. Though he had seen none of it, he saw it all: the setup, perfect for a predator; the girls, like low-hanging fruit; the other workers bound by fear. But there was one aspect of the conspiracy that didn't quite fit— the complicity of Hamad and his general manager.

"So this is where he does it," Cameron said, interrupting the owner.

Hamad frowned in confusion. "I don't understand."

"Siraj." Cameron studied the owner's face as comprehension dawned.

In desperation, Hamad tried to play the fool. "What do you mean?"

"How often does it happen?" Cameron asked. "Once a month? Once a week?" When Hamad just stared at him, he went on, "Who was it the last time? Was it Alya Begum?"

At the mention of the young woman's name, Hamad's hands began to tremble.

"You know who she is," Cameron said, watching the owner's nose twitch. "Yet you have a thousand workers on the floor. I'm curious. Have you raped her too?"

The question struck Hamad like a hatchet blow. He shook his head and waved his arms, protesting that he had never touched the girl, or *any* girl, that it was only Siraj, that he had no idea about the manager's appetites when he hired him, and that he had tried to intervene but Siraj had threatened to go to the Anti-Corruption Commission and accuse him—falsely, of course—of bribing public officials. By the end of his defense, the owner was frothing at the mouth. It was pathetic and disgusting, but exactly what Cameron needed.

He took out his iPhone and put it on the table. "Everything you just told me is on this recording. If you have a prayer of keeping Presto as a customer, this is what you're going to do. By the end of the day, you are going to terminate Siraj's employment. By the end of the week, you are going to put him on a plane to whatever godforsaken place he came from. Your next production manager will be a saint. After that, you are going to double the pay of Alya Begum and every other girl that Al-Karama has identified as a victim. And if any of those girls happens to get pregnant, you are going to pay for their medical care and six weeks of maternity leave. You are not, under *any* circumstances, going to deport them. From now on, you will give Al-Karama full access to your factory. If they find anything amiss, they will report it to me."

"Yes, yes, of course," Hamad simpered. "I will do it."

"Oh, and those bribes you didn't make," Cameron said, his eyes boring into the owner. "If I ever find out you're lying to me, we will pull all of our business immediately."

"I am a good man, a *religious* man," Hamad replied. "I do not pay bribes."

Right. You just help your friends. "I'm finished here," he said, taking his phone off the table and walking out of the room.

Hamad ran after him, catching up in the hallway. "Where are you going?"

"I'm going to walk the floor," Cameron replied and did just that.

With the owner on his heels, he took long strides down the sewing lines, searching the faces of the workers until he found her. It was her beauty that gave her away. Even without makeup, her hair back in a bun, Alya was one of the loveliest young women he had ever seen. She was also young enough to be his daughter. She stared back at him, at once inquisitive and anxious. For a quixotic moment, Cameron wished he could take her home with him, buy her a flat in Washington, and give her all the opportunities that the world had denied her—tutors, language lessons, college, graduate school. But that was impossible. She had a life already. He had done everything he could for her.

He moved on down the line before drawing attention to her, but on the way back he met her eyes a final time. She regarded him for a second or two, then blinked and focused again on her work. As he returned to the offices, he felt a profound sense of satisfaction. Words came to him then, words he could never speak but that perfectly expressed the attitude of his heart.

I'm sorry, Alya, for all of it. But it's over now. As long as you are here, my word will keep you safe.

CHAPTER THREE

Cameron was sitting in the dining room in his hotel suite tapping out an e-mail when he heard the reminder on his iPhone. It was six in the morning in Boston—the only appointment on his calendar he was loath to miss. Even seven time zones away, he had arranged his schedule to accommodate it. He sent the e-mail and took a breath, steeling himself against the dread. Then he placed the call. His mother answered on the second ring.

"Good morning, darling," she said, her tone as tender as it was tremulous.

"Hi, Mom," he replied. "What's the word from Dr. Radcliffe?"

By the way she hesitated, he knew the prognosis wasn't good. Despite four months of chemotherapy, the cancer had metastasized again, spreading through her lymphatic system to other parts of her liver and both of her lungs. Her doctors had tried other drugs, but they did nothing to arrest the downward spiral of the disease. Every week her mind was a little bit slower, her voice a tad frailer, and another piece of Cameron's heart died.

"It's in my bone marrow," she replied. "I don't know how much more they can do."

Cameron closed his eyes, the pain a dull ache in his gut. "Dr. Radcliffe is the best oncologist in New England. She isn't the kind to give up."

"She isn't giving up," Iris said. "I'm the one having doubts."

Her words reflected her weariness. She had battled the cancer for over a year, submitting her body to the knife and the heat and the poison, but the treatment had gotten her nowhere.

"You have to keep going, Mom," Cameron urged. "We need you."

She sniffled once, and he knew she was crying. "I'm sorry. You're right. It's just hard to accept." She collected herself. "Anyway, enough about me. How are you?"

"I'm fine," he said, still reeling from the news. "Keeping busy, as always."

"I'm not talking about your job. How is your heart?"

He knew precisely what she meant. The second anniversary of Olivia's death was fast approaching. But he didn't want to go there. The thought of talking about it exhausted him.

"Are you sleeping?" she persisted. "Or are the dreams coming again?"

He steadied his hands. He wanted to flee the questions, but he knew his exertions would prove futile. She would wait until he told her the truth.

"The other night I saw it again," he finally admitted. "Like I was there."

He listened to her breathe and imagined her thinking what many of his friends had said over time. *It could have been any of us. You didn't kill her. You loved her. You did everything you could to stay awake. It's not your fault.* But they were wrong. What could have happened to anyone had happened only to him. And Olivia was dead because of it.

"Cameron," Iris said, reaching out to him across the miles. "I said this a year ago, and I'll say it again every year for as long as I'm alive. What you lost that night you can never get back. But Olivia would not want you to hate yourself. She loved you as much as any woman can love a man. What happened to her will never change that."

The ache in his gut climbed into his head. He massaged the bridge of his nose. "I know, Mom," he agreed, wanting nothing more than for her to stop talking.

But his mother wasn't quite finished. "She also wouldn't want you to live the rest of your life alone. I know that because she told me. Did she tell you?"

"Yes," he whispered.

"It doesn't have to be now, or even soon," Iris said, "but please don't forget that."

"Okay," he replied, conceding the field. "Look, I have to go. I have a meeting."

"At six o'clock in the morning?" she asked curiously.

"I'm in Jordan. It's afternoon here."

This gave her pause, but only for a moment. "I love you, Cameron. Your sisters love you. Your father loves you. We're here for you, whatever you need."

"I know," he said again. "Just promise me you'll keep fighting, no matter what."

"I promise," she replied, then ended the conversation on a lighter note. "Send me a picture. I've always wanted to see the Middle East."

Half an hour later, Cameron left his room and found his way to the hotel courtyard. He walked past the azure swimming pool surrounded by palm trees and found a table on the stone terrace some distance away from the handful of guests enjoying a late lunch. Though the table was in the shade, he didn't take off his sunglasses. The light in the courtyard was dazzling, and in his present emotional state, he didn't quite trust himself to remain impassive.

As angry as he was about Sun Star, he had to stay under control. The problem wasn't just the Dubai office and its director, Hosni Shaaban. Like Presto's offices in Dhaka and Bangkok, Dubai was a symptom of a more insidious disorder. Cameron no longer had any doubt that compliance failures were rife in Presto's sourcing system. The only question that remained was whether the corruption was parasitic or an essential feature of Presto's business model.

He watched as Declan led Shaaban across the terrace to the table. They had summoned the Dubai director to Amman on the pretense that they were conducting a compliance review of Presto's overseas offices. Shaaban had accepted the invitation with gusto, particularly when Cameron sweetened the deal by dispatching the Gulfstream.

Cameron stood and shook Shaaban's hand. The man was impressive at first glance—tall and lanky with a chiseled Arab face, imperious eyes, and a salt-and-pepper beard. His résumé was equally striking. Egyptian by birth, he was the son of a diplomat and had spent his formative years in London, obtaining degrees in economics from Cambridge and management from Bath before taking the helm of the Dubai office at its inception in 1998.

After exchanging pleasantries, they took their seats, and a server appeared with menus. Cameron was about to speak when Shaaban turned the tables on him.

"Are you a fan of Middle Eastern food, Mr. Alexander?" he asked, speaking the Queen's English. "We can eat family style if you like."

Cameron nodded, playing along. "Why don't you order for us?"

Shaaban did so with flair, engaging the waiter in a dialectical exchange—part English, part Arabic—that synthesized in a diverse array of selections.

After the waiter left, Cameron said, "Declan and I have reviewed our sourcing data. I wouldn't have guessed it, but it seems that Presto has deep roots in Jordan."

"We do indeed," Shaaban replied energetically. "We were one of the first companies to take advantage of the Qualifying Industrial Zones established by President Clinton. Even today, some of our most reliable factories are in the QIZs. The free-trade agreement gives Jordan a distinct advantage over other garment-exporting countries. Because their shipments are tariff-free, they can charge us less and pay their workers more."

Cameron kept his tone light, buttering up Shaaban. "I imagine that makes our regional sourcing director quite happy. What's his name again? Bentley Adams?"

"Yes," Shaaban replied. "He's quite fond of our relationships in Jordan. Under his leadership, we've encouraged our suppliers to modernize their equipment, and we've supported them by expanding our orders year after year."

The waiter appeared again with water goblets and appetizers.

Shaaban pointed to a ball of spiced cheese. "This is shanklish. It's Lebanese."

Cameron spread the cheese on a piece of pita and tasted it, enjoying the savory and pungent flavors. As soon as the waiter departed, he homed in on his first point. "Some years ago, we set a limit on the percentage of a factory's total capacity that our offices are allowed to book. That limit is 40 percent. We've heard through the grapevine that some of our suppliers here in Jordan are receiving orders at a higher percentage. Do you know anything about that?"

Shaaban finished chewing an olive. "We are very careful to observe that policy. With all due respect, I believe your sources are incorrect."

"What if I told you my sources are workers?" Cameron asked.

Shaaban didn't break stride. "There must be some mistake. Might I ask which factories? I know many of the owners personally."

"Sun Star Enterprises," Cameron said.

Shaaban's smile had every appearance of being genuine. "Ah, yes, one of our oldest partners in Jordan. Hamad Basara is a good man, and quite dependable."

"So what you're saying is that the workers at Sun Star are wrong."

"They must be," Shaaban replied, showing no hint of deception. "I approve all the orders myself. What other explanation is there?"

Cameron kept his face impassive. *Either he is an extremely adept liar, or he takes me for a fool.* "Do you know the name Ghada Azizi?"

The office director hesitated a fraction of a second. "I can't say that I do."

"How about Al-Karama?" Cameron pressed, scrutinizing Shaaban's face. He saw it then, a twitch just above the man's left eyebrow. He was good, but not that good.

"I think I've heard of them," Shaaban admitted. "Aren't they an activist group?"

Cameron allowed his lips to spread into a thin smile. "What if I told you that Ghada Azizi, Al-Karama's director, sent you an e-mail last week and called you twice to follow up, going so far as to confirm with your receptionist that you were in the office?"

Shaaban was caught, but he didn't concede. "I would say you are here for reasons other than what you disclosed to me. There is no global compliance review, is there?"

"No," Cameron said, admiring the director's brazenness. "I'm here because Ms. Azizi is a persistent woman. She was about to go to the press."

Shaaban shrugged. "Activists are always whining about something. Most of the time the media ignores them. And when they listen, the story comes and goes in a heartbeat."

"So you ignored her," Cameron said, barely veiling his rage.

"Mr. Alexander," Shaaban replied, "I direct an office that sources half a dozen product lines in four countries. I don't have time to worry about every grievance brought by groups like Al-Karama. My job is to ensure that our suppliers deliver our merchandise on time at a price point that maximizes Presto's profits."

In a moment of introspection, Cameron realized that six months ago he would have said the same thing. But his dismissiveness had been the result of blindness. His focus had been on satisfying the regulators, dispensing advice to Vance and his stable of executives, directing the train of corporate litigation, keeping up with the paper mill of contracts and deals and memos and policy statements, and inventing ways to streamline the compliance and administrative systems to make them more cost-effective. Perhaps Shaaban's oversight had been legitimate. Or perhaps he was concealing a more deliberate form of blindness.

"If you had listened to her story," he said, "you wouldn't be so cavalier."

Shaaban's brow furrowed. "And what story would that be?"

"It's about a production manager with a fetish for pretty female workers."

As Cameron watched, Shaaban's left eyebrow twitched again. *He's heard this before*, Cameron thought. *Does he know about Sun Star? Or does it go beyond that?*

The director held out his hands in a gesture of reasonableness. "Is that such a scandal? When men and women work in close quarters, things happen."

In an instant, Cameron's anger boiled over. "It's a scandal when it's rape."

Shaaban was taken aback, but he recovered his poise quickly. "Who's saying that? The workers? Al-Karama? And what factory is it? I'm sure if we heard both sides of the story we would see that it was all just a harmless misunderstanding."

Cameron twisted his wedding ring under the table, his blood pressure in the stratosphere. Shaaban was either a misogynist or the densest human being on the planet. Cameron was about to reply when more food arrived. This time, however, Shaaban made no attempt to explain the cuisine. Instead, he fingered his napkin distractedly.

When the waiter left, Cameron lowered his voice until it was almost a growl. "You asked what factory? You tell me. I can see this isn't the first time you've heard about this."

Shaaban shook his head, undisturbed. "What do you want me to say? It's the oldest instinct on earth. I bet if you could take a candid survey of every factory in the world, you would find workers and managers having sex. Especially in places like Jordan, where most workers and managers are from foreign lands and don't see their families for years at a time."

"I'm not talking about sex," Cameron said slowly. "I'm talking about sexual assault. How many allegations of rape have arisen from our factories in this country?"

Shaaban didn't answer right away, so Cameron repeated his question more insistently. Finally, Shaaban said, "Over the years, there have been a few. Each time my compliance team has looked into the claims and found no merit in them."

Cameron's eyes bored into Shaaban. "Did any of those allegations come from Sun Star?"

When the office director's eyebrow twitched a third time, Cameron said, "I'll take that as a yes." He turned to Declan. "Have you heard about any of this?"

"Never," Declan said, fury in his eyes. "No official report from our Dubai office has ever referred to allegations of sexual assault in Jordan or anywhere else."

"How do you explain that?" Cameron asked Shaaban.

Shaaban calculated every word of his answer. "We didn't deem the allegations significant enough to demand the attention of the corporate office. We took care of them ourselves."

"By doing what?" Cameron demanded. "Talking to the owners?"

"Yes," Shaaban replied. "Like I told you, we know many of them quite well."

Cameron felt sick to his stomach. "I have something you should hear." He reached into his pocket and took out his iPhone. After a few touches, he played the recording of Hamad Basara's panicked confession. The owner's voice sounded tinny through the miniature speakers, but his words were as clear as the Jordanian sky. While Shaaban listened, Cameron cataloged the changes in his face, tracing his emotions from surprise to dismay to revulsion to antipathy.

After it was over, Cameron took off his sunglasses and locked eyes with Shaaban. "So here's the way this is going to work. I am going to ask you some questions, and you are going to tell me the truth. I can see when you're lying, and quite frankly, it sickens me. You may be the longest-standing office director in this company, but I have Vance Lawson on speed dial. If I need to, I will place a call, and he will dismiss you on the spot. Do you understand?"

For the first time that afternoon, Shaaban looked afraid. "I understand," he said quietly.

Cameron ticked off his points one by one. Was Siraj Ahmed the focus of any rape allegation in the past? What were the names of the other factories where allegations had arisen? Why did the factory audit reports, compiled by a supposedly independent auditor in Jordan, reveal nothing about rape at Sun Star or any other factory? How had the auditors found no hint of forced labor among foreign guest workers, when numerous international agencies had reported such abuse? Wasn't it true that Presto was booking Sun Star at a rate far higher than 40 percent of capacity? And how was it possible that not a single factory overseen by the Dubai office had been called out for material violations of the Code of Conduct and demoted to the Red List?

Shaaban's answers were tepid but sincere, at least as far as Cameron could see. The problem in Dubai was not just a Middle Eastern preference for politeness over honesty. Shaaban thought of himself as invulnerable because he was doing exactly what Presto's sourcing director for the Middle East and Africa, Bentley Adams, had asked of him. Jordan was a honeypot of inexpensive, high-quality garment production. Shaaban's task was to keep the engine well oiled and unencumbered. Unless absolutely necessary, he ignored complaints from the outside and handled all internal issues without involving corporate. Also, to avoid bumps in the road, he had hired an auditing company known for its slapdash approach and justified it on the basis that all of Presto's factories received supervision and training from the ILO's Better Work Jordan program.

"Your candor is a breath of fresh air," Cameron said in the end. "On account of it, your position is no longer in peril—as long as you do exactly as I say."

He outlined his terms and obtained Shaaban's assent to each one. Sun Star would remain a supplier at current levels; the Dubai office would reduce all other orders to 40 percent of a factory's capacity; the current auditing company would be fired and replaced with a credible auditor; the new auditor's first order of business would be to evaluate the merits of all sexual assault allegations, no matter how stale, except for Sun Star, which Cameron had already handled; and from now on, any complaints raised by a reputable agency or media outlet would be forwarded to Declan's office for immediate review.

"There is one final matter before we can enjoy the food," Cameron said.

The office director gave him a look at once chastened and wary. "What is that?"

"You keep this to yourself—this conversation, this visit, everything we've discussed. And if your office's performance numbers go down and Bentley Adams ever asks why, you tell him that you've had a change of heart, that compliance matters for a whole host of reasons, and that if he has a problem with your priorities, he can take that up with me. Got it?"

"Yes, sir," Shaaban replied wearily.

Humility becomes you, Cameron thought. "Excellent. Let's eat."

CHAPTER FOUR

PRESTO TOWER, 16TH FLOOR

ARLINGTON, VIRGINIA

MAY 30, 2014

4:51 P.M.

All was still and quiet in Cameron's office, so quiet, in fact, that he could hear the march of the second hand on the wall clock across the room. Outside his door and in the fifteen floors below him, the workday vortex continued to spin, holding thousands of people in its orbit and churning out reports and memos by the terabyte to meet end-of-month deadlines. The swirl had consumed Cameron until thirty-one minutes ago when he shut the door, issued instructions to his secretary to turn everyone but Vance away, spread out the contents of the Black File on the great slab of Berkshire walnut, and picked up the Targeted Risk Assessment he had received from Kent Salazar, reading all twenty-eight pages until the findings were cemented in his brain.

From Malaysia: (1) strong documentary evidence of forced labor and debt bondage among migrant workers in Presto's apparel supply chain, thanks to a corrupt and exploitative system of outsourced labor; (2) minor documentary evidence, but strong suspicion, that Presto's suppliers routinely use unauthorized subsidiary factories, bringing Presto's supply chain into further contact with human rights abuses and corruption; and (3) minor documentary evidence, but strong suspicion, that Presto's suppliers, and outsourcing agents acting on their behalf, have used bribes and other forms of illegal inducement in the course of business.

From Jordan: (1) strong documentary evidence of forced labor and debt bondage among workers in Presto's factories; (2) minor documentary evidence, but strong suspicion, that Presto's Jordanian partners have bribed public officials to gain commercial advantage; and (3) strong oral evidence that female workers in an unknown number of Presto's supplier factories have suffered sexual harassment and rape while making clothes for Presto.

From the "spot" audits of Red List suppliers outside South Asia: minor documentary evidence, but strong oral evidence, that factories on the Red List have continued to receive occasional Presto orders in spite of their prohibited status, though it was unclear whether Presto's local offices were complicit in the unauthorized subcontracting or unaware of it.

Cameron then turned to the three-page addendum and read its opening paragraph:

> After conducting a series of interviews in the Ashulia district of Dhaka, Bangladesh, and the village of Kalma, Bangladesh, researchers from Atlas were able to determine that the girl depicted in the photograph taken anonymously on the night of the Millennium Fashions factory fire is Sonia Hassan, age fifteen, the daughter of Ashik and Joya Hassan; that Joya Hassan and Sonia's sister, Nasima, age twenty-four, perished in the fire; that Sonia is still living, though she suffered damage to her brain that rendered her blind, deaf in one ear, perpetually exhausted, and incapable of work. The following is an account of the fire and its aftermath delivered to Atlas researchers by Ashik Hassan.

It had been less than twenty-four hours since Cameron received the report, but he knew Sonia's story by heart. He was so consumed by it, in fact, that he had scarcely slept the night before. He had imagined the narrative from beginning to end—the heat of the flames, the fabric of the Piccola pants, the acridness of the smoke, the cries of jumpers, the climb onto the ledge, the descent along the makeshift rope, and then the fall. Somewhere in the throes of insomnia, the story had taken on an existential dimension in his mind. Sonia's fear became his fear. Her suffering became his suffering. In that moment, more than in any that had come before it, he knew he had to *do* something. He couldn't bring Joya and Nasima back to life. He couldn't restore Sonia's broken body. But he, Cameron Douglass Alexander, could do his damnedest to make sure it never happened again.

He put the report down and stood up, looking out the window at the Lincoln Memorial in the distance. He remembered the day his father had first taken him there with his sisters, to the shrine of the Great Emancipator, and brought history to life.

"Do you see these people?" Ben had asked them, sweeping his hand over the tourists milling on the steps. "Most of them will never understand this place. I don't fault them for that. It's beyond them. Only the free children of slaves can truly appreciate the gift—and the burden of all the work that remains to be done."

After that, Ben led them into the hall, pausing only briefly before the statue of Lincoln before drawing them into the north chamber.

"This," he had said, pointing up at the wall and the engraved words of Lincoln's Second Inaugural Address, "is the greatest speech ever delivered in the English language. Read it. Let your heart hear the words as he spoke them."

And Cameron had. He was only twelve, but he was old enough to understand that justice had a price, and that price was sometimes more awful than men could bear.

"One month after Lincoln gave this speech he was murdered," Ben had said. "The life he lived and the death he died leave us with questions. Will we—will *you*—continue the work? Are we—are *you*—willing to make the sacrifice?"

Cameron glanced at his watch and realized that five o'clock had passed. He picked up the phone on his desk. "Linda, please remind Rebecca Sinclair about our meeting."

He waited, statuesque, as the second hand on the wall clock circumnavigated the dial. Irritated, he picked up the phone again. "Linda?"

"I'm trying, sir," his secretary said. "She isn't answering."

Cameron shook his head, rankled by the sourcing VP's rudeness. Rebecca had been with the company for twenty years, and every CEO since Bobby Carter had worshipped at her feet. The board treated her like the goose that laid the golden egg. Her blasé attitude toward time was but one feature of her legendary arrogance. She was only certain to be punctual for the directors.

As the minutes multiplied, Cameron began to pace alongside the window. He couldn't let her get to him. The Black File put him in the driver's seat. But, of course, it didn't. In Presto's organizational chart, Rebecca's office was on par with his. And in the hierarchy of company politics, she was fifteen years his senior and had a far more lucrative compensation package.

At last, at twenty minutes past five, Rebecca breezed in, tossing him a half apology about a meeting that ran over and seating herself in one of the wingback chairs without being invited. Cameron suppressed his annoyance and sat down across from her. Over the years, he had heard many words used to describe her, but one of them summed up the rest—severe. She was like a one-woman magnetic field, inspiring almost religious zeal in her admirers and near superstitious dread in her detractors. She cared nothing for consensus, only competence. She believed that fortune was a choice, not a matter of chance. In a contest of wits, a clash of personalities, or an argument about business strategy, he had never seen her lose.

"So I hear you've been poking around," she said, stepping into the silence as if Cameron had intended it. "I was wondering when you were going to inform me."

Her preemptive strike shocked Cameron as thoroughly as if she had dropped a cobra in his lap. It took all his internal discipline to throttle the instinct to lash back at her.

"Oh, I know your little inquest was supposed to be confidential," she went on. "But my people are loyal. They know I can protect them."

"Your people," Cameron said calmly, "have made sourcing decisions in disregard of our Code of Conduct, our Red List, and the standards of compliance that have been the hallmark of Vance's tenure as CEO. The 'little inquest,' as you call it, was his idea, not mine."

This gave her pause, but only for a moment. "I have one question for you, Cameron. Have my people done anything illegal?"

He tried not to smile. "As a matter of fact, the suppliers your people have chosen solely for the benefit of the bottom line have been involved in corruption, bribery, and forced labor and human trafficking, all federal offenses for which this company could be held liable."

For a long moment, Rebecca was speechless. "You have evidence of this?" she said.

He held his hand out toward his desk. "It's all in the Black File."

She wrinkled her nose. "Does the board know?"

"I've kept Blake Conrad apprised. But he isn't fully briefed. Nor is Vance. I wanted to talk to you first."

Her eyes pierced him. "What do you want from me?"

"I want you to send a letter to every member of your sourcing team. We'll draft it together. I promise to be reasonable, as long as you do too. The letter will establish a new ethical baseline for sourcing decisions that respects all prevailing laws and company policies. After that, I want to give a speech at your annual sourcing meeting. Without your endorsement, your people won't listen to me. But with it, things will change."

"Done," she conceded. "Anything else?"

He took a slow breath. "I also want to talk to you about your performance incentives."

She didn't reply, just gave him a look that said, *You're starting to step on my toes.*

He went on. "Aran Wattana in Bangkok has been borrowing money from my compliance team to reward his sourcing staff for putting his office at the top of the global heap. The letter is going to make clear that that kind of budgetary reshuffling will be cause for termination."

"That's fine with me," she said, "so long as I get to keep Wattana. He knows the Thai factories better than anyone."

"He's all yours," Cameron agreed, lowering his voice to lend it gravitas. "My concerns are actually much deeper. I have doubts about the calibration of the sourcing system itself."

Rebecca's eyes flashed with indignation. "As I see it, that's dangerously close to saying you have doubts about the character of my children. You attack me, and I fight fair. You attack my sons . . ." The line drawn, she continued, "But, please, enlighten me."

Cameron leaned forward and waded into the thicket. "It's like this. You put a normally functioning nineteen-year-old boy on an island with a dozen under-age girls. What's going to happen? Unless the boy is Jesus himself, he's going to commit a crime. The same is true of our suppliers. Your people push them to drive their prices down, to shorten their lead times, to invest in new technology. You threaten them with competition from factories in other countries. The consequences are as predictable as the boy on the island. Decent managers start cutting corners, paying bribes, squeezing wages, shirking on overtime. They fire women who get pregnant, hire shady outsourcing agents to bring foreign workers from distant lands, and then ignore the fact that those agents are making false promises and ensnaring the workers in debt bondage. It doesn't matter if we have auditors. It doesn't matter if we have a Red List. It doesn't even matter if your people abide by every jot and tittle in the Code of Conduct. Unless the incentives change, the crimes will continue. We won't be committing them. But we'll be responsible because we created the climate that made them inevitable."

Rebecca shook her head condescendingly. "You've crossed the line. Those incentives you hold in such disdain are the lifeblood of this company. They give us competitive advantage. Why do you think I make twice the money you do? Why does my department get a Learjet? It's because I make the rain. When customers buy something from us, it's not because our stores offer an enjoyable shopping experience or our website is user-friendly. It's because we give them the quality they want at an unbeatable price. That's the holy grail of retail. You dismantle that and you might as well shutter the company."

Cameron returned her gaze without blinking. "When was the last time you read the company handbook?"

She laughed irreverently. "I didn't read it the first time. Hank and Dee Dee Carter are dead. Their business model lost its mojo in the 1980s."

"I figured as much," Cameron said. "So what you're telling me is that our philosophy of 'People First'—the philosophy that dragged us out of the abattoir of the Millennium fire by the power of historic goodwill—only applies to customers and investors. Is that right?"

Her laughter turned contemptuous. "Pardon my French, Cameron, but the market doesn't give a shit about self-righteous mottos or sentimental PR campaigns. We're a public company. Our owners are investors. We sell things to consumers. At the end of the day, we do and say whatever it takes to keep them happy."

As brutal as her logic was, Cameron couldn't disagree. The market was a system with no master, regulated by governments and corporate legal departments like his own, but governed by the blind and impersonal laws of economics. If Presto's sourcing system yielded exploitation, it did so because the market rewarded self-interest. They worked in a ruthlessly Darwinian world, where the hammer of creative destruction shaped the future and where fortunes were more easily lost than made. But that gave Cameron leverage.

"I'm going to take this to Vance and the board," he said. "I don't want to undercut our competitive advantage. But there are tweaks we could make that would diminish our exposure. I might make half your salary, but I'm the guardian of this company's reputation. Without the trust of the marketplace and the regulators, your rainmaking doesn't mean a damn thing."

She gave him a wintry look. "If you do this, I'm going to make opposing you a matter of personal pride."

He clenched his teeth, thinking of Sonia Hassan, and Jashel Sayed Parveen, and Alya Begum, and the words etched in marble in the north chamber of the Lincoln Memorial. "I'm glad we had a chance to talk," he said, rising from his chair. "You know the way out."

She stood without another word and headed toward the door.

"Rebecca," he said and returned her glare with a grin. "Good luck."

CHAPTER FIVE

The wind was up on the Potomac, blowing out of the east at twenty-five knots. Despite her oceangoing draft and heavy keel, the *Breakwater* was heeling hard and hammering through the waves, sending plumes of spray high into the air. Cameron was at the helm, holding the sailboat steady on a beam reach at almost eight knots. Vance was behind him in the cockpit, working the winches and adjusting the sails with the quiet competence of a professional racer. He was the best yachtsman Cameron knew, his touch delicate yet firm, and his judgment unerring. He moved with the instinct of a man born under sail. He might as well have been. He had spent every summer of his childhood plying the waters off Nantucket.

"She's a beauty today," Vance yelled over the wind.

"More like a beast," Cameron called back, gripping the wheel as a thirty-knot gust sent the *Breakwater* heeling even harder to starboard.

In contrast to Vance, he hadn't stepped foot aboard a sailboat until business school. It was Vance who had taught him to love blue water. A week before their first spring break at Harvard, he had invited Cameron to join him and a couple of buddies at his family's place in Saint Croix. The house came with a thirty-foot yacht, the *Bohemian*, that Vance sailed with the mastery of an old salt and the panache of a playboy. There were four of them in the house when the week began, but after a day on the island their number grew to seven. The newcomers were young ladies, all beautiful and available. Only Cameron refrained from the bacchanal that followed. In the company of anyone else, he might have felt jealous. But Vance was a born leader who prided himself on making and keeping friends. While the other men drank and cavorted with the ladies, Cameron spent time on the *Bohemian* with Vance, learning how to handle lines and sails and anticipate the changing sea. Harvard brought them together, but sailing cemented their bond—and deepened it across three decades of friendship.

"I'm going to tighten her up and head toward the creek," Cameron shouted.

Vance nodded and trimmed the headsail as Cameron brought the sailboat closer to the wind. After securing the winch, Vance picked up the mainsheet and hauled in the boom. They maintained a close reach to the entrance of Mattawoman Creek. Then they came about, shortened their sails, and glided under partial power into the protection of Sweden Point Marina.

When the sails were down and the anchor set, they went below and prepared sandwiches in the galley. Afterward, they grabbed bags of chips and bottles of beer and took the meal topside, eating together in the shade of the canopy.

"It's been too long, Cam," Vance said, chewing a bite of his sandwich. "Remember when we used to go out every other weekend?"

"Yeah," Cameron replied, feeling his friend's nostalgia. Then he laughed. "Olivia hated it. I don't know if I ever told you that."

Vance grinned. "It was written all over her face. But she was tough. I never saw her get green around the gills. I can't say the same for the ladies I brought along."

Cameron shook his head. "Don't you ever get tired of it? All the flirting and dating and breaking up." *With women half your age*, he wanted to add, but didn't. "Wouldn't it be easier if you found another Jackie and settled down? It would give Annalee something to come home to."

"Another Jackie would be the end of me," Vance quipped. "I'm defective in the domestic department. No woman would stay married to me for long." He paused and turned reflective. "What you had with Olivia was special. I've never been the sentimental type, but seeing you guys together was something beautiful."

Cameron looked out at the water, his eyes misting behind his sunglasses. In the two years since his wife's death, he couldn't remember a time when he and Vance had shared a moment like this, just the two of them, under sun and sky, away from the Presto pressure cooker. It was a shame he couldn't just relax and enjoy it. But there were matters he had to discuss with Vance, matters of grave consequence that could destabilize their peace, even destroy it.

"I know how much you miss her," Vance went on, unaware of Cameron's musings. "Even though I wasn't her favorite person, I miss her too. She was sharp and sensible, generous and trustworthy—a lot like you, in fact, although much better looking."

Cameron smiled at the joke, but his preoccupation didn't abate.

Vance regarded him thoughtfully. "Something's on your mind."

Cameron put down his sandwich. "Back in November you asked me if I'd discovered anything about the Millennium fire that you needed to worry about. I said I'd loop you in when I had an action item. Well, I have one now, but you're not going to like it."

Instead of looking puzzled, Vance replied bluntly, "Does it involve Rebecca Sinclair?"

Shit, Cameron thought, admiring the sourcing VP's resourcefulness and loathing it at the same time. "What did she tell you?"

"She called me Friday night," Vance replied, "but I stopped her before she could say anything. I didn't want to hear it secondhand. As long as I'm CEO, you get first dibs."

Cameron felt a rush of gratitude for his friend.

"Out with it," Vance said. "Whatever it is, we'll deal with it."

So Cameron told him about his trips to Bangladesh and Malaysia and Jordan, about the rot he had discovered in the sourcing system, about the damning results of the Atlas audit, and about Sonia Hassan, the girl in the photograph. Vance listened to everything without a word. Since his eyes were hidden behind mirrored lenses, Cameron couldn't follow the trajectory of his thoughts, but he knew Vance like he knew his own soul. He knew the earth was shaking beneath his friend's feet, and that he would do anything to stop it.

When Cameron finished, Vance took a noisy breath. "I'm starting to understand why Rebecca sounded so desperate. This is unprecedented." He took a long swig of beer, then said, "You'll have to permit me a little skepticism; I wasn't quite prepared for this. But I'm wondering how much of this can actually be changed, assuming we keep our current business model, which is the only model we've ever had."

For a moment, Cameron was astonished by Vance's insouciance. Cameron hadn't pulled any punches. He had used the words *slavery* and *serial rape*. He had described in detail Sonia's fall and Nasima's leap from the ledge. Then he recalled something from the past, the only time he had seen Vance face a personal crisis. The girl was a twenty-two-year-old staffer at a late-night show in Manhattan. Vance had bumped into her at a bar in Chelsea. What happened next was just a weekend fling. He took her to dinner at Eleven Madison Park, showed her his suite at the Mandarin Oriental, and then parted ways. When she called him a month later claiming she was pregnant, Vance was surprised that she even had his phone number. But his response was swift and decisive. He sent Cameron to New York with a briefcase full of cash and a simple question: How much? He never asked about the baby or whether she planned to keep it, just made her an offer to stay quiet and leave him alone, which she accepted, all two hundred and fifty thousand dollars of it.

"Some of the problems are endemic, I agree," Cameron said, trying to shore up the bridge between them. "But there are steps we can take. We can tighten up compliance and improve auditor oversight. We can recalibrate incentives in sourcing, so performance reviews are based on more than delivery, margin, and costing. We can hire Atlas to do a thorough evaluation of our supply chain. We can run a new PR campaign making 'People First' a global priority."

Vance looked across the water at the boats floating in the marina. He arched his eyebrows and scratched his chin. "I take it Rebecca disagreed with you."

"Not in every particular," Cameron replied, "but about the core of it, yes."

"No surprise there." Vance took off his sunglasses and regarded Cameron openly. "Look, I understand how you feel. You did exactly what I asked. You've been out in the field. You know what you're talking about. I doubt any other general counsel would have gone so far to protect his company. Thank you for that. I mean it."

He took a breath, and Cameron heard the swish of the blade as it fell.

"But the timing isn't right, not for anything major, anyway. The shareholder meeting is in two weeks. The board is still holding its breath, but I think we're in the clear. We climbed out of last year's hole and followed it up with a good showing in the first quarter. If sales stay strong, we'll deliver investors even better news in August. The fire was an awful tragedy. It sickens me that our clothes were the last thing those poor girls made. But we didn't make the factory blow up. We did nothing more than send them an order in violation of our own policy. I don't mean to be callous here, but Millennium is yesterday's news. The world has moved on."

Cameron sat in stupefied silence, grateful that his friend couldn't see his eyes. Vance had not only ignored his advice, he had spit in his face, and in the faces of Declan and Kent Salazar and Victoria Brost, and the entire global compliance staff, and every worker across the world making apparel for Presto under conditions of danger, violence, and abuse.

"This isn't just about ethics," Cameron finally managed. "This is about liability. The potential for a verdict is huge, to say nothing of the damage to Presto's reputation."

Vance nodded, trying to defuse the tension. "I get it. I really do. You have my blessing to bolster compliance. If you need more money, I'll get it for you. But right now we just don't have leverage in the market to rethink our sourcing practices preemptively."

"And if someone files a lawsuit?" Cameron persisted.

Vance smiled magnanimously. "Then you can say 'I told you so.' And we'll do what we always do—confront it head-on and find a way to survive."

Cameron weighed his options and placed his final card on the table. "I have an obligation to advise the independent directors," he said, feeling the gravity of the words as he spoke them.

Vance sat back against the bench and cast his gaze upward at the clouds. "You're right," he admitted. "Take it to the board. They should have the last word."

Cameron searched his friend's face for a sign of exasperation but saw none. To his amazement, Vance held up his beer bottle. "You know, I think this calls for a toast. We've been working side by side for five years, and this is the first time you've gone over my head. I bet that's a record in the Fortune 50. I've never been prouder to have you with me."

Cameron accepted the olive branch because it was the only way forward. But he couldn't deny what he felt in his heart. A rift had opened up between them. Vance hadn't just dismissed the women of Millennium. He had trampled on their graves.

He touched Vance's bottle with his own and said, "Cheers." But he knew it wasn't over. Not by a long shot. One way or another, he would find a way to make things right.

CHAPTER SIX

The Hank Carter Memorial Auditorium was at capacity and brimming with investor energy—a thousand bodies in a thousand seats in terraced rows. Vance Lawson strutted across the stage in front of a forty-foot wall of curved glass, a lavalier microphone over his ear, delivering his annual State of the Company speech with assistance from a state-of-the-art sound system and a colossal fifteen-by-twenty-five-foot screen. Cameron was in the second row with the rest of the C-suite. His seat was closest to the center aisle, the most privileged location. It was Vance's doing—one of his attempts to mend what had happened between them on the sailboat, then what had happened in the boardroom five days later.

It was a fait accompli. Cameron had seen it coming as soon as he walked through the door and glimpsed the faces of the directors arrayed around the table. Their minds were already made up. The ringleaders, as he had suspected, were Lester Grant and Jim Dunavan, both veterans of Wall Street, both hard-boiled acolytes of Milton Friedman, both millionaires many times over. The senior-most member of the board, Grant was seventy-two and the erstwhile CEO of Laffin-Stone, America's fourth-largest investment bank. Dunavan was his unofficial wingman and president of the Philomel Group, a hedge fund managing seventy billion dollars in assets.

They countermanded the meeting almost immediately, giving Cameron only five minutes to outline his proposal before lodging their objections. Their talking points sounded like dictums from Rebecca Sinclair's playbook. At times, they almost parroted the sourcing VP, confirming Cameron's hunch that they had strategized with her.

"In retail, cost is drag," Grant emphasized, his pale forehead wrinkling beneath wispy hair brushed back in unruly curls. "Our sourcing people shave off fractions here and there, but they add up to big savings. We give our customers more than they think they should be able to get for the price. That's magic you don't mess with."

Then Dunavan chimed in. "The supply chain is an ecosystem that exists in delicate balance. Interference anywhere can disrupt the system everywhere. It's the butterfly effect. I have tremendous respect for you, Cameron. But the job of compliance is to keep Presto on the right side of the law, not to play God with the market. Leave that to the damn regulators."

Of the eight independent directors, only one—Paula DeMille, a fifty-year-old executive from the tech sector—defended Cameron against the Grant-Dunavan juggernaut. She spoke about corporate citizenship and the need to balance investor returns with the rights of stakeholders in the global community, noting the growing public demand for businesses to protect workers and the environment in the absence of regulation. But her arguments were drowned out by the naysayers. Even Blake Conrad, who usually ratified Cameron's advice on principle, took exception to meddling with the status quo. He articulated his concerns judiciously, but among the remaining directors his judgment was damning.

"I hate to sound cliché, Cameron, but if it ain't broke, don't fix it. Fix the Red List. Fix the auditors. Fix communications between sourcing and compliance. All of that makes sense from an institutional standpoint and as a shield against liability. But this is no time to tinker with the profit center of the company. It's like you're asking us to do heart surgery when diet and exercise would work just as well. I'm with Lester and Jim on this one. I can't agree with it."

At that point, Cameron's only refuge was a bit of gallows humor. "Are there any other metaphorical pearls you'd like to share before you scuttle my proposal?"

Of those at the table, only Paula smiled.

In the auditorium, Cameron turned his attention back to the stage and watched as Vance clicked to the last slide—the Presto logo against a white background. "At McKinsey," the chief executive was saying, "I watched companies soar and companies crash. From those experiences, I learned the four pillars of success—a clear-eyed vision of the marketplace, a smart and versatile management team, an ethos that puts customers first, and a strategic plan for long-term growth. Challenges come and go. But if a house is built on a sure foundation, it will stand firm. Presto is that kind of house. The state of our company has never been stronger."

When the shareholders erupted in applause, Cameron joined them, but inside he was seething. By all appearances, Presto was back on its feet. Sales and stock were up, investor confidence hadn't been higher since the 2008 crash, and the new website was actually starting to compete with Amazon. But Cameron knew the rebound was tainted, the bonny news stained with blood. Perhaps Vance could walk away from the plight of Sonia Hassan; perhaps the board could justify its inaction with aphorisms. But Cameron couldn't. He'd barely slept since the sailing trip. Each night he had lain awake listening to the sounds of the marina and hatching delirious plots to force Presto's hand, all of which were either illegal or insane. He had done everything in his power, but it wasn't enough. Nothing had changed.

His iPhone vibrated. He retrieved it from his pants pocket as Vance was leaving the stage, waving and shaking hands. When Cameron saw the text message, he felt a pang of dread. It was from his father.

"Please call ASAP."

He turned to Kristin Raymond and raised his voice over the din. "I have something I need to deal with. It's a family matter."

Kristin nodded and spoke into his ear. "I'll let Vance know."

Cameron walked quickly up the aisle, ducking his head and hoping none of the investors noticed him. Outside the auditorium was a reception area lined with windows. He walked toward one of them and placed the call. "Dad," he said when his father picked up, "what's going on?"

"It's your mother," Ben replied, his tone darker than Cameron had ever heard it. "She's taken a turn. You need to come home."

✲

It took Cameron three hours to get to Logan Airport and another thirty minutes to reach his parents' house in Cambridge. He spent the trip in a state of barely suppressed agitation. He hadn't felt so destabilized since the days after Olivia's death. The helplessness unsettled him the most. He had spent his life perfecting the art of control—of himself and his surroundings. Control was a function of wisdom and skill and connections and favors, all woven together into a web of self-knowledge and self-protection. All risks were calculated, some bypassed, others taken but hedged. No path was pursued without a viable alternative. These were the rules he had followed in all aspects of his life, except one—love. It was his undoing.

The taxi left him on the driveway outside the house. He stood there for an unconscious moment, gazing up at the window of his old bedroom, his heart like a sluice gate letting in a flood of memories—his father in the study, glasses perched on his nose, a book in hand, lost in a world of rhetoric that afforded little space for children; his sisters playing together in the yard, always gleeful, never alone; his mother like a benevolent spirit moving through the rooms, keeping things tidy and hearts tended, speaking with grace, helping him find his place. He was there among them as a child, as an adolescent, as a young man, but he was also separate from them, the son who feared his father more than respected him, a third wheel with his sisters, the boy who took shelter with his mother until his mind made sense of the world.

He approached the door in a daze, pressing the latch and finding it unlocked. The house was quiet when he stepped into the foyer. Both of his sisters were still in transit. He set his bag down in the living room and laid his coat and tie over the back of the couch. After rolling up his sleeves, he climbed the stairs, counting the creaks as he had when he was young. He looked at the pictures on the wall—family portraits from Cape Cod that marked the progression of time. His mother was at the center of all of them. He couldn't imagine the world without her.

His father met him at the top of the steps, his eyes leaden, his handshake limp. In the seven months since Thanksgiving, Ben had aged years. Cameron followed him into the master bedroom, its shades drawn but its curtains tied back, allowing in diffuse light. When he saw the frail figure on the bed, only her face visible among blankets and pillows, his heart came apart in shards, like a glass ornament fallen from the hand. He knelt beside her and saw that her eyes were open. His mother turned toward him, her smile a lark in passing.

"Cameron," she whispered. "It's good to see you."

He couldn't believe how fast she had deteriorated. Only eight days ago she had drifted off during their Thursday call, dropping the phone and leaving him with a dial tone. Ben took her to see Dr. Radcliffe right away, and the oncologist ordered an MRI along with a bone marrow biopsy and blood tests. The results were dismal. Her tumors had doubled in size; her platelet, hemoglobin, and red cell counts had dropped precipitously; her lungs were collapsing, her liver failing; her marrow was all but destroyed. Dr. Radcliffe offered her the option of further chemotherapy, but Iris declined. Instead, Ben took her home and informed Cameron and his sisters that it wouldn't be long. Still, Cameron hadn't expected the summons so soon.

He touched his mother's face and blinked back tears. He didn't know what to say. She had always been stronger than him, like the ground beneath his feet, as solid as anything in creation. To see her like this, her face so gaunt, her skin so sallow, her eyes dim and sunken in, her hairless head covered by a wool cap, was to see a shadow, a person departing.

"It's good to see you too," he said at last. The words felt hollow on his lips, but he spoke them anyway because they were true.

"Come closer," she said. "I have something to tell you."

He leaned toward her, angling his head so his ear was inches from her mouth.

"I'm sorry," she said softly, and his stomach clenched. "I'm sorry for all the ways that life has hurt you. But I believe that goodness is waiting for you, if only you'll reach out and take it. Trust your heart, Cameron. I trust it. Trust . . ."

Her voice trailed off and her eyes closed. He worried for an instant that she was gone, but then he saw her nostrils flare and knew she was asleep. He stood up and found his father in the hall, talking in low tones with a hospice nurse, an old book in his hands.

"She's sleeping," Cameron said, wiping a tear from his cheek.

The nurse nodded compassionately. "It'll probably be a few hours before she's cognizant again. Are you hungry? I'll make you something to eat."

He felt his stomach rumble. He'd eaten nothing for lunch. But he didn't want to leave his mother's side. "I'm all right. I'm going to sit with her for a while."

"I'll bring you something just in case," the nurse said kindly, descending the stairs.

He stood awkwardly in front of his father, the years of misunderstanding like a chasm between them. There was a time long ago when he would have craved Ben's support—a hand on the shoulder, a tender word, an encouraging smile. But his father never offered any of these things, and Cameron stopped wishing. He was about to turn away when Ben reached out and handed him the old book.

"She asked me to give you this," he said. "I'm not sure why."

Cameron took the volume and ran his fingers over the tattered cover. "What is it?"

"Something from the past. About the man I'm named after."

In a flash of memory, Cameron recalled his mother's words at Thanksgiving. *I have Cornelius's diary. He wrote it all down, Esther's entire story, but he kept it secret, and all of his heirs kept it secret . . . I'd like you to read it sometime.*

"I have work to do," Ben said. "I'll be in the study if you need me."

Cameron watched his father trundle down the steps, leaning heavily against the railing. In spite of himself, he felt empathy for the man. He knew what it was like to lose the best person in his life—like the world had come after him with a meat cleaver, hacked open his chest, and cut off a piece of his heart, just enough to make him bleed, little by little, for the rest of his days.

He took the old book into his mother's bedroom and sat down on an armchair by the bay window. One of Olivia's cats—Bella—appeared at his feet and eyed him curiously, then climbed into his lap and began to purr. He stroked her fur and scratched her behind the ears, just as he had done in the evenings at their old apartment in DC, a glass of wine in hand and Olivia across the room with Grayson, reading a magazine.

In time he opened the book and saw the handwriting of a bygone age. Cornelius had inscribed his full name inside the cover, along with a place— Beacon Hill, Boston—and a date—September 1867. Beneath that, he had written, "Herein lies the story of Esther Marshall Alexander, beloved wife and mother, now resting with her ancestors, awaiting the Resurrection. A eulogy and a lament."

Cameron read the opening pages, expecting the brittle prose of a barrister, but instead he found the soul of a man laid bare in letters. Esther had come to Cornelius as an escaped slave. But her ordeal went far beyond the indignities of servitude. The daughter of a Mississippi house girl and her master, a cotton planter, she grew up in the big house, was tutored by her mistress, and learned to read the Bible and mend clothing. When she was thirteen, the planter's crop suffered a blight, and he sold a dozen slaves to pay his debts. Esther was the first on the block in Vicksburg. Because she was beautiful and virginal and a mulatto, she fetched a high price. A trader bought her, bound her neck in a coffle, and marched her and twenty others to the slave market in Atlanta, stopping only when he had the urge to sleep or fornicate. Every night for weeks on end he raped Esther, sometimes in the woods, sometimes in a field, sometimes in an abandoned barn. He called her a "fancy girl" and promised to find her a master who would enjoy her "very superior qualifications."

In Atlanta, he sold her to a Georgia plantation owner named John Henry

Fletcher. From the day she stepped foot on Fletcher's property, he treated her as a sex slave. Over thirteen years, she bore him three children, all of whom he sold as soon as they were weaned. Then the war came, and General Sherman captured Atlanta. When the news arrived, Esther fled in the night to the Union lines and lived in a contraband camp until Sherman marched on Savannah. Esther went with the army, reading Scripture to the wounded and mending uniforms. In Savannah, she stowed away on a Boston-bound ship with other escaped slaves. She met Cornelius at the African Meeting House in Beacon Hill, and he fell for her over the objections of his family, all prominent members of the free black community. They married in the last days of 1865, shortly after the Thirteenth Amendment was ratified.

Cameron glanced at his watch and realized that an hour had passed. His mother was still asleep in the bed, a sandwich brought by the nurse untouched on the windowsill. He scarfed it down and returned to the story. What came next astonished him. Cornelius devoted only two pages to his marriage to Esther and the birth of their son, Jeremiah, which Esther didn't survive. Instead, Cornelius recounted the journey he had taken with the Freedman's Bureau through the byways of the Old South, to the plantation of John Henry Fletcher, then to the chaotic streets of postwar DC where Fletcher had taken refuge, and finally into a courtroom and before a judge who heard Cornelius's suit for reparations. In that courtroom, Cornelius had made the argument that the freedom now guaranteed by the Constitution was not compensation enough for the long years of Esther's toil and abuse. The only way the scales of justice could be balanced was if Fletcher was forced to pay. The judge, however, kicked out the case, allowing Fletcher and his family to maintain their comfortable living in the capital and sending Cornelius back to Boston with a wound to his conscience that never healed.

By the time Cameron finished the diary, he realized that Cornelius's "lament" was not about the death of his wife, but rather about the America that he loved and loathed at the same time, a country that had liberated his brethren from their chains only to abandon them in poverty, make amends with their former captors, and allow the centuries of their bondage to remain unrecompensed. The last paragraph Cornelius wrote left Cameron with the haunting feeling that his great-great-great-grandfather had known, in some mysterious way, that this day would come, that one of his heirs would read his words in a place of doubt and anger and grief and need a little nudge to take a step that could change things.

Cameron set the book aside and tented his hands beneath his chin. He recalled Kent Salazar's words in Malaysia: *What you need is a vaccine.* At the time, he doubted such a thing was possible. But now his mind had changed.

He heard a car pull into the driveway outside. His sisters were coming. His mother was dying. His heart was breaking. But at last he saw it clearly—the light in front of him, the chance to redeem something of his life. It was more perilous than any path he had ever taken. There would be casualties and collateral damage. But the potential reward was commensurate with the risk. If anyone could pull it off, he could.

And if he failed, at least he would go to his grave with the knowledge that he had tried.

PART SIX

Joshua

March–May 2015

CHAPTER ONE

"Would you like some water, sir?" asked the flight attendant, balancing a tray on her hand.

Josh took a bottle from her and twisted off the cap, taking a sip. He glanced at Rana in the seat beside him. His friend's eyes were closed, his head propped against the headrest, the faint sounds of reggae emanating from the earbuds in his ears. For a moment, Josh considered joining Rana in sleep. He was exhausted after nearly twenty-four hours in transit. But he resisted the instinct. They would be on the ground soon. He could sleep at the hotel.

He reached for his backpack and took out his iPhone and noise-canceling headphones, searching for the recording in the memo app. He knew every word of the conversation by heart. He had done most of the talking. His source had spoken only in riddles and occasionally for clarification. In the past month and a half, he had listened to the recording a dozen times. There was nothing left to glean. But the enigma of the man's motives continued to gnaw at Josh. He pressed Play and sat back against his seat, remembering.

The rain fell like flour sifted from the lightless sky. All was wet and cold, the kind of cold that shivers skin and seeps into the bones. Had he not been so distracted, Josh would have noticed that his teeth were starting to chatter. But his mind was on graver things. He huddled deeper into his anorak, his fists bunched inside damp pockets. His footsteps were the only sounds intruding upon the silence of the National Mall. It was two in the morning on a Monday in February. Before long, six million Washingtonians would rise from their beds and greet another gray winter workweek. For now, though, the city was only awake in the shrines of the dead.

Which was why Josh was here. His source had chosen well.

The Lincoln Memorial stood before him, robed in brilliance, like the shining citadel on a hill that had fired the dreams of the first Americans and haunted their progeny ever since. He scaled the steep steps in pairs, the faces of lions and eagles watching him from their granite chalices. At the top of the staircase, he slipped through the colonnade into the north chamber.

A man stood with his back to him, looking up at the text of Lincoln's Second Inaugural Address. He was dressed in a dark suit, a wool topcoat, and a matching fedora—the sartorial stereotype of Washington's professional class. But his skin set him apart. Even in 2015, the vast majority of DC power brokers were white. The man was black.

"Joshua Griswold," the man said, turning toward him, his voice resonating in the vaulted space. "You look different in the flesh. The stubble becomes you."

When Josh saw the man's face, his stride broke in surprise. He had spent the last thirty hours turning over rocks on the Internet and reading everything he could find about Presto and the Millennium fire. He had guessed the source was a disgruntled midlevel functionary, either recently terminated or passed over for promotion. He could not have been more wrong.

"I could say the same for you," Josh replied, finding his voice. "I expected—"

"Someone else," Cameron Alexander interjected. He gave Josh an opaque look, then his lips spread in a wry smile. "An understandable mistake."

Josh stared at him for a moment longer, then tried to make conversation. "When I was at Harvard, I had your father for constitutional law. All of us were mesmerized."

Cameron's smile disappeared. "Spells are curious—they conceal more than they reveal."

It was a peculiar statement, and Josh allowed it to hang in the air until the pause became awkward. It was a trick he had learned from a negotiator he once interviewed—stare at a person long enough and he'll fill in the silence with something more than he meant to say. Cameron, however, seemed immune to the discomfort. Or perhaps he knew the technique.

"What are we doing here?" Josh asked at last, realizing with a shudder how cold he was. The wet winter chill had circumvented his jacket, permeated his jeans, and risen up through the soles of his sneakers until he felt like he was standing in a refrigerator. He folded his hands and warmed them with his breath.

"I'd have thought that a man with a pair of Pulitzers would tell me," Cameron said.

Josh looked past the barb and realized that Cameron was telegraphing something critical about the game they were playing. There were limits to what he could volunteer. But Josh's questions—and the inferences he drew—were unconstrained.

"All right," Josh replied. "I'll talk and you tell me where I'm wrong." He organized his thoughts. "The Millennium fire was an accident, no sign of foul play. But the factory was a death trap. One entrance and exit through the storeroom on the ground floor. Three generators online, all within yards of flammable fabric. A short in a wall socket set the fabric ablaze. The generators exploded and sent flames up the stairwell. The workers on the lower floors escaped through the windows. But the people on the upper floors had no chance. The death toll, by last count, was three hundred forty-three."

"A nice soundbite," Cameron said. "But nothing original."

"I'm just getting started," Josh rejoined. "What makes the fire interesting is why the workers were at their stations at nine in the evening with the power out. Here the stories diverge. Activists alleged they were fulfilling a last-minute order for Presto. But Presto claimed that it hadn't done business with Millennium in months. Reporters tried to get into the factory, but the owner sealed it off. The only evidence we have implicating Presto is the photograph of the girl."

Cameron looked down at the ground, his expression obscured by the brim of his hat. Josh waited. Moments passed. Then Cameron spoke again, and his voice was different somehow.

"Sonia Hassan."

Josh narrowed his eyes. "What?" His heartbeat increased. "Is that her name?" When Cameron didn't respond, he went on. "No one was able to identify her. There was too much blood and soot, and the pants were over her nose and mouth. Are you saying you found her?"

Cameron was silent again, but this time he appeared to be calculating.

"Is she alive?" Josh asked. "Where is she?"

At last, Cameron said, "Her father is Ashik Hassan. Find him and he will tell you."

"It *was* your order, then. Millennium was making clothes for Presto."

The general counsel didn't answer, so Josh took his reasoning a step further. "You *knew* how dangerous it was. You lied to the press. You covered it up."

Cameron seemed to bristle. "That's too simple. And too small."

"So you *didn't* know about it?" Josh demanded, allowing his incredulity to show.

Cameron stared back at Josh, his eyes unfathomable. "We're not a bad company. We're more conscientious than many of our competitors. But we've lost our way."

Josh clenched his jaw, suppressing his frustration. "I didn't come out here in the middle of the night for platitudes."

"You can walk away," Cameron replied, holding out his hand toward the darkness and the rain. "Or you can accept this for what it is."

"And what is that?"

Cameron spoke his answer evenly, without judgment. "How long has it been since you last wrote a column? Almost a year?"

Nine months. But Josh didn't say it.

Cameron went on. "I came to you because I respect your work. I also happen to believe that everyone deserves a second chance. But I can't make you take it."

Josh steadied himself. "I'm listening."

"No, you're not," Cameron said. "You're talking."

"Right." Josh stood for a moment, thinking. He looked up at the wall inscribed with Lincoln's luminous words and replayed in his mind everything Cameron had said. It was then that an idea struck him. It was outlandish, but it had a certain incontestable logic.

"This isn't about Millennium, is it? This isn't even about the fire. This is about Presto. It's about your supply chains, the way you make the things you sell to consumers." Josh followed his intuition further. "Or perhaps it's bigger. It's about the business of retail in the global economy."

Cameron raised an eyebrow. "A bit grandiose, but not completely off base."

Josh took a short breath. At last he was beginning to understand. "You gave me a name—Ashik Hassan. I assume he's still in Bangladesh. I can find out. But if this is about Presto, I'm guessing there are other names, other stories."

For a brief moment, Cameron's wry smile returned. Slowly, almost reverently, he spoke two more names: "Jashel Sayed Parveen, Rightaway Garments, Kuala Lumpur, Malaysia. Alya Begum, Sun Star Enterprises, Cyber City, Jordan."

"I need to write this down," Josh said, reaching for his notebook.

"No, you don't," Cameron contradicted him. "You're recording."

Shit, Josh thought, even as the iPhone in his pocket converted his silence into binary code. "I'm surprised you don't object."

Cameron shrugged. "You won't use it. Not in public, at least."

"How do you know?"

"Because your sources are the last people in the world who still trust you. And because I have these." Cameron reached into his topcoat and produced a small manila envelope. "I imagine you'll want me to guard them with equal diligence."

Josh took the envelope and opened it. What he found inside stunned him. They were photographs, close-ups, and absolutely damning. He was with Maria in the lobby of the Hotel Caesar Park in Rio de Janeiro. She was wearing the sheer viridian dress that turned her eyes into blue-green lagoons. She was holding his hand, imploring him not to leave. She was leaning into him, and he was letting it happen, his fingers on her arm. And then she was kissing him, and he was kissing her, the good-bye he intended getting away from him, as so much had before.

He closed his eyes. "How . . . ?" he stammered.

"It doesn't matter," Cameron replied. "I know that's where it ended. She left and didn't come back. But that was only three months ago." He reached into his coat again and handed Josh a folded piece of paper. "I also have this."

Josh stared at the page with trembling hands. It was a record of a wire transfer in the amount of ten thousand dollars. The name on the originating account was his. The destination account was Maria's. The date was just before Christmas.

"I don't fault you for it," Cameron said. "In spite of her indiscretions, the work she's doing is commendable. But perception is reality. No one would understand."

Josh took a labored breath. "What do you want me to do?"

Cameron met his eyes. "I want this to matter."

"The *Post*? *60 Minutes*?"

Cameron shook his head. "The media has the attention span of gnats. And the public is overwhelmed. It would get lost in the clutter."

Josh's head began to spin. The meeting, the cold, the pictures—he felt depleted, almost despairing. If not the media, then who? What was he missing?

"When I was a young man," Cameron said, "my father told me about the great civil rights lawyer at the Justice Department, Robert Ames. They met at the March on Washington in 1963. Lewis was there too. He was just a boy. It seems he followed in Robert's footsteps."

For a moment, Josh was confounded. What did Madison's father and grandfather have to do with Presto? He racked his brain for an answer. The memorial. Lincoln's Second Inaugural Address. The names, the factories, the foreign lands. Suddenly it came to him. It wasn't Lewis's past that interested Cameron. It was his present work—the public-interest lawsuits Lewis had brought against Goliaths in the government and the private sector and won against all odds.

"You want me to start a war," Josh said. "In the courtroom."

Cameron said nothing, but in his eyes Josh saw the truth.

"I'm not a lawyer," Josh protested. "I don't know the law."

"You knew it once," Cameron replied. "My father taught you. And you have your wife. From what I've heard, she's a damn smart attorney."

Had, Josh thought. *I had her. How in the world will I convince her—let alone her father—to spearhead a legal campaign against a multibillion-dollar corporation?* But the longer he pondered the idea, the more he warmed to it.

"And you?" Josh asked. "What's your role in all this?"

Cameron smiled again. "Don't misunderstand. I'm not your friend. I'm going to use every lawful means at my disposal to oppose you." He paused. "But you must prevail. We have blood on our hands."

***

When the recording ended, Josh shook his head, as bewildered as he was before. He understood the guilt beneath Cameron's words. He had met Sonia and Jashel. But he was just as certain that their exploitation was not the general counsel's fault. Cameron was a Harvard-trained attorney. Presto was not only his company; it was his client. By disclosing information to a journalist and inciting a lawsuit against Presto, he had shattered more laws than Josh could count. What could possibly have compelled him to do it? And what, exactly, was his ultimate objective? If the lawsuit took Presto down, Cameron would go down with it. Yet his charge hadn't seemed like a suicide pact. He was after something that Josh couldn't see. But what?

Josh put his headphones away and looked out at the night. The stars always looked different from the air, like snowflakes frozen in an obsidian globe. The desert below was an abyss as deep as space, the darkness total in every direction. Josh watched the horizon out the window, waiting for the appearance of light. They were scheduled to land in Amman in twenty minutes. Another flight, another country. But not any country—Jordan.

The Middle East had changed profoundly since his last trip. The Iraq War had come to an end. The Arab Spring had ignited hopes of democracy and then dashed them again, toppling dictators only to open up vacuums of power that had drawn in villains under half a dozen black flags. The peace talks in Israel were in tatters, but the Iranians were negotiating a nuclear deal with the US. Syria was perpetrating its own holocaust, creating a humanitarian crisis beyond comprehension. Oil was gushing from shale wells in North Dakota, undermining the influence of petrostates like Saudi Arabia. Every week, it seemed, the world was treated to another Islamic State beheading. Across the Levant, the brutal stability of Cold War realpolitik had given way to uprisings, bloodshed, and chaos. Only a handful of states remained unscathed, chief among them the Hashemite Kingdom of Jordan.

Since the 1990s, when King Hussein agreed to end hostilities with Israel, Jordan had been a bulwark of peace, modernization, and reason in the region. Its citizens were largely educated, industrious, and tolerant, its women working in the marketplace, holding positions of power, and dressing how they wished— some in hijabs, others in the latest Western fashions. Its religion was Islam, but the faithful tended toward moderation. The barbarians of the Islamic State were literally at the gates, but they had yet to breach the Jordanian firewall. In all these ways, Josh admired the country. But there were exceptions to the rose-colored story. Freedom of press was an illusion and corruption was endemic. It wasn't surprising, therefore, that Cameron had directed him here. Underneath Jordan's polished gleam, all manner of injustices lay festering.

At last, Josh saw the lights of Amman sprinkled like stardust on the horizon. The plane came in low and fast and landed with barely a bump. When they began to taxi, he took out his iPhone and connected to a network. A number of notifications showed up, but he noticed only one of them—a missed call from Madison. Had it been anyone else, he would have ignored it. But a call from his wife meant one thing—something wasn't right with Lily.

"Hey," he said when she answered. "Is everything okay?"

She took a breath, and he heard its weight. "No, everything is not okay. Where are you?"

His heart clutched in his chest. "Amman."

He could almost see her shaking her head. "Bangladesh, Malaysia, Jordan. When will it end?" She paused. "Forget it. Don't answer that. I'm calling because of Lily. She had her clinic visit on Friday. She wanted you to be there."

The blade of guilt buried itself deep. "I wanted that too," Josh said softly.

Madison took another breath, and he heard her unspoken question. *Then why didn't you come home?* But he didn't answer it. He couldn't. Not yet. Instead, she said, "Today was a bad day—the worst in a while. She misbehaved at school. She was mean to another girl. Her teacher called, and I picked her up early. I took her out for pizza. She asked where you were, and I told her I didn't know. She flew into a rage. She threw her cup at me."

Tears collected in Josh's eyes. "It's the Dex. It's not her."

"I *know* that," Madison snapped. "But the medicine didn't put words in her mouth."

He felt the knife twisting in his gut. "What did she say?"

Madison sniffled, and he knew she was crying. "She blamed me for sending you away."

He massaged his face. "Shit," he finally managed. "I'm sorry."

Madison laughed tersely. "And I thought you'd come up with something eloquent."

He accepted the jibe. He had earned it. "Is she there? Can I talk to her?"

"Not now. She's out at the stables with her grandmother."

He closed his eyes, at a loss for words. "Madison, I—"

"I don't need an excuse," she cut in, sounding more grounded again. "I get it. You're on a mission. If I were in a better mood, I might even say I'm happy for you. But you need to remember something. You have a daughter. And she needs a father. She needs you here."

He sighed. How was it possible that a woman could deliver kindness and censure in the same breath? "I know," he said as the plane braked to a halt. "I'll be home soon."

"Soon?" She sounded doubtful.

"I have to find someone," he said, running a hand through his hair. For a moment he wavered in indecision, then he followed the voice in his heart. "This isn't just for me. This is for you, for Lily. I can't tell you why. But I will. I promise."

"Okay," she said, the slightest tremor in her voice. "We'll wait for you."

Her use of "we" struck Josh like a lightning bolt. A wave of warmth surged through him, even as his inner cynic declaimed it as nothing. He ignored the cynic and threw caution to the wind. "I miss you, Madison. Being out here has reminded me of that."

The silence that followed felt like an eternity. He conjured her face, the dramatic contrast of fair skin with eyes and hair the color of mocha and lips as pink as cherry blossoms. He tried to imagine her mouth as she thought about his words. It was her most expressive feature, a prism for her emotions. Was it tense or soft, pursed or tender? Might its corners even be hiding the imperceptible trace of a smile?

At last, she spoke again, her tone gentler than anything he had heard in months. "That's good to know. I'll see you soon, Joshua."

CHAPTER TWO

The road stretched out into the windswept distance, traversing grassy plains and dappled hills with olive groves and medieval towns and ruins from Roman times. The sky above was royal blue and dotted with woolen clouds. They were driving another rental SUV—a Toyota Prado. Rana was behind the wheel, and Josh was in the passenger seat, navigating the route to Habaka with his iPhone. They were alone and flying blind in a land Rana had never visited and Josh knew only in passing. Unlike in Malaysia, they had no fixer, but it wasn't for want of asking.

At Rana's request, the director of Kebaikan in Kuala Lumpur had introduced them to Al-Karama, a labor rights organization in Amman. But when Josh tried to schedule a meeting with the director, Ghada Azizi, she had rebuffed him with perfunctory bluntness, claiming to know nothing about Sun Star Enterprises and offering no help in locating someone who did. Her behavior was so standoffish that Josh wondered if she was concealing something. His suspicions grew after he reached out to his friend Tony Sharif in DC, and Tony had called him back with the name of none other than Ms. Azizi, who, according to the *Post*'s bureau chief in Beirut, was "hands down the finest human rights activist in Jordan."

Rana, too, had drawn a blank with his contacts. Jordan was a relatively recent vintage in global garment production. Its export sector had been modest until 2000 when it implemented a free-trade agreement with the United States, allowing Jordanian companies to gain tariff-free access to the American market. Almost overnight, the sector had exploded into life, fueled by investments from foreigners who brought managers and guest workers along with them. The best Rana had been able to arrange was a meeting with Hamad Basara, the owner of Sun Star. The cover Rana had invented was simple. He and Josh were buyers for a new American label set to launch next year, and they were conducting a search for factory partners for their debut line. With a reference from Rana's father, Hamad had welcomed them with open arms.

After a lunch stop in Irbid, they drove east to Cyber City, an industrial area surrounded by agricultural fields. They entered by the main road, passing dormitories on the right and factories on the left. At the gate to Sun Star, Rana spoke to the guards in Arabic, and they told him where to park. Hamad was waiting for them beside the office entrance, dressed in a suit and tie. His face was on the fleshy side of round and crowned with a thick crop of salt-and-pepper hair. Josh and Rana introduced themselves using identities they had invented on the drive, and Hamad welcomed them with an extended handshake.

Josh let Rana take the lead, guiding the conversation away from their fictitious company and toward Sun Star. It was a natural dynamic. As "buyers," they held all the cards. If Hamad hoped to win their business, he had to convince them not only that Sun Star had the capacity to make their designs at the quality and scale they desired, but that he could offer them an advantage over his competitors, a calculation that almost always came down to price.

After a tour of the offices, Hamad showed them the sewing floor. The contrast between Sun Star's ultramodern facilities and the squalid hothouse at Class 5 in Malaysia could not have been starker. Everything here was clean and white: the walls, the rafters, the vaulted ceiling, the floor, even the stations and the sewing machines. There were piles of unused fabric, cuttings, and half-finished clothing—men's pants, by the look of it—but they were neatly arranged and afforded space for movement. The operators—almost all young South Asian women—were a model of efficiency, their motions sparse, their work precise. Hamad treated Josh and Rana to a demonstration of pants making: the joining of leg seams, the marriage of fly and zipper, the construction of the waistband, the incision of the buttonhole.

"These are Porto Bari," Rana said, holding up a piece of seersucker fabric. "I have always appreciated their lines—the combination of style and affordability."

"Yes, yes," Hamad replied. "Presto is one of my best customers. They have been with me many years. I do everything for them. The buyers come to me and say, 'Hamad, we want such and such,' and I say, 'Send me the pattern, and I will do it.' My workers are the best in Jordan."

During the tour, Rana busied the owner with queries about fabric sourcing and lead times and customs regulations and sample making. He kept his tone businesslike, but dropped just enough hints of interest to convert Hamad into an unwitting ally. By the time Rana moved the conversation from economics to ethics, the owner was so excited about the prospect of landing a new American customer that he would have answered questions about his own children.

"Your workers are not Jordanian," Rana said. "How do you find them?"

"The agents come to me," Hamad replied. "They know what I like." He swept his hand over the floor. "Bangladeshis, Indians, sometimes Sri Lankans. They have to be young and smart and in good health. I hire mostly women. Men make trouble. Women are compliant."

Rana asked him about passports and visas and work permits.

"I don't like dealing with the government," Hamad said. "I leave that to my GM. I handle the buyers, the buying agents, people like you."

Rana inquired about audits and inspections, and Hamad smiled generously. "The brands, the audit companies, the ILO, I make all of them feel at home. I show them pay slips and time sheets, whatever they want. They talk to workers and supervisors. They look around. I don't care. I want everyone to be happy."

As the conversation progressed, Josh found himself increasingly baffled by Cameron's final instruction. *Alya Begum. Sun Star Enterprises.* The first two names on the general counsel's list had revealed transparent veins of exploitation. But Sun Star didn't seem like a haven of abuse. Hamad seemed honest enough. His workers were foreign and furnished by outsourcing agents, which almost guaranteed some form of bonded labor and probably the occasional bribe. But Josh couldn't believe that Cameron had guided them to Jordan merely to reprise their findings in Malaysia. Involving Sun Star in the lawsuit wouldn't enhance its impact unless the factory—and Alya Begum—offered a novel glimpse into Presto's supply chain.

"Please, this way," Hamad said. "Now that you have seen how my workers perform, let me show you the products they make."

He led them down a hallway and through a door into a wide, windowless room with a waist-high wooden table beneath halogen bulbs. Along the walls were metal racks stocked with every kind of woven apparel imaginable. Hamad spread a selection of clothes out on the table, pointing out design features and encouraging them to touch the fabric.

While Rana discussed craftsmanship, Josh looked at labels. Half were from Porto Bari, everything from resort fare to workaday pieces. The rest were a survey of midlist brands. The more garments Josh studied, the more convinced he became that they were missing something.

It was then that he noticed faint scratch marks on the painted surface of the table not far from the edge. He examined them closer. They were clustered in groups of two and three, each mark separated from the next by about a centimeter. Some of the scratches were accompanied by tiny indentations, as thin as an eyelash. Josh glanced at Hamad and saw that the owner was paying no attention to him. He looked back at the table. On a hunch, he put his fingers on the table, nails down, and clenched his hand. He felt the wood give way. He removed his hand and examined the marks he had made. They mirrored the others.

He walked slowly around the table, pretending to examine garments but looking past them at the wood. He saw more scratches in clusters. But the spacing was uneven—sometimes wider, sometimes tighter. He frowned, perplexed. If they were indeed fingernail marks, there should have been some kind of pattern—unless the responsible parties left them unconsciously, in which case they made no sense. What sort of circumstances could have caused people to press down so hard? Josh took a breath and cleared his mind, making space for free association. But no explanation came to him. His frustration deepened.

"Your operation is impressive," he said, rejoining Rana and Hamad. "I have no doubt we would be in good hands. I can also tell that you are a man of exemplary character. It is important for us to know the people we work with, not just the products they make."

Hamad beamed. "Of course, of course. This business is all about relationships."

Josh nodded. "Since we are a small company trying to break into a big market, we intend to focus on the people who work for us. We're going to feature our employees and suppliers in our catalogs. We want to give our business a human face."

By now Hamad was nodding along enthusiastically, no doubt picturing his photograph in an American apparel magazine. "A very good idea."

Josh delivered the punch line without blinking. "We've had a chance to get to know you. But before we leave I'd like to talk to a couple of your workers. Would that be okay?"

Hamad's eyes narrowed a fraction, but his reply was smooth. "I would be happy to make such an arrangement, but today is not good. The Porto Bari order is almost due, and the workers cannot be distracted. How long will you be in Jordan? Perhaps we can do this in a day or two."

Josh traded a glance with Rana. "I think we can rearrange our schedule."

"Excellent," Hamad said, showing them out of the product room. "Now let us go back to the office and discuss terms."

Twenty minutes later, Josh and Rana left the factory and climbed into the Prado. They waited until they passed through the gates before speaking.

"He's hiding something," Rana said. "He didn't want us to talk to the workers until he had a chance to prepare them."

Josh nodded and told him about the marks on the table. "We need to find a way into the dormitories. We need to find Alya Begum."

"I think I know a way," Rana replied and explained himself.

Josh smiled grimly. The risk was substantial, but the reward if they succeeded would more than make up for it. "We go tomorrow night."

CHAPTER THREE

OUTSIDE SUN STAR ENTERPRISES

CYBER CITY, HABAKA, JORDAN

MARCH 19, 2015

8:25 P.M.

The desert was quiet beneath the night. The stars were distant, feeble things, and there was no moon. Against such a backdrop, the artificial brilliance of Cyber City was almost eerie. At half past eight, the streets were devoid of life. There were no pedestrians about, no cars arriving or departing, no trucks making deliveries or taking on freight. Most of the factories had sounded their closing bells an hour ago, sending waves of workers streaming toward the constellation of multistory dormitories on the outskirts of the area. But not Sun Star. Its doors remained closed, its workers still at their machines. So Josh and Rana waited.

They were parked down the road within sight of the office entrance. They had spent the past thirty hours conducting surveillance and learning the workers' schedule. To avoid suspicion, they had moved often, never parking in the same space twice. During the day, there had been enough activity to give them cover. But now, after hours, they were exposed. To Josh's relief, no one seemed to be paying attention. All eyes at Sun Star were focused on fulfilling Presto's most recent order from across the ocean.

At 8:43 p.m. by Josh's watch, the closing bell finally rang. The workers filed out in lines but fanned out as soon as they left the gate, walking down the road toward their dormitories. At the head of the pack were three male supervisors in work shirts. They were the main obstacles to Rana's plan. Under other circumstances, it might have been possible to pay them to look the other way. But without a local fixer to broker a deal, the risk was too great. So Rana had decided on a different play—to hide in plain sight.

"See you in a few," he whispered, opening the front door of the Prado and slipping out into the crowd. He was dressed like a worker in faded jeans and an open-collared shirt two sizes too large for his lanky frame. His shoes were old sneakers acquired at a secondhand store, his hair was unkempt, and he'd trimmed his beard into a moustache to alter his appearance.

Josh watched him go from the backseat. In his hands he held the digital receiver he had purchased in Malaysia. This time Rana was wearing the wire. Before long, the stream of workers flowing down the street turned into a trickle, and Josh focused on the sounds coming through his earbuds—the scratch-scuff pattern of moving feet, muffled words, and Rana's steady breathing. His heart skipped a beat when he heard a supervisor bark out an order, but nothing changed in the pace of feet and breath. *You can do it*, he urged Rana. *Make yourself invisible.*

In time, the footsteps and voices took on a new echo, as if the workers had moved inside. He heard doors opening and Rana speaking in Bengali. A man replied in a friendly tone. Their exchange lasted almost a minute. Josh held his breath. If the workers rejected Rana's entreaty, not only would his plan fall apart, but he would find himself in physical danger.

At last, Josh heard the sound of a door closing, and Rana said in soft English, "I'm in. Sit tight. I'll let you know when to come."

Josh grinned even as his heart began to hammer in his chest. The burden of risk had shifted to him. Unlike Rana, he couldn't blend in with the workers. His skin was a beacon even with a beard. He had to pass for a supervisor, which was why he was wearing a work shirt, jeans, and boots. He sat in the darkness for long minutes, preparing his mind. He watched the Sun Star supervisors return from the dorms and depart in their vehicles. Still, Rana didn't summon him. *Come on*, Josh thought, his nerves as taut as piano strings. *I'm ready to go.*

Finally, just after nine o'clock, Rana spoke to him again. "Last dorm on the left, second floor, third door. I saw no guards. Good luck."

Josh put down the receiver and stepped out into the night. Sun Star was behind him, its security lights illuminating a vacant parking lot. He kept his pace steady, moving as if he belonged there. He searched the buildings for signs of human presence but saw nothing. The absence of guards at the dorms sur-prised him, but the more he thought about it, the more sense it made. The

CHAPTER FOUR

JAYMANIRGOL VILLAGE

KHULNA DIVISION, BANGLADESH

MARCH 25, 2015

4:25 P.M.

How hard was it to find one missing girl in a country of 156 million? It turned out not to be that hard, so long as the girl was born in a village, held a valid passport, and Rana Jalil was the person searching for her. When Josh and Rana left Jordan, they had nothing more to go on than a name—Alya Begum—and an age—no older than eighteen. Within days of their arrival in Dhaka, however, they had much more than that. Friends of Rana's father greased the wheels of the government bureaucracy and delivered the name of Alya's birthplace—Jaymanirgol—and her date of birth—February 15, 1996—which made her nineteen, but just barely. They also confirmed that she had cleared immigration at the Dhaka airport on January 24, 2015.

The village of Jaymanirgol was located on a remote peninsula between two rivers just outside the Sundarban nature preserve. To get there, Josh and Rana had taken an early flight from Dhaka to Jessore, hired a car for the drive through the countryside, taken a ferry across the Mongla River, then hired another car for the trek to the village. In Jaymanirgol, Rana approached a vendor and obtained directions to the home of the village headman. After sharing a meal with him, they learned that Alya's mother, Saima, lived with her four younger children in a house down the road. The headman showed them the way and made introductions, repeating their cover story that they were American journalists researching migrant labor.

So it was that Josh found himself sitting with Rana on a thatched mat in a mud-brick dwelling, sipping tea with Saima Begum while her children peered in from the bedroom. From the lines on the woman's face, she looked to be in her late forties, but Josh guessed she was a decade younger. He had seen the same effect across the developing world. The strain of subsistence living in the tropics without access to running water or proper sanitation accelerated the aging process dramatically. Yet for all the advantages that nature had denied Saima, it had blessed her with beauty. It was fading around the edges now, but Josh could still see it in her high cheekbones and full lips and large eyes.

She sat with them on the mat, her legs tucked under her, her hair covered by a scarf. With Rana translating, she gave them a sketch of her husband—just enough to reveal his dereliction—and told them about the merchant in Mongla whose house she kept. She told them how Alya had assisted her until the agent came and wooed her with tales of lucrative employment in the Middle East. The prospect of sending Alya abroad had terrified Saima, but her children were growing and she had no other support. Her family needed the money, plain and simple.

So Alya went and sent her earnings back. Not right away, but eventually. The money was a godsend. It paid for clothes and school fees and house repairs and transport to Mongla. For the most part, Saima's story was unremarkable, but two things stood out. Her words were laced with piety. She believed firmly that Alya's employment in Jordan was a gift from God. When Rana probed, asking if Alya had experienced trouble in Jordan, Saima gave no indication of knowing about the abuse. Nor did she understand that Alya had returned to Bangladesh. She talked as if her daughter were still sewing clothes at Sun Star.

"When did she last hear from Alya?" Josh asked.

Rana had a brief exchange with Saima. "Three weeks ago. She called to say she'd deposited money in Saima's mobile banking account."

"I assume the money arrived?"

Rana nodded. "The same amount she always sends."

Josh frowned. How in the world was she making that kind of money with a baby? Then it dawned on him. She was nineteen and beautiful. And she was alone.

He opened his mouth to ask another question, but Rana preempted him, saying something in Bengali. Saima stood up and went to a chest of drawers, returning with her phone. After a moment, she showed them a photograph. The resolution was limited, but the resemblance was obvious. Alya was a teenage version of her mother.

Rana turned to Josh. "Saima took this just before Alya went to Dhaka with the agent. It's not great, but it'll do the trick."

Josh looked at him in bewilderment. "What are you talking about?"

"Alya has a cousin who lives in Dhaka. I'll explain in the car."

❋

Two days later, at eleven o'clock in the morning, Rana's driver, Anis, collected them from the Westin in Dhaka and drove them to the border of the Korail slum. Situated on the fringes of some of the most expensive real estate in Bangladesh, the slum was like an island in the city, a shantytown of mud, bamboo, and corrugated iron dwellings, and home to more than forty thousand people—the poorest of the urban poor.

At the end of the last paved road, they left the car and hailed a boy driving a bicycle rickshaw. The boy carried them down a dirt lane, weaving in and out of pedestrians and stalls and rubbish heaps. The density of makeshift development was overwhelming. The buildings, such as they were, had two and sometimes three stories, and were crammed together in a three-dimensional jigsaw puzzle with almost no airspace between them. Most of the paths that intersected the lane were barely wide enough for two people to pass on foot.

Somewhere deep in the maze, the boy stopped and pointed at a green door. Rana knocked and a man stepped out. He was dressed in a white panjabi—a shirt that fell below the knees—and a matching skullcap. He shook their hands, then led them across an open sewer and down a footpath overshadowed by clotheslines. The path led to two more, then the man stopped and gestured at a structure with a bamboo ladder that extended upward into a loft space.

He called out a greeting and waited. Eventually sandaled feet appeared on the ladder. Legs soon followed, then arms and a sari-wrapped torso, and last of all a face. Alya greeted the man with a demure smile that seemed to brighten everything that was grim about the world. The man held out his hand toward Rana and Josh, vouching for them, and Alya turned her smile toward them, inviting them to come up.

As he followed Rana up the ladder, Josh felt a hint of apprehension. He knew how unusual this was—two men entering the home of an unmarried Muslim woman to discuss something exquisitely painful and personal, something she had probably not talked about with anyone else. They had considered bringing along a woman, one of Rana's cousins, but they had decided against it for reasons of privilege. They were lawyers—though Josh had never practiced, he was a member of the Virginia Bar—and Alya was a prospective client.

When Josh poked his head through the opening, he was astonished by what he found. Alya's living area was as cramped as a prison cell. Her mattress occupied 80 percent of the floor. The only other piece of furniture was a wood bureau in the corner. To create storage, the builder had layered the walls with plywood shelving, which Alya had filled with necessities. A tiny baby with a shock of dark hair was lying on the bed, wearing only a diaper. His eyes were open and he was staring at the ceiling, cooing.

Alya climbed onto the bed and held the baby out for them to see. Josh offered her a smile, but his heart was at war with itself. She hadn't chosen motherhood. It had been forced upon her by violence. He tried to imagine what it felt like to wake up each morning bearing such a burden, but his empathy didn't reach that far. She was young and vulnerable in a society where men ruled, women lived at their mercy, and an illegitimate child was a permanent stain on the family honor. Rana had explained it on the drive back from Jaymanirgol. Alya hadn't told her mother about her return to Bangladesh to avoid bringing Saima more grief. It was disgraceful enough that Saima was raising her children without a husband. But for Alya to come home with a child born out of wedlock would have doomed Saima to a purgatory of shame.

So Alya had stayed away and contacted her cousin in Korail, and he had found her this loft and introduced her to a friend who made arrangements for men looking for companionship, businessmen who had wives and families but no compunction about paying for pleasure on the side. And she had gone with this friend, and done what the men asked, and taken their money, and deposited it in Saima's bank account. These last details were speculation, but Rana had confirmed her cousin's connection to the sex trade.

Josh took a seat at the foot of Alya's bed, and Rana did the same. Rana said something in Bengali, and the girl nodded, glancing at a window covered by a hinged screen. Rana pushed the screen out and propped it open, allowing a wedge of daylight to illumine the space.

"Do you speak English?" Josh asked.

"Little," she replied. "Not much." She spoke a few more sentences in Bengali.

Rana interpreted. "She only made it through grade eight before she had to leave school."

"Thank you for having us," Josh said. "Your son is beautiful."

Alya offered him a grateful smile. "Welcome. *Dhonnobad.*"

Josh let Rana take the lead. They had scripted the conversation as far as they could see it, but much of it lay in uncharted territory. He heard Rana say the word *Presto* twice, and Alya began to wag her head, signaling that she was following the narrative. Before broaching more sensitive topics, they had decided to lay the groundwork with their core contention—that companies like Presto had an obligation to ensure that the people making their clothing were treated fairly. For workers like Alya, the inference was axiomatic. They weren't making clothes for the factory. They were making for the brands.

Eventually Alya spoke again, and Rana said, "Most of the items she made at Sun Star were for Presto. For a while, she thought the company owned the factory. Their quality-control people were always there checking on orders."

"Is she on board with our theory?" Josh asked.

"She is," Rana confirmed. "Sun Star paid her wages, but the money came from Presto."

"Good," Josh said, feeling the suspense of what came next. "Go ahead, then."

Rana nodded and took the plunge. When Alya heard Siraj's name, she shivered, as if touched by a frozen hand. Rana spoke quietly for about a minute, then gave her time to process the shock of his revelation. As the seconds passed, Josh watched the birth of her tears. They shined in her eyes and spilled down her cheeks, dripping onto her child's stomach. She didn't move or make a sound for so long that Josh worried that they had lost her. At last, she blinked and took a breath. She met Rana's eyes and began to speak.

"What they did to me was wrong," Rana said, translating in real time. "I didn't think anyone cared. I don't know who you are, but I can see that you care by how far you have come to find me." She paused and shed fresh tears. "Please tell me why. What do you want?"

And there it was, the question on which everything hinged. But the answer was the gift. They hadn't just come with a request. They had come with a proposition. When Rana explained, Alya stared at him in amazement.

"I don't understand," she said, shaking her head. "Why would you do that for me?"

"It's simple," Josh replied. "Because we can."

Still, she had doubts. "How can I trust you?"

Josh gave her a tender smile. "You can come with us and see."

She looked down at her baby. His tiny eyes were shut, his nose flaring as he breathed. It was then that she made her decision. She put the child on the mattress and tied a sling over her shoulder. Then she lifted the baby and slipped him into the sling without waking him.

"*Ami prastuta*," she said. "I am ready."

❋

The house was only fourteen kilometers away, but with traffic the drive took an hour and a half. The grounds were in Farashganj, in old Dhaka. The guards at the gate waved to Rana and admitted them without delay. The stone driveway looped through a garden of shade trees and flowering bushes and ended at the front steps. A butler escorted them into the parlor. The place was a museum of antiques—a brass lamp made from a saxophone, an engraved mahogany trunk, chairs upholstered in brocade, painted porcelain vases and gilt-framed paintings. Alya looked around in wonderment, as did Josh. Only Rana was unimpressed. He had grown up here.

After a brief wait, a regal middle-aged woman entered the room, wearing a sari and an exuberant smile. She hugged Rana and welcomed Josh in English. "I am Nadia Jalil, so nice to finally meet you." Then she greeted Alya in Bengali. The girl seemed overwhelmed by the attention, but Nadia put her at ease, sitting beside her and complimenting her baby.

"My son tells me you had a good job at a garment factory in Jordan," Nadia said kindly as Rana translated for Josh. "Have you found another job here?"

By the way Alya blushed and studied the floor, Josh knew their surmise about her recent "employment" had been accurate. "No," she said, shaking her head. "It is difficult with Fazul. My family is far away."

Nadia nodded gently, one mother to another. "Would you be interested in a position in my household? My housekeeper has been looking for help. Rana says you have experience."

Although they had prepared Alya for this, she still looked astonished.

Nadia smiled. "I will pay you 50 percent more than what you were making in Jordan. Your meals and accommodation will be provided. When you are working, one of my attendants will look after Fazul. But you will always be free to care for him when he needs it."

Alya blinked and bowed her head respectfully. "It would be my honor to serve you."

"It's settled then," Nadia said happily. "I will send a car to collect your things. Now I have a phone call to make. As soon as I'm finished, I will give you a tour."

When Nadia stepped out of the room, Alya looked down at Fazul and stroked his tuft of hair. Josh met Rana's eyes. It was an odd moment, but it was also a delicate one. There was a final matter they had to discuss, but to raise it unbidden didn't seem proper.

After what seemed like an eternity, she spoke again. "I am glad I trusted you. Thank you for what you have done. In Korail, you talked about Presto and the American courts. Presto did not make Siraj do what he did, but they let it happen. For that I hold them responsible. If it would help the other women in Jordan, I will go to America and talk to the judge."

Josh grinned, feeling a victory as personal as it was professional. Alya would make a glorious witness. Presto could hire a battalion of jury consultants and the best lawyers in the world, but she would be untouchable on the stand.

Now all they had to do was get her there.

CHAPTER FIVE

For the first time in as long as he could remember, Josh was early to pick up Lily. He parked in front of the school and took a seat by the entrance beneath the covered walkway. Other parents soon joined him, waiting for classes to let out. The air was brisk yet warming beneath a sky shot through with sunshine. It had been a long winter in Virginia, but the signs of spring were abounding—green buds in the forest, blooms in the pear trees, daffodils joyous in their beds.

He stood up when the doors opened and children streamed out. Seconds passed as the river of red-and-white uniforms parted around him. At last he caught sight of Lily. Her wavy chestnut hair was pulled back in a ponytail that bounced as she walked.

"Daddy!" she shrieked, racing toward him and giving him a hug. "You're home!"

He stroked her hair and felt the weight of that word like a memory stone in his hands. *Home.* He had been so many places that his allegiance was a divided thing. But home was just as real. Instead of a place, it was a face, this face staring up at him, and another one like it but older and wiser and wounded by his failures. In his forty years, he had felt love many times, but never more than in the presence of this girl and her mother.

"I thought you were coming tomorrow," she said, stepping back and taking his hand.

"I wanted it to be a surprise," he replied as he led her toward his car. "Your grandmother is getting the horses ready. I thought you might like to go for a ride."

"Yay!" she exclaimed. "I've been practicing my jumps. Did you bring me a present?"

He chuckled. "It's in the passenger seat."

She dashed to the car and threw open the door, squealing with girlish pleasure. The gift was a stuffed Arabian camel with an outsize head and plush fur. He had seen it in Amman and bought it on the spot, knowing it would fit perfectly in Lily's menagerie of "friends."

"I love it!" she said, squeezing the camel to her chest. "Thank you."

He slid into the seat. "You're welcome. Now buckle up. Betsy and Tommy are waiting."

✲

In the springtime, the drive out to Painted Hill Farm was one of the most scenic in Virginia, the rolling hills carpeted with new grass and budding trees, the fences and barns sparkling in the sun, and the winding road stretching into the distance. Josh cracked the windows and let in ribbons of wind. He drove in a leisurely manner, enjoying the bucolic landscape, until Lily put her window all the way down and said, "Faster, Daddy!"

He laughed and hit the gas, accelerating until her hair began to dance. After ten glorious minutes, he slowed down and turned into a pebbled drive with a boxwood gate and a wrought iron sign that read PAINTED HILL, 1878, the year Madison's great-great-great-grandfather—a lawyer, land speculator, and Virginia assemblyman—had bought it on the courthouse steps and converted it from a bankrupt plantation into the elegant estate it was today.

The drive meandered up the hill between rows of maples, then wrapped around past the barn and springhouse (repurposed into a chicken coop) and the servants' kitchen (now a guest quarters) before ending at a turnaround outside the manor house. Josh saw only one car in front of the steps, an Audi driven by Madison's mother, Caroline. That meant that Lewis was still at the office, as Josh had hoped. Ever since his affair had become public, he had been persona non grata in the Ames household. His banishment, handed down by Lewis in a painful exchange, extended to everything but the barn and the horses, and that solely for Lily's benefit.

Josh parked in the shade of a massive oak tree, its bottom limbs as thick as poplar trunks, and trailed Lily into the shadows of the barn.

"Grandma!" she cried, her voice echoing through the stalls. "Daddy's home!"

Josh heard Caroline before he saw her. "I know," she said, her cultivated southern drawl as smooth as silk and brightened by a lilt that sounded unfeigned. "Isn't it exciting?"

Madison's mother emerged from the tack room and met him in the soft dirt of the center aisle, a silhouette against the rectangle of light at the far end of the barn. A nervous tremor coursed through him. Their last meeting had been barely cordial.

"Joshua," she said hesitantly. "It's good to see you again."

Caroline was tall and long-limbed like her daughter, with a countenance that had aged gracefully, her skin opalescent and gently blushed in the cheeks, her eyes round and dark.

"That's kind of you to say," Josh replied, standing awkwardly.

She stopped three feet away and smiled, though her eyes were flecked with pain. "Lily wants you to wear the outfit she got you. I put it in the riding lounge."

He nodded. "I've been looking forward to it."

She was silent for a moment. "You know, we all make mistakes. But life goes on." She winced, revealing her discomfort. "What I'm trying to say is that I haven't given up on you and Madison. I just thought you should know."

Her words, while not quite an absolution, went further to heal the rift between them than Josh could have imagined. "Thank you," he said quietly, moved but not sure how to express it. Then something came to him. "It's good to be home."

Caroline touched his shoulder. "Go get ready. I'll saddle up the horses."

❀

The path curved away through the understory of the forest, the ridgeline hidden behind a veil of trees. Caroline was in the lead on Lexi, a gray Lipizzaner and Madison's favorite mare. Lily was behind her on Betsy, a palomino pony with a white mane and golden coat. And Josh was bringing up the rear on Tommy. The quarter horse had welcomed him warily, pawing the ground and huffing when he climbed on. As a result, Josh was treating him with deference, holding the reins loosely and letting the horse set the pace.

As birds chirped in the branches above him, Josh adjusted himself in the saddle, trying to ameliorate the pinch of his new riding breeches. He wasn't used to the feel of fabric so close to the skin. He looked toward the crest of Painted Hill and tried to appreciate the scene without seeing every rock on the trail as a cudgel that could crack his skull if Tommy decided to throw him. It was ridiculous how fragile he felt on the back of a thousand-pound animal. In the saddle his goal was simple—to make it back in one piece.

In time, the path opened up on a highland meadow strewn with boulders and patches of early wildflowers. Caroline rode Lexi toward a cluster of rocks that piled up and jutted out just enough to offer a view of the piedmont over the tree line. Madison had christened the rocks "Old Man's Nose" when she was a child, and the name had stuck. Caroline dismounted and helped Lily and Josh down, then tied the horses' leads together and gave them carrots to munch on.

"Why don't you go on up?" she suggested, giving Josh and Lily some space. "I want to see how the blackberry bushes fared over the winter."

When she was gone, Josh took his daughter's hand and climbed carefully to the pinnacle of Old Man's Nose. They found a seat and looked out over the forest to the countryside beyond. The green hills and vales of Keswick reminded Josh of the way he had imagined Tolkien's Shire as a boy. It was a kind of American Eden, a watercolor landscape so easily rhapsodized that it gave definition to the dream of the New World.

He draped his arm over Lily's shoulder and drew her close. "I'm sorry I missed your last clinic visit," he said softly. "I wanted to be there."

"It's okay," she replied, and he knew from her tone that she had forgiven him. "You can take me this month." She looked up at him then. "Unless you're going away again."

He shook his head reassuringly. "Not for a while."

"What were you doing in all those places?" she asked with the gravitas of a grown-up.

He thought about how to describe it and then realized that pictures would be better than words. "Here," he said and took out his iPhone, showing her photos of Ishana in her home in Dhaka; of Ashik and Sonia by their huts in Kalma; of the Bangladeshi workers in their dormitories in Malaysia and Jordan; of Rana dressed in clerical robes as Imam Mehtar's acolyte; of Ajmal and Jashel at the hotel in Kuala Lumpur; of Saima Begum and her children in Jaymanirgol; and, finally, of Alya and Fazul in Nadia Jalil's parlor in Dhaka.

"Some of them we talked to," he said. "Others we helped. We got Jashel out of a bad situation. And we found Alya a new job."

Lily gave him a featherlight smile and nestled her head on his shoulder. "I talked to Mommy. I told her I want you to live with us again. She said she'd think about it. Last night I saw her looking at pictures of you. You need to ask her. I think she'll say yes."

If only it were that simple, Josh thought. Yet Madison's foray into their photo albums was auspicious. It meant that she was open to remembering what the world looked like before the bridges were burned and the war broke out and the specter of Maria stood between them.

"I know how hard this has been for you," he said. "I want to live with you again too. But you need to know something. What happened isn't your mother's fault. It's my fault. When you're older, you'll understand. I need you to be patient."

"Just promise me you'll talk to her," Lily insisted. "Please, Daddy."

He looked toward the far-off hills. "I'll talk to her," he finally said, even as he wondered where he would find the courage.

Madison's car was in the driveway when they returned to the barn. Josh couldn't decide whether to be relieved that he had survived another equine adventure or terrified that he had to face his wife. As he rode toward the hitching post, he imagined her sitting in the riding lounge in her favorite armchair, her mind a jumble of racing thoughts, a thousand questions unasked and feelings unexpressed, trying to piece together a vision of what her future might look like and whether she wanted him to be a part of it.

He barely noticed when Caroline took the reins from him, barely registered the sound of Lily's voice when she shouted, "Mommy!" and ran into the barn. All he could see were faces—his face, Madison's face, Maria's face. And all he could hear were the words that brought him here. Maria in Rio when he told her the affair was a lie: *You can say it isn't real, but you are wrong. I love you. You can go to the other side of the world, but that will never change.* Madison in their farmhouse down the road, the *O Globo* story dangling from her hand: *I hate you. I hate you! Go away. I don't want you here. Leave me alone.*

He didn't realize she was standing in front of him until she said his name. "Joshua." He stopped and stared at her, saw in the span of an instant that she wasn't mad at him, or troubled by his presence, or nursing hidden pain. She looked like the girl he saw for the first time in Langdell Reading Room at Harvard Law

School, standing in a group of 1Ls but alone with her thoughts, reading the inscription from Cicero on the crown molding: LEX EST SUMMA RATIO INSITA IN NATURA. "Law is the highest reason implanted in nature." How much life stood between then and now. How much he cherished. How much he regretted.

"I think your mother gave Tommy some Valium," Josh said, deflecting the moment with humor. "He was unusually sedate."

"Or maybe he's just starting to like you," she replied with a lopsided grin.

"After all this time?" he asked sardonically. "I find that hard to believe."

Sunlight twinkled in her eyes. "Horses are like people. They can change their minds."

He studied her carefully, toying with a cautious optimism. She was dressed in one of the outfits she kept in the lounge—skinny jeans, Frye boots, and a knit shirt that complemented her pale complexion and trim figure. Her thumbs were hooked in the back pockets of her jeans, her weight balanced on one of her boots. He spoke the idea before he could talk himself out of it.

"Take a walk with me."

This time her smile spread to both corners of her mouth. "I was thinking the same thing."

They strolled across the grass and down a hill to a pond surrounded by willow trees. A few Canadian geese were floating on the water, taking a rest from the journey to their summer breeding grounds. Beside the pond sat a bench. They sat down and watched the wind stir the water. After a while, Josh began to speak. He started at the beginning and told her where he'd been and what he'd seen and what he'd done. And then he told her why. She listened until he fell silent, his proposition hanging like a trial balloon between them. In time, she touched his hand.

"You want to work with me," she said, as much a statement as a question, as if she had never considered it before. "You traveled all that way to build a case."

He nodded, watching the geese waddle up onto the far bank. "I did the research before I left. The claims are a stretch, but this could be historic."

"You'll have to convince my father of the merits," she said, opening the door, but not all the way. "He's more of a skeptic than I am."

"I'll talk to him if he'll talk to me," he replied, trying not to appear too eager.

"I'll tell him about the people you helped," she said. "That will go a long way."

He felt her fingers spreading out across his hand, felt the surge of warmth in his stomach, and decided to take the final leap. "This is about more than the case," he said, speaking the truth plainly. "I want this to work."

She turned and looked into his eyes. "I'm not sure I'm ready yet."

"Will you think about it, at least?" he asked, brushing a strand of hair over her ear.

The smile she gave him then was as tender as a kiss. "You've been talking to someone."

He rubbed his thumb across her fingers. "She wants what I want."

"I'll think about it," she promised and gently took back her hand.

CHAPTER SIX

The house stood at the top of the hill like a lantern on the mast of a sailing ship. Around it all was dark, the woods and mountains and fields effaced by the cloak of night. But inside the house lamplight beckoned. The windows of Josh's car were halfway down, the brisk wind of spring running fingers through his hair as he drove up the pebbled drive, preparing himself for the interrogation that was sure to come. He hadn't shared a drink with Lewis Ames since his marriage fell apart. That his father-in-law had summoned him meant two things: that Madison had turned on the charm and that the old barrister was intrigued by his proposition, despite his oft-spoken disdain for "men of lackluster will and rebarbative character" who broke their vows.

The Ames family was a paradox. They came from old money, as old as the Old Dominion itself, yet none of it, as far as Josh could tell, had come from slaveholding. In Lewis's line, there were politicians and judges and speculators and merchant entrepreneurs, men whose portraits adorned courthouses and capitols and whose names had christened philanthropic projects across time—the Millard Ames Library in Richmond, the John Jacob Ames Performing Arts Center in Washington, the Shelby Ames Museum of Virginia History in Charlottesville. His ancestors had dined with Thomas Jefferson and James Madison, anchored the Southern Unionist block in the US Senate before the Civil War, and voted against secession at the convention in Richmond in 1861. In its three centuries of prominence and public service, the family's greatest transgression was also its most glaring—the reluctant decision of George Lewis Ames, a two-term US senator, to support Virginia in the Confederacy despite deep personal reservations. The memory of that decision had motivated Lewis's father, Robert Ames, to lead the charge at the Justice Department in enforcing the Civil Rights Act, and to name his son after a man he considered a traitor to humanity. Lewis's name was both a curse and a call—a reminder of the sins of the past and a profession of faith in the redemptive possibilities of the future.

Josh left his keys in the car and walked up the steps, past planters where marigolds and zinnias would soon bloom, across the flagstone portico, and through double doors hewn from oak as heavy as iron. Madison was waiting for him in the foyer, dressed casually in jeans, flats, and a cardigan sweater unbuttoned just enough to reveal an enticing hint of what lay beneath it. She smiled at him delicately, the light of the chandelier above her glistening on her lips and in the diamonds on her ears and around her neck, gifts he had given her on her fortieth birthday. He hadn't seen her wear them since the separation.

"He's waiting for you in the drawing room," she said.

Josh nodded. "Any advice?"

Her gentle laugh sounded like wind chimes. "Would it help?"

He followed her down the oak planks of the hallway, past the living room, dining room, and kitchen, and through a molded archway into the one room in the house that Caroline's penchant for modern style had hardly touched. The drawing room still looked like it belonged in the nineteenth century. The furniture was all dark wood and brass, much of it original. There were heavy curtains on the windows, lamps with painted shades, a couch and Queen Anne chairs in red velvet, and an enormous Oriental rug that spanned the length and breadth of the floor. Lewis stood before the hearth, moving logs with a poker. He was as dapper as he was imposing, his tall frame clad in a blue Harris tweed suit that brought out the glow in his white-whiskered chin and silver hair. He turned toward them and fixed his gaze on Josh. His iceberg-blue eyes were what people most remembered—and what Josh most feared. They seemed to look through a person. Before them, Josh had never been able to hide.

"Will you join me in a glass of gin?" he began, moving toward the wet bar. "Or would you prefer something else? A Heineken, perhaps?"

His first sentence a challenge, Josh thought. "Gin is fine," he replied.

Lewis took his bottle of Burrough's Reserve off the shelf, plunked cubes of ice into two old-fashioned glasses, and poured the golden liquid generously. He handed one of the glasses to Josh and poured a glass of wine for Madison. Then he took a seat on one of the Queen Anne chairs, and Josh and Madison sat on opposite ends of the couch. Josh took a sip of the gin and found it more tolerable than he remembered.

"I read your memo," Lewis said with a trace of irony. "I found it surprisingly well crafted. I had to remind myself that in another life you attended my alma mater."

Josh kept his expression blank, not allowing the blow to land. That he had graduated near the top of his class at Harvard Law and then taken a job as a Metro reporter for the *Post* was as much a scandal to Lewis as his decision to drag Madison around the globe chasing stories and prizes. In Lewis's mind, the media was a kangaroo court, and journalists were its self-appointed jesters. Time, however, had tempered his scorn, as had Josh's zeal for the poor. By the time he wrote *The End of Childhood*, Josh had managed to gain his father-in-law's grudging respect. Then the news of the affair broke and all of Josh's gains were suddenly erased.

"Your analysis of forced labor and the trafficking act was spot-on," Lewis said. "We've been looking for a corporation to sue for years, but we haven't found the right target. We've never given serious thought to an international case because it's hard to find plaintiffs and evidence overseas. But it appears you've done that for us. As much as I hate to admit it, I admire that. You've built a solid foundation in a remarkably short period of time."

Josh hazarded a question. "What did you think about the Bangladeshi law claims?"

They were the weakest links in his case—the wrongful death and worker injury claims on behalf of Sonia, Nasima, and Joya Hassan—but they were crucial to the broader narrative of Presto's sourcing practices and as a matter of simple justice. Before passing his memo along to Madison, he had shored up his own research with an opinion from a law firm in Dhaka. The Bangladeshi lawyers were of the same mind—it was a long shot, but not impossible.

Lewis took a swig of gin. "To be frank, I think they're losers—"

"But, Dad," Madison interjected, dismay written on her face. "You said . . ."

Lewis held up his hand, and her voice trailed off. "Having said that, I *like* them. They're bold and creative, and the law of employer liability is as much of an anachronism as this drawing room. I can't think of a good reason to leave it alone beyond precedent, which, as you know, gave us Dred Scott and Jim Crow and segregated schools and a host of other morally repugnant policies that happened to enjoy the imprimatur of history."

Lewis's ringing validation came within a hairsbreadth of making Josh smile. But he knew his father-in-law too well not to anticipate the blowback. Lewis was a devotee of Damocles, a man who lived in the perilous shadow of his own power. He took no action without assessing all the risks. And he gave no compliment without qualification.

"I have no problem with your claims," Lewis went on. "I also have no problem with your plaintiffs. What concerns me is how you found them so quickly. Madison tells me you have a source, someone inside Presto. Anonymity doesn't cut it with me. I need a name."

As prepared as Josh was for this confrontation, he still had to fold his hands to keep them from trembling. "I can't tell you. But if I did, you wouldn't doubt his reliability."

Lewis's eyes flickered in the firelight. "You must think I'm a fool. Did you *really* come here thinking that I would bet my reputation and the organization I've built on a lawsuit against one of the most admired companies in the history of American business without knowing the identity of your source and understanding the game he's playing?"

Josh took a slow breath and let it out. He glanced at Madison and saw the tension written in lines on her face. *If only you knew what he has on me*, Josh thought.

Lewis stood up suddenly, his agitation apparent. He set down his glass on a table and held out his arms like he did when he was in court. Immediately, Josh saw what was coming—a lesson in the art of oratory and a dressing down worthy of a drill sergeant.

"Let me spell this out for you. Let's say we file this lawsuit in federal court. Presto will go out and hire a marquee law firm to defend against it. The firm will charge Presto a retainer of a hundred and fifty thousand dollars up front, because, of course, they're going to put fifteen lawyers on it and bill for every fraction of a second they're thinking about the case, even if they're on the toilet, or in the middle of sleep and dreaming. At Presto's behest, the first thing the firm is going to do is put together a sanctions motion. They're going to make us look like neophytes and opportunists and maybe even communist sympathizers, and they're going to ask the judge to dismiss the lawsuit and make us pay Presto's legal fees, plus some unspecified additional amount to deter other plaintiffs from wasting the court's time in the future. And then

CHAPTER SEVEN

The plane lurched in the sky, banking one way, then the other. The turbulence rattled tray tables and unsettled carts in the forward galley and sloshed water in the bottles on the console between Josh and Madison. They were in the first row of the plane, the window to their right. Madison's eyes were glued to the pane, watching for the lights of Dhaka to appear in the clouds. Her long fingers were curled into balls, her lithe frame tense as a coiled spring.

Josh smiled sympathetically and reached for her hand.

"I bet I've flown a quarter of a million miles," she said, glancing at him. "But you'd think this was my first flight."

At last, the clouds broke and the city appeared in flecks of light. The plane leveled out and descended toward the runway, landing without a hitch and taxiing to the terminal.

At the gate, Madison retrieved her hand and gave Josh a grateful smile. "It's been a long time since I went anywhere like this. It's good to do it again."

"I'm glad you decided to come," Josh replied.

They collected their rollaboards from the overhead bin and left the aircraft. Because they were at the front of the crowd, the queue at immigration was brief. Josh led the way out of the terminal to the sidewalk. Taxi drivers swarmed them, offering to drive them into the city, but Josh carved a path to the battered Corolla at the curb.

"Mr. Josh!" Anis called out. "Welcome back to Dhaka!" He approached them swiftly and took their luggage, securing it in the trunk. "No more bags?"

"Short trip," Josh replied, opening the door for his wife and sliding in beside her.

"Is he a friend of Rana's?" Madison whispered.

Josh nodded. "Along with everyone else in this town."

In the past month, Josh had brokered the connection between Lewis's team at CJA and Rana's team at LA Legal. They had flown to Los Angeles for a meet-and-greet, and then Rana had brought his boss, Peter Chavez, to Virginia to hash out a framework for collaboration. LA Legal would take the lead on client relations and evidence gathering overseas, and CJA would spearhead the litigation and arrange for law firm support during the discovery process. Madison had reached out to her old firm, Keller Scott, and pitched the case to them, knowing they were always on the lookout for pro bono opportunities, but Keller had declined, citing a conflict of interest. So Madison had aimed her sights lower and trolled her contacts at regional firms. In time, she found Remington & Key, a forty-lawyer outfit in Richmond that specialized in product liability cases. They were masters of complex civil litigation and fearless in the face of corporate opponents. They were also media hounds who relished the spotlight. To them, Madison's offer was like an all-expense-paid trip to legal Disneyland.

"Westin again?" Anis asked, driving toward the circle outside the airport.

"Yes," Josh confirmed.

He gazed out the window at the clamorous night, stained amber by the city lights. He was surprised when he felt Madison take his hand. He looked at her in the shadows and saw the smile gracing the corners of her mouth. He heard it again like an echo inside him, the quiet voice of hope. Their singularity of purpose in building the lawsuit reminded him of the early days in their relationship when she had left behind the comforts of her familiar world and followed him around the globe because she believed in his dream of writing stories about the poor.

"Do you think Lily's all right?" she asked.

"She's fine," Josh said. "She knows her medicine better than anyone. And your mother is meticulous. We'll be back before her next clinic visit."

It was the first time since Lily's diagnosis that Madison had been away from home for more than a few hours. Josh had tried everything to convince her to come—reason, charm, the allure of world travel, the significance of meeting the plaintiffs in their own country—but in the end it was Lily who liberated her mother to take a risk again. *I want you to go with Daddy,* Lily had said. *It's silly to worry about me.* For Josh, looking at Madison now, her face framed by the blur of Dhaka traffic, was like looking at her years ago, before the leukemia and the ghost of Maria had driven her inward into a cloister of anxiety and control.

Twenty minutes later, Anis pulled up to the hotel and unloaded their luggage. Josh tipped him and confirmed his availability in the morning. Then he and Madison walked to the front desk. The clerk checked them into two rooms on the sixteenth floor. Madison yawned as they waited for the elevator, and Josh caught the contagion. They had forced themselves to stay awake on the flight from Dubai. It was morning in Virginia, but their bodies were ready for rest.

When they reached their floor, Josh walked Madison to her door and bid her good night. She smiled at him tiredly and went into her room. He found his own just down the hall and began to unpack. As he put his clothes in the closet, his thoughts wandered into an arcade of memory—places they had traveled together, hotels they had stayed at, beds on which they had frolicked, turning love into the most exuberant of verbs. He pictured her in her room washing her face and getting undressed, turning out the lights and slipping under the covers. He imagined her closing her eyes, relaxing, letting go.

He was so distracted that he almost didn't hear the knock at the door. He blinked once and listened. The knock came again. A cascade of thoughts crashed through his mind. He went to the door and pulled it open. Madison was still in her travel clothes, her long hair flowing down around her neck. Her lips parted, and her eyes formed a question that had only one answer.

He reached out for her and grazed her cheek with his fingertips. Then he took a step and drew her into his arms. Their lips met and their bodies came together by instinct, moving back into the room, past the bathroom, and onto the bed. Their clothes came off and their hands found each other without thinking, guided by the grace of much practice, elevating need and desire into an apotheosis of delight. There were moments in the midst of his pleasure when Josh realized how lucky he was, when the gift of Madison's beauty and devotion broke through his rapture and filled his heart with gratitude. But the rest was all haze and joy and feeling and bliss, until the wave crested and the fragments washed into memories.

When it was over, Madison turned to him and ran a fingernail through the hairs on his chest. "I have only one request," she said softly. "Please don't hurt me again."

He wrapped his arm around her and kissed her forehead, loving her more now than he ever had before. "I won't," he whispered. "I promise."

n't.

g-

The ne.—
The day
ers. Rana w
his suggest.
at ease.

Rana
for you in .
statements a
fact that you'

"Have y.
trailed him

Rana n.
long and ha.
of them sai.
would."

Josh gri.
that togeti.

"Ho.

Rana
brain. TI
damag.
sight
pay f.

J
work s.

"I c.
One mo.
licenses I
fire. A lot

Madis

"See
Banglad.

Ra.

them to Old Dhaka, to the home of Nadia Jalil.
nd the gardens inside the gate festooned with flow-
em in the foyer, wearing jeans and a polo shirt. At
dison had also dressed casually to put the plaintiffs

hug and Madison a kiss on the cheek. "We're ready
set up the video camera in the parlor. We'll get their
fixed his eyes on Madison. "I'm glad you came. The
ill help."

the contracts with them?" she asked as she and Josh
ble entry hall to a pair of imposing mahogany doors.
le sure they understood that lawsuits in America are
many plaintiffs never receive a monetary verdict. All
do it for no money. But they wanted to know why we

ison, thinking about the night before. "We can answer
e nodded and turned away, a slight blush on her cheeks.
h asked.

oice. "She has a lesion that's putting pressure on her
onsulted are recommending surgery. A lot of the nerve
nent, but there's a chance she could recover some of her
therapy. Her father's willing to do it, but he wants to help

it the huts in Kalma where Ashik lived. "Tell him we'll
out we're not going to take food off his table."

l. "We'll dignify him, and my parents will cover the rest.
dad worked some magic and got copies of all the interbond
mani Apparel and Millennium for two years before the
e Presto orders."

d softly. "You're making this look easy."

ld you?" Josh said, proud of his friend. "The sultan of

That would be my father. Are you ready?"

lded, he swung open one of the giant doors. The living room

was more commodious than the parlor and lined with windows. There were tapestries on the walls and earth-toned rugs on the floor—teak, Josh guessed. The furniture, all collectibles and antiques, was arranged to encourage conversation. Josh saw Jashel sitting in a chair that looked like a throne. Across from him on a sofa were Ashik and Sonia. The girl's eyes were closed, and she was resting her head on a pillow. Alya was standing by one of the windows, watching a gardener tend to a flower bed. They turned as one and stared at Josh and Madison.

"*Suprabhata,*" Josh said, greeting them with the Bengali words he'd been practicing for a week. "Good morning. It's good to see you again. This is my wife, Madison." He knew as he was speaking that he had butchered the pronunciations. But it didn't matter. Their faces, initially uncertain, softened and began to glow.

Madison shook their hands and sat in an armchair beside Jashel. Josh and Alya found seats opposite them, and Rana took a place beside Ashik on the sofa. For a moment, Madison waited, making eye contact with each of them. Then she took out her phone and showed the plaintiffs photos of Lily and her parents and the Virginia countryside. By the time she finished, they were smiling easily, comfortable in her presence.

When she took a seat again, she caught Josh's eye and nodded. He took a breath and began to speak. "I know all of you are wondering why we're doing this. Why did Rana and I travel to Bangladesh and Malaysia and Jordan to find you? What's in it for us? We're interested in the chance, however unlikely it may seem, to change the way the world works. Right now back in America it's nighttime. All 2,543 Presto stores are closed. When they open in the morning, people are going to show up and buy all sorts of things not knowing where they came from or who made them. They're not going to think about that because they—and all of us—have been conditioned not to think about it. That's part of the great deception in the global economy. Things just appear on our shelves, pretty things, desirable things, things we need and want. They're right there in front of us, made and assembled, all shiny and new. We give a company like Presto our dollars, and we walk away with them, never considering that they might be the fruit of abuse and exploitation."

Josh paused and allowed Rana to catch up. "Workers like you are invisible to people in the United States, and Presto and its competitors are happy to keep it that way. They don't want their customers to see you because their customers aren't all that different from you. They're just people, fathers and mothers, aunts and uncles, grandfathers and grandmothers. They would never allow their kids to work in places like Millennium, Rightaway, or Sun Star. The reason they buy the clothes made in those factories is because they don't see the truth. Your pain and toil and tears have been erased from the picture. All that's left is the transaction, which makes Presto money, and keeps the engine of the economy humming, and gives politicians their power, and allows Presto's CEO to take home twelve million dollars a year. I could go on and on. Now imagine what would happen if the deception were exposed. Imagine what would happen if Presto actually had to account to the world for its sourcing practices."

Josh traded a look with Madison and handed off the baton. He watched as she leaned forward in her chair and straightened her back like a lawyer preparing to speak. *She's in her element,* he thought as her eyes began to glitter. *This is what she was made for.*

"I'm newer to all of this than Josh is," she said, looking at Alya first, then Jashel, Ashik, and Sonia, "but for the last month, I've been thinking about almost nothing else. I remember where I was when I saw the photograph of Sonia on the TV. I was helping Lily with her schoolwork." Madison's eyes moistened. "I remember looking at that picture, and looking at Lily, and hoping that *finally* the corporations who profit off the mistreatment of workers like you would be forced to admit the truth. But it didn't happen. The media milked the fire for ratings and moved on. Presto flooded the airwaves with propaganda. I remember watching the news a few weeks later and hearing that Presto's sales on Black Friday had been 20 percent higher than the year before. Then the story disappeared. No one talked about it. No one cared."

Madison took a breath and gave Rana time to translate. "Unfortunately, this is often the way the world works. This kind of truth is ugly and painful and inconvenient. It doesn't help people pay their bills, or care for their kids, or get a better job, or go on a nice vacation. But the truth is essential. Because our blindness allows Presto to treat people like you horribly, people who are *also* just trying to feed their families and improve their lives. Across history, the powerful have enriched themselves by exploiting the poor. The only power greater than theirs is the law. That's why I went to law school. That's why Josh and Rana went to law school. That's why we're here. In a courtroom with a good judge and great lawyers and solid evidence, you will no longer be invisible. The truth will be safe, and Presto won't be able to hide."

God, I love her, Josh thought. *It's never that simple, but her passion is beautiful.*

By the time Rana finished interpreting, Alya's eyes were shining and Jashel and Ashik were nodding along. There was an extended period of silence as they processed what they had heard. Then Alya adjusted her headscarf and began to speak. Tears ran down her cheeks, but she didn't wipe them away. Rana listened to her words carefully and translated them verbatim.

"When I was at Sun Star, I prayed every night for Siraj to leave me alone. Then one day a man came to visit the factory. I don't know who he was, but the next day Siraj was gone. I was so grateful. I thought that was enough. But then Fazul born and my contract ran out, and I came back to Dhaka and realized I had no one to take care of me. Those days were very hard. Then you found me and brought me here and gave me a job I love. I will come to America and speak to the judge. But whatever happens, I want to say thank you. May God bless you."

Josh met Madison's eyes and knew that she, too, was thinking about Cameron. None of it could have happened without him. "You're very welcome," he said for all of them. "We're going to do everything in our power to see that justice is served."

PART SEVEN

Joshua & Cameron

November 2015–April 2016

CHAPTER ONE

The lounge was like a film set in a dystopian future, a rustic-glamorous fusion of old brick and neon light, shiny metal and unpolished stone. Josh was sitting in one of the alcoves, a martini glass in hand, earbuds in his ears, the digital recorder clipped to the inside pocket of his blazer, tracking the sounds picked up by the tiny microphone under Madison's shimmering red dress. She was at the bar not far away nursing a Long Island iced tea, her dark hair swirling around bare shoulders, her legs silhouetted by flamingo-pink light. The effect of the three-hour makeover—done by a makeup artist who once worked for *Vogue*—was transformative. Instead of forty, she looked twenty-five, a siren among the singles aiming for a drink or a dance or a score. The hook was baited, the lure just right. Their target wouldn't be able to resist.

They had planned this moment for more than two months, hiring a private detective to track his movements, to plot the points when he was in a public space without his bodyguard at his side. It had been a jigsaw puzzle. He lived in a penthouse on the Potomac, had a chauffeur who drove him from there to his office—garage to garage—had a housekeeper who went shopping for him, never took a predictable walk, and never seemed to dine in the same restaurant twice. But he had one routine that verged on habit: his Saturday trip to the L2 Lounge in Georgetown, and afterward, if he was lucky, to the Hay-Adams hotel with a girl half his age.

233

Josh watched the bodies moving in the dim light and kept an eye on his wife. She had been at the bar less than a minute, but already she had had to rebuff a thirtysomething finance-type who tossed her a clichéd compliment and slipped an arm around her waist. Josh wasn't a fan of the setup, but it wasn't his idea. It was Madison's brainchild. He had objected, but she had overruled him: *It's my body. Try to stop me.* In the end he conceded because she was right and because he understood her anger. Ever since their trip to Bangladesh, she had thrown herself into the lawsuit with a zeal that bordered on obsession. She needed to do this for herself almost as much as she needed to do it for Sonia, Jashel, and Alya. She needed to make this personal.

Josh's iPhone vibrated with a text from the detective. "Target en route and alone."

They didn't have long to wait. Josh spotted Vance Lawson at the same time that the chief executive saw Madison. He was wearing a blue suit and a white shirt unbuttoned at the collar, his salt-and-pepper hair cut short like an athlete's, a trace of stubble on his chin. He stepped up to the bar and ordered a martini, then glanced around like he was waiting on a friend. The first time he caught Madison's eye, it happened almost in passing. The second time he did it more intentionally—as did she. He left his seat and glided over to her, a casual smile on his face.

"I'm Vance," he began as Josh listened in from twenty feet away. "I'd offer to buy you a drink, but that would be redundant. You already have one."

Her eyes twinkled. "I think that's the least original pickup line I've ever heard."

Vance's grin widened. "I can do worse. I was tempted to say you're a vision."

"Yes." She laughed, playing with an earring and leaving him hanging.

"Yes, what?" he persisted, meeting her eyes.

She softened her gaze, inviting him in. "You can buy me a drink."

Vance summoned the bartender. "Vodka martini for the lady, shaken with a twist." He turned back to her. "So what do you like to talk about, Miss . . . ?"

"Sophia," she replied. "And the answer is everything. How about you?"

If before he was merely attracted, now he was intrigued. "Where is home, Sophia?"

"I've lived many places," she said. "But Paris is where I feel most alive."

"The city where every scene is a story. Like waking up in a novel."

Her surprise was unaffected. "Is that yours? Or did you read it in a book somewhere?"

He smiled wryly. "My pickup lines may be uninspired, but the rest of me is not."

"A double entendre hidden in a double negative. How's that for panache?"

Damn, she's good, Josh thought as their chatter turned to badinage and she matched him wit for wit. They covered politics and business, philosophy and art history, dabbling and dueling, agreeing and disagreeing. Josh was astonished by Vance's erudition. He knew opera and ballet, Kant and Sartre, horses and Tokyo hotels. After one martini multiplied into three, his hand found Madison's arm, and he suggested they move somewhere more comfortable. Josh watched as they passed him, angling toward one of the alcoves. He saw Vance's bodyguard out of the corner of his eye, repositioning himself but staying discreet. *Almost time.*

He listened through his earbuds as Vance ordered another pair of drinks. He knew his cue, but she had yet to speak it. She had taken her performance beyond setting the hook. Now she was burying it with relish. Minutes passed, and their conversation deepened to relationships. He told her about his ex-wife, Jackie, and his daughter, Annalee—the origins of his Francophilia. She gave him a fictional account of her own "misbegotten marriage," the cheating husband, the painful separation and divorce, and the move to DC. She spoke with such verisimilitude that Josh knew some of it was authentic. *I hear you,* he thought with no small dose of guilt.

It had been eight months since his call with Maria, and he still hadn't figured out what to do about her girls. When he wired her more money, he knew he would hear from her again. She made his gift last until June, then sent another request. He had gnashed his teeth for a week before sending twice as much and telling her it was all he had—which wasn't quite true, but would be soon enough if nothing changed. To Lily's delight, he had ditched his apartment and moved back home. But he had no income beyond dwindling book royalties and no job prospects that interested him. Maria's third e-mail, which arrived three weeks ago, had prompted yet another tranche and yet more soul-searching. He knew he had to cut the cord. But Maria's girls were orphans. If he abandoned them, he didn't know how he could forgive himself.

Madison's words brought him back to the present. The cue was improvised, but it was his summons all the same. "Will you excuse me for a minute? I need to use the ladies' room."

Josh stood up quickly and collected her coat and messenger bag from the seat next to him. He meandered through the crowd and met her in the shadows outside the restrooms.

"How'd I do?" she whispered.

He smirked. "If I were a talent agent, I'd take you to Hollywood."

The smile she gave him was brief. "Are you ready?"

"I've been ready for a week."

She pursed her lips, psyching herself up. "Let's get this over with."

They strolled back to the alcove together, hand in hand. Josh watched Vance's eyes when he caught sight of them, saw the glaze of lust deaden into shock. He opened his mouth as if to ask a question, but Madison preempted him, channeling her nervousness into indignation.

"My name is not Sophia. It's Madison. This is my husband, Joshua." She took the perfect-bound, 104-page complaint from Josh and dropped it in Vance's lap. "This is a lawsuit for fifty million dollars on behalf of garment workers in three countries who suffered terribly making clothes for your company. Consider yourself served."

With that, she turned away and they fled the lounge, ignoring the stares of the patrons who looked at them as if they had stolen something. They headed east down Cady's Alley, then up 33rd Street, dodging late-night revelers and laughing like teenagers who had just pulled off the world's biggest practical joke.

"That was incredible!" Madison exclaimed, her breath forming clouds of vapor in the chilly November air. "He's never going to forget it."

"I think that may go down as the brassiest opening in the history of civil litigation," Josh exulted. "Remind me never to get on your bad side."

She stopped abruptly and turned toward him, taking his hands. "You did this," she said brightly. "You made it possible." She leaned in and kissed him, then whispered in his ear, "Now we go to war."

CHAPTER TWO

"What the hell is this?" Vance said, thrusting the lawsuit into Cameron's hands as soon as he entered the corner office. It was early on a Sunday, and the building was deserted. Cameron had woken from a rum-tinged sleep to find Vance's summons on his phone—sent in the middle of the night. He knew what it meant. He had been anticipating it for weeks. He looked at the complaint, heart thudding in his chest, as Vance paced the floor like a caged beast.

"Someone gave them information," the chief executive was saying. "They *had* to. The workers, the factories, it doesn't make sense—"

"Slow down," Cameron interjected, taking a seat on the couch. "Whatever this is, we're going to handle it like we always do, professionally and deliberately."

But Vance didn't seem to hear him. "We're three weeks from Black Friday. It's like some kind of demented déjà vu. And they've got a reporter on their side—Joshua Griswold. The guy won two Pulitzers. The media is going to eat us for lunch."

Cameron scanned the complaint with a practiced eye, the tranquility on his face masking the turmoil he felt inside. Joshua's research had been even more painstaking than he expected. The allegations were excruciatingly detailed, the language at once precise and flamboyant. There were more quotable lines than Cameron could count. Yet somehow, in all of its invective, it didn't overreach. Everything in it was true—and damning.

237

"I know who the mole is," Vance was saying, his eyes flashing.

Cameron took a steady breath. "Who?"

"Declan Mays."

Cameron chose his words with care. "Vance, think about it. By the time I gave my report to the board, a lot of people knew about it. Even if you're right about a leak, it could have been any of them. It could have been Paula or Anderson. It could have been me."

Vance shook his head contemptuously. "It was Declan. He's a zealot. I had that thought when I first met him. He has no appreciation for nuance. And he was privy to your investigation from the beginning. Come on, Cam. I bet he was livid about the board's decision."

"Declan is an officer of the company," Cameron objected. "What you're talking about isn't just a breach of fiduciary duty. It's a crime."

Vance rubbed his face with his hands. In their thirty years of friendship, Cameron had never seen him so unglued. "I want you to find proof. I want him out."

Cameron kept his tone measured. "The last thing the company needs right now is a witch hunt. We'd never keep it quiet. It would destroy morale."

"*Damn it!*" Vance exploded. "I don't care if we don't have proof. *Somebody* has to take the fall for this. If you can't do it, I'll fire him myself."

Cameron allowed the threat to hang in the air, giving Vance an opportunity to climb down from the ledge. The scene was unfolding as he had expected. Vance was the accusatory type and Declan the obvious target. No one—not even Rebecca Sinclair—would question Cameron's own fidelity. After his ill-fated meeting with the board, he had followed their orders, shoring up compliance, overseeing the selection of new auditors in every country, speaking at Presto's sourcing conference, and drafting a letter, with Rebecca's input, to the office directors overseas about the consequences of violating the Red List. After that, he had returned to his duties—or so he had made it appear—distinguishing himself as a valued adviser, voice of reason, and defender of Presto's honor. No one had a clue about how he had spent his free time, how meticulously he plotted his course, how cautiously he planned every move before he made it. He had long since crossed into uncharted waters, but he felt no fear, only sorrow and guilt.

"I understand how angry you are," he said. "But we can't act precipitously. The world is going to judge us by what we do from this moment forward."

Vance pounded his fist in frustration. "How is it that I can be the CEO of a sixty-five-billion-dollar company and there isn't a damn thing I can do?"

Cameron ignored the outburst. "How did you get this? Lawsuits usually come to me."

Vance grimaced. "They served me at the L2 Lounge. The lead attorney—Madison what's her face—was at the bar dressed like a vamp. She acted like she was into me." He shook his head again, as enraged at himself as anyone else. "I can't believe I didn't see through it."

The Griswolds have a taste for theater, Cameron mused. Then he guided Vance into productive action. "I'll get Kristin to put the critical incident team together. I'll also call Rusty Blackwell at Slade & Barrett and engage his litigation team. You assemble the board for an emergency meeting. We have to prepare for a full-scale media blitz."

Vance started nodding, his executive instincts finally overcoming his reptilian brain. "I want everyone in on this. We're going to salvage the fourth quarter, whatever it takes. And we're going to hit back. I want these people to feel the pain they're causing."

"That's the Vance Lawson I know," Cameron said.

He closed the complaint and studied the cover page. They had filed the case in the Western District of Virginia, which meant that Rusty—the nastiest courtroom brawler he knew and a card-carrying member of the Mensa genius club—would have to conjure a literal rabbit out of a hat to contest venue. Cameron read the caption with a mixture of anticipation and dread.

Ashik Hassan, as Parent and Guardian of Sonia Hassan, a Minor Child, and as Administrator of the Estates of Nasima Hassan and Joya Hassan; and Jashel Sayed Parveen; and Alya Begum, All Residents of the People's Republic of Bangladesh v. Presto Omnishops Corporation, a Virginia Stock Corporation.

Cameron smiled grimly. *Game on.*

CHAPTER THREE

The sky was overcast, the wind blowing briskly off the Potomac, but so far the forecasted rain hadn't made an appearance. The same couldn't be said of the media crews. Every outlet with a role in shaping national headlines had someone in the audience. Griswold & Associates—the PR firm founded by Josh's father after he left the Carter White House—had erected a stage on the sidewalk outside the entrance to Presto's headquarters. Twenty microphones now adorned the podium, bent in all directions like a bouquet of black roses.

The gathering was at least a hundred strong. There were television vans parked on curbs, satellite dishes beaming signals into the heavens, guardrails and police officers keeping people separate from traffic, and gawkers all around—across the street, at nearby intersections, and inside the tower itself. Josh could see the shadows of Presto employees as they moved in front of the windows. He knew Cameron was watching. *How's this for a show?*

The press conference had been conjured by a brilliant group of media strategists—Frank Griswold, Tony Sharif, and John Remington, managing partner of Remington & Key. Their pitch, delivered to every contact in their combined address book, had been shockingly effective. The girl in the photograph had a story to tell, and her family was suing Presto in federal court.

At precisely ten o'clock, Lewis Ames stepped to the podium. Clad in a chalk-stripe suit and cobalt tie, he looked like a diplomat or a royal. Behind him stood Madison and Josh, Rana and the plaintiffs, and a phalanx of staff from CJA, LA Legal, and Remington & Key. Ashik and Jashel were wearing suits Madison had bought them for the occasion, and Alya was dressed in a crimson sari. Only Sonia was not present. The flight from Bangladesh had exhausted her, and she was resting at the hotel with a Bengali-American occupational therapist Rana had hired.

As flashbulbs lit the air, Lewis introduced the plaintiffs. His voice, amplified by speakers, carried easily above the wind. Afterward, he took a poster-size enlargement of the photograph from the fire and placed it on a tripod. A number of the reporters winced.

"All of you remember this picture," Lewis said gravely. "It captivated us for a time, and then we let it slip away. We stopped asking questions and demanding answers. The protests that happened on this sidewalk melted into memory. We turned to other things, and we forgot. But Sonia didn't forget. That's her name, Sonia Hassan. Her father, Ashik, didn't forget. Her mother, Joya, and sister, Nasima, didn't have a chance to forget. They died in the fire."

Lewis placed another poster on the tripod—a photo of Sonia in Nadia Jalil's parlor.

"Sonia was thirteen when she started working at Millennium. She was fourteen when she climbed out of a burning window and fell to the earth, sustaining injuries that have yet to heal. She's sixteen today. She's legally blind, deaf in one ear, and has trouble staying awake. If this disaster had taken place in America, there would have been a massive lawsuit, and Millennium and Presto and all the other brands that made clothes inside the factory would have been forced to pay. The law wouldn't have restored Sonia's health, or the lives of her mother and sister, but it would have forced Presto to admit the truth—that the merchandise they offer us under the banner of 'People First' is manufactured under conditions that put their workers last, conditions that endanger, exploit, and enslave."

As Lewis paused for effect, Josh felt the first misty raindrops begin to fall.

"If *only* the Millennium fire had happened in this country," Lewis went on. "But it didn't. Sonia was injured in Bangladesh. And Jashel was forced to labor in Malaysia, and Alya was raped in Jordan, all while Presto employees were *aware* that abuses were taking place in their supply chain, and all while Presto executives and shareholders profited from them. Yet neither Sonia nor Jashel and Alya—nor thousands of others like them—have received a cent for their injuries. If it weren't for my son-in-law, Joshua Griswold, and Rana Jalil of LA Legal, their stories never would have been told. But we're going to tell them. We're taking Presto to court to prove that justice knows no borders, that Bangladeshi lives matter as much as American lives, and that at least *some* of our laws follow multinational companies into the darkest reaches of their supply chains, making ignorance no longer a defense."

Lewis held up a copy of the lawsuit. "We're not going to argue our case today. But our allegations are in the public record. We called this press conference to make sure you didn't miss them, and to invite you to join us in demanding justice—for the plaintiffs, and for millions of exploited workers around the globe." He surveyed the crowd. "I'll take a couple of questions."

As cameras flashed, two dozen hands shot into the air, among them Meredith Blakely from CNN, Tim Robinson from Bloomberg, James Foster from the BBC, Latasha Owens from the *New York Times*, and Tony Sharif from the *Post*. Lewis called on Tony first. The question was staged, the answer a carefully crafted soundbite they wanted viewers to hear.

"With the holidays coming, there are people who are going to wonder whether they should shop somewhere other than Presto," Tony said. "While the lawsuit is company-specific, I'm guessing the abuses you're talking about are not. Can you offer consumers any reassurance that the clothes they're going to buy for their loved ones weren't made in a sweatshop, or a death trap, or by the victims of forced labor or sexual assault?"

"I wish I could say yes," Lewis replied. "But I can't. There are good companies out there selling ethically made products. But other companies are not. The real question is how do you and I, as consumers, tell the difference? I have no idea. But it's time we start asking."

"Mr. Ames! Mr. Ames!" The voices reached a crescendo before Lewis motioned to Meredith Blakely.

"When stories like this have surfaced in the past," she said, "companies like Presto have always said the same thing: 'We didn't know what was happening. We don't control our suppliers.' Are you telling us they're lying, that they *do* know what's happening?"

Lewis's eyes flashed. "Let's not talk generically. Let's talk about the company behind me." He held up a sheet of paper. "This is the statement Presto issued a week after the fire. In it they said, and I quote, 'As a company founded upon the principle of putting people first, Presto works tirelessly to ensure that its suppliers around the world operate in accordance with all local laws and international norms. Presto rates its suppliers by color, and those that fail to meet the company's exacting standards are placed on its Red List for one year. During this probationary period, all orders are suspended. At the time of the fire, Millennium Fashions had been on Presto's Red List for six months. It was not authorized to make clothing for any of Presto's brands. If Presto clothing was being made there, it was in violation of the company's Code of Conduct and without its consent.' That last part about consent was a lie. Whatever the Red List said, Presto was one of Millennium's biggest buyers, and had been for some time."

As hands went up again, Lewis pointed to Tim Robinson. "Last question."

"Mr. Ames," said the Bloomberg correspondent, "your allegations carry the whiff of scandal. Are you worried about a countersuit for defamation?"

Lewis laughed softly. "The beauty of defamation law is that the truth always wins. We're giving you the truth. Don't let it get away from you again."

CHAPTER FOUR

Cameron entered Vance's office nineteen minutes before the chief executive would go before the cameras and speak to the world. He found his friend sitting in his desk chair, his eyes fixed on something across the river. Cameron walked to his side and looked out at the Mall. It was a glorious November day, the kind of day that made him nostalgic for autumns past, when he had taken Olivia south to Kiawah Island, and they had unplugged and relaxed on the beach and eaten seafood and played golf on the Ocean Course—him badly, her better—and made love to the percussion of the surf filtering in through open windows. He felt the misery inside of him, the sense of sadness and loss, but it wasn't just about Olivia.

Despite all of his meticulous planning, he had underestimated the whirlwind the lawsuit would unleash. No, that wasn't quite correct. He had underestimated the brazenness of Lewis Ames. He had known that Lewis would go to the media, but he had expected a written press release, as Lewis had done before. He had anticipated that the major outlets would pick it up and drop some quotes into their nightly newsreels, along with clips from the fire. He had expected the columnists from progressive papers to run op-eds accusing corporate America of a cover-up. He had expected Presto's stock price to take a hit. He had even expected the Justice Department to send him a letter expressing concern about Presto's compliance with federal law.

But then Lewis had arranged a press conference on Presto's doorstep and invited everyone on earth with a megaphone, and all of them had come and listened and tweeted, and gone back to their offices and written columns and filed stories that made it seem like a bomb had gone off in Arlington and Presto was behind it. In two days of trading, Presto's share price had plummeted by 35 percent. The board had gone berserk. Investors were calling for Vance's head. Customers were jamming the phones, asking if their kids were wearing slave-made clothing. Lester Grant and Jim Dunavan were agitating for a purge of the compliance department and a lawsuit against Atlas Consulting on the instinct that *someone* had leaked the findings of the investigation. Facebook and Twitter were awash with calls for a nationwide boycott. Protesters had descended on Arlington like a plague, fulminating through bullhorns about "child killers" and "slave masters" and "corporate rapists." And the Justice Department hadn't just sent a letter. They had called Cameron directly, threatening to open a criminal investigation.

"I was just thinking about Abraham Lincoln," Vance said, his voice subdued, matching the stillness of the office. "The country was coming apart at the seams. An entire generation was dying on the battlefield. This is a cakewalk by comparison. But I'm not sure I can manage it."

It was one of the humblest things Vance had ever said. But the irony only added to Cameron's melancholy. This "cakewalk" had started beneath Lincoln's solemn stare.

"I'm going to give you some advice," Cameron said. "Kristin would flip if she heard it, but you know the stakes. If we don't neutralize this, the company could go down. Ditch the script. Speak from the heart. Don't give a disclaimer. It'll only make things worse. You need to give Presto a human face. People need to see that we're not monsters. We're just like them."

Vance took an audible breath, then let it out. "I'll do it."

His phone beeped, and Eve came on the line. "They're ready for you downstairs."

The chief executive went to the couch and donned his suit coat. "It's showtime," he said to Cameron and led the way to the elevator.

The C-suite was eerily quiet for a Thursday morning, but everyone was in the conference room, watching the proceedings on CNN. The elevator whisked them to the lobby, then the doors opened and they were caught in the shutter of a hundred cameras.

Vance strode to the podium, which stood atop a flight of steps. Cameron took his place behind him with Eve and Kristin and the board. He watched as Vance surveyed the assembly, smiling hospitably as if the media had come for a celebration, not a scavenging expedition.

"I had a speech," he said without preamble, "but I'm not going to give it. I'm just going to talk for a few minutes about this company and what it means to me, what it means to every one of the three hundred and fifty thousand people we employ—people like you, people like the folks watching at home. We're a family company, not family-owned anymore, but family-born. Hank and Dee Dee Carter had a vision for giving people quality goods at an unbeatable price. Their timing was right, and America embraced that vision, and the rest"—he swept his hand toward the vaulted ceiling—"is a bright spot in the history of business. In the past few days, a lot of terrible things have been said about Presto. A lot of accusations are swirling around. I know you want answers, and we intend to give them. But there's a lawsuit pending, and my attorneys tell me I can't get into all that, not here at least."

Vance took out his wallet and retrieved a photograph, displaying it for the cameras. "But this much I *can* tell you. I have a daughter about the age of Sonia Hassan. Her name is Annalee, and she's the light of my life. I would do anything to protect her from the pain that Sonia feels right now. As a father, I feel deep empathy for Ashik Hassan. I don't blame him for his anger. If I were in his shoes, I'd feel the same way. On behalf of Presto, on behalf of everyone who cares about this company, I want to say to Ashik and Sonia and Jashel and Alya that I'm sorry. I'm sorry for everything you have suffered. But I didn't cause it. Presto didn't cause it. We will respond to the allegations in court, and we will defeat this attempt to defame and destroy a great American success story. Thank you all for coming."

When Vance left the podium, the lobby erupted in a riot of noise. Reporters shouted questions, bystanders hurled epithets, but Vance paid them no heed. Instead, he walked back to the elevator with Cameron, Eve, Kristin, and the board. After the doors closed and the uproar receded, Lester Grant put a papery hand on Vance's shoulder.

"That was the most courageous speech I've ever heard from a CEO."

Vance sighed, his relief palpable. "It was Cameron's idea."

The old banker gave Cameron a look of unvarnished respect. "Well, my friend, you may have just saved the company."

Cameron met Lester's eyes, guilt and satisfaction at war within him. *No*, he thought. *I haven't saved it yet.*

CHAPTER FIVE

OUTSIDE PRESTO SUPERSTORE

TYSONS CORNER, VIRGINIA

NOVEMBER 26, 2015

7:46 P.M.

In the America of modern consumerism, Tysons Corner Center was one of its capitals. Its anchors were two colossal malls with four hundred stores and restaurants, fifteen thousand parking spaces, and a dozen hotels that offered shoppers shuttle service to the bonanza. But it didn't end there. The whole area was a cash register. If a shopper took a break from her quest and listened, she could almost hear the sound of money being spent, the chatter of card readers turning credit into commerce, the cries of children begging parents for one more toy, the squeals of those who were rewarded, the pouts of those who weren't, and the millions of thoughts running through the minds of people on the edge of decision.

On any ordinary Saturday, the shopping scene was harried but orderly. On Thanksgiving weekend, however, the place turned into an anthropological spectacle, part human zoo and part city on speed. For anywhere from twenty-four to forty hours, depending on the start times set by the retailers, the paved-over paradise became paradisiacal again—for bargain hunters, at least. Judging by the bedlam outside Presto's flagship superstore, that included half of Virginia.

Josh was there in the throng along with Tony Sharif and two female reporters from the *Post*, interviewing shoppers anticipating the eight o'clock opening. The coverage had been Josh's idea. He had pitched it to Tony, who had cleared it with his editor on the condition that Josh's name would be nowhere in the byline.

Madison had resisted at first, because it meant Josh would miss Thanksgiving dinner at the farm. But Lewis had overruled her. The story was too tempting to pass up. It had been only two weeks since the dueling press conferences, and the lawsuit had been all over the media. No American with a television or Internet connection could have missed it. Yet here they were in a crowd of nearly a thousand, clamoring for the chance to exchange their hard-earned dollars for products on Presto's shelves.

Josh had expected resistance to his questions, but he had encountered none. Excitement, it seemed, loosened tongues as effectively as alcohol. He had sought out a diverse sample of interviewees, chatting with them about their buying habits, their opinions of Presto, and their concerns, if any, about the working conditions of the people who made the things they were about to buy. Their comments had been freewheeling, often engaging, and always enlightening.

From Donald—white, midfifties, CPA, father of two: "I saw the story. It's shameful what happened to those people. But I didn't come here for the clothes. I came here for the 60-inch 4k TV. It's the deal of the century. I'm not sure how all the hullabaloo relates to me."

From Jamila—black, midtwenties, hairstylist, toddler at home: "Yeah, I saw the boycott thing on Facebook. I thought about it, but, you know, boycotts don't do anything. Presto couldn't care less what I think. I'm just trying to make a living and raise a kid with no help from my ex. My son wants that new tablet. You've seen it, right, the DreamTab? It's half off. Crazy!"

From Louisa—Latina-Asian, schoolteacher, mother of three: "What happened to those people is very disturbing, but so is everything else going on in the world. ISIS. Syria. Russia. North Korea. If I made more money, I could shop somewhere else, but would that really change anything? My kids know Christmas is coming. What am I supposed to do?"

From Victor—Hispanic, forty-two, delivery man for a shipping company, accompanied by his two children, both teenagers: "I heard it on the radio. Hope the girl wins. Big companies are always squeezing the little guy. I bet my company is doing the same. You won't quote me on that, will you?"

From Rashad—black, nineteen, community college student: "I think the allegations are probably true. But we've got bigger problems in this country. You should do a story on Black Lives Matter. If people talked as much about racism as they do about all these other things, we might actually make some progress."

From Rohit—Indian American, late forties, small-business owner: "I bet the lawyers made the whole thing up. Lawyers are bloodsuckers. Businesses like Presto are the American dream. They create jobs. They give people what they want."

From Aylan—twenty-four, law student, Lebanese ancestry, within earshot of Rohit: "I don't know what that guy's problem is. Lawyers are the good guys. Corporations only care about the bottom line. I'm not here for myself. I'm here for my girlfriend. She's dying to get this green handbag that looks like Prada. I hope it doesn't sell out."

The most insightful commentary, however, came from a pair of women who at first glance could not have been more different from one another. Alisa was a suburban housewife from Falls Church with a husband in middle management at a tech company, two kids in private school, an Internet business, and a master's degree in child psychology. Donna was a college dropout and recently divorced, whose ex-husband, a long-distance truck driver, was always late on his alimony payments. She worked two jobs to feed four kids and could barely afford to lease a townhouse in Front Royal. When Josh approached them, they were strangers, united only by the crush of the crowd. But his questions bridged the gap and got them talking.

"My daddy worked in meatpacking," Donna said. "He was always getting injured on the job, always going to the ER. Then he had a heart attack. Now he's living on disability. His company did nothing for him, even after twenty years. But companies are like that. They do what they do to make a profit, and the rest of us don't think about it. I'm that way. Bet you are too. That jacket you're wearing—nice leather. You know where it came from? How about those loafers? Heard bad things about shoe factories. See what I mean? We're all in on it."

"She's right," Alisa affirmed. "I've actually done research on this. This isn't just about Presto. A lot of companies have gotten into trouble making products overseas. And not just clothes either. It's everything. But consumers are clueless—all of us are. How do we tell what's good from what's bad? When I go to the grocery, I look at the labels. I buy organic and stay away from GMOs. When I buy a dress or a toy for my kids, it's not the same. It makes me angry that people are being exploited making some of the things I buy. It makes me angry that companies are selling those things to me without telling me. But, honestly, what am I supposed to do about it? Stop buying things? Even 'Made in the USA' isn't always clean."

Just then, lights flashed and sirens wailed inside the store. The doors slid open and the crowd surged ahead, sweeping Alisa and Donna and Josh along with the current. When they reached the bank of blue Presto shopping carts,

Alisa tossed them a "Happy Thanksgiving" and disappeared down an aisle. Donna, however, stopped short, causing a collision between two other shoppers. She stepped out of the melee and found a place by the wall, watching the action with a quizzical frown. Josh joined her, notepad at the ready.

"You know what?" she said. "I've changed my mind. I don't think I'm going to shop here tonight. I'm going to do a little research myself. Maybe she's right and there isn't anything we can do. But I don't like the feeling of buying things blind."

"Mind if I quote you on that?" Josh asked.

"Go ahead," Donna said as shoppers whizzed by. "It'll make my daddy proud."

CHAPTER SIX

The road to Charlottesville was winding and scenic, a divided highway through rolling farmland fringed by the Blue Ridge Mountains. It was a route Cameron knew all too well. It was the road on which Olivia had fallen asleep in the dark hours of an April morning, never imagining that the tarmac illumined by the headlights was the last thing her eyes would see.

The irony was so rich it was almost ridiculous. For as long as *Hassan v. Presto* remained on the docket, Cameron would have to make the trip south for every hearing, would have to pass not once, but twice, the infuriatingly flat, arrow-straight stretch of pavement where exhaustion had drawn his eyelids shut, where the wheels of his SUV had veered off the road, and where his sleep-addled instinct had caused him to overcorrect, sending the vehicle into three barrel rolls that scattered glass over a hundred feet and stole the most wonderful woman he had ever known.

That Lewis Ames had filed the lawsuit in Virginia was another thing Cameron hadn't anticipated. He was intimately familiar with the contours of domestic law—what law there was—governing the overseas treatment of workers by US corporations. He had predicted that Lewis would file in California. The courts there were among the most liberal in the nation and had presided over the biggest triumvirate of lawsuits in the history of apparel manufacturing,

Does I v. The Gap, Inc., which had yielded a twenty-million-dollar settlement in favor of exploited workers from Saipan. Virginia, by contrast, was a pro-business state. To Cameron, Lewis's choice had seemed like a gift—until Rusty Blackwell called him with the news.

"I heard from the judge," the lawyer had said, his voice low and raspy, the product of a pack-a-day lifestyle that only the patch had helped him kick. "We didn't get the guy who normally sits in Charlottesville. We got Ambrose Chandler, chief judge of the district. He and Lewis have a history together. Their families go way back."

Shit, Cameron thought. "Is there any way to get him recused?"

Rusty grunted. "We're going to give it a shot. If nothing else, we can rein him in, keep him careful. He wants to see us in chambers tomorrow. No public, no press. I think you should be there. If you'd like, we can drive down together."

Cameron had accepted Rusty's invitation but declined the ride. He didn't want Rusty to see what happened when the memories came back.

The site was just minutes away now, half a mile south of the town of Opal. He had considered taking a roundabout route, but he knew he couldn't avoid it forever. Better to get it over with. He gripped the wheel tighter, shame and self-hatred entwined around his heart. He wrestled with them in silence as the autumn countryside flew by, trees bending in the wind, leaves swirling beneath his tires. Then he saw it—the guardrail and telephone poles and steep grassy median. He looked away and felt the pain afresh. It was the first time he had been back since the accident, the first time since the ambulances had carried them away in a terror of lights and sirens, Olivia on a gurney, Cameron behind her with only lacerations and bruised ribs.

He let off the gas and pulled to the shoulder, his eyes burning, his face wet. He rested his forehead against the wheel and forced himself to breathe. *Why didn't you just stop? Why did you have to keep pushing?* They were questions he had pondered a thousand times, but as always he came up empty. There were no reasons, just the brute fact of what had happened.

"I'm so sorry, Livie," he said through clenched teeth. "I'm so sorry."

Minutes passed and cars drove by, but Cameron remained still, his mind besieged by memories. A patrolman on the radio with dispatch: *Single vehicle. Cadillac SUV. The driver's okay, but the passenger's in bad shape. I can't find a pulse.* The ER doctor, female, thin lips and sad eyes: *She didn't make it. I'm so sorry.* Olivia's mother at the funeral, hands shaking, voice crumbling: *It was an accident. We don't blame you.* And, finally, his own mother a year later: *You have*

a choice to make, Cameron. You can die with her every day. Or you can make the
rest of your life mean something. What would she want you to do?

He had known the truth, of course, but not what to do with it. He was at
the summit of his career, but what did it matter? Where was the meaning in anything? In time he had submerged his perplexity in productivity, driving himself
to the limits of his power to protect the people he had left—Vance, the board,
Presto. He had vowed to himself that he would never fall asleep again. Then
Millennium went up in flames and Presto washed its hands. That was when the
answers came. Presto didn't just need protection. It needed a new conscience.

Cameron opened his eyes and brought his emotions under control. He
looked into the distance and saw the sign to Charlottesville. Ambrose Chandler
wasn't the judge he wanted, but the law was the law. He and Rusty would find
a way to make it work.

Help me, Livie, he said in his heart. *Give me the strength to turn this ship*
around.

✾

Fifty minutes later, Cameron parked in the garage on Water Street and walked
up the pedestrian mall to the courthouse at the top of the hill. In the pantheon
of federal buildings, it was an obscure demiurge, a rectangular block of red brick
with no grand entrance or marble halls, just a metal detector and an elevator that
led to a spiderweb of corridors and the chambers of the district judge. Rusty was
waiting for him in the sitting area with two associates.

Cameron greeted them and gave Rusty a laconic smile. "I miss the days
when you smelled like an ashtray. It always inspired confidence."

Rusty's laugh turned into a cough. "The world has gotten too damn
civilized."

He showed Cameron to a windowless conference room with a table and
chairs.

"Is Lewis in with the judge?" Cameron asked when they were seated.

Rusty nodded. "He was swapping stories with Chandler's secretary when we
showed up. They're quite chummy, but it won't matter." He patted his briefcase.
"We've got enough to put the judge on his heels."

Cameron leaned forward in his chair, his eyes ablaze with intensity. "I don't
have to tell you how much this means. The past three weeks have been the most
volatile in Presto's history. Black Friday didn't reassure the market. We've got

activist funds taking aim at the board. We need to kill this case on the pleadings. If we go to trial, all hell is going to break loose."

"You've got my A-team," Rusty assured him. "We're going to find a way to stop it."

Cameron heard a knock at the door and opened it, and a uniformed bailiff said, "The judge is ready for you. Plaintiffs' counsel is already situated."

They stood together and followed the bailiff down the hall to chambers. The Honorable Ambrose Pickens Chandler was waiting for them in front of an antique bookcase. He invited them in with handshakes and a welcoming grin that looked more politician than judge. His features reinforced the impression. He had a round, fleshy face with bushy white eyebrows, a balding pate, and sky-blue eyes that sparkled when he smiled.

Lewis was standing beside the judge's desk, chatting with Madison. Cameron had met him only once, at an award dinner fifteen years ago. Lewis was older now, his hair silver, his cheeks a ruddy pink, like a man too fond of his liquor. But his gaze was stiletto tipped.

"Cameron," Lewis said, pumping his hand and giving him a look that seemed almost appreciative. "I'm so sorry about your mother. How is Ben holding up?"

"He's hanging in there," Cameron lied, feeling unnerved. He hadn't spoken to his father since his mother's funeral. But it wasn't the thought of Ben that bothered him. It was Lewis's too-familiar demeanor. *He knows,* Cameron intuited, keeping his expression friendly despite his irritation. He wasn't completely surprised. He had put the odds at fifty-fifty that Lewis would demand the truth before signing on to the lawsuit. Still, the added exposure was unsettling. Josh was a manageable risk; the photos and wire transfer slip guaranteed his silence. But Cameron had nothing to keep Lewis and Madison quiet beyond the regard they had for Ben.

"A pleasure, Mr. Alexander," Madison said. "Your father was my favorite professor."

"Glad to hear it," Cameron replied, forcing a smile.

"Sit down, sit down," said the judge, motioning for a young woman in a pantsuit to join them. "This is Ashley, one of my clerks. There should be enough chairs."

The bailiff had arranged the seating in an arc around the judge's desk. When everyone was situated, Judge Chandler held out his hands toward the windows behind him.

"This courthouse is an Orwellian disgrace," he said wryly, "but at least they gave us a view." In an instant, his grin disappeared. "This is a monumental case. It has implications not just for Presto but for thousands of American companies that source their products overseas. I called you here because I'm not happy with the way it began." To Cameron's surprise, the judge looked at Lewis sternly. "That was quite a stunt you pulled with the media. I don't want to see it again. Either you try this case in court or in the press. You can't have it both ways."

"Understood, Your Honor," Lewis replied.

Just as quickly, the judge turned his displeasure toward Rusty. "As for your motion for sanctions, I'm overruling it now. It offends me when big-firm lawyers throw Rule 11 around like a bludgeon, intimidating plaintiffs with the threat of legal fees. The complaint is creative but not beyond the pale. We'll resolve this case on the merits. Is that clear?"

Rusty cleared his throat, undaunted by the judge's glare. "Your Honor, if I may, our sanctions motion raises questions of fact that can't be resolved without a proper hearing. A perfunctory dismissal would be a violation of due process."

Judge Chandler peered at him without blinking. "What exactly are you referring to?"

Rusty spoke the accusation candidly. "We have reason to believe that the plaintiffs' counsel drafted the complaint for the media, not the court; that their intention in pulling that 'stunt' on my client's doorstep, to use Your Honor's phrase, was to incite the media to harass Presto and damage its image at a critical moment in the business cycle; and that the plaintiffs' 'creative' legal claims are nothing more than cover for a brazen attempt to extort a settlement."

"That's outrageous," Lewis hissed. "You have no right—"

The judge held up a hand. "Mr. Blackwell, you're talking about sharp practice—the worst kind of bad faith. I've known Lewis Ames for most of my life. His reputation is unimpeachable. A hearing will only waste the court's time."

"I disagree," Rusty pressed. "It will give me a chance to cross-examine witnesses—Mr. Ames, Ms. Ames, her husband, Joshua Griswold, and Mr. Griswold's father who runs the PR firm behind the press conference. Mr. Griswold is a journalist of dubious character. His involvement is prima facie evidence that this case was manufactured for the media."

Cameron saw Rusty's angle. It was a perfect trap.

Judge Chandler sat back in his chair. "Lewis," he said, his tone subdued, "what is your relationship to Mr. Griswold, beyond the obvious?"

"He's an investigator and consulting attorney," Lewis replied evenly. "He did the initial overseas research, and he found the plaintiffs."

The judge nodded. "Did he have anything to do with drafting the complaint?"

"No, Your Honor," Lewis said. "He only reviewed it for accuracy."

"And did you file the complaint to harass, injure, or extort a settlement from Presto?"

Lewis shook his head. "Of course not. Do we want this case to count? Yes. Do we want the public to know about it? Absolutely. But we've done everything by the book."

Judge Chandler shrugged. "That's all the testimony I need. The motion for sanctions is overruled. Now, let's talk about a hearing on Presto's motion to dismiss—"

"Your Honor," Rusty interjected, pulling a document out of his briefcase. "I didn't want to do this, but I'm afraid I have no choice." He placed the document on the judge's desk and handed a copy to Lewis. "This is a motion for recusal. No one's seen it yet, but I'll file it tomorrow unless you agree to reassign the case."

The judge stared at the motion as if it were leprous.

"You said it yourself," Rusty went on. "You've known Mr. Ames most of your life. In fact, your families are very close. You've vacationed together at the beach, played golf together, and attended the weddings of each other's children. Had I requested a hearing on sanctions before any other judge, I would have gotten it. But you took Mr. Ames at his word after virtually no questioning—which confirms what I suspected. You're biased, Your Honor. Whether you intend to do it or not, you're going to give the plaintiffs an edge."

For a long moment, no one in chambers seemed to breathe. Cameron studied the judge. He saw the anger burning in his eyes. It was righteous anger but not completely pure. Behind it was something darker—the faintest shadow of guilt.

At last, Judge Chandler spoke, his voice as brittle as ice. "You better have something more than that, Mr. Blackwell, or I'm going to hold you in contempt."

Rusty pointed at the motion on the judge's desk. "It's all in there, Your Honor. You've been on the bench for ten years, yet this is the first case you've ever taken in Charlottesville. You have a soft spot for plaintiffs and a prejudice against corporate defendants. In cases between individuals and corporations, you've ruled for the individuals 68 percent of the time. You're an intelligent man and a learned jurist. But Presto is not going to get a fair hearing in your courtroom, not with Lewis Ames on the other side."

As Cameron watched, the judge wavered. He looked down at the motion, his thoughts imponderable. Then his lips curled into a smile. "File the motion, Mr. Blackwell. Preserve the point for appeal. But I have every intention of keeping this case. Unless you have proof of misconduct, the Fourth Circuit will run you out on a rail."

Rusty stared at the judge for pregnant seconds, then nodded and said no more.

He made his point, Cameron thought. *Lewis's advantage is gone.*

"Now that we're all on the same page," the judge said, opening his calendar. "Let's talk about scheduling. How does March 1 look for a hearing on Presto's motion to dismiss?"

CHAPTER SEVEN

UNITED STATES COURTHOUSE

CHARLOTTESVILLE, VIRGINIA

MARCH 1, 2016

12:52 P.M.

The courtroom was lost in time. Built at the end of the 1970s, it straddled the divide between the soulless brutalism of the postwar years and the more fashionable marriage of classicism and modernism that followed. The ceiling was high and coffered, the furnishings hewn out of dark wood. But the historic veneer was only skin deep. There were no windows, no brass accents, no scroll-work on the molding as in older courtrooms. The place looked hastily designed and half-created, like a museum exhibit or a movie set, which was also, at that moment, the way it felt.

The gallery was crammed with bodies, most of them holding notepads and sketchbooks. Apart from the occupants of the first two rows, everyone was a reporter or a spectator fortunate enough to have survived the gauntlet outside the courthouse. Josh was sitting by the wall just outside the bar. Madison and Lewis were in front of him at the counsel table with John Remington and Peter Chavez. Lily was beside Josh on the bench, having inveigled her mother and her teacher to turn the hearing into a class project. Next to Lily sat Alya, clad in a blue sari and headscarf. Jashel was beside her, and then Ashik, both dressed in suits, hands in their laps, staring silently forward. Sonia sat next to her father, her frail body swaddled in green. Rana was at the end of the row, sporting a headset connected wirelessly to earpieces worn by the plaintiffs. For the duration of the case, he would serve as translator.

When everyone was in place, Josh glanced across the aisle at Presto's legal team. There were nine of them down from Washington, a cadre of tailored suits and lambskin briefcases. Cameron Alexander was in the first row, doodling on a legal pad. Josh had tried to catch his eye when he walked in, but Cameron ignored him. It had been more than a year since Josh had last seen him. His hair looked slightly grayer, but that was probably an effect of the lighting. Josh puzzled again over the mystery of his motives. Over the past months, he'd done some digging and solved the only riddle in Cameron's public life—the cause of his wife's death. The obituary published by her family had given no details, referring only to a "tragic accident." But Josh had followed a hunch, called in a favor at the Metro police, and ferreted out the truth. Yet it didn't explain anything. What did Cameron's guilt over Olivia have to do with Presto?

"All rise!" the bailiff intoned, and Josh stood. "The Honorable Ambrose Pickens Chandler, Chief United States District Judge, presiding. Please be seated and come to order."

Judge Chandler entered the courtroom with two law clerks in tow. He climbed the steps to the bench and sat down in a tall black chair. He smiled sardonically, surveying the gallery. "It's always a joy to see so many people interested in the justice system. Mr. Ames, I see you've brought some guests from Bangladesh. Would you please introduce them?"

Lewis stood and gestured toward the first row. "Your Honor, this is Sonia Hassan and her father, Ashik Hassan. This is Jashel Sayed Parveen, and this is Alya Begum. This is their first time in a courtroom. They asked me to thank you for hearing their case."

The judge gave the plaintiffs an inviting smile. "It's a pleasure to meet all of you." He turned to the defense table and his expression flattened. "Mr. Blackwell, we're here on your motion. We're all waiting with bated breath to hear why this case is misconceived."

As Rusty stood and went to the podium, Josh suppressed a smile. Madison had told him about the dust-up in chambers over Presto's recusal motion. The judge had overruled it in a one-paragraph order the day after Rusty filed it, and there the story died. No one in the media cared about the judge's family connection to Lewis or his penchant for siding with the underdog. The judge's decision had proven Lewis a prophet. It was he who had argued over the objection of Rana Jalil and Peter Chavez that they should file the case in Virginia, not California. *If I'm going to put my name on this lawsuit,* he'd said, *we're going to keep it here. Ambrose Chandler will take it, and he'll give us the best chance we'll get anywhere in the country.*

Rusty opened his notebook and spoke in a somber tone. "Your Honor, before I get into the more technical aspects of our motion, I'd like to reiterate something that Vance Lawson told the public back in November. Everyone at Presto sympathizes with the plaintiffs. I think we can all admit that *someone* deserves to pay for the terrible things that happened to them. But that someone is not in this courtroom. That someone is not the defendant."

Rusty cast a sideways glance at Lewis. "This is a straightforward case of mistaken identity. Presto is a retailer, not a manufacturer. It contracts with suppliers all over the world to produce the clothing it sells. It exercises no control over the operations of those suppliers. It doesn't tell them how to manage their employees or produce their garments. The only control it exercises is over quality. As independent contractors, the suppliers *alone* are responsible for what happens at their factories. If conditions are dangerous or abusive, if workers are lured into employment on false pretenses, if their labor is less than voluntary, it is not Presto's doing—"

"Pardon me, Counsel," the judge interjected, "but the plaintiffs included Presto's Code of Conduct in the complaint, along with language from the company's website informing the public of its dedication to sustainability and ethical sourcing. Are you telling me that the Code exists solely to cover Presto's derriere, not to benefit the workers who make its products?"

Rusty came up short, caught on the horns of a dilemma. "That question was answered by the Ninth Circuit in *Doe v. Wal-Mart*," he said at last. "The Code of Conduct is part of the bargain between Presto and its suppliers. The workers who are employed by those suppliers, including the plaintiffs in this lawsuit, are not parties to that bargain. They benefit from it indirectly. But they are not *intended* beneficiaries, from a legal standpoint, at least."

The judge frowned. "So what you're telling me is that Presto's commitment to worker welfare is just fodder for the PR department?"

The defense lawyer chose his response with care. "All of Presto's public statements are accurate reflections of the company's moral commitment to worker safety and human rights, but they are not part of its supplier contract. That is correct."

Josh heard whispers behind him, along with the sound of pens scribbling furiously. If he knew Tony Sharif, that quote would appear above the fold in the *Post* tomorrow morning.

"Folks," the judge said to the spectators, "I'm glad you're paying attention, but please keep your thoughts to yourself. Mr. Blackwell, you may proceed."

"Thank you, Your Honor," Rusty said. "The most basic question raised by the complaint is whether, under US or Bangladeshi law, Presto is the plaintiffs' effective employer. On this point, their argument is threadbare. While many facets of this case remain unclear, what *is* clear is who employed the plaintiffs. Their factories did. In the eyes of American law, employment has always been a function of managerial control, and I've seen no authority from Bangladesh to convince me that their law diverges from long-standing precedent on this point—"

Again, the judge interrupted him. "The basic legal concept of employment is an anachronism that owes far more to the nineteenth-century notion of masters and servants than to the economic realities of the twenty-first century. What about the concept of joint employer liability? Under the *Hearst Publications* and *Rutherford Foods* line of cases, factory workers who are part of an 'integrated unit of production' can be the legal employees of an off-site contractor like Presto. From my reading of the complaint—which is all we're talking about—your client's supply chain looks pretty integrated to me."

Rusty shook his head forcefully. "Your Honor, the joint employer theory is limited to *domestic* cases brought under the National Labor Relations Act and the Fair Labor Standards Act. Those statutes, as the court is well aware, do not apply overseas."

"So I'm clear," the judge replied, "what you're saying is that had the plaintiffs been making clothes for Presto in *American* factories, they could have availed themselves of the joint employer theory. But because they were laboring *outside* the borders of the United States, I should kick their case out of court. Is that your position?"

As uncomfortable as Rusty appeared, he spoke without wavering. "That is our position, Your Honor. I didn't set the boundaries of the law. Congress did."

"And Presto benefits from it enormously," the judge said sharply.

While Rusty fumbled for an answer, Josh glanced at Cameron. The general counsel was sitting ramrod straight, staring implacably at the bench. Josh searched his face for a glimmer of pleasure but saw none. He recalled Cameron's sangfroid at the Lincoln Memorial, the complete absence of discomfort or fear. Cameron was one of the most self-disciplined human beings Josh had ever seen. Still, he found it strange. This whole spectacle was Cameron's creation. Yet he looked more like the accused on trial than a playwright watching his masterpiece unfold.

"I have to take exception with that characterization," Rusty said at last. "There *are* legal limitations on how Presto can behave when operating abroad. It must abide by all local laws and all federal laws that apply extraterritorially, such as the Federal Corrupt Practices Act."

"It seems to me," said the judge, "that the plaintiffs have made out a prima facie case under the corruption act. But that's not something I can consider, is it?"

Backed into another corner, Rusty cleared his throat. "Congress saw fit to leave the FCPA in the hands of the Justice Department. The plaintiffs have no cause of action."

The judge nodded. "All right then, let's talk about the trafficking act. Assuming the plaintiffs' allegations are true—as I must at this stage—the terms of Mr. Parveen's and Ms. Begum's recruitment and employment constitute forced labor. What I'm wrestling with is whether the allegations are sufficient to implicate Presto. Clearly Presto benefited from the way its suppliers obtained workers on the cheap. But did Presto benefit knowingly or recklessly?"

In an instant, Rusty's confidence reasserted itself. "I'm happy you raised that, Your Honor. That is the critical inquiry under the trafficking act and a fatal flaw in the complaint. What did Presto *actually know* about its suppliers' hiring practices? *Who* at Presto knew? *How* did they know? *When* did they know? The complaint offers no details about my client's knowledge. As the Supreme Court has stated time and again, a complaint that rehearses bald-faced legal conclusions is not entitled to the assumption of truth. It should be dismissed."

The judge wrote something on his pad, then focused on Rusty again. "Anything else?"

"No, Your Honor," said the defense lawyer. "That's all I have for now."

Judge Chandler focused on Lewis. "Mr. Ames? Let's hear from you."

"Actually, Your Honor," Lewis said, lifting himself halfway out of his chair, "I'm going to let my daughter handle this. She's not only smarter than I am, she's better looking."

The judge grinned, and people in the gallery laughed softly. "Very well. Ms. Ames?"

Madison stood up and caught Josh's eye, then Lily's, as she moved to the podium. She was wearing a white pantsuit with black accents, along with a string of pearls around her neck. She had almost put her dark hair back in a clip, but Josh convinced her to leave it down. *Let the world see you as a woman,* he'd said. *Not just a lawyer.*

"Your Honor, it's a privilege to be here," she began, speaking without notes. "I have to admit the longer I've lived with this case, the more it's gotten to me. My daughter is here today. She's nine years old. In the lottery of birth she was pretty fortunate. She was born into a family of means in a country of laws and opportunity. She suffers from leukemia, but it's treatable and she's getting top-notch care. Her school is exceptional. She'll go to college one day. Unless the sky falls, she'll never have to labor in a firetrap like Sonia Hassan. She'll never be forced to work as a slave like Jashel Sayed Parveen. She'll never be raped by a supervisor like Alya Begum. These are the thoughts that comfort me when I'm falling asleep at night. The world is full of misery, but at least my daughter is safe. Then it hits me. I shop at Presto. I've bought pants *for Lily* like the ones Sonia Hassan wore as a mask. When the fire happened, Sonia's sky *did* fall, and because of it I know the truth. And so do all of you."

She swept her hand over the courtroom. "Look around us, Your Honor. Some of these people are here for a story, but most of them are here because they're fascinated by the world my husband uncovered, the world that exists under our noses, that creates the things we love to buy, that fuels our economy, that props up our retirement accounts, that makes some of us very rich at the expense of the very poor. They're here because the matrix has malfunctioned and the illusion that keeps us buying more and more as if the products just magically appear has been revealed as false. And this implicates all of us, not just Presto. It implicates me. It implicates you."

Madison took a breath, her eyes shining with emotion. "All too often, we lawyers act as if the law exists for its own sake. It doesn't. It exists to protect people. It exists because without it factory owners get away with murder, and labor brokers entrap and enslave workers, and managers abuse young women. We're not here arguing about abstractions. We're here because real people have been terrorized by a system of commerce that is, in many respects, exploita-tive, and from which the defendant has profited handsomely. We've crafted the complaint as carefully as we can, recognizing that we're stretching the bound-aries of existing law. But as Your Honor pointed out, existing law is lost in the past. Indeed, the law pertaining to the production of goods abroad is barely a law at all. It is up to this court to give that law teeth."

"Ms. Ames," the judge said, "I appreciate your words. But this court has no legislative or executive power. If gaps exist in the law, there is very little I can do to fix that. I understand your joint employer argument on the negligence claims. But on the Code of Conduct, I'm struggling to understand how you can infer that *Presto* was obligated to maintain the plaintiffs' working environment when the Code places that burden squarely on the shoulders of Presto's *suppliers*."

Madison nodded. "As Your Honor pointed out, the Code is, in a certain sense, a cynical piece of window dressing. At the same time, it is part of a binding agreement between Presto and its suppliers that is only rational if Presto intends to *enforce* it. And, indeed, Presto *has* enforced it with auditors and inspections and its color-coded list. It would be one thing if Presto simply sent orders to its suppliers and paid for shipments without saying anything about the way its products were being made. But Presto *does* care. At least, it *says* it cares. Its promise to pay is conditioned upon its suppliers' agreement to treat their workers with dignity. That treatment is intended by the agreement, even if it isn't the central feature of it."

Judge Chandler angled his head thoughtfully. "I see where you're going, and I'll take it under advisement. Let's talk about the trafficking claims. I agree with Mr. Blackwell that Presto's knowledge is the only issue at the pleadings stage. In the old days, I would have upheld your claims without a second thought. But now we have *Twiqbal*, a set of rulings as ugly as they sound. It isn't enough for you to allege that Presto knew what their suppliers were doing, or that they recklessly disregarded the obvious. You have to give me more."

Madison picked up a copy of the complaint and flipped to a page near the end. "We were acutely conscious of *Twiqbal* when we drafted the pleadings, Your Honor. Like all companies, Presto is highly secretive about its internal procedures. What we obtained in our research gave us a basis for our last two counts. We allege that 'Presto employees and executives in legal and/or compliance departments in the United States and overseas either actively knew or had reason to know about the deceptive and exploitative manner in which foreign workers from Bangladesh were being supplied to its factories in Malaysia and Jordan. Presto employees and executives allowed such abuses to take place, and Presto benefited financially from those abuses.'"

"I'm familiar with the language," the judge replied. "But I don't see the detail."

Madison pursed her lips, her composure starting to slip. "With all due respect, detail is the purpose of discovery."

At this comeuppance, Judge Chandler raised an eyebrow. "Fair enough. I'll give it a second look—or a fourth." He grinned. "Anything else, Ms. Ames?"

"Just this," Madison said, holding up the complaint. "If these pages, all one hundred and four of them, and the stories of these people"—she held out her arm toward Sonia and Jashel and Alya—"aren't compelling enough to force Presto to come clean about the way it sources the clothing it sells to people like me, what will ever be compelling enough?"

When Madison sat down beside her father, Lily tugged on Josh's blazer and leaned in close. "I think she did great," she whispered.

"She's a terrific lawyer," he replied softly.

Lily tugged on his sleeve again. "I'm not sure the judge agrees with her."

He gave his daughter a squeeze, but her doubt was a precise reflection of his own. He examined Madison from behind, saw the tension in her shoulders, sensed her dismay about the way her colloquy had ended. The question of Presto's awareness was another issue they had debated ad nauseam. Josh had played them the recording of his meeting with Cameron, and they had gleaned from it what they could. But it wasn't much. So they had leveraged Cameron's position in the company without implicating him directly. The judge, however, had homed in on their weakness. From the way he had grilled Rusty, it was obvious how he wanted to rule.

The question was, what would he do when the law contradicted his conscience?

CHAPTER EIGHT

HAMILTONS' AT FIRST & MAIN

CHARLOTTESVILLE, VIRGINIA

APRIL 1, 2016

12:36 P.M.

The chandelier-lit table in the private dining room was empty except for two place settings, one for Cameron, the other for Vance. Cameron was at his seat, munching mindlessly on crab cakes. The food was irrelevant. The only thing that mattered was the conversation happening across the room on Vance's mobile phone. The chief executive was standing by the windows, his face a mask of tension. The phone was on speaker. Lane Donaldson, founder of the world's third-largest investment fund, was on the line.

"Lane," Vance was saying, almost humbly, "I hear where you're coming from, but you're not being reasonable. The lawsuit is a distraction. Sales are starting to rebound. Share price is up 2 percent this week, 4 percent in the past month—"

"Vance," Lane Donaldson interjected, his voice hard-edged, "you're *not* hearing me. It's the uncertainty that's getting to us. There was a day when Presto was a blue chip stock. You paid predictable dividends. Your growth rate was well above inflation—"

"That was before the crash," Vance interrupted, showing a hint of desperation. "Back then Presto could sneeze and make money. You're talking apples and oranges."

"I'm not," Donaldson disagreed testily. "I'm talking about the last year and a half since that damn factory went up in flames. Your market cap has been a

Ping-Pong ball. Your growth has flatlined. We gave you a pass last year. You pulled the company out of the hole. But the lawsuit changed the game. The instability has reached an unprecedented level."

Vance shook his head. "This is about the *New York Times*."

"Hell, yes, it's about the *New York Times*! They're calling for divestment, like Presto is apartheid South Africa. Look, you know I'm not squeamish. I've never minded a little egg on my face. But this thing is different. I feel like I'm swimming in a pond of shit. If the court lets the case go forward, the pond is going to turn into an ocean. That's the end of the line."

Across the room, Cameron's neck began to tingle. He could feel the voltage in the air. He focused on Vance's face, his breath trapped in his throat, his hands twitching.

"What are you saying?" Vance demanded.

"I'm saying the funds are in agreement. If this case doesn't disappear, we're going to clean house—the board, the C-suite, everybody. We can't let our value erode any further."

"Thanks for nothing," Vance said acidly and terminated the call. He stood frozen in place as if time had taken a pause, then from his lips came a long string of curses. He looked for a moment like he was going to dash the phone against the floor, but he caught himself and slipped it into his pocket. He sat down at the table and speared a piece of steak, chewing deliberately.

"I saw Declan Mays last week," he said in time. "I had half a mind to toss him out the window. He's in a relationship with Victoria Brost, you know. I hired an investigator to track his movements. They've been seeing each other for a while. Maybe she turned him against us; maybe he turned on us himself. It doesn't matter. If the judge rules against us today, I'm going to take great delight in firing his ass. I might even sue him just for the hell of it."

Cameron had been Vance's friend for half his life. He could name all of his vices—pride, lust, vanity, and intemperance—but he had never known Vance to be malicious. In the past few months, however, his fortitude had started to fray, his speech had lost its lilt, and his eyes had turned shifty, almost paranoid. He had shrunk into a shadow of the leader Cameron knew him to be—the McKinsey-trained savant who had taken Presto from an antique ship adrift in a digital sea to the only retailer challenging the Internet hegemony of Amazon. Yet the lawsuit had turned it all into a house of cards, one judicial opinion away from total collapse.

Cameron took a slow breath and steadied his hands. He may not have seen how far this would go, but it wasn't over yet. He glanced at his watch. "It's time."

Vance drained the last of his wine and picked up the bottle. "This is good. Shame we can't take it with us. Make a peace offering to the judge."

They met Hector, Vance's bodyguard, on the street and walked together down the pedestrian mall beneath the shade of willow oaks. The media swarmed them when they angled toward the courthouse. Reporters pelted Vance with questions, some confrontational, others inane. Cameron and Hector ran interference, putting their arms out and sweeping people aside. At last, they reached the glass doors and stepped inside. After passing through security, they took seats in the courtroom beside Rusty Blackwell's army of attorneys.

As the clock marched toward one thirty, journalists and spectators filed in. Cameron glanced across the aisle and saw Josh Griswold on the far end of the first bench, his daughter, Lily, beside him. Alya, Jashel, and the Hassans were next to her, along with their interpreter. Cameron was surprised to see the plaintiffs in attendance. The judge had scheduled the hearing only a week ago, informing counsel that he wanted to deliver his decision in person before filing it electronically. It was a rare move for a district judge. Yet it had a certain portentous logic. The case was in the national spotlight. The judge wanted the media to hear what he had to say.

At the bottom of the hour, Judge Chandler appeared with his law clerks, and the bailiff called the court to order. From the dark circles under the judge's eyes, Cameron could tell that the decision had bedeviled him.

"Thank you all for coming," he began. "This is an important moment in the life of this court and, more broadly, in the life of our society. Over the last three hundred years, America has built its legal system on the concept of equal justice for all. A case like this shows how far we have to go to attain that ideal."

The judge's eyes sparked. "I've never said this from the bench before, but I'm going to say it today. I'm angry. I'm angry because I feel like the wool has been pulled over my eyes. We live in an age in which materialism has become our highest value—to have the look, the stuff, to keep up with the Joneses, and, if possible, to exceed them. I'm a part of the problem as much as anyone. And now I see the consequences. They're sitting right in front of me, these lovely people whose language I don't speak and whose suffering I can't imagine."

Judge Chandler shifted in his chair. "In the last month, I have struggled enormously with the decision before me. The law governing US companies who make their products overseas is shockingly ill defined. But is it my role to clarify it? That's the question that's been keeping me awake at night. What does a judge do when justice demands more than the law can give? I wish I could say I found a satisfying answer. I didn't. And that, too, makes me angry. But my decision is not a result of my anger. It comes from another place, from the oath I gave."

When the judge paused, Cameron cast a sideways glance at Lewis Ames. A minute ago, he had been a model of poise. Now his forehead was creased, his fingers drumming on a pad. He was waiting for the ax to fall, as Cameron was. But here their hopes divided, like rivers seeking different oceans. Here the cause of individual justice had to bow before the greater good.

"In the context of the global economy," the judge said, "I find the paradigm of master-servant in employer liability as offensive as master-slave. But I didn't write the laws of Virginia, let alone Bangladesh. I must apply them as I see them. Unless the plaintiffs can plead that Presto had a daily role in managing the work performed by Sonia Hassan, I can't allow the negligence claims to proceed. The same is true of the third-party claims. Presto's Code of Conduct is a self-serving document, placing the entire burden of workplace safety on the shoulders of Presto's suppliers. As a consumer, I find it repugnant that Presto would use the Code to burnish its public image and then hide behind its skirts in court. But hypocrisy is not actionable at law. Given the pleadings before me, the claims on behalf of Sonia, Nasima, and Joya Hassan must fail."

The judge took a heavy breath. "As for the claims of Jashel Parveen and Alya Begum, they, too, have a defect, but it need not be fatal. Mr. Parveen and Ms. Begum have sufficiently pleaded that their labor was obtained by force and threat of force, and by the abuse of legal process. They have pleaded that Presto benefited from this scheme. However, the allegations about the defendant's *knowledge* lack a plausible foundation. The plaintiffs allege that persons in Presto's legal and/or compliance departments were aware or should have been aware of forced labor in the company's supply chain. But the plaintiffs offer the court no more information about such persons. They also fail to allege *when* Presto acquired that knowledge. Was Presto aware of Mr. Parveen's and Ms. Begum's abuse while it was happening, or did the company find out later on? Absent such detail, the allegations are not entitled to deference."

The judge turned his troubled eyes toward the plaintiffs. "Mr. and Miss Hassan, the way you have been treated is a disgrace. I would like nothing more than to send your case to trial. But the rule of law is not the rule of men. Without a proper complaint, I can't do it."

Finally, the judge looked at Lewis. "As for the claims of Mr. Parveen and Ms. Begum, Counsel, I'm dismissing them without prejudice. You have until May 16 to make out a plausible story of corporate knowledge or recklessness. If you satisfy the standard, I will allow you to proceed. If not, I will leave Presto's fate in the hands of the public. This court is adjourned."

Cameron closed his eyes and opened them again. He had survived. Vance and the board had survived. His reading of the law had been vindicated, and his plan was still in motion. But the victory inspired no joy in him, only the hollow ache of his betrayal. This time it wasn't Presto he had deceived, but the plaintiffs and their lawyers and Joshua Griswold.

He shook hands with Rusty Blackwell, then walked down the aisle with Vance and Hector, following the bodyguard through the clot of reporters outside the gallery and ignoring the barrage of questions. Neither he nor Vance spoke again until they were outside the courthouse and down the street, out of the earshot of anyone who cared to listen.

"We made it, Cameron," Vance exulted. "I'm going to make Donaldson eat crow."

"Accompanied by a glass of hemlock." Cameron laughed wryly despite the gall churning in his gut. "Look, we were fortunate. But we're not out of the woods yet. If there's a mole in the company, we could be back here in May."

The sunshine faded from Vance's face. "I know. There's something I need you to do."

CHAPTER NINE

The parlor was as quiet as a mausoleum, until Madison took a breath and broke the spell.

"You have to talk to him again, Joshua," she said from beside the fireplace, its logs black and cold. "You need to get more detail."

Josh gripped the back of the couch, consumed by an inexpressible rage. He couldn't believe he had circumnavigated the earth, spent tens of thousands of dollars, risked his safety, and offered hope to three of the poorest people he had ever known only to be turned back by a principle of legal pleading so technical that Rana had found it impossible to explain to the plaintiffs' satisfaction. All of them were convinced that the judge had chosen not to believe them, that he had sided with the rich and powerful, as courts did every day in Bangladesh. Their faces haunted Josh, their words of sorrow and disbelief, as did Madison's now.

"I'll get in touch with him," he replied. "If he's still on our side, he should come to me."

"I don't care whose side he's on," Lewis said. "What matters is whose side *we're* on. If you can't get more information, we're going to have to put his name in the pleading. We have an obligation to our clients that supersedes our concern for Cameron and his family."

Josh thought of Maria and the pictures from the Hotel Caesar Park. He thought of the e-mail he had received from her a week ago, apologizing profusely but begging him for more money. Curses flooded his mind, as if a sewer line had broken inside of him. He wanted to let them out, to turn his anger toward someone or something, but he couldn't find a target.

"I need some time," he said. "The judge gave us six weeks."

Lewis nodded. "You can have five and a half. Then we'll make a decision."

✻

Josh sped down the driveway and tore out of the boxwood gate, flooring the accelerator and flying across the hills of Keswick. He drove that way for a few miles, passing slower vehicles as if they were standing still. He knew what would happen if the police caught him—the loss of his license, the jail time. But for a handful of minutes he simply didn't care.

At last he slowed down and pulled over to the side of the road, staring out the windshield at the tall grass waving in the wind. In an instant, he unleashed his pent-up frustration, shouting expletives and pounding the steering wheel until his fists began to hurt. Then he rolled down the windows and let the breeze waft through the cabin, soothing his nerves.

He took out his iPhone and opened Maria's last message. "Joshua," she had written, "I know you do not want to hear this, but the roof of the Casa has a bad leak. I ask our maintenance man to help, but he says no, unless I do favors. I know this problem is not yours. But the money is gone. Please. I do not like to beg. But I will beg for my girls. *Beijinhos.*"

Josh tossed the phone on the passenger seat and massaged his temples. His bank account was bleeding. He hadn't made a deposit in six months. Another royalty check would arrive any day now, but *The End of Childhood* had been off the bestseller list for over a year. The wave of stardom had passed, and the scandal had dried up what remained of his goodwill. He had already dipped into his emergency fund to help Madison with the bills. She didn't need his assistance. She had more money in her grandfather's trust than Josh would make in a lifetime. But he was her husband, and he couldn't imagine letting her pull the weight of their family alone.

He shook his head, trying to figure a way out of the mess. He needed to talk to Tony Sharif about getting his job back. He could work a copy editor's desk. He could ghostwrite for another columnist. He was too valuable for the *Post* to cut him loose permanently. He also needed to find Maria a new benefactor. He had to sever ties. But there was something else he needed to do first, something far more immediate and urgent.

He had to get in touch with Cameron.

CHAPTER TEN

The skyline of Washington was bright in the morning light, the Potomac wind tossed and slate gray. Cameron stood at his office window preparing himself for the duty Vance had given him. He thought of his mother and the grave that was her final resting place. He remembered the promises he had made to her beneath the blue and white sky of Boston, the promise to trust his heart and make his life count. He thought of the look he had traded with his father, the question he had seen in Ben's grief-laden eyes. *What will people say of you when you follow her into the earth? What will they remember?* He didn't know the answer yet, but he was on a path to find out. For the first time in a long time, he was doing something that could make his father proud.

And that, quite unfortunately, required this.

"Declan, come in," he said when his compliance director knocked. "Take a seat."

"I have a call at ten," Declan said, sitting across from his boss. "Should I reschedule?"

Cameron waved his hand. "We'll be finished by then. It's been awhile since we had a chance to catch up. How is Victoria?"

Declan's expression shifted from officious to pleased. "She's well. We're going to Rome in June. I'm actually going to take a vacation."

Cameron grinned. "Declan Mays, away from the office for more than a weekend, strolling through the Eternal City with a beautiful woman. It's almost hard to imagine."

"I know," Declan replied. "I won't know what to do with myself." He took a breath and changed the subject. "I heard it was quite a scene at the courthouse. I wish I could have been there. What are the chances the judge will let the case go forward?"

Cameron's gaze turned calculating. He despised what he was about to do, but it was necessary. From this point forward, he needed Vance firmly on his side. "That depends."

The compliance chief tilted his head quizzically. "On what the plaintiffs allege?"

"On what they *can* allege." Cameron allowed the silence to linger before he lowered the boom. "It isn't clear where they got their information in the first place."

For a moment, Declan sat in shock. Then just as quickly he recoiled. "You have to be kidding. After all we've been through, you don't actually think . . . I can't *believe* this."

Cameron kept his face a mask. "I don't think you had anything to do with it. But my opinion isn't the only one that matters."

Declan's green eyes began to burn. "Who's accusing me then? Rebecca? Vance? One of the old bastards on the board? I'm not going to take this sitting down."

"I'm afraid you don't have a choice," Cameron said evenly.

"Like hell I don't." Declan stood up and walked to the window. "I'm not going to lie to you. I enjoyed reading the complaint. I thought *at last* the truth about this industry might actually come out. Presto didn't start the fire, but we had a role in it. The system is rigged. We care far more about price than we do about people. But I wasn't the leak. I'd never betray this company."

Cameron stood up too. "It doesn't matter. I'm giving you notice. If the plaintiffs file an amended complaint, I'm going to put you on administrative leave until we sort this out."

Declan turned toward him and spoke in a voice just above a whisper. "If that happens, I'll tender my resignation. Have a nice day, Cameron. I hope it's better than mine."

With that, Declan stalked out of the office, slamming the door behind him. Cameron took a breath and held it until he felt light-headed. His eyes wandered to the Lincoln Memorial, shining like a beacon in the sunlight. He thought back to the night two Februaries ago when he had heard Josh Griswold's footsteps scuffing the marble of the main hall. He thought back a little further to the Sunday before that, when he had sat down at a computer terminal at the library in Rosedale, created an anonymous e-mail account, and sent Josh a message. He remembered how the key had sounded when he hit Send. He knew that people would get hurt. It was inevitable. But their pain would be his pain, and his pain a passage.

He took out his iPhone and placed a call on which everything hinged.

"Cameron," the man said in a crisp New England accent, the sounds of the ocean behind him. "I saw the news. I was wondering if I might hear from you."

"How are you, Stephen?" Cameron asked. He pictured the investor as he was when he met him in California, the broad, avuncular face and thoughtful smile, the combed-back white hair and owl-like eyes that took everything in at once, the blaze of clairvoyant intelligence that had made him billions in the market, defying every prediction of the Wall Street cognoscenti.

Stephen Carroll gave a breezy laugh. "I'm sitting on my deck with a double espresso and a copy of the *Journal*, watching pelicans skim the waves at the beginning of another day in paradise. How do you think I am?" He allowed the question to dangle for a moment, then said, "I suppose you're wondering if I've lost my appetite."

Cameron stared at his own reflection in the glass, saw the depth of his weariness etched in the lines of his brow. "The thought had crossed my mind."

"I'm not that fickle," Carroll said. "I still see opportunity here. But the kind of value that interests me is incompatible with chaos."

Cameron kept his voice measured, hiding his relief. "The lawsuit is as good as dead."

Carroll grunted. "Call me back when the coffin is in the ground."

CHAPTER ELEVEN

THE LINCOLN MEMORIAL

WASHINGTON, DC

APRIL 4, 2016

4:34 P.M.

The east face of the memorial was thronged with students and tourists when Josh arrived. He climbed the steps to the colonnade but skirted the main hall, rounding the building to the side that faced the Potomac. He found Fitz Conlin sitting between columns, munching on a granola bar. Conlin was an old friend from the Metro police who had parlayed his contacts and deductive skills into a thriving private investigation practice. It was he who had trailed Vance to the L2 Lounge and inspired in Madison the idea of delivering the lawsuit with a personal touch.

Josh sat down next to him. "What do you have for me?"

Conlin took an envelope out of his jacket. "Your friend is elusive. He used to live in an apartment at the Wyoming, but he sold it after his wife died. Now his mail goes to a PO box in Arlington. All his IDs still show the old address. The doorman at the Wyoming is new, and the supervisor wouldn't talk. The only phone number I found went to Presto's receptionist. He owns two vehicles—a Lincoln sedan and a sailboat he keeps at the Gangplank Marina. The harbor-master wouldn't let me in to see the boat. I spent some time at the yacht club, but everyone was coy. It's possible he's renting a place in the area. It's also possible he lives on the boat. If I had another twenty-four hours, I'd follow him from work and know for sure."

"That's good enough," Josh said. "I'll take it from here." He took Conlin's envelope and passed along one of his own. "Good to see you again, Fitz."

Josh walked back the way he came, through the trees along the Reflecting Pool, around the Washington Monument, and along the Mall to the Smithsonian Metro station. He hopped aboard a Blue Line train and got off at Rosslyn in Arlington, following the crowd up to the street. The parking garage where he had left his car was a short distance away.

He checked his watch. It was just after five. He doubted Cameron would leave the office for a while, but he couldn't afford to miss him.

Over the weekend, he had sent a message to the e-mail address Cameron had used, but the account was inactive. There was still a chance that the general counsel meant to contact him, but the more Josh thought about it, the less likely it seemed. Cameron's behavior at the last hearing gnawed at him. He had watched as Cameron left the gallery with Vance. He had searched his face for a hint of disappointment but seen nothing. What if Cameron hadn't wanted the lawsuit to succeed? What if he had used Josh and the plaintiffs for purposes all his own?

Josh drove out of the garage and parked in a lot across the street from Presto Tower. The tower had its own parking structure with a guard post and traffic spikes. As the end of the workday approached, the stream of cars leaving the building increased. Josh kept watch for Cameron's Lincoln sedan, but the general counsel was not among them.

Half an hour turned into an hour, then two. Around seven thirty, the tower began to glow as the sun sank toward the horizon. By eight, Josh started to grow impatient. He hadn't eaten since lunchtime. *Come on, Cameron. Turn it in.* But Cameron didn't, and another hour passed. Josh's stomach started to growl in earnest.

Finally, at four minutes before ten, a black Lincoln sedan emerged from the gate and headed south at a fast clip. Josh was so addled by boredom that it took him a second to register the license number and punch the ignition. By the time he left the lot, the Lincoln had almost disappeared. Josh gunned the engine, then slowed to make the turn at Wilson Boulevard, settling in three car lengths behind. Cameron took the George Washington Parkway to the Rochambeau Bridge and crossed the Potomac into DC.

Josh watched the signs for the waterfront, certain now that Cameron was living on his sailboat. But the Lincoln stayed in the left lane and passed the exit, traversing the tunnel under the National Mall and taking the exit to D

Street. When Cameron passed Senate Park and turned left on First Street, Josh pounded the armrest. *Damn it! He's going to Union Station.*

Cameron entered the garage and parked near the train terminal. Josh found a spot two rows away and watched as the general counsel locked his car and walked toward the escalator. Josh put on a baseball cap, flipped up his jacket collar, and followed in Cameron's footsteps. Outside the car, he felt totally exposed. If Cameron turned around or saw his reflection, he would lose his only advantage—surprise. He had no interest in making a scene. He wanted nothing more than to catch Cameron in a private moment and ask a few questions.

Cameron strolled through the hall of brightly lit shops and took the staircase down to the main floor. Josh hesitated at the top of the steps. The staircase made a wide turn, such that at the bottom Cameron was almost facing in Josh's direction. Josh watched pensively, hoping the general counsel wouldn't see him. What happened next left him thunderstruck. On the last step, Cameron looked up and held Josh's gaze. Then he lowered the brim of his hat and disappeared.

As soon as Josh overcame his shock, he raced down the stairway and caught sight of the general counsel weaving through clumps of passengers. Josh fought to keep up, nearly knocking over a girl with a suitcase who veered into his path. He tossed a "Sorry!" over his shoulder and kept his eyes on Cameron. The general counsel made his way toward the Amtrak waiting area and vanished around a corner. Josh began to sprint. A security guard stepped into his path and barked, "Slow down!" but Josh made an end run around him.

At the intersection where Cameron had disappeared, Josh looked around frantically, searching the crowded corridor and the stores and restaurants that lined the waiting area. Around him passengers swarmed as trains disembarked and others prepared for departure. Bodies moved and faces shifted, coming in and out of focus. *Which way did he go? Make up your mind!*

Josh spotted a dark hat atop a black head about thirty feet away. He started off again, threading his way through the crowd. The man in the hat reached the end of the hall and turned the corner to the Metro station. Josh picked up his pace, jostling shoulders and handing out hasty apologies. He pulled out his wallet and waved his SmarTrip card at the scanner. Then he followed the line of commuters down the escalator to the tracks.

A Red Line train was in the station, doors open, passengers filing in. Josh saw the man in the hat step into a car midway down the platform. In desperation, Josh ran headlong through the milling passengers, reaching the car just in time to slide a hand between the doors. The doors jammed, then parted. Josh searched for Cameron through the windows, but he couldn't see him.

He made his decision and stepped onto the train. As the doors closed, he scoured the inside of the car, and his heart sank. The man in the hat wasn't Cameron. Josh turned around and looked out the window. What he saw sent shivers down his spine.

Cameron was on the platform, hat in hand, watching him go.

CHAPTER TWELVE

The freedom of an endless horizon, the solitude of an empty sky, time away from the office—they were pleasures Cameron had allowed himself to forget. Without Olivia, his life had turned into a tunnel of progressive myopia in which Presto's needs and Vance's needs and the board's needs had eclipsed his own. In some ways the transition had been inevitable. In other ways, it had been intentional. But the result had been singularly debilitating, compressing his vision and cannibalizing his soul. So little remained of the man he once was that the idea of freedom now left him floundering. That morning when his eyes had opened, he hadn't known how to greet the dawn. But that was exactly the point. It was time to remember.

He was sitting in the cockpit of the *Breakwater*, sipping coffee from a mug and watching the wind kick up spray on Mattawoman Creek. The sun had risen half an hour ago, but it was doing a tango with a cloudbank on the horizon, casting long shadows across the water. The air temperature was just above freezing, but his body was toasty inside his foul-weather gear. The sailboat was stuffed with provisions, the perishables purchased over the weekend, the rest acquired over the past few months in preparation for this day. The forepeak berth was now a storage locker, holding charts and equipment, spare rigging and emergency beacons, and a hundred other items. The voyage on which he was about to embark was unlike anything he had attempted before. But he was ready for it. He had been ready a long time.

When he finished his coffee, he started the engine and allowed it to warm up. Then he winched in the anchor and motored out of the marina before hoisting the mainsail and taking on wind. The yacht leaped forward like a gazelle, cleaving the chop and heeling ten degrees to port. Cameron held the wheel lightly, pointing the bow toward the Potomac. The wind stung his cheeks, probing the seams at his neck and wrists, but the exhilaration he felt was more than a salve for the pain. His plan was coming together, despite all the twists and turns and terrifying moments. The end game was in sight. All he needed now was time—time for the judge's leave to expire, time for Josh Griswold to wrestle his wife and father-and-law into a reluctant silence, embracing the media victory but conceding the legal defeat. And time was what the sea had to offer, along with so much else. Beyond the blue horizon, Josh would never find him.

It was hard to believe that only eight hours had passed since he recognized the white BMW in his rearview mirror. But he had been ready, his escape route in place. From Union Station he took a taxi to the yacht club, where he gave his keys to the harbormaster along with a tip to collect his car. Thirty minutes later, he cast off the sailboat's lines, motored quietly out of the harbor, and headed downriver beneath the stars.

Before the sun rose, he sent four e-mails—one to his father and sisters, one to Vance and the C-suite, one to Anderson, Declan, and Linda, and one to the board—confirming what he had explained in advance: that he needed a break, that he had twelve weeks of vacation in the bank, that with the lawsuit on ice, now was a perfect time to use six of them, and that he would stay in touch via e-mail. Only Jim Dunavan had expressed reservations. The rest had wished him well, even his father, who said it was about time he did something for someone other than Presto.

Now, at the mouth of the creek, Cameron turned the *Breakwater* to the southwest on a course parallel to the riverbank. He set the autopilot and sheeted out most of the headsail and main. Without the buffer of land, the wind clocked up to nineteen knots, filling the sails until they were taut. He switched off the engine and let the sloop run fast and true through three-foot swells, its raked bow and performance hull cutting the water with speed and stability.

Before long, he rounded the headlands at Stump Neck and set a course to the south. At seven knots, he would pass Point Lookout and enter the Chesapeake sometime in the afternoon. He planned to spend the night in Horn Harbor, north of Mobjack Bay, topping off his fuel tanks and getting his last full night of sleep for some time. After that, he would navigate south toward Old Point Comfort and the open sea. Around noon tomorrow, he would cross the bar and sail out into blue water, charting a course north, then east, and following the path of the fairest winds. His next landfall would be Flores Island in the Azores, fifteen days away.

Fifteen days and four years from the night his world had died. He planned to spend the anniversary on a beach with a bottle of Château Lafite—Olivia's favorite—telling her stories from the voyage as if she were there listening to him, a half smile on her lips, her love just beneath the surface. Her body was in the ground, but her spirit was still with him. She was watching over him, as was his mother. Together, they would carry him across six thousand miles. Together, they would bring him home again.

Then, when the lawsuit was dead and Vance and the board were right where he needed them to be, he would go back to Presto and finish what he had started.

PART EIGHT

Joshua & Cameron

April–June 2016

CHAPTER ONE

The flight from Washington descended through a thick layer of rain clouds. Josh watched the ground approach, feeling every bump in his stomach and thinking about Madison and their trip to Bangladesh almost a year ago. He had taken her to meet the plaintiffs with such a sense of expectation, knowing the challenges that awaited them but believing they would find a way to prevail. That optimism seemed so foolish now, so woefully naïve. He should have pushed Cameron harder at the Lincoln Memorial. He should have demanded an explanation of the rules of the game. But he hadn't. How credulous he had been, how amateurish his mistake.

The aircraft landed with a jolt, then taxied for a while before pulling into the gate. Josh sent a text to Madison informing her of his arrival and an e-mail to Lily apologizing for yet another trip out of town. Before the disaster of the last hearing, the three of them had worked out a new domestic rhythm. They ate meals together. He took Lily to school. Every Friday night he and Madison went out to dinner and saw a movie. On Sundays they attended church with Lewis and Caroline. They were a family. Josh was at home and he was present, a husband and father who cared at least as much about his wife and daughter as he did about his career.

But now here he was again, living in the whirlwind. He hated the guilt even as he loved the rush. He was in Boston because Cameron was gone, and he had run out of leads. Fitz Conlin had worked every angle, fishing for information around the yacht club, interrogating Cameron's secretary on the phone, even contacting Cameron's sisters posing as a friend from Harvard. But no one had talked. It was remarkable the way people protected him.

Josh walked off the plane and followed the signs to ground transportation. He hailed a cab and gave the driver the address in Cambridge. It came down to this, a desperate appeal more likely to blow up in his face than yield a miracle. But he couldn't allow Lewis to put Cameron's name in the complaint. If the evidence of his ongoing relationship with Maria came out, it would shred every last stitch of harmony that he and Madison had so carefully reconstructed. He cared too much about his wife, too much about his daughter. He had to find Cameron.

He had to convince Ben Alexander to talk.

The drive to Berkeley Place took just under half an hour in the downpour. Josh hadn't been back to Cambridge since his law school graduation. The tour through Boston was nostalgic, but his years at Harvard felt like another life. The cabbie dropped him off at the driveway, and Josh raced through the rain to the covered porch. He waited a moment, then knocked on the door. Ten seconds passed, then twenty, but Ben didn't appear. A car was parked in the drive. In such weather, the old professor couldn't be out for a walk. Perhaps he was taking a nap.

Josh knocked again and waited a while longer, listening to the rain. The porch wasn't wide enough for him to sit down. At last, after nearly three minutes, he heard the latch retract. The door slowly opened, and then there he was, the vaunted Benjamin Alexander, looking like a man with one foot firmly in the grave. His hair was white, his ebony skin papery, his imposing frame reduced by the stoop of aging.

Ben frowned at Josh for a poignant moment, the creases in his brow like the ridges of a washboard. "You look familiar," he said, his voice still intimidating. "I know you."

"I'm Joshua Griswold. I was your student two decades ago."

Ben shook his head. "That's not what I'm remembering. You're a journalist with the *Washington Post*. Or you were. You wrote that book, *The End of Childhood*. I read it. It was good, if a bit sentimental. Then that story came out about the Brazilian woman. Quite a beauty, but she was abusing kids, using them for prostitution. A grand mess, if you ask me."

Josh just stood there, skewered like a pig. Finally he managed, "That's a reasonably accurate summary. Your memory is as sharp as I recall."

Ben's eyes took on a humorous cast. "Ah, I see from your choice of words that the press got something wrong. What was it? Were they unfair to you? Or maybe they were unfair to her. They sensationalized the story, trumped it up to sell papers. How accurate is that?"

"Pristinely," Josh replied. The man was so smart it was scary.

"I hate to say it, but the media is a flock of vultures," Ben said, looking like he didn't hate to say it at all. "Perhaps you were an exception, but most of your colleagues live to peck at dead meat." Ben blinked and his face softened. "Pardon me. I've lost my manners. Please come in."

Josh stepped into the foyer and glanced around. The living room was to his left, the dining room to his right, and the kitchen down the hall. The house was a curious paradox, a trove of antiques and original art yet as cozy as a cottage, as if all the beautiful things were in place not just to elicit admiration but because beauty made a home to which people wanted to return.

"This way," Ben said, leading Josh on a slow walk to a den at the back of the house. A fire was blazing in the hearth. Ben gestured to a chair and sat down in another. "I'd offer you coffee, but I'm afraid the pot is empty." He peered at Josh intently. "So what brings you out to Cambridge on such an unpleasant day? Certainly not the desire to keep me company."

On the flight, Josh had debated with himself about how to broach the topic of Cameron. He decided on an indirect approach to build credibility. "I assume you're aware of the lawsuit pending against Presto. I'm married to one of the lawyers representing the plaintiffs—Madison Ames. I believe her father is an acquaintance of yours."

Ben scratched the stubble on his chin. "I've followed the case in the papers. Lewis was a star student in my early years. And his father was a great friend of the black community. I recall seeing your name in the coverage. You had a part in the research, am I right?"

Josh nodded. "I tracked down the plaintiffs."

Ben pondered this. "So what can I do for you? As I understand, the judge dismissed the claims with leave to replead."

Josh leaned forward and spoke the truth gently. "We didn't just dream up the lawsuit. Someone came to us with information. I met him at the Lincoln Memorial in the middle of the night." He gave Ben a piercing look. "It was Cameron."

Long seconds passed in a silence so dense that the air seemed to have frozen solid. Ben sat rigidly in his chair, as if his joints had ceased to function, yet his eyes sparked with vivid life.

"I'm going to pretend this conversation isn't happening," he said at last, his words like steps through a minefield. "And when you leave, I'm going to forget it—the curse of being an old man. But for a moment, I'm willing to listen. Tell me what this has to do with me."

Josh looked into the fire and told Ben about the summons and the meeting and the names. He told him about Cameron's aloofness at the last hearing, his evasive action at Union Station, and his disappearance in the weeks since. "I did what he asked," Josh said. "I don't know what his reasons were, but I don't care anymore. I need to find him."

Ben raised an eyebrow. "And if you don't?"

Josh shrugged. "Then Lewis will put his name in the amended complaint. None of us wants that to happen. But we have an obligation to the plaintiffs."

Ben cleared his throat, his eyes smoldering. "You have got a lot of nerve. You come to my home on a Sunday afternoon and accuse my son of conspiring against his own company, and then you attempt to extort information from me by threatening him. You can see yourself out."

Ben's words hit Josh like a punch in the gut. But he was prepared. He pulled a slip of paper out of his pocket. "I understand how you feel. But, please, think about it. We have until May 16. Call me if you change your mind."

Josh placed his phone number on the chair and left through the front door.

CHAPTER TWO

THE ATLANTIC OCEAN

NEAR CAPE VERDE

MAY 8, 2016

11:07 A.M.

The ocean was like a creature from a fairy tale, its sinuous form always in motion, animated by the wind. Its nature was as winsome as it was tempestuous, soothing with one breath and scorching with another. Cameron had been at sea for over a month now, and no two days had been the same. He saw periods of calm where the ocean was a mirror for the sun. He saw squalls that clotted the skies and dumped rain in buckets before vanishing over the horizon. And he saw fair winds that blew like a benediction from the gods. Whatever the weather, he stayed on the move, sometimes sailing with the engine off, sometimes with it on.

His timetable was loose, but his course was set. He had landed in the Azores on April 21 and uncorked the bottle of Bordeaux on a patch of sand as the sun sank into the sea. In a moment of inspiration, he took Cornelius's journal from his backpack and wrote his thoughts on a blank page in the form of a letter. He told Olivia about the flying fish and dolphins and cloud shapes he had seen. He told her how much he wished she could have seen them too, how much he missed her, how much he loved her. After draining the bottle, he rinsed it and placed the letter inside, then filled a third of it with sand, plugging the top with the cork.

After Flores Island, he had sailed to the Canaries. He topped off his tanks in Tenerife and restocked his refrigerator. Then he hired a local to drive him to the rim of the crater on Mount Teide. He climbed to the summit beneath a spotless sky, collected pumice in a jar, and then transferred it to the bottle of Lafite back at the port. He stayed on Tenerife for two days, catching up on sleep, and then set sail again along the course of the trade ships from centuries past, following the coast of West Africa toward Cape Verde.

The islands were out there in the wild deep, beyond the canyons of waves carved by the harmattan wind blowing off the deserts of Mauritania four hundred miles to the east. Cameron had never seen a wind like it. It was the spirit of the Sahara, superheating the atmosphere and draining it of every stray drop of moisture. The blazing current was so powerful, in fact, that the *Breakwater* was sailing at hull speed with two reefs in the mainsail. The anemometer had been pegged at twenty-five knots since the sunrise, and gusts had sent it above thirty.

Cameron was at the helm in shorts, a faded T-shirt, and aviator shades. The Beatles were crooning over the speakers, but he could barely hear them over the wind. His eyes were on the horizon, looking for a color other than blue. His charts said it should be there, but the dancing waves diminished his visibility. He waited and waited some more, the patience coming to him naturally now, worn in by nights and days of solitude.

Then he saw it—a yellow spar above the water. The cry erupted from his lips like from the mariners of old. "*Boa Vista!*" It was the easternmost island in the archipelago, christened by the Portuguese in their seafaring joy—"*boa vista!*" was the equivalent of "land ahoy!" He pointed the bow toward the leeward side of the island. When he passed the headlands near Sal Rei, the wind fell off to fifteen knots and the waves settled down. Beyond the jetty, the water flattened out, and Cameron started the engine, motoring into the harbor.

Three other sailboats were at anchor in the bay, along with a host of colorful fishing craft scattered near the shore. People were sunbathing on a rocky stretch of beach and swimming in the turquoise water, their skin a few shades lighter than Cameron's own. He watched the depth gauge until it dropped below twenty feet, then released the anchor and worked the throttle back and forth until the flukes held firmly in the sand.

He took out his iPhone and connected to a network. Then he went below and fired up his MacBook, checking his e-mail via satellite. There were thirty messages in his in-box, down from two hundred when he arrived in the Azores. The majority were from Anderson and Declan, legal matters that required his advice. One was from Noel, asking for an update and pictures. Another was from Vance with up-to-the-moment financial statements and a draft letter to the board. The most recent e-mail, however, sent Cameron reeling. It was from Josh Griswold and had been sent to his personal address. He opened it, cursing his trembling hands.

Cameron,

I have no idea where you are, but it's obvious you have no intention of returning until after May 16. What I don't understand is why. Why did you ask me to start this if you didn't want me to finish it? I can't believe it was all for nothing, but perhaps you never meant me to understand. Perhaps you just meant to use me. Perhaps you just meant to use Madison and Lewis. We're all adults. We will move on. But Sonia, Ashik, Jashel, and Alya are different. Their lives will forever be scarred by what they've experienced.

The court's decision aside, we both know the truth. Even if Presto doesn't control its suppliers, it bears responsibility for its supply chain. It's like food and medicine. If the ingredients are bad, it doesn't matter where they came from or who made them, only that the product that included them made people sick.

I believe you care about the plaintiffs. I know about what you did to save Alya from Siraj. But right now I don't know what to tell her. I don't know what to tell the others. I don't know what to tell my wife. I was hoping you could give me an idea. I was hoping you wouldn't just walk away like your company did. I think you're better than they are. But your disappearance has put that instinct to the test.

The question I can't answer is what I'm supposed to do now. I suspect you want the lawsuit to die. But I'm not sure I can let it go. Someone once told me that I had to prevail, that Presto had blood on its hands. I'm counting the cost of following through.

What do you think I should do, Counselor? What would you do?

Josh

Cameron stared at the screen, his stomach in knots. He remembered another moment like it, when he had watched from his office window as Lewis addressed the media, conjuring a spectacle nearly as dramatic as the Millennium fire itself. He didn't fault Josh for his zeal any more than he faulted Lewis. They were traits he had deliberately chosen in allies he had carefully selected. Yet for his mission to succeed, they had to concede. If they didn't, the whole plan he had worked two years to construct would fall apart.

He clenched his teeth so tightly they began to ache, and then he typed nine words. He couldn't believe he was doing this, but Josh had backed him into a corner. He had to reply. He stared at the message in anguish, then shook off his indecision and hit Send.

"Let it go," he wrote. "I have a plan. Trust me."

CHAPTER THREE

There was a reason it was called Painted Hill. Every spring the hilltop turned into a riot of color. The wildflowers were kaleidoscopic—black-eyed Susans, geraniums, violets, thistle, and spring beauties. Lily chased the rainbow like a leprechaun, dancing through the grass with her guidebook in hand. Josh and Madison watched her from the top of Old Man's Nose, delighting in her delight. After church, Lily had suggested a horseback ride, and Madison agreed, daring Josh with a look that said, *Any other response would be infantile, and we'd drag you along anyway.* So, of course, he acceded, playing nice with Tommy long enough to survive another ride up the mountain. He wasn't looking forward to the return trip.

"Sometimes I think she's just like any other kid," Madison said, picking at a clump of grass. "And then I remember how close we came to losing her." She took a breath and glanced at him. "Do you think she's going to be okay?"

Josh saw the vulnerability in his wife's eyes. "She's going to beat it," he said softly.

Madison reached out and touched his hand. "I can't imagine the world without her."

He slipped an arm around his wife and pulled her close. She was a gift, the avatar of his conscience and the lover of his soul. He woke up every day regretting what he had done to her and vowing he would never do it again. Yet its consequences were still haunting him. Maria's last e-mail was buried in his in-box, its twin beside it, sent a week ago when he didn't respond. He didn't know what to do. He wished he could ask Madison's advice, but that would require a confession he didn't want to make. He knew it might come to that. But there was still a chance he could pull this off without wounding her again.

"We're down to a week," Madison said. "We could ask the judge for an extension, but he won't grant it. He already gave us more time than anyone else would have."

Josh shook his head. "I keep hoping Ben will come to his senses and call me."

"That assumes Ben knows where he his."

"*Someone* knows where he is." Josh's hand moved to his pocket. Then he hesitated. Madison's rule was firm—no technology during family time. He gave her his most solicitous look. "Do you mind if I check my e-mail? Cameron might have sent a reply."

She let out a wry laugh. "Go ahead."

Finding Cameron's personal e-mail address had been a coup. Conlin had dredged it up. Josh had no idea how, but he had the good sense not to ask. He opened his in-box and held his breath. When he saw the general counsel's name at the top, a jolt of adrenaline shot through him. *Thank God!* he thought. Then, just as quickly, the letdown came.

"Shit," he muttered, holding the screen for her to see. "He wants us to quit."

"Bastard!" Madison erupted, loudly enough to startle Lily forty feet away.

"What is it, Mommy?" she called out, sounding worried.

Madison brought herself under control. "Nothing, sweetie," she said. She stood up on the rock, bleeding nervous energy. "We need to talk to my dad."

Josh grimaced. *Much obliged, Cameron. You just ruined a beautiful moment. One way or another, I'm going to return the favor.*

The grandfather clock tolled in the hallway as Lewis entered the parlor, his expression grave. Josh and Madison were waiting for him on the couch. He sat across from them and draped one leg over the other, ever the patrician, even in an earthquake, even at the epicenter of his rage.

"So Cameron has been leading us on," he said. "It was always a possibility, but I allowed myself to believe otherwise." Madison leaned forward, poised to speak, but Lewis gave her a look and she held her tongue. "Right now I don't feel like giving him the benefit of the doubt, but I will for his father's sake. Let's imagine he's telling the truth and has a plan. Let's imagine that plan has something to do with leveraging the fallout from the lawsuit to make changes inside Presto. I'm just spitballing, but if I'm in his shoes, that's what I'm thinking. Let's imagine that plan will go haywire if we name him in the complaint. I sympathize, but it doesn't change our obligations. We need something more before I can ask the plaintiffs to walk away from this."

"I'll be more than happy to tell him that," Josh said acerbically.

"E-mail is not going to cut it," Lewis rejoined. "We need a meeting." He slid his iPhone out of his pants and swiped the screen.

"What are you doing?" Madison asked.

"I'm doing what I've been thinking about for the past two weeks. I'm calling Ben."

Josh couldn't hide his astonishment. "You have his number in your contacts?"

Lewis smiled drolly. "Assuming he hasn't moved, yes. I didn't tell you before because I wanted to see how he would react to your story."

He put the phone on speaker and listened as the call went to voice mail. Halfway through the recorded message, Ben picked up.

"Hello?" he asked, sounding slightly disoriented. "Is that you, Lewis?"

"Hi, Ben," Lewis said, imbuing his voice with affection. "It's been too long."

"About seven years, I think," Ben replied. "Back in the days when I could still captivate an audience. Now I can barely get up the stairs. Getting old is a curse."

"I heard about Iris," Lewis continued. "I'm so sorry. She was a magnificent person."

Ben took a ponderous breath. "The best woman I ever met." The old professor paused, then presented his question with care. "So what can I do for you?"

Lewis spoke the words gently. "I'm calling about Cameron."

After a brief silence, Ben said, "I figured as much."

"We have to talk to him, Ben. If we don't, some bad things are going to happen. We don't want that any more than you do. But he's put us in a bind."

Ben snorted. "That damn company of his. I told him when he took the job that he was dancing with the devil. But he's got a brick on his head. He's never listened to me a day in his life."

Lewis waited a beat before saying, "I don't know about the past, but I believe he's trying to do the right thing now. I think that's what this is all about. But we can't ask our clients to drop the claims unless we talk to him. The filing deadline is in eight days."

"What makes you think I can help you?" Ben asked.

Lewis's lips spread into a thin smile. "Call it a hunch."

Ben grunted, then wheezed, as if he was laboring to stand. Josh heard scratching sounds and breathing, then a muffled thump, like he had set the phone down. A moment later, he heard the click of a mouse, then a series of keystrokes. Eventually Ben came back on the line.

"He has a sailboat, the *Breakwater*. He took it offshore about a month ago. He sent me a link to a website that gets satellite data from the boat. I've been watching him on Google Earth. Before I tell you where he is, I need you to promise me something."

"Anything, old friend," Lewis replied.

Ben's voice cracked with emotion. "Cameron and I have had more than our fair share of differences. But he's my son. If it comes down to it, I want you to trust him. I'm not asking you to throw away your case, just that you give him a chance to make this right."

Lewis gave Madison a triumphant look. "We will."

"He's in Cape Verde," Ben said, "an island called Boa Vista. He just arrived today."

Josh clenched his fists, scarcely able to contain his elation. Cape Verde was only five time zones away. He took out his phone to check on flights, even as Ben spoke a final word.

"When you see him, tell him I'd love to talk to him when this is all over."

CHAPTER FOUR

The old Toyota pickup bounced along the dirt track, its springs and struts groaning from the impact of potholes the size of craters. The blue-green ocean was in the distance, and at its edge lay Praia de Santa Monica, a great sweep of unspoiled sand that some had called the most beautiful beach in the world. Cameron was in the passenger seat, feeling the discomfort of the ride in every joint of his body. A gregarious young Cabo Verdean named Sergio was driving him. Cameron had found him in the town of Sal Rei, or, more accurately, Sergio had found Cameron, approaching him with a toothy grin and the offer of an island tour. On the trip to the beach, Sergio had introduced him to Cabo Verdean music, cranking up the volume until the truck rattled as much from the booming speakers as from the rutted ground.

In time they emerged from a thicket of scrub trees and crossed an expanse of dirt and sand dotted with colorful ground cover. The harmattan wind pressed against them, rocking the truck and howling through the open windows. When they reached the beach, Sergio gunned the engine, and the truck shot across white-gold sand as fine as salt. The gemstone sea stretched out before them. There was not a person to be seen for miles around.

Sergio stopped the truck and jumped out, trudging toward the shoreline. Cameron grabbed his backpack and followed, leaning into the wind and smiling without thought. His weeks at sea had retrained the muscles in his face, reminding him what it was like to discover happiness in unexpected places. At moments like this, he wished he could stay away forever. He had a home on the *Breakwater*. He had enough money to live out his life in comfort. He could keep sailing and leave the world behind. But, of course, he couldn't. The world would find him. And even if it didn't, he could never outrun his sense of responsibility.

He strolled toward the water and sat down on the sand, listening to the thunder of the pounding surf. He imagined Olivia sitting beside him in her bathing suit, Jackie O sunglasses on her face, her long ebony legs soaking in the sun. He imagined her smiling with him, telling him how good it was to see him so relaxed. *You're too serious*, she had said more times than he could count, and made it her mission to loosen him up. Whatever cheerfulness he possessed, it was her gift. God, how he missed her.

As Sergio dived into the waves, Cameron found a glass jar in his backpack and filled it with sand. Then he took out Cornelius's journal and opened to a dog-eared page. He read the passage reverently, drawing strength from his ancestor's pain and the clarity of his vision.

It was called Windover, and it was as pretentious as its name, the plantation house three stories high, with lofty ceilings and crystal chandeliers and a grand staircase that looked like it belonged in an English court. The handsome floors were heart of pine and once had been polished to a gleaming shine, or so I assumed. The whole place was haunted now, like a grave robbed of bones, weeping dust like blood.

I walked through the rooms and imagined the Fletcher family as they went about their affairs: John doing business in the parlor; his wife, Matilda, sharing tea with a neighbor on the porch; the boys running about in the yard. And then I pictured the slaves, seventy of them according to the ledger in Fletcher's desk—the butler and foreman and cooks and maids and farmhands. Her name was among them, as were the names of the children he stole from her arms. Esther Marshall. Born 1838 in Mississippi. Purchased 1851 in Atlanta for $1,135. It was a princely sum, a premium for her charms.

I climbed to the third story and found the bedroom she had described, the small room by the end of the banister, decorated simply with an iron bed and a wood chest and a table by the window with a view of the oak tree, beneath which five generations of

Fletchers were buried. I sat on the bed and dust rose up around me. It was there on that mattress where John had plundered the dignity of my dear departed wife that I shed my first tear, and my last. The house was a monument to the monstrous cruelty of an entire way of life. But by the mercy of God that way of life was gone. Now was the hour of its judgment. And judge it I did. I could not resist.

I poured out my venom on that place. I raised my fist into the air and gave voice to my pain. And then I left it behind, walking back the way I came, to the horse I had tied to a maple tree. Many roads stretched out before me, but all of them led to one place and one man, a man who had fled the advance of Sherman's cannons and taken shelter in the capital of the nation with men who would sooner grant amnesty to the slaveholders than justice to their former slaves. Those were the men I had to persuade with the ledger and the stories Esther had told me, the stories I have written in this diary. I did not know if I would be successful in my quest, but I knew one thing beyond peradventure—I had to try.

Cameron closed the journal and returned it to his backpack, zipping the pouch closed. Then he stood, took off his shirt, sandals, and sunglasses, and ran with the abandon of a man half his age into the surging arms of the sea. The waves pummeled him as he swam, but he didn't care. He was alive. His purposes were true. There was work to be done, justice to be served.

But not quite yet.

❀

Two hours later, Sergio returned Cameron to the port at Sal Rei. His dinghy was waiting where he left it, lashed to a piling on the dock. He climbed aboard and started the motor, thinking about the passage that awaited him tomorrow. At ninety nautical miles, it would take him no more than thirteen hours to reach Santiago, assuming the weather held. He would leave at sunrise and make landfall just after sunset. Santiago was his last stop in the islands and the launching point for a voyage that had lived in his imagination since he was a boy. He had never dreamed that he would make it, that he would sail the Middle Passage on the trail of his ancestors. But then he had read Cornelius's journal, and his future had come to him as if inspired.

The dinghy bounced across the bay, sending spray into the air and dousing Cameron's hot skin. The *Breakwater* was at anchor beyond a cluster of yachts, her hull gleaming in the sun. He approached the sailboat from behind and released the throttle, allowing the dinghy to glide to a stop by the ladder on the transom. After tying the line to a cleat, he opened the air cocks and allowed the bladders of the dinghy to deflate. Then he detached the motor and climbed into the cockpit of the sailboat, stowing it in a locker.

"Hello, Cameron."

Cameron whipped around and stared up in disbelief. The face was so unexpected, and the shock so deep, that for an excruciating moment his mind ceased to function. Then the moment passed and he recovered his composure. He sat down on the bench and looked back at the man, taking in the tousled curls, the day-old stubble on his cheeks, the soulful blue eyes.

"You found me," he said.

Josh Griswold stepped down from the rail. "I'm done playing games. We need to talk."

CHAPTER FIVE

Josh had waited an hour for Cameron to return. The wait gave him an opportunity to plan his surprise. He watched the dock through binoculars and saw Cameron start out across the bay. He stretched out along the beam and hid behind the rigging at the base of the mast. He felt like a prowler, but he didn't care. Cameron deserved it.

He listened to the motor and heard it cut off. He felt the sailboat rock as Cameron climbed aboard. He lifted himself into a crouch and stepped quietly along the rail, his heart thundering in his chest. When he reached the dodger, he waited a second or two, relishing the suspense. Then he spoke Cameron's name. Oh, the delight he took from the look on Cameron's face. For once he had the advantage.

"I'm done playing games," he said, stepping into the cockpit. "We need to talk."

Cameron shrugged his shoulders. "So talk. Out here, we have nothing but time."

Josh sat down on a bench. "But that's where you're wrong. You have six days to stop Lewis Ames from exposing you to the world."

Cameron's brow furrowed. "I thought that was your job."

"It's out of my control," Josh replied. "The lawsuit has taken on a life of its

303

own. The claims are legitimate. The plaintiffs should prevail. And the world should know the truth."

"The truth comes at a price the world is rarely willing to pay," Cameron said evenly.

Josh shook his head, irritated. "I'm not here for bromides. I'm here to make a deal."

Cameron smiled opaquely. "You said something like that the last time we met. Tell me, why should I negotiate with you? The law isn't just, but it *is* clear. Even if you name me in the complaint, you still can't answer the question of *when*. Here's some truth for you: I knew nothing about what was happening in our supply chain until after the fire. I didn't know about the problems in Malaysia and Jordan until later. If you plead that I did, you'll be staking your claim to a lie. And I can tell you from experience that Rusty Blackwell has a habit of turning groundless allegations into sanctions awards. If that's something you can live with, along with the disclosure of the documents I have, then be my guest. I'll resign from the company, transfer my assets to an offshore account, and stay out here permanently. Do you know how many nations lack extradition treaties with the United States? We're in one of them right now."

Josh's irritation escalated into anger. "If you do that, you'll lose everything. You'll tarnish your family's reputation. Your father will die in shame."

For the first time, Josh's words hit home. Cameron took a careworn breath. "You don't understand. I've lost everything already. As for my father, the world will always love him."

"I went to Boston," Josh said, pressing in relentlessly. "I met with him."

Cameron blinked. "I assumed as much. Only he and Vance knew where to find me."

Josh nodded, imbuing his appeal with all the passion in his heart. "He didn't help us right away. He took some convincing. And when he gave us your location, he made a request. He asked us to give you a chance to make this right. I don't want your name anywhere near the complaint. It's not just my marriage I'm concerned about. I respect what you did in coming to me. It was an act of profound moral courage. You have a plan. Great. I want to help you. But you have to let me. You can't do this on your own."

Cameron's gaze fell to the deck. "What exactly are you proposing?"

"I'm proposing that we settle the case *before* the deadline, confidentially, so that when May 17 comes it will look like the case just died. The press will walk away with nothing, but the plaintiffs won't. I didn't come with any authority, and I know you don't have any. But if you can convince your side, I'm sure I can convince mine."

Cameron pondered this as the waves lapped against the hull. Finally he said, "You would have made a fine lawyer. But your reasoning has a flaw. Presto never settles after a case is filed. It's a matter of company pride."

"This wouldn't *be* like any other settlement," Josh retorted. "We're talking about zero exposure. We won the media war. We'll fall on our sword in the courtroom. The plaintiffs don't want to get rich. They want to make a difference. So Presto doesn't like to settle. Fine. Make an exception. I doubt you'll see a case like this again."

Cameron stood abruptly, his face a mask of concentration. "I need some space," he said and walked forward along the rail to the foredeck. Josh sat back against the bench, playing the odds. There were dimensions of Cameron's thinking that went far beyond his understanding, the calculus of leverage inside the company, the personalities and vanities of Vance and the board, matters of finance and market viability and investor confidence. Frankly, Josh didn't understand how any general counsel of a multinational corporation kept his sanity. Yet if he knew anything about Cameron, it was that he could take the heat. The suffering he had experienced would have crippled most men. But he had allowed it to sharpen him, to turn him into a weapon. In spite of his anger, Josh admired that about him. He admired it immensely.

After a while, Cameron returned to the cockpit and spoke bluntly. "I'm willing to work toward a settlement, but only if we do another deal first."

Josh frowned, unsure what was coming. "I'm listening."

"Before I contacted you, I learned everything there is to know about you—your adoption, your parents, your education, the stories you wrote, the awards you won. I also learned about Madison and her family, and about Maria. I realized that your greatest strength is also your greatest weakness—your empathy. It's what makes you such a gifted storyteller. It's also what made you unfaithful. I hired someone to follow you when you went to Rio the last time. I had a hunch. It turned out I was right. A woman like Maria is hard to walk away from. But the photos made me angry. I would give *anything* to have what you have"—here, Cameron's voice faltered—"to be able to take back the mistake I made. But Madison deserves more than the part of you you've given her. She deserves all of you."

As Josh reeled, Cameron's eyes shined with feeling. "Here are my terms. If I'm going to walk through the fire with Presto, you're going to walk through the fire with your wife. Go home and tell her the truth. I'll talk to Vance and the board. If we burn, we'll burn together."

CHAPTER SIX

OFF LONG ISLAND

ANTIGUA AND BARBUDA

MAY 11, 2016

4:48 P.M.

The speedboat blazed across the water of Winthorpes Bay, its engine thrumming with a deep-throated growl. Cameron was hunched behind the windshield, his shirt and pants billowing in the slipstream. The last thirty hours had been madness. After an overnight voyage to Santiago, he'd barely had time to pack a duffel bag, pay the harbormaster to watch his sailboat, and catch a taxi to the airport. The Gulfstream had been waiting for him on the tarmac. The flight across the Atlantic had taken five hours. From the airport on Antigua, Cameron had hailed a taxi to the marina where Jenson, one of Vance's handymen, had collected him in Vance's Porsche-designed Fearless 28. The speedboat was more than a little ridiculous—it looked like a prop in a Bond film—but the adrenaline rush distracted Cameron from the fear of what he had to do.

Josh's appearance in Cape Verde had thrown all of his plans into jeopardy. Yet it wasn't the journalist's ultimatum that had astonished him the most; it was the deal he had proposed. In all his months of preparation, Cameron had never considered leveraging the lawsuit into a settlement prior to the dismissal of the complaint. He had expected to make his move after the dust had settled, to leverage the damage caused by the case and the threat of future litigation to press Vance and the board for systemic reform. The success of his gambit had never been guaranteed, but with the memory of the lawsuit fresh, the deck was stacked in his favor. The old guard had been weakened and the new guard emboldened. Then in a moment that still seemed surreal, Josh had tossed him a live grenade. The pin was gone, the explosion inevitable now. The only question was what Cameron would do with the blast.

The speedboat made a turn and rounded the tip of Long Island, heading toward Vance's villa on the north shore. Every May, Vance retreated here, leaving the rest of Presto gearing up for the annual meeting of the shareholders. In the years since Olivia's death, he had invited Cameron to join him, but Cameron had declined, unwilling to yield the reins for even a week.

Jenson pulled back the throttle and guided the boat to Vance's pier. After securing the lines, he helped Cameron onto the dock, then led him down a boardwalk and through a stand of palm trees. The villa beyond the palms was arranged in two wings with a swimming pool in between. A girl was sunbathing on a lounge chair, earbuds in her ears. She looked no older than sixteen. For an instant, Cameron felt the sting of indignation, thinking that Vance's libido had led him into forbidden territory. Then he saw her face.

"Is that Annalee?" he asked Jenson.

The captain spoke with the lilt of the islands. "Mr. Lawson brought her along this time."

Cameron was astounded by how much she had grown since the last time he saw her. She looked just like her mother now.

He gestured toward a cabana surrounded by flowering plants. "I'll wait out here," he said.

When Jenson disappeared into the house, Cameron climbed the steps to the cabana and sank into a plush armchair. He closed his eyes, wishing he could take a nap. Before long, a man in a servant's uniform brought him a coconut with a straw and a tray of sliced mango.

"Welcome to Antigua, Mr. Alexander," he said kindly. "I am Cecil. Will this be enough, or shall I have something more prepared? Dinner will be served at six."

Cameron took a sip of the milk. "It's perfect, thank you."

Cecil nodded. "Mr. Lawson just finished exercising. He will be out shortly."

Cameron ate the fruit and waited, his stomach churning with dread. In time, Vance appeared on the terrace and sauntered across the lawn. He was dressed in Bermuda shorts and a linen shirt, his feet bare and his skin tan.

"Look at you," he said with a smile. "No suit. No laptop. I barely recognize you."

Cameron stood up and embraced his friend, laughing as naturally as he could. "The sea has been good to me. I feel like a different person."

Vance sat down and reached for a piece of mango. "I'm glad you got away. I mean it. You deserved it more than anyone. But your six weeks aren't up yet. What's going on?"

"Annalee's growing up," Cameron said, deflecting Vance's question.

Vance laughed. "She's beautiful, isn't she? I bet half the boys in her school are trying to get into her pants. It's terrifying."

And a taste of your own medicine, Cameron thought. "Is it just the two of you here?"

Vance's eyes glinted with humor. "This week is hers. But when she goes home, I'm going to throw a party or two, bring some friends over from the mainland."

Cameron waited a beat, then chastised himself for dithering. There was no pleasant way to do this. It just had to be done. "Unfortunately, I don't think that's going to happen. Unless we act in the next five days, everything you've built will go down the drain."

Vance's smile faded. "What are you talking about?"

"You were right," Cameron said. "There's a mole in the company. But it isn't Declan."

Vance frowned. "Who is it then?"

Cameron returned his gaze without blinking. "It's me."

Vance reeled back, wounded and uncomprehending. "Please tell me you're kidding."

Cameron shook his head, riven by guilt and anger. "The lawsuit was my idea. I went to Josh Griswold. I gave him the names and told him what to do with them."

Vance launched to his feet and stared out at the water, the muscles in his cheeks twitching, his rage barely contained. "I feel like Julius Caesar. 'Et tu Brute?'"

"This was never about you," Cameron shot back. "It was about something so right that even a child could have seen it. Two years ago, a girl no different from Annalee jumped out of a burning factory wearing Presto's pants like a mask. You asked me to find out why. I did. I told you what we needed to do so it wouldn't happen again. But you walked away. The board walked away. The threat wasn't palpable enough. Well, it's palpable now."

Fury burned in Vance's eyes. "I can't believe I'm hearing this. Do you have *any idea* the harm you've done?"

Cameron stood up and gripped the railing. "I saw it all from the beginning. I just didn't realize how far they would go."

"Speak plainly, for God's sake."

So Cameron laid it out for him. "In five days, Lewis Ames is going to put my name in the complaint. I don't think it's enough, but I suspect the judge will let the case go forward. At that point, Donaldson and his allies will take down the board, and all of us will be out of a job. I'll be sued by the shareholders and investigated by the Justice Department. If I don't leave the country, I'll end up broke and behind bars. You'll be sued too, and hounded by the press. You'll never have another job like this. And Presto? By the time the jury delivers its verdict—which I guarantee will be massive—the company will be dead in the water. I doubt it will survive, even with restructuring. This wasn't my intention. I expected the lawsuit to fail. I expected the plaintiffs to walk away. But they're not going to, unlike us."

Vance let out a string of expletives. Then he lapsed into tense silence. "How much do they want?" he asked at last. "Whatever it is, I'll pay it."

"It's not just money they're after. They want change."

Vance rubbed his face, and the anger bled out of his skin until it seemed to turn gray. "So what you're saying is that they're giving you exactly what you want, except that this way *you* don't have to force the issue because *they* are. This is *unbelievable*."

Instead of answering, Cameron took out his iPhone and found the video. "I'm going to take a walk. I want you to watch something. It's not long. When I get back, I'm going to tell you how we can survive this, and then I'm going to ask you to take a leap. Right now it's hard for me to see, but underneath your arrogance and narcissism is the soul of a decent human being. I met him at Harvard, and he became my best friend. I saw him at the press conference last November—the man, not the CEO. I see him when you talk about Annalee. You need to dig deep and find him again. He's the only one who can save us now."

Cameron handed the phone to Vance. Then he turned around and left the cabana for the sand. He didn't know where he was going, but he didn't care, for the pain that had festered inside of him for so long—the pain of Olivia and his mother, the pain of Sonia and Jashel and Alya, the pain of Cornelius and Esther—had given birth to hope. In spite of his blindness, Vance had seen the truth. In risking his own future, Josh had offered Cameron the surest path to achieving what he had sought all along. Indeed, the solution Cameron saw taking shape before him was more permanent than the vaccine he had envisioned.

Josh had given Presto a chance at redemption.

When Cameron returned to the cabana, he found Vance slouching in his chair, head tilted to the side, staring listlessly at the sea. His friend looked chastened, even ashamed. Cameron's iPhone was on the table in front of him, Alya's face frozen on the screen, her dark eyes shining, her cheeks coated with tears. Cameron sat down across from him and waited for him to speak.

"Where did you get that?" Vance asked, pointing at the phone. The video Cameron had given him was an edited cut of the plaintiffs' personal stories, spoken in their own words with a voiceover in English. It was one of the most affecting things Cameron had ever seen.

"Josh Griswold gave it to me in Cape Verde," Cameron replied.

Vance sat up slowly and glared at Cameron. "I should fire you right now and sue you for everything but the shirt on your back. Doing anything else makes me an accomplice."

Cameron held his tongue. He knew Vance's dilemma, for it had been his own. There were hazards on all sides. To take any action was to invite mortal danger. But to do nothing was impossible. He studied his friend's face, saw the calculation in his eyes, the painful shape of his internal struggle. He watched for long seconds as the wind rustled the palms above them. He watched until Vance made his decision and Cameron knew he'd won.

"So what's your plan?" Vance asked darkly. "What's the leap I have to take?"

"You'll find out in California," Cameron answered.

Vance stared at him, perplexed. "What's in California?"

"Not what, who." A smile spread across Cameron's lips. "Stephen Carroll."

CHAPTER SEVEN

The lights were low in Lily's bedroom, her coterie of stuffed friends watching Josh from their perch in the bay window. Josh was conscious of them as he finished reading to Lily. He looked at them as Lily slid off the bed and went downstairs to take her medicine. Many of them were gifts from his travels, apologies expressed in the shapes of animals, real and imaginary. He recalled little of the occasions that had prompted them, but he remembered the sound of Lily's delight. Her joy had always lifted him, even when his marriage fell into shambles and Madison banished him from the house. Those months had been the loneliest of his life. He wanted desperately to leave them behind. But now he wondered if that was possible.

Soon, Lily returned with a water glass in hand. Her hair was still damp from her shower, her nine-year-old body clad in a cotton nightdress. She placed the glass on the nightstand and slipped under the covers. Josh pulled the comforter up to her chin and turned off the lamp. He sang to her then, a lullaby that had soothed her in early childhood. His voice wasn't good enough for bad karaoke, but Lily had never minded. His presence was all that mattered.

When the song ended, he kissed her forehead and brushed her hair with his fingers. "Good night, sweetie," he said softly. "I love you more than anything."

"I love you too, Daddy," she whispered, leaving him with the shadow of a smile.

He left the room and went downstairs, the century-old steps creaking beneath his weight. All was quiet in the farmhouse and on the cul-de-sac outside. Nights in the countryside were too quiet for Josh's taste, growing up as he had in the heart of the city, but this was Madison's place in the world, as much a part of her as if it had been woven into her DNA. Now that she was home, he knew she would never leave again.

She was on the couch when he found her, a copy of *The Atlantic* in her hands, her feet bare and curled under her, the light of a reading lamp burnishing her skin. She looked up at him and swung her feet to the floor, putting the magazine down.

"Are you okay?" he asked, seeing the pensive look in her eyes.

"I can't stop thinking about Cameron," she said. "Do you think he was ever going to tell us, or did he believe we'd just go quietly into the night?"

Josh sat down on an armchair and traced the lines of her face. She was more beautiful to him at forty-two than she had been in her twenties and thirties. The wrinkles that framed her eyelids when she smiled were like filigree on jewelry, the visible manifestation of love and time. He wanted nothing more than to protect her from what he had to say.

"He wanted me to convince you to walk away," Josh replied.

She gave him a peculiar look. "What do you mean? Did you promise him something?" When Josh said nothing, she took a sharp breath. "What did he have on you, Joshua?"

Josh looked down at the coffee table, his heart a chalice of guilt. "He knew something about Maria," he confessed. "She isn't gone. After the *O Globo* piece came out, her donors fled. She got desperate and came to me for help. My relationship with her was over, but I didn't know how to walk away from her girls. I was foolish. I agreed to meet with her one more time. I was headed to Peru for a story. I stopped over in Rio and she met me in the lobby of my hotel. I told her it had to stop—the e-mails, the texts, the pleas. She begged me not to leave. She kissed me. It didn't go further, but someone was watching with a camera. Cameron showed me pictures at the Lincoln Memorial. He also had the receipt of a wire transfer I made at Christmas. I don't know how he got it, but it doesn't matter. I sent Maria ten thousand dollars for the Casa. That was his leverage. If we ever went public about him, he'd return the favor."

Madison sat perfectly still, only her tears in motion. After the longest silence that Josh could remember, she found her voice. "I have some questions for you. Don't even think about lying to me. The only reason I'm holding it together is for that little girl upstairs." She choked up, then collected herself. "When did you last sleep with Maria?"

"The fall of 2010," Josh replied softly. "I told you that before."

"I don't believe you," Madison retorted. "There were galas, fund-raisers, and conferences here and in Brazil. I didn't always come with you. I can't believe nothing happened."

Josh shook his head slowly. "Nothing did."

"Did *she* want something to happen?"

"I don't know. We never talked about it."

Madison swallowed. "She did when the pictures were taken."

He nodded. "But I said no, and she left, and I haven't seen her since."

A moment passed into the void of all that was unspoken between them. Then Madison asked the question Josh feared the most. "Have you *talked* to her since then?"

He braced himself for her judgment. "Yes," he admitted. "Once on the phone, a few times over e-mail, always because she needed money for the Casa. I tried to ignore her, but she just kept coming back. Her last request came about a month ago. I haven't responded. I wanted to tell you before, but I didn't know how to do it."

Madison crossed her arms over her chest. "Joshua Griswold, I'm going to say something that is true whether you believe it or not. Maria is *not* your responsibility. Her girls are *not* your responsibility. We *are*." Again, Madison wavered. "You have to choose."

It was then that Josh broke down. "I choose *you*. But I know what's going to happen when I cut her off. She'll go back to the bars, and she'll take another girl, not because she wants to, but because it's the only way they can survive. If I can stop that, how can I walk away?"

Madison went to the nearest window and looked out at the night. Eventually she faced him again. "You can't save them. You could try, but you would fail. You have to let them go."

Josh stood from his chair and approached her hesitantly, looking into her eyes and seeing her strength and vulnerability. He loved her more than he could express. Whatever she needed him to do, he would do, even if it broke his heart.

"If I do that, will you forgive me?" he asked.

She sighed and turned away, staring at the floor. "I'm not sure."

Josh winced. "If you need time . . ."

"It's not that," she said, shaking her head sadly. "You promised not to hurt me again. I don't know if I can."

Lester Grant, Jim Dunavan, Paula DeMille, and Blake Conrad—the committee chairs whose assent to the plan would sway the rest of the board—was scheduled to start in five minutes.

"You remember before the press conference when I compared myself to Lincoln?" Vance said. "It was a preposterous thing to say. I owe you an apology. I should have listened to you that day on the sailboat. But I didn't want to deal with it. I wasn't ready."

Cameron met his friend's eyes, wondering at his conversion but comprehending it at the same time. Vance was a consummate businessman, a born winner, but underneath the suit and polish and accomplishments, he was a member of the human race. And Cameron, with Stephen Carroll's help, had given him a way to win that affirmed the whole package.

"You're ready now," Cameron said, glancing at the clock. "It's time."

They stood together, and Vance clapped Cameron on the shoulder. "We're going to make history today. I think Hank Carter would be proud."

Cameron smiled. "Damn straight."

❀

The boardroom was quiet when they entered it. The four directors were seated in their usual chairs on the far side of the long table, Lester first, then Jim, then Paula, and finally Blake. They were somber and serious, like the family at a funeral wake. Gone were the banter and small talk that usually preceded such meetings. Before them on the table were copies of the Black File memo Vance had sent along with his emergency summons. By their expressions, Cameron knew they had read it. Lester and Jim were indignant. Blake was troubled. Paula was intrigued.

"Thanks for coming on such short notice," Vance said, sitting down at the head of the table with Cameron beside him across from the other directors. "What we have to discuss today concerns nothing less than the future of this company. Last week plaintiffs' counsel in the *Hassan* case notified us that they intend to file an amended complaint. They also made a settlement offer. As all of you know, this company takes a dim view of settling lawsuits. But the plaintiffs gave us some additional information to encourage negotiations. The amended complaint will name one of our own as the instigator of the case."

"I knew it!" cried Jim Dunavan, pounding his hand on the table. "Who is it?"

"We don't know," Vance answered without a hitch. "Just that it's someone senior. They intended to keep the source a secret. But the judge's decision forced their hand."

The directors glanced at each other with sudden mistrust.

"Obviously this raises the stakes of the lawsuit immensely," Vance went on. "It also raises fundamental questions about the integrity of our leadership. Cameron and I think it would be prudent to conduct an internal investigation to find the whistleblower. If possible, we'd like to handle the matter in-house. Outside counsel would demoralize our employees."

"This is asinine," Lester spat, his porcelain cheeks purpled by anger. "I don't want some weasel from the legal department poking around in my e-mail. We all know who sympathizes with the other side." He looked down the table. "Paula, do you have something to tell us?"

"How dare you," Paula rejoined.

But Lester didn't relent. "We've sat here for years listening to your sanctimonious bullshit about corporate social responsibility. I want to know. Did you sell us out?"

Paula put her hands on the table like she was about to stand up. "I don't have to dignify this. Either we discuss this productively, or I'm resigning now."

"That's not necessary," Vance interjected. "Lester, you're out of line. Besides, it's highly unlikely that it's anyone in this room. If you're concerned about the legal department handling the investigation, we can bring in Rusty's team at Slade & Barrett."

"There's another possibility," Jim offered. "We could ask the plaintiffs to give us the name of the whistleblower as a settlement condition."

Cameron's breath caught in his throat. This was a twist he hadn't foreseen. He knew Lewis would never expose him. But the idea that Presto might demand it made him queasy.

"Cameron and I talked about that," Vance said quickly, "but plaintiffs' counsel made clear that the source's identity isn't on the table."

"*Everything's* on the table," Jim retorted. "We should discuss it with the full board."

At this point, Cameron broke his silence. Jim's idea was too dangerous to allow it to go any further. "With all due respect, plaintiffs' counsel said this point is *non*negotiable. They've given us a settlement framework. The terms are in the memo. If the board prefers, we can bring in outside counsel to find the turncoat, or Blake and I can manage the investigation ourselves." He glanced at

Blake and saw him nod, then locked eyes with Jim. "Unless, of course, you think one of us had something to do with it."

Jim wrinkled his nose and looked away, unwilling to accept Cameron's challenge.

Lester, however, was more brazen. He stared down the table. "Did you, Blake?"

"Of course not," Blake said heatedly.

In a blink, Lester focused his paranoia on Cameron. "How about you? After that fire, you made some sweeping recommendations. You told us if we didn't act, we'd be risking a lawsuit just like this. Now that I think about it, it seems like a hell of a coincidence."

It was a moment Cameron had been anticipating for two years. He answered cleanly, his expression unfazed. "I had nothing to do with it. But I have suspicions about who did."

Lester sat back, thrown off balance. "Who? Somebody in legal?"

"Until I have proof, I won't name names," Cameron replied. "But with Blake's help, I'm confident we can handle this quietly."

After a pause, the old banker shrugged bitterly. "Fine. Let's move on."

Thus, with a single riposte, Cameron succeeded in deflecting attention from himself and focusing it on a subordinate who would never be found. Declan was safe because he hadn't been involved. And Cameron was protected because all incriminating evidence had been destroyed. As of two days ago, he had a new personal e-mail address. His prior address had been hacked, and he had wiped it clean before closing the account—or so the story would go if anyone asked. His tracks, too, had been covered. After his meeting with Josh in Cape Verde, Lewis, at Josh's request, had reached out to Rusty with a settlement demand. Rusty, in turn, called Cameron on the water, and Cameron promised to inform Vance. It was only after Rusty's call that Cameron requisitioned the Gulfstream. The only loose end was Stephen Carroll, but Vance and Cameron had agreed upon an approach that would preempt an inquiry.

Vance took the helm again. "Let's talk about settlement. In light of the judge's decision, it's Cameron's view that an amended complaint naming a senior-level insider would stand a good chance of surviving judicial scrutiny, leaving us with the prospect of a searching discovery process and a very public trial. All of us know what that would mean."

"The funds would call for our heads," Jim remarked.

"Exactly," Vance affirmed. "The plaintiffs' ten-million-dollar demand is a drop in the bucket compared to the potential of a jury verdict. But the money isn't really what they're after. They want us to change the way we source our clothing. I have to confess, when I heard that, I felt like someone had put a gun to my head. But then I saw the silver lining. For some time, Cameron—at my behest—has been in conversation with Stephen Carroll. We went to him after the Millennium fire because times are changing. Our industry is in a vast shake-up, and it isn't just about Amazon anymore. It's the mood of the culture, what Carroll calls an epochal shift in the zeitgeist. Society is demanding greater transparency. More and more consumers are asking questions about the products they buy. This is especially true among Millennials. If we stand any chance of capturing their demographic, we have to appeal to their ethics. I've outlined Carroll's proposal in the memo. His investment would radically improve our market standing, especially with the litigation behind us. But his buy-in is contingent upon our decision to embrace a more aggressive vision of Presto's responsibility in the world. Over the years, a lot of people have argued that corporate citizenship is antithetical to the bottom line. Stephen is a living refutation of that argument. What he's suggesting is not an overhaul of our business, but a priority shift that would solidify our public reputation and boost our profits. By how much? I don't know, but Carroll's betting nearly ten billion dollars that he's right."

Vance held out his hands. "Comments?"

His first contender was Lester Grant. "Stephen's record is unassailable, but he's not God. I want to know what Rebecca Sinclair thinks about this."

Vance traded a look with Cameron. "Rebecca isn't privy to the settlement offer. But I talked with her yesterday about Carroll's proposal. She told me she had no interest in doing her job with one hand tied behind her back. She informed me that if the board votes in favor, she's going to tender her resignation."

Jim slapped the table again. "This is insane! We have a traitor in our midst. We have the *New York Times* calling for divestment. We have bossy money telling us to rearrange our face. And now the only person who knows the secret in the Presto sauce is threatening to quit. What kind of twilight zone is this?"

"I couldn't agree more," Lester said. "Without Rebecca, Presto doesn't have a chance. I can't support this. I say we roll the dice with the lawsuit."

"I couldn't *disagree* more," Paula said, swiveling toward Lester. "I think it's a once-in-a-lifetime opportunity. For over a generation, this industry has been defined by a dog-eat-dog race to the bottom. Carroll's not asking us to jump off a cliff here. He's asking us to break that cycle and start a race to the top. In

exchange, he's offering us ten billion dollars, along with his name and imprimatur. As far as I'm concerned, we'd be fools not to accept it."

Lester mumbled something that Cameron couldn't hear.

"If you mean it, say it out loud," Paula said, her face livid.

"I said, 'Bleeding heart bitch,'" Lester rejoined. "This company isn't a charity. If Bobby Carter were here, he'd put you in your place."

"Bobby Carter's world was the Land Before Time," Paula said, "and you, Lester
Grant, deserve to join him there. I want to talk to Stephen and see the financials."

Blake chimed in next. "Given the status of the lawsuit, the board would
be derelict not to give his offer proper consideration. Either way we vote, we'll
probably see a shareholder suit. I don't want a target on my back."

"Tim is finishing up the financials now," Vance said. "Stephen is with him. I
expect them any minute. But in the meantime, I want you all to see something."

On cue, Cameron turned on the television, switched off the lights, and lowered the shades over the windows, throwing the room into semidarkness.

"We received the video from plaintiffs' counsel," Vance went on. "It's what
the jury and the public will see if the case goes forward. If it comes to that, God
help us."

Vance touched his iPad, and Sonia Hassan appeared on the television. Her
doll-like face was tilted slightly forward, her eyes limpid as she looked in the general direction of the camera. She clasped her hands together and began to speak.
Her voice was quiet, just above a whisper, but the translator, a Bengali woman,
spoke with gentle yet melodious clarity.

"My name is Sonia," she said. "I was fifteen when the fire happened. I was
with my sister, Nasima, on the top floor. That night we were making pants for
Piccola. There were loud noises and shouting. The lights went out. Nasima led
me to a window where we could breathe. It was hot. People were screaming and
crying. Some of them jumped from the windows. Nasima put pants around my
face that helped me breathe. She made a rope out of pants and put it out the
window. She told me to climb down. The fire was on the stairs. I was afraid. I
didn't want to die. I climbed down like Nasima told me to do. Then I fell. That
is the end of my memory."

Cameron looked at Lester and Jim and Paula. All of them were overachievers
at or near the pinnacle of wildly successful careers. Yet as they listened to Sonia's
story, they were unmasked. Lester's face, seconds ago constipated by fury, had
gone slack. Jim and Blake were watching Sonia, spellbound. Paula was blinking
away tears.

Sonia rocked forward in her chair, then back again. "I can't see much any-more," she said. "I can see shapes. I know if it is light or dark. I hear nothing out of this ear." She touched her left cheek. "I feel pain sometimes, like my head is boiling. Then I have to sleep. I have dreams. I talk to my sister." The video cut again, and Sonia began to list to one side. "I wish I could be with Nasima," she said so softly that only her lips seemed to move. "I wish I had died. This is no life."

Cameron turned off the television and returned light to the room. Then he sat down and met Vance's eyes. *Go for the jugular*, he urged his friend silently. *Finish this.*

"So you see," the chief executive said, "the choice before us isn't theoretical. It's about telling this girl and our customers and the rest of the world that we care about how our products are made. Until now, we've pretended. But the jig is up. We don't get to pretend anymore."

The silence at the table was long and deep. Finally, Lester cleared his throat. "I don't like being put in a corner. But Stephen Carroll is a smart man. If he thinks there's a way out of this mess that doesn't compromise our integrity, I'm willing to listen."

Jim grunted his approval. "Let's hear what he has to say."

Vance smiled with his eyes and glanced triumphantly at Cameron. "That's all I ask."

CHAPTER NINE

The formal dining room at Painted Hill Farm had space for twelve. At holidays, when Madison's younger sisters brought their families to visit and Caroline whipped up a feast, the room was the hub of a bustling house, full of chatter and activity. Minutes before five o'clock on the day of the court's filing deadline, however, it was as quiet as a crypt. Madison was sitting at the head of the table, her MacBook in front of her, editing the amended complaint she had drafted just in case they needed it. Lewis was seated at the other end, reading a book and waiting for a call from DC. Josh was in the uncomfortable middle, scanning the news on his iPhone.

It had been four days since his confession, and his wife was still distant toward him. He had sent a reply to Maria the following morning, declining her request for help and wishing her the best. Writing it had pained him greatly, but he did it out of love for his family, and because he knew it was the only way to seal his good-bye. After sending it, he informed Madison, hoping to see a sign of warmth. But she showed no interest in granting him absolution.

Josh heard the trill of Lewis's phone and glanced at the clock. It was five o'clock exactly. Lewis answered and put the phone on speaker.

"Hi, Judge," he said casually. "How are you this afternoon?"

"A little older, but I can't complain," replied Judge Chandler. "I'm also curious. The last six weeks have been awfully quiet. I thought we'd hear some-thing from you."

Lewis gave Madison a half smile. "The deadline isn't until midnight, Your Honor."

"Of course," said the judge. "But I've never known you to wait until the last minute."

"This is an unusual case," Lewis replied, offering no elaboration.

Judge Chandler took an audible breath. "Well, I thought I'd call before I head home for the day. I'll be checking my e-mail."

The other corner of Lewis's mouth turned upward. "Sounds good, Judge."

"Lewis," said the judge, "I'm going to say something I'll probably never say again. If you bring me a complaint that would survive appeal, I'll throw the doors wide open to discovery. I don't know what you'll find, but I'd be fasci-nated to see it."

"I know you would, Your Honor," Lewis affirmed. "So would we."

"All right, then," said Judge Chandler reluctantly. "Have a good evening."

When Lewis put down the phone, he laughed. "We're never going to see a friendlier bench. It almost makes me regret the thought of settling this."

"The board may not give its consent," Madison said. "They're nearly out of time."

Lewis ran a hand through his silver hair. "If Cameron can play all of us like pieces on a chessboard, he can get to checkmate." He stood up. "I'm hungry. Your mom made us some chicken salad before she left. Why don't you stop messing with that thing and join me?"

Madison sighed, closing her computer. "Sorry. I'm just nervous."

Just then, Lewis's phone rang again. "Speak of the devil," he said and answered the call, putting the phone on the table. "Rusty, we were just talking about you."

"Lewis," rasped the defense lawyer, "I just sent you an e-mail with a counter-offer and a draft agreement. We couldn't get to ten million, but the board authorized seven. We want it to be paid into a trust, so there's no trace of payment from Presto to any of the plaintiffs. We also need a bulletproof non-disclosure agreement. They can't tell anyone that the money came from Presto. If they talk, we get the money back. Plain and simple."

While Rusty spoke, Madison accessed the e-mail and took the laptop to her father.

"I've got the document," Lewis said, scanning it quickly. "The counteroffer is acceptable. The trust won't be a problem. Neither will the nondisclosure agreement. They can tell their friends and family we took up a public collection for them. What about the rest of the terms?"

Rusty coughed twice, then wheezed heavily. "This is totally confidential—you didn't hear it from me—but the board is working on a major stock deal with Stephen Carroll. There's going to be an announcement at the shareholder meeting next month. Until then, I can't tell you more, but Cameron assured me you'll be happy."

Lewis looked at Madison, his blue eyes alive with delight. "I like how all of that sounds, but I don't see any of it in the agreement."

"We can't put it in writing," Rusty replied. "You're going to have to trust us on this. As a gesture of good faith, Presto would like to bring the plaintiffs to watch the live streaming of the shareholders' meeting from Vance Lawson's office. No one outside the board will be aware of your presence. The press can't get wind of this. I can't stress that enough."

Lewis took a breath, holding his exuberance in check. "I'll look over the agreement and get back to you with any changes. As soon as the language is set, we'll call Dhaka. Rana Jalil is over there now. We should be able to get signatures from all of the plaintiffs by midnight."

"Works for me," Rusty wheezed. He waited a beat. "Lewis, give it to me straight. Did one of Presto's senior people really betray the company?"

Lewis let out a wry laugh. "Now, why would I lie about something like that?"

"I don't know," Rusty replied with a chuckle. "Because I might have. Talk soon."

CHAPTER TEN

The doors to the executive elevator closed with a mechanized *whoosh*, sealing Cameron in mahogany and glass. He was alone, as he wished to be, the C-suite empty except for Vance, the rest of their colleagues already seated in the Carter Auditorium, listening to Kristin Raymond greet the shareholders. He closed his eyes as the elevator began its descent, thinking back to the day of the fire. He remembered the way Vance had been standing in his office, mesmerized by the sight of the flames. He remembered Vance pointing at the photo of Sonia on the screen. *It's going to go viral. The whole world is going to see it.* And the whole world had. One girl lying on a patch of dirt in a country many Americans couldn't place on a map had shaken a sixty-five-billion-dollar corporation to its foundations. For everyone in the Presto universe, there was the world before Sonia Hassan, and there was the world after her. Nothing would ever be the same.

When the elevator reached the garage, the doors slid open and Cameron saw the plaintiffs and their attorneys standing together, the men dressed in suits, the women—except Madison—clad in festive colors. He wasn't quite prepared for the wave of emotion that overcame him. He welcomed Josh and the lawyers by name—Lewis, Madison, Peter Chavez, John Remington, and Rana Jalil. Then he bent at the waist and greeted the plaintiffs.

Jashel was first. Cameron shook his hand firmly and nodded to the woman beside him. "Is this Farzana?" he asked as the woman looked at him shyly. "*Shagotom.*"

Ashik was next, and Sonia beside him. Cameron took the man's hand and shook it, then knelt and looked up into the girl's eyes. "*Shagotom,* Sonia."

Finally, he turned to Alya, who was holding a little boy in her arms. He smiled at her and she smiled back, tilting her head demurely in a gesture of gratitude. "It is good to see you again," he said in Bengali, pronouncing each word carefully.

"*Dhonnobad,*" she replied, and he understood. "Thank you."

He held out his hand toward the elevator. "Come. We don't have much time."

They piled in, and he pressed the button for the sixteenth floor, transporting them to the pinnacle of the tower. When the doors opened, he led them through the lobby and the lounge and down the wood-paneled hall to the corner office. Vance stood outside the double doors, dressed in a blue suit and silver tie, his hair freshly cut, and his eyes aglow with the magnetism that had drawn Cameron to him at Harvard and so many others to him through the years.

Vance escorted them into the office and offered the plaintiffs the couch. He and Cameron had rearranged the furniture in front of the TV screens on the wall and brought in additional chairs. When everyone was situated, Vance spoke from the cuff, with Rana translating.

"It's an honor to have you with us today. I said this once before, but I want to say it to you personally. On behalf of everyone at Presto, I'm truly sorry for everything you've suffered. I know words are not enough. They can't erase your memories. They can't change the past. But they can set this company on a new course. And that's what I'm about to do."

He took a remote out of his pocket and turned on one of the televisions. Kristin Raymond stood at the podium, the massive screen behind her displaying a highlight reel of victories from the past year—the opening of new stores in California and Washington, the LEED certification of the last of Presto's distribution centers, the carnival atmosphere on Black Friday, customer comments from Facebook and Twitter, selfies from Snapchat and Instagram.

"That's where I'll be in just a minute," Vance said. "I've given a lot of speeches in my life, but this is going to be different. It's going to make a huge splash, and not everyone is going to like it. But I'm convinced we're doing the right thing. I wish all of you the very best."

With that, Vance headed toward the door. Cameron had a quick aside with Josh, then caught up with the chief executive at the elevator. They stepped inside, and Vance pressed the button for the auditorium. Cameron stood at his side, fighting back tears. For reasons he couldn't fathom, his mind was alive with words from the past, words spoken by the people who had brought him into the world and by the woman who had held his heart in her hands. Ben, at Thanksgiving: *I know the boy I raised. He was a gentle boy, a sweet boy, with one of the most finely tuned moral compasses I have ever seen. He stood up for the powerless. He defended the weak. I don't believe that boy is gone.* Iris, on her deathbed: *I'm sorry for all the ways that life has hurt you. But I believe that goodness is waiting for you, if only you'll reach out and take it.* And Olivia, on the night she died: *It's time, Cameron. It's time to go.*

Vance touched his shoulder. "Are you okay?" he asked, a flash of worry in his eyes.

"I'm fine," Cameron said softly.

Vance faced the doors again. "Any pearls of wisdom before I address the mob?"

Cameron blinked and a thought came to him. He spoke the words from memory. "'With malice toward none, with charity for all, with firmness in the right as God gives us to see the right, let us strive on to finish the work we are in, to bind up the nation's wounds, to care for him who shall have borne the battle and for his widow and his orphan, to do all which may achieve and cherish a just and lasting peace.'"

Vance gave him a look that mixed curiosity and gravity. "Is that Lincoln?"

A smile spread across Cameron's face. "Now it's right."

CHAPTER ELEVEN

PRESTO TOWER, 16TH FLOOR

ARLINGTON, VIRGINIA

JUNE 10, 2016

10:18 P.M.

After Vance and Cameron departed, Josh took a moment to survey the chief executive's office. The baronial décor, dominated by reds and browns and dark leather and Oriental rugs, triggered something in his memory—the Harvard Club in New York. He hadn't been there in years, but he remembered it distinctly, all the lamps and sconces and portraits on the walls, the weight of privilege in every gilded frame. That was the world in which Vance had been reared, a world of mansions and servants and summer houses on Nantucket. He hadn't climbed his way to this lofty perch overlooking the Washington skyline as much as he had been born to it, in the same way that Lewis and Madison had been born to a lineage of social reformers and Cameron to a pedigree of Boston lawyers. It was the way of the world. But the world wasn't immutable. Things could change, as Vance himself was about to prove.

Josh looked at the plaintiffs and tried to imagine their thoughts as they sat in the corner office of the global headquarters of a company they had once known only through the clothes they made. Thanks to the settlement, they were all millionaires now, but the news of the payout and the trusts had left them more perplexed than anything else. After Rana had explained the details, they accepted the bewildering fact that they now had more money than anyone they knew in Bangladesh. Ashik had three wishes—to build a house large enough for his family, to obtain the best therapy for Sonia, and to give his sons the chance to attend university. Jashel planned to buy a dump truck and a backhoe and start an excavation company. He also intended to give Farzana many children. As for Alya, her greatest hope was to care for her mother and sisters, to offer Fazul all the advantages she had been denied, and perhaps one day to earn the right to manage Nadia Jalil's household. She had no interest in getting married. She had confessed that to Nadia over tea, and Nadia had shared it with Rana, and Rana with Josh, in a transcontinental daisy chain of humor. *If a woman is already happy*, Alya had said, *what good is a man?*

At twenty minutes after ten, Kristin Raymond wrapped up her retrospective and gave Vance a slick, spark plug introduction. As soon as she said his name, Vance walked out from behind the screen, a lavalier microphone millimeters from his cheek. He thanked Kristin and walked to the front of the stage amid boisterous applause. He smiled brilliantly, his teeth glistening beneath the lights, and waited for the applause to die down.

"You know, folks, I'm a lucky man. It's been seven years since I first stood on this stage, seven years since I got the call from Lester Grant offering me the chance to lead this great company. He told me then, in a way only he can, not to screw it up. For the past seven years we've grown our market share, we've expanded into new segments, we've figured out how to challenge Amazon, and we've proved the doubters wrong. But the excitement I feel about the past doesn't begin to compare with the excitement I feel about the future."

Vance reached into his pocket and took out his iPhone. "Anybody have one of these?" The crowd laughed. "Of course you do. That means you've seen the news. Everybody's talking about it. One hour ago, Stephen Carroll spent a little money—9.5 billion dollars, to be exact. The shares he bought? Presto! It's the largest single investment in the three decades this company has been listed on the New York Stock Exchange. In the last hour, the value of your shares increased by 15 percent. Not bad, eh?"

Vance paused while spontaneous cheers erupted from the audience. "As all of you know, Stephen doesn't just throw money around. He believes in Presto's future. And over the past month, with the guidance of the board, we have come up with a plan to make the future brighter than ever. Hank Carter founded this company on a simple idea: 'People First.' He did that by creating a store that offered Americans quality goods at prices no one could beat. He did it by creating a company that took care of its employees. He did it by creating the Presto Foundation to channel profits into charity. Over the years, the foundation has invested billions of dollars in improving communities across America."

Vance held out his hand toward the screen and focused the shareholders' attention on a slideshow of blue-shirted Presto volunteers cleaning up trash and planting trees and opening parks and escorting celebrities to hospitals to visit sick kids.

"All of this has made America a happier place. If Hank were still with us, he would be proud. But the world has changed a lot in fifty years. When he opened Presto's flagship store in 1963, there were only a few thousand products on the shelves, all sourced from North America and Europe. Today, we offer over a million products in stores and online, almost all of them sourced from the developing world—China, Vietnam, Bangladesh, Thailand, Malaysia, Jordan, the Philippines, the list goes on. The impact of Presto's business is no longer confined to the United States. Yet we have done little to improve communities in the countries where we send our orders. As of today, that is going to change."

Again, Vance gestured toward the screen as faces began to flash across it—garment workers in Bangladesh, toymakers in China, agricultural workers in California.

"As of today, 'People First' applies to everyone our business touches, from the people who shop at our stores to the people in over thirty countries who make products for us. Just last week I authorized a team from Atlas Risk Consulting to begin a project with extraordinary ramifications for our business. Over the course of the next three years, Atlas will create a map of our supply chains, showing where everything comes from. In clothing, that means the fibers, the thread, the textiles, and the finished garments. In toys, electronics, and furniture, that means component parts as well as final assembly."

Vance gave a self-deprecating shake of the head. "In this building, we know a lot about our business. But one thing we really don't know—how our products are being made. We aren't in the factories to see it. And when we send auditors, they report only a tiny fraction of what's going on. This isn't just true of Presto; this is true of our entire industry. We all have supplier codes of conduct. But our ignorance is vast. Labor groups, governments, and NGOs tell stories of abuse. We see fires and factory collapses. But we don't really know what's happening on the ground. That's going to change. Atlas is going to tell us the truth about our supply chains. They are going to help us place our orders more ethically. In addition, at the end of this year, we are going to publish our supplier list. We are going to tell our customers where we do business overseas. A few companies already do this. Kudos to them. Most don't. That's got to change."

Vance walked to the podium and took hold of it with his hands. "For years, Presto's brand promise has been 'Everything you need at the snap of your fingers.' Today that promise is expanding. We just launched a multimillion-dollar ad campaign rebranding Presto as the company 'outfitting a better world.' I told you about supply-chain mapping. As soon as that map is complete, we are going to launch our own fair-trade clothing label under a new brand we just trademarked—Elysium. Our goal is to maintain affordability while ensuring that the people making our garments are treated fairly. The faces you have seen behind me will soon appear in our stores. They've been invisible for far too long. As of today, they are part of our brand promise. With their help, and yours, we are going to redefine the term *responsible retailer*. And we are going to grow our bottom line. This is the future. I invite you to be a part of it."

The applause that followed was a far cry from the ovation that had greeted Vance when he took the stage. *The shareholders aren't convinced*, Josh thought.

Then something happened that took everyone by surprise. A man suddenly appeared behind Vance. He was clad in a gray suit a few shades darker than his combed-back hair, and his trademark smile was as welcoming as that of an old friend. Vance turned from the podium and took the man's hand, then held it up toward the shareholders in a gesture of solidarity.

It was Stephen Carroll.

As if a wand had been waved, the applause increased until it filled the room. The CEO and the billionaire stood there together for a long moment, enjoying the spotlight, then Carroll held up his hand and the shareholders grew quiet. He took a step forward and spoke into a lavalier microphone, his voice as resonant as his conviction.

"Since Vance started talking ten minutes ago, Presto's share price has climbed another four points." His eyes glinted with humor. "Maybe he should *keep* talking." Laughter rippled through the audience, and he greeted it with a chuckle of his own. "No, I've heard enough, and I bet you have too. Execution is all that matters now." He waited a beat, holding the shareholders in suspense, then delivered his valediction. "I'm here today because I believe in this company and I believe in all of you. We're on the right side of history."

When Vance and Carroll walked off the stage, Josh glanced at Madison and saw the soft smile on her lips. He matched it with one of his own. Then he stood and walked to the window, looking out at the monuments. Lewis came to stand next to him.

"Inspiring view," Josh said, making conversation.

Lewis grunted. "Ironic, actually. But I suppose Vance knows that now."

Josh didn't know what to say, so he said nothing, just stood there feeling like a fool and wondering what Lewis would do if he knew the whole truth about Maria. Apparently Madison hadn't told him. In that way, at least, she had shown Josh mercy.

Suddenly Lewis laughed. "You did a good thing here, Joshua. I don't know how much Presto is really going to change, but you've given it a chance." Lewis turned and opened his arms, his eyes glittering with feeling. "Come here, son. I'm glad you're in the family."

Josh stared at his father-in-law in surprise, then moved hesitantly into his embrace. He couldn't remember the last time Lewis had hugged him. The moment didn't linger, but it lasted long enough to convey Lewis's meaning. His father-in-law had forgiven him. Josh smiled. Perhaps one day Madison would forgive him too.

At that moment, Cameron strode into the office. "I'm sorry," he said, "but we have to move quickly. Follow me, please."

The general counsel shepherded the group to the elevator, then down to the garage and the caravan of four Chevy Suburbans that Presto had rented for the occasion. When everyone was seated inside and all the doors were closed, Cameron took Josh aside.

"This is for the plaintiffs," he said, handing Josh an unmarked white envelope. "Share it with them when the time is right." After Josh slid the envelope into his pocket, Cameron went on. "I've also got a proposition for you."

Josh gave him a humorous look. "The last time I took you up on something, I ended up bouncing around the world for a year and a half and spending all my money."

Cameron smirked. "Don't tell me it wasn't fun."

Josh laughed. "Fun doesn't pay the bills."

In a flash, Cameron grew serious. "Let me make it up to you then. The guys at Atlas are a little overwhelmed by what we've asked them to do. I thought maybe you could help them out."

"You want *me* to help with your supply-chain biopsy?" Josh asked, playing coy despite the excitement he felt. "Isn't that like giving your adversary the keys to the kingdom?"

Cameron put a hand on his shoulder. "We've always been on the same side. Besides, we need somebody to tell our story."

Josh was dumbstruck. "You want me to *write* about it?"

Cameron grinned mischievously. "It'll get a good reading from legal, but yes. There are a lot of doubters out there. The only way this works is if we turn them into believers."

When Josh started to smile, he found he couldn't stop. He put out his hand, and Cameron shook it. "You have yourself a deal."

CHAPTER TWELVE

The black sand was as sharp as pumice between Cameron's toes. Little remained of the five-hundred-year-old harbor except for a rocky stretch of beach framed by promontories that jutted out into the sea, taking the brunt of the wind. The waves rolling in off the Atlantic were three feet from crest to trough by the time they crashed onto the rocks. The *Breakwater* was anchored in the bay, pitching on the swells. If he had more time, Cameron would have taken a stroll through the streets of the old city, founded by the Portuguese at the dawn of the slave trade. But sunset was only an hour away, and he didn't trust the anchor to hold the sailboat much longer.

He knelt down and took the glass jar out of his backpack, filling it with sand. Then he put it away and opened his heart, imagining the harbor in 1761. He saw the English slave ship riding high in the water, its hold half-empty, waiting for the cargo it would take aboard in Guinea. He saw the captain bartering with the natives, trading bars of iron for rolls of cloth dyed with indigo and orchil, a native lichen. He saw the captain take an interest in one of the weavers, a teenage girl. The captain admired her while he handled the cloth. Then he spoke to her master and struck an unusual bargain. When he took the cloth, he took the girl with it. The tale was a mere footnote in Cornelius's journal, a legend handed down through the generations until Esther's mother had passed it along

335

to her. The girl was Amelia Marshall, Esther's first ancestor in America. After traversing the Middle Passage with a hold full of slaves, the captain had sold her to a planter named Marshall, a name she had taken for herself and given to those who came after, all children of slavery, until Esther had escaped and found her way to Boston and taken the name Alexander.

The journal was in Cameron's backpack, but he decided not to read from it today. He felt no sense of leisure in this place, only the urge to return to the sailboat. He walked across the sand to the dinghy waiting by the waterline. He searched for a break in the waves, then shoved the boat into the water and jumped aboard, dropping the motor and crossing the bay. When he climbed aboard the *Breakwater*, he stowed the dinghy and pointed the sailboat toward the open sea. As soon as he was clear of the land, he hoisted the sails and ran before the wind, his hands light on the helm, his eyes on the horizon, looking west toward home.

The sun fell quickly toward the sea, its haste a feature of the tropical latitudes. Cameron watched it from behind his sunglasses as the sails luffed and the deck moved beneath him. When the sunset drew near, he turned on the autopilot and went below to retrieve the bottle of Lafite, now as heavy as a brick with his collection of sands. He brought it up to the cockpit and loosened the cork, then took the jar from his backpack and poured the black sand into the bottle. When it was full, he reset the cork and carried the bottle forward to the pulpit. There he sat, one leg on either side of the bow, feeling the spray on his skin and the warmth of the dying light on his face.

As the sun touched the hem of the ocean, he conjured Olivia's face as she was on the last night of her life. He pictured her smile in the candlelight, heard her say the words, *We need to do this more often*, and heard himself agree. It was a promise they had made many times and broken just as often, the dream of a quieter life they never managed to make. When the sun fell beneath the waves, Cameron began to speak. He gave voice to the words he couldn't say at her funeral, the words that had been buried in him like a thorn since he heard she was gone.

"You were everything to me, Livie. You were my truest joy. You saw the best in me. I could search the whole world and never find another like you. I wish I could go back and tell myself not to get into the car, but I can't. Please, I beg of you, forgive me."

He held up the bottle and saw the letter he had written inside, lines of white occluded by sand. He kissed the rim as lovingly as if it were his wife's lips, then lifted the bottle over his head and cast it into the sea. It made a great splash and disappeared from sight. He closed his eyes and imagined it descending into the depths, through shades of blue and black, until at last it settled down on a bed of soft silt where it would remain until the end of days. Tears stung his eyes, but he didn't mind. For the first time in years, he felt peace.

"Good-bye, Olivia," he said. "I will always love you. Perhaps one day we'll meet again."

CHAPTER THIRTEEN

The guests started arriving at half past seven, parking their cars along the pebbled drive within walking distance of the house. There were twenty in all—seven staff members from CJA; four from Remington & Key; Peter Chavez and Rana Jalil; Jashel and Farzana; Alya and Fazul; and Ashik, Sonia, and Sonia's occupational therapist. They were the only people outside Presto who knew about the settlement. The media was still in the dark, despite the dogged persistence of a few reporters. Lewis and Cameron had headed them off, and eventually they tired of asking. The judge had been the hardest person to satisfy. He called Lewis again after the deadline passed and even made a trip out to the farm, entreating his old friend for a morsel to satisfy his curiosity. But Lewis stood firm, and in time the judge, too, left the matter alone.

The summer sky was dusky blue as the sun descended toward the horizon. The lawn behind the house was dressed as if for a wedding, with white tables spread out upon the grass, topped with floral centerpieces, flatware, and china; a dance floor beneath the limbs of a great oak tree; and string lights and lanterns and candles all around. Josh met the guests in the turnaround with Lily and directed them to the backyard, where Madison and Caroline were handing out drinks.

When the plaintiffs arrived, escorted by Rana and Peter Chavez, Lily gave

Sonia, Alya, and Farzana bracelets she had made with daisies from Caroline's flower bed. The women accepted the gifts with childlike delight. Josh marveled at their resilience. All of them had experienced enough anguish to make them bitter toward the world. Yet their eyes held no darkness, not tonight. Even Sonia, who could see the flowers only by touch, smiled brightly, giving Josh a glimpse of the effervescent girl she was before the fire.

Rana shook Josh's hand. "This is one gorgeous piece of earth."

Josh nodded and waved for everyone to follow him around the side of the house. "It's Arcadia. But I miss the city. If I spend too much time out here, I get restless."

Rana grinned. "From what Cameron said, that shouldn't be a problem."

Josh laughed. "I have to say, I never saw that one coming."

"What are you going to tell Tony? He's been pushing hard to get you a job."

"I talked to him yesterday. I told him I got a commission for a book. He was relieved. The editors didn't really want to bring me back." Josh paused. "So what are you going to do now? Go back to bagging fast-fashion bandits?"

Rana shook his head. "I'm going to find another Presto. Judge Chandler opened the door. Someone needs to walk through it."

Madison and Caroline welcomed them into the backyard with flutes of champagne and sparkling water. Josh watched as his wife embraced Sonia and Alya and spoke to them in halting Bengali. He caught Madison's eye and she smiled softly as Lily ran to her side. In the past two weeks, she had begun to warm to him again, engaging him in conversation and treating him like a member of the family. As the days passed, her smiles came easier, and she returned his spontaneous hug after the shareholders' meeting. The master bedroom was still off-limits, but every evening Josh grew more hopeful. He took a flute of champagne from her hand and kissed her on the cheek.

"You look gorgeous," he said.

"Shush," she replied, blushing beneath her makeup.

When everyone was assembled, Lewis spoke a few words, then pointed the way to buffet tables brimming with the fruits of the Virginia summer—beef tenderloin, Cornish game hens, heirloom-tomato salad, corn and bean succotash, watermelon—and an assortment of Bengali offerings prepared by an Indian restaurant in Charlottesville. With music wafting through the air, everyone ate with gusto, and Josh filled his stomach until he had no room to spare.

After dessert, Lewis stood at his seat and waited until the crowd grew quiet. "There are a lot of things in my heart at this moment, but I won't bore you with a speech. I just want to say that it has been an honor to work with all of you on this case, and especially with you, Ashik, Sonia, Jashel, and Alya. I can only imagine how disorienting this has been. But by coming here and showing people in this country that you are real, that your pain is real, you did something heroic. You not only brought a giant corporation to its knees, you brought it to repentance." He held up his glass, half-full of Chardonnay. "I salute you. We all salute you."

A chorus of voices rang out in agreement. "Hear, hear!"

When Lewis took his seat again, Rana stood up. "I have something to add. I've been talking with our Bangladeshi friends, and they'd like to do something special with the settlement money. From what we can tell, there were 604 workers who were injured or lost their lives in the Millennium fire. A lot of those families are now destitute. In a just world, the factory owner and the brands who made clothes there would have paid them compensation. Short of that, Ashik has proposed—and the others have agreed—to share the settlement with them. Each family will receive four lakh taka, or about five thousand dollars, from a foundation my mother set up. It's not enough to secure their future, but it will help them meet basic needs." Rana's eyes began to shine, and he held up his water glass. "To generosity."

Again, the crowd gave its approbation.

Finally, Josh stood and surveyed the faces around him, warmed by the glow of candles and lamplight. A wave of memories washed over him—Cameron at the Lincoln Memorial, Rana at Gladstones, Ashik and Sonia by the river in Kalma, Jashel fleeing the sweatshop at Class 5, Alya inviting them into her loft in Korail, Madison arguing before the court, the fire in Judge Chandler's eyes, Cameron on the sailboat in Cape Verde, and Vance on the stage, speaking with the zeal of the reformed. He tried to give order to his thoughts, to express them eloquently, but in the end the words tumbled out of him in a stream of consciousness.

"Very few of you know the whole story about how this came about, or where I was when it began. I've been a journalist my whole career. I've covered stories around the globe. Nothing compares with this. People talk about reversals of fortune. This defines the term. I want you to know how thankful I am for you"—he took a sharp breath—"how truly thankful. This case has given me a new lease on life. Without you, I don't know where I'd be." He raised his glass of wine. "So here's to second chances, clean slates, and friendships old and new. Cheers!"

Once again, everyone spoke with a single voice. "Hear, hear!"

Josh was about to sit down when he remembered something. "One more thing," he said, fishing in his jacket for the envelope. "This is from Cameron Alexander." He opened the flap and removed the contents. "There's a note here. It says, 'To Sonia, Jashel, and Alya: Vance and I thought your original request was more than fair.' With the note is a check for three million dollars." As the crowd gasped, he finished his thought. "There's a part of this story that many of you will never know. But I can honestly say, this is a good ending."

At last, Josh collapsed in his chair, his head swimming with feeling. Lily slipped her hand into his and squeezed. "Are you okay, Daddy? You're crying."

He wiped his eyes and smiled. "I've never been better. Are you having fun?"

She nodded with girlish delight. "This is the best party ever."

It was then that he heard the voice of Louis Armstrong rise above the chatter. He knew what he had to do. He turned to Madison and held out his hand. "Would you like to dance?"

Her eyes widened when she recognized the song. Then she blinked and began to smile. She took his hand and walked with him to the dance floor. The lights above them twinkled as he drew her close and began to sway with the music. It was the song they had danced to at their wedding—"What a Wonderful World." For precious seconds, Josh's universe compressed into two square feet of polished wood and a woman who stood almost as tall as he did, a woman he knew better than any other, who had allowed him to follow his dream and write for the world, who had borne him the most beautiful child and welcomed him home when he had lost his way. She nestled her head against his shoulder and held him tight. He felt her breath on his neck, smelled the scent of her perfume. His heart began to race and desire coursed through his body. It seemed impossible, but somehow he felt as if the clock of time had rewound itself and they were twenty-five again, and the pain of his betrayal wasn't just gone, it didn't exist, and the path before him was open, and the future was everything he had hoped it would be.

After a while, the song faded and blended into another, but they didn't leave the floor. It came to him then that there were others around them—Lewis with Caroline; Lily with Mark, a paralegal at CJA whom she secretly adored; Ashik with Sonia, holding her steady; and Jashel with a self-conscious Farzana. He glanced toward the tables, worried that Alya had been left out, but then he saw Rana at her side, asking her to dance. She put Fazul down, letting him scamper around the grass, and trailed Rana to the floor.

"Let's go," Madison whispered in his ear, taking his hand and leading him through the trees toward the barn. When they were alone, she said, "I have something to tell you." She searched his eyes in the dim light. "I had a talk with my father. I told him about the girls at Casa da Amizade. He's willing to help, but he has conditions."

Josh just stared at her, unable to comprehend the depth of her kindness.

"He'll handle everything," she went on. "You will never speak to Maria again. And you'll assign him all future royalties from *The End of Childhood*. It's only fair. That was her book as much as it was yours."

"Of course," he managed when he had collected his wits. "Does that mean—?"

She touched his lips to silence him. "That night in Bangladesh, I decided to trust you again. The last few weeks I've doubted my judgment. But I don't think I was wrong. I'm willing to give you one more chance. You remember the promise you made. Say it again."

He put his forehead against hers and spoke the words as a solemn pledge. "I'll never hurt you like that again."

"I believe you," she whispered. She lifted her chin and kissed him, then smiled with mischief and drew him toward the barn.

Boston

Thanksgiving Day 2016

BERKELEY PLACE

CAMBRIDGE, MASSACHUSETTS

NOVEMBER 24, 2016

4:01 P.M.

The afternoon was crisp and breezy and festooned with sunlight filtering through the branches of trees mostly bare. Cameron stood on the porch of his father's home and watched leaves skitter across the lane, then cartwheel into the sky, caught by a gust of wind. Noel had offered to collect him at the train station, but he declined and took a taxi instead, knowing that without his mother to run the kitchen, Justine needed all the help she could get. It was just as well. He was glad to have a few more minutes of silence before stepping into the joyous pandemonium of another Thanksgiving with his family.

The last five months had been a runaway train as the Atlas team launched its supply-chain mapping expedition, and Kristin Raymond and her communications team fielded endless media requests about Presto's new manifesto, and Vance did a tour of the Sunday-morning talk shows, and gave an interview to *Forbes*, and saw his face splashed on the cover of *Time* beside the caption: "The Iconoclast: Will the Poster Boy of Big Retail Inspire a New Industrial Revolution?" Cameron hadn't left the building before ten p.m., and when he had carved out a window of free time, he had spent it outfitting his new condo in Georgetown, two floors below Vance. He had made the decision to move a week after his return from the sea. The *Breakwater* had served him well, but it wasn't a permanent home, not if he intended to have guests over, and perhaps, when the time was right, to enjoy the company of a woman again.

After filling his lungs with refreshing air, Cameron opened the door and gave himself over to the task of socializing. His niece Rita Mae met him with a hug. "We're so happy you could come!" she exulted, her eyes glittering over dimpled cheeks.

His smile broadened. "How is it possible that you don't have a boyfriend yet?"

She laughed unself-consciously. "As Olivia used to say, 'The right man is worth the wait.'"

Cameron caught his breath, moved by the memory. "Good girl," he said softly.

Rita Mae took his coat and placed it in the closet, then drew him into the kitchen to greet Justine and Noel. He looked over the countertops, admiring the dishes that would soon grace the sideboard in the dining room. He took a pinch of stuffing with his fingers, and Noel swatted his hand. He grinned at her and followed Rita Mae into the family room, greeting the husbands and nephews. Then he turned toward the hearth and met his father's eyes.

"You don't need to get up," he said when Ben labored to stand.

"Nonsense," Ben replied gruffly. "What good are legs if you don't use them?"

When at last he creaked to his feet, his wrinkled face came alive and he shook Cameron's hand. "It's good to see you again, son. Thank you for making the trip."

Cameron touched his father's shoulder. "You're welcome. It's good to see you too."

"Here, Uncle Cameron," said Rita Mae, handing him a glass of Chardonnay. "You should ask Granddad about the book. It's coming out next spring."

So Cameron did, and his father beamed with pride and launched into a synopsis of *Hope Deferred, Hope Rekindled*, an autobiographical journey through the Civil Rights Movement, its tectonic cultural aftermath, and his many storied years teaching at Harvard Law. Little, Brown and Company had slated it for release in May. It was, as Ben put it, his magnum opus.

In time, Justine summoned the family to the dinner table. Cameron glanced at Olivia's old chair and felt the familiar ache. The guilt, however, was gone, washed away by the sea. He pictured her lovely face, and then, for reasons he couldn't discern, another face came to him—that of Kanya Nguyen, Presto's compliance director in Bangkok. The memory of her sent flutters through his stomach, much to his private embarrassment. But something else grew out of it, a sense of anticipation. After the New Year, he was scheduled to embark on a tour of Presto's offices with Adeline Wellman, Rebecca Sinclair's replacement. The Bangkok office would be their second stop. Perhaps, if Kanya was still unattached, he would buy her a drink.

After the family held hands and Ben said grace, they made their way through the line and piled food onto their plates. Their conversations over the meal were festive and uncomplicated, a spiderweb of stories from school and work and chatter about the recent presidential election.

Eventually Ben touched his fork to his wineglass and got their attention. "It gives me great joy to have all of you here. The only thing missing is my wife beside me. But I know she's with us in spirit. I see her love in all of your eyes. I thought we could do something in her honor. I want us to go around and say something we're thankful for. I'll start."

He fixed his eyes on Cameron, who stared back at him transfixed. "I'm thankful for my son. I'm thankful for the boy you once were and for the man you've become. I haven't always understood you. But this year has helped me appreciate you in a new way. I don't have a lot of time left to make it up to you. But I want you to know that I'm proud of you. That's it."

The astonishment at the table was evident in the silence. No one seemed to know exactly how to respond. Noel sniffled and wiped an eye. Rita Mae, who was sitting next to Cameron, squeezed his arm. Justine put her hand on her father's. The husbands fiddled with their napkins. The young people glanced around, hoping for someone to end the awkwardness.

Finally Cameron spoke, his gratitude undisguised. "Thanks, Dad. That means a lot."

At once, Ben cleared his throat and turned to Justine. "You're next."

Later that evening, when everyone but Ben was down in the basement watching a movie, Cameron slipped out and found his father in the study, a thick blanket draped over his legs, a space heater at his feet, and a mug of cider in his hand.

Ben looked up from the book he was reading. "I was just thinking of you," he said, gesturing toward the armchair next to him. "It's been awhile since we've talked."

"I'm sorry for that," Cameron replied, taking a seat. "I plan to visit more often."

Ben set his book aside and fixed Cameron with an inquisitive gaze. "I know there are things you can't tell me, but I'm going to say what I think. I think you settled the case. I think they used you as leverage, and you used it with Vance, and Vance turned the board. That's what I would have done, at least. But what I can't figure out is how you managed to turn Vance from a self-impressed egomaniac into a defender of workers in the developing world."

Cameron bit his lip, wishing for a moment he could cast off the mantle of general counsel and tell his father the whole story. But he couldn't. So he did the next best thing. "People are complex. There's more to Vance than meets the eye. He has a daughter he loves. He has a creed he believes in—that private enterprise is one of the most productive forces in society. I happen to think he's right. He just needed to give that vision a broader frame."

Ben's eyes glistened behind his wire-rimmed glasses. "I imagine Stephen Carroll's buy-in helped. Was it you who charmed the billionaire?"

Cameron said nothing, allowing a half smile to convey his answer.

"Damn," Ben said, shaking his head in wonderment. "I've got one more question for you, and I don't think it's out of bounds. What made you do it? What made you go to Joshua? I don't care how I felt, I don't think I would have had the guts to put myself on the line like that."

Cameron nodded and stood, part of the answer a few steps away. He found his briefcase in the entryway closet, Cornelius's journal in the back pocket. He took it out and ran his thumb over the cracked cover. He remembered the way his father had given it to him outside his mother's room hours before she died. He remembered reading it by the window and seeing the path charted out for him in the footsteps of his ancestor, not the details, but the shape of the quest. The book had taken him to a place far beyond himself, and he had made it his own, smudging the pages with his fingers, stretching the fraying spine. But it didn't belong to him. It belonged in this house. He had brought it home.

He returned to the study and handed the journal to his father.

"I remember this," Ben said, examining it. "I never read it. I take it you want me to now."

"Just the last paragraph," Cameron said and watched his father turn the pages. "He wrote it after Esther's death, after he had found the man who had last enslaved her holed up like a fugitive in DC and sued him for reparations. The judge laughed him out of court."

Ben regarded Cameron over his glasses, his look rich with poignant feeling. Then he began to read out loud.

"When I left the courthouse clutching nothing but the skin of my fist and the rage curled up like a stillborn child in my heart, I looked out across the city and saw the truth. Even if the judge had hearkened to my plea and granted Esther justice, it would not have been enough to satisfy the demands of men, let alone God. Even if the scales fell from the eyes of all the courts of this nation and they handed down judgments in favor of every newly freed slave, forcing their former masters to pay them honest wages for all the years of their toil, it would not be enough. For the debt of slavery is stitched into the fabric of this great land, from the hallowed halls of Congress to the New York Stock and Exchange Board to the textile factories and clothing shops in my own beloved Boston. This whole country has been enriched by the blood and sweat of the slave. We have reaped the harvest and enjoyed its fruit, ignoring the fact that it is a harvest of thorns. The very shirt on my back was stitched with cotton fibers harvested from southern plantations. All of us are implicated in our nation's sin. What are we to do with this? What am I to do? What would it take to right this wrong? The world would have to be made anew. And so I say with the prophet Amos words written about the last days. 'Let justice roll down like waters, and righteousness like a mighty stream.'"

By the time Ben stopped reading, his voice had dropped from its resonant pitch to a half whisper, and tears had formed in his tired eyes. He closed the journal gently and cradled it in his lap, breathing in and out, his musings beyond reckoning. He looked Cameron in the eye. "That boy I raised, he never left, did he?"

Cameron shook his head slowly, saying the words that came to him like the blessing he intended. "Whatever I am, whatever good I have done, I learned at your feet."

Ben's tears fell down his whiskered cheeks. He grasped the arms of his chair and levered himself to his feet, shrugging off Cameron's attempt to stabilize him. When at last he stood at full height, he stepped toward Cameron and embraced him with the full force of his waning strength. In Cameron's fifty-four years, he had no recollection of such a moment—not the hug, for there had been others, but the acceptance and devotion it expressed. It was as if Ben had finally claimed him as his own, the son of his flesh, the firstborn of the line that would come after him, and heir to his call as a servant of the law, a servant of mankind.

When Ben let him go, he was as vulnerable as Cameron had ever seen him. He gathered himself and grunted. "I love you, son. It's been too long since I said that."

Cameron closed his eyes, knowing his father meant it. Then he opened them again and spoke his own benediction, his soul finally at rest in his own home.

"I love you too, Dad."

AUTHOR'S NOTE

On November 24, 2012, a fire broke out on the ground floor of the Tazreen Fashions factory in Dhaka, Bangladesh, and quickly spread up the stairwell, cutting off the only safe escape route available to the more than sixteen hundred workers laboring overtime at their machines to fulfill a last-minute order. The eight-story building had no fire escapes, no emergency exits. Its corridors were littered with fabric. When the workers heard the alarm, they had nowhere to go except to the windows, which were blocked by iron bars, cloth netting, and panes of glass. Eventually the lights went out and the factory was plunged into darkness.

With the fire raging in the stairwell, many workers made the fateful decision to break through the barricades on the windows and leap into the abyss. Some workers were impaled on the bars and cut by the glass. Others died in the fall. Still others survived with permanent disabilities. According to official reports, at least one hundred seventeen workers perished that night, and over two hundred were injured. But many bodies remained unclaimed and were buried without a name—likely villagers whose families were not in the city to identify them.

Before the dust had settled, a public-relations battle broke out between the media and Walmart, the world's largest retailer. Despite an attempt by the factory owner to shutter the site, the press confirmed that clothes destined for Walmart stores were inside the factory when the fire started. Walmart, however, claimed that Tazreen was no longer an authorized supplier and blamed another supplier for sending orders to Tazreen without its approval. When the *New York Times* reported that multiple Walmart suppliers had been sending orders to Tazreen over the past year, Walmart pleaded ignorance and denied responsibility. (The *Times* also claimed that Tazreen had been making clothing for Sears at the time of the fire. Sears made similar denials.)

In March of 2015, I traveled to Bangladesh and met a group of Tazreen survivors not far from the burned-out factory. I will never forget the stories they told me: the way they felt when they realized they had no way out; the work it took to break the windows and dislodge the bars; the thoughts that passed through their minds before they jumped; and the miraculous ways they survived—falling through roofs that cushioned the impact, landing on bodies that were softer than the ground. They also described the extent of their injuries. One young woman who broke her back in the fall was about to be evicted from her home because she could no longer pay rent. Another woman who cracked her skull had episodes every day in which her head felt like boiling water. A third had a broken back, neck, and skull. A fourth had an injured back and a dislocated hand. None of these women could work again. All were desperately poor.

When I asked if anyone had offered them compensation for medical expenses and basic needs, they told me the shocking truth. Apart from individual gifts from the nonprofit Caritas and the buying agency, Li & Fung, they had received no compensation from the factory owner or the brands that sourced clothing from Tazreen. A well meaning non-profit had given each of them a manual sewing machine, but for those with permanent disabilities, the gift was impractical. One of the women told me she was using the sewing machine as a coffee table.

Gratefully, this unconscionable situation changed in September of 2015 when a group of brands and civil society organizations joined forces to create the Tazreen Claims Administration Trust. Spearheaded by the ILO, the brand C&A, the C&A Foundation, the IndustriALL Global Union, and the Clean Clothes Campaign, the TCA was modeled after the compensation scheme developed in the wake of the Rana Plaza factory collapse. By the end of 2016, the TCA had paid out $2.17 million to 582 Tazreen beneficiaries. Regrettably, since this assistance did not arrive until three years after the fire, it was too late to help many of the victims with the worst injuries.

After I listened to the women tell me their stories, I asked them to name the brands whose clothes they had made at Tazreen. They reeled off a laundry list of major American and European labels. I asked them whose clothes they were making on the night of the fire. All of them said, "Walmart." The fire happened on a holiday. The workers were only there after hours because they had to finish a last-minute order for Walmart. I asked them how they could be sure. They told me they knew all of the buyers. They said Walmart's buyer was in the factory until lunch that day.

Given the complexity of the global apparel industry, they may have been partially mistaken. The buyer they saw might have been an *agent* of Walmart's, not an employee. The buyer might also have been a representative of Walmart's primary supplier. Indeed, Walmart's sourcing team may have sent the original order to a different supplier and that supplier may have subcontracted the order to Tazreen without Walmart's permission, just as the company later claimed in the media. Nevertheless, the stories I heard at Tazreen coupled with the reporting I read in the *New York Times* shaped the novel I was developing. I came away from my visit with more questions than answers. I talked to a long list of experts—garment workers, factory owners and managers, auditors, buying agents, journalists, lawyers, activists, and academics— trying to understand how it was possible that clothes destined for the US market (for stores my family and I shop in) could be made under such awful conditions and then, when disaster struck, disavowed by the brands whose labels were on them.

In my research, I learned something truly disturbing. Most of the clothing offered for sale in North America and Europe comes from what Sarah Labowitz at NYU called the "Independent Republic of Global Supply Chains," which means that nobody really knows how it is made or by whom or under what conditions. It's possible that the sweater I'm wearing right now was made by a slave. My shirt could have been made in a sweatshop by a young teenager working eighty-hour weeks. My pants could have been made by a girl whose manager raped her. My shoes might have been made in a factory about to collapse or erupt in flames. As consumers, we're in the dark. And so are the brands we trust. Or so they claim. A number of people with deep insight into the industry told me that the brands know more than they let on. But the extent of their knowledge is a mystery. Most corporations protect their secrets like the NSA guards its ciphers.

At this point, I should make one thing clear. Presto Omnishops Corporation is not a fictional rendition of a real company. It is a product of my imagination. Nevertheless, my description of Presto's business model and practices, the mind-set of its executives and directors, its sourcing methodology, the tension between its sourcing and compliance departments, and the perverse incentives built into the system is based on my research around the world. In writing *A Harvest of Thorns*, I hoped to raise questions about the soul of the global economy, about the responsibility and irresponsibility of global business, and about the need for companies, investors, governments and consumers alike to take proactive measures to ensure that the products offered for sale in our markets are being made under conditions that any decent person would consider humane.

Since the book was released in January, 2017, I have heard one question more than any other from readers: How can we tell the difference between brands that are sourcing ethically and those that are playing fast and loose with worker rights and the environment? I wish I had a definitive answer to that question, but I don't. A chasm exists between how brands actually behave and what they tell the public. The best we can do is rate them by a proxy standard—transparency—which assesses their willingness to submit their internal policies and practices to public scrutiny. Groups like Know the Chain and Fashion Revolution have created transparency benchmarks that show how the brands stack up. You can find these benchmarks online at: https://knowthechain.org/benchmarks/3/ and www.fashionrevolution.org/about/transparency. Unfortunately, a brand's commitment to transparency says little about its business model. Some fast fashion companies are quite transparent, yet their cutthroat approach to sourcing encourages exploitation at the supplier level.

In addition to the transparency benchmarks, I have three tips for conscientious consumers. The first is a list of companies I admire based on my own research. I can't guarantee that the products sold by these companies are free of the kinds of abuse revealed in this story. (Almost no brand can make such a guarantee.) But all of these companies have responded to the societal call for greater corporate responsibility by improving their internal processes and sourcing strategies, by working with their suppliers to eliminate the worst forms of labor abuse, and, in some cases (though not nearly enough), by advocating that the workers making products in their supply chains be paid a living wage, not just the minimum wage required by local law.

Patagonia is the gold standard for social responsibility in apparel. They have numerous lines that are Fair Trade certified; they are working to map their supply chains down to the raw material level; and they are remarkably candid about the challenges they have faced in cleansing their supply chains of forced labor. Indeed, when they found evidence of forced labor in the Taiwanese mills fabricating their material, they went to *The Atlantic* and made the challenge public. There are also a host of smaller, socially conscious brands like Eileen Fisher, PACT, Everlane, Prana, and Visible. Clothing lines one can shop with particular confidence. For a curated list, check out Remake.world.

Among the sporting giants, Adidas is the standout. It consistently garners the highest transparency ratings among major brands; it has the respect of watchdog organizations; and it is working hard to end forced labor in its supply chains. In addition, Nike has developed an impressive reputation for social responsibility in recent years, an about-face from the challenges it faced in the 1990s.

Of the mid-tier brands, Gap, Inc. (which owns Banana Republic, Gap, Old Navy, Athleta, and Piperlime) has made commendable strides toward eliminating forced labor and abuse from its supply chains. I have reservations about Old Navy's fast fashion business model, just as I have reservations about European fast fashion brands like H&M and Zara. (For a more in-depth exposé of the fast fashion industry as a whole, check out Lucy Siegle's groundbreaking book, *To Die For*, and the excellent documentary, *The True Cost*.) As a company, however, Gap rates highly on the transparency benchmarks, and its people have impressed me with their commitment to responsible sourcing.

With respect to the big discounters, Target is head and shoulders above the rest. The company recently launched a line of Fair Trade clothing (and has plans to expand it); the Chinese wall between sourcing and compliance doesn't exist at Target; and it has some incredible people working to combat forced labor and other forms of abuse at the supplier level.

My second tip is a rule of thumb. If a deal looks too good to be true, it probably is. Brands are in business to make a profit. If a store's prices are so low that you wonder how the company could possibly be making money, the answer could be exploitation.

Third, avoid the lures of fast fashion. Buy fewer items and invest in higher quality workmanship. Purchase beautiful clothes you will be proud to wear over time. If we truly want to clean up fashion supply chains, we need to wean ourselves from our cultural addiction to mass quantities of cheap merchandise. We need to revolutionize fashion in the way we have revolutionized food. We need to slow fashion down. Twenty years ago, the Big Mac was all the rage. Now, McDonalds is selling kale salad and fighting to compete with Chipotle. I am convinced we can do the same with clothing. But it won't happen unless all of us do our part. Will you join us?

Corban Addison
September 2016

ACKNOWLEDGMENTS

As with all my novels, I never could have written *A Harvest of Thorns* without the steadfast love and patience of my wife, Marcy, and the generous support of a battalion of friends who gave me time on the phone and online, fielded my endless questions, made strategic connections for me, and offered me assistance in my research overseas. If I have learned anything in my eight-year journey of writing stories about injustice, it is that the world, despite its sometimes grotesque ugliness, is also brimming with kindness. It never ceases to amaze me when people I have never met welcome me into their circles, open doors for me, and put their safety on the line to help me get my stories right. I am truly honored and humbled by their friendship.

In the United States, I wish to thank Michael Shively at ABT Associates for your insights into labor trafficking and excellent research ideas; John Grisham for making connections and critiquing the manuscript; Mary Bauer at Legal Aid Charlottesville, Dan Werner at the Southern Poverty Law Center, and Gus May at Bet Tzedeck for educating me about human trafficking and labor litigation in US courts; Shawn MacDonald and Quinn Kepes at Verité for giving me a glimpse into the underside of global supply chains; Barbara Briggs at the Institute for Global Labour and Human Rights for offering me insight into the misbehavior of suppliers and brands in Bangladesh and Jordan; Ben Skinner for opening doors for me in Bangladesh, opening my eyes to the role of activist investors in driving corporate change, and being such a steadfast champion for the book; Sarah Labowitz at NYU's Stern School of Business, Justin Dillon at Made in a Free World, and Steven Greenhouse at the *New York Times* for educating me about business and human rights; Peter, Ida, and Brandon Caramanis for sharing with me your family's experiences with childhood leukemia; and Blaec Kalweit at Sunshine Sachs for your insights into PR campaigns in times of corporate crisis.

In Malaysia, I wish to thank Scott, Palm, and Barbara Feist for hosting me in Kuala Lumpur, and for your friendship; Dr. Kian Ming Ong for your insights into the politics of human rights in Malaysia; Soo Choo and Aegile Fernandez at Tenaganita for your generous support during my time in KL; Ashik Khan for escorting me to Cheras and for your insights into forced labor in the Malaysian apparel industry; Kabita Upreti for sharing your stories about life on the sewing line, Hari Budhathoki for translating, and Shirley Tan for arranging the interview; the Bangladeshi garment workers in Cheras for opening your hostel to me; Harun Al-Rashid at CARAM Asia for talking to me about labor abuses in the apparel industry in Southwest and Southeast Asia; and Sahul Hamid Bin Hussain, Haji Badul Nasser Bin Abd Hamid, and Mohamad Fauzi Ibrahim of the Malaysian Trades Union Congress, Penang Division, for your insights into the role of labor unions and their leaders in cleaning up global supply chains.

In Bangladesh, I wish to thank Sharif Alam for being a fabulous fixer; the women of Tazreen for sharing your stories from the fire and showing me the true face of courage; Khalilur Rahman Sohel of Bureau Veritas for your insights into factory fire safety and auditing; Rana Farhad, Olilur Rahman, Sadaf Saaz Sidiqqi, and Rubana Huq for your expertise in so many areas of the Bangladesh apparel industry; K. Anis Ahmed for making critical connections for me and embodying the spirit of corporate social responsibility; and Faruque Ahmed of Warbe for sharing with me the challenges confronted by Bangladeshi migrant workers laboring abroad.

In Jordan, I wish to thank Phillip Fishman and Nisreen Bathish of the ILO's Better Work Jordan program for an overview of the Jordanian apparel industry; and Linda Al-Kalash of Tamkeen for talking with me about the way factories, brands, and auditors operate in Jordan.

Finally, I wish to thank my tireless agents, Dan Raines at Creative Trust, Danny Baror at Baror International, and Brian Lipson at Intellectual Property Group, for believing in me and my work and for representing me with such zeal. I am honored to have you as friends and mentors. To my publishers in North America and the UK, Daisy Hutton and Doug Richmond at HarperCollins and Jane Wood at Quercus, I am ever grateful for the passion you bring to my stories. And to my publishers around the world, thank you for getting my words into the hands of readers. Every book I write is a chapter in my life and a piece of my heart. I am so grateful for the tender way all of you hold it, and care for it, and bring out the shine.

DISCUSSION QUESTIONS

1. In the opening chapters of the story, Cameron travels to Bangladesh and meets with Habib Khan, owner of Rahmani Apparel. After being caught in a lie, Habib confesses to Cameron that he colluded with Presto's local office director in subcontracting part of the order to Millennium in violation of Presto's Code of Conduct. By way of explanation, Habib tells Cameron about the dilemma he faces. His profits are falling. His competitors outside Bangladesh are undercutting him with superior technology, cheaper labor, and vertical integration. At the same time, Presto is demanding lower prices and faster turnarounds, or it will take its orders elsewhere. In this environment, he has no choice but to agree to Presto's terms and then to find a way to deliver. What does this dilemma reveal about the power dynamics within the global fashion industry? In your mind, which party (a supplier like Rahmani, or a brand like Presto) bears more responsibility for working conditions and worker safety at the factory level?

2. In Josh's meeting with Tony Sharif in Washington, DC, Tony introduces Josh to Rana Jalil. As Tony puts it, Rana is shining a light into the dark hole of American fast fashion. When Josh asks for an explanation, Tony expounds: "You know those teeny bopper stores in the mall, the ones that dress their mannequins like hookers and make you want to keep Lily under lock and key? . . . A lot of the clothes they peddle are made in sweatshops in L.A. The fashion companies know about it, but they don't give a rat's ass. So long as they keep feeding American teens a fad a week, they see it as the cost of doing business." What does this revelation say about the label "Made in the USA"? Does it surprise you that worker abuse is rife in fast fashion garment production in the United States? What, if anything, do you think should be done about it?

3. What were your initial impressions of Cameron at the beginning of the story? How did those impressions change as his investigation proceeded and

he began to advocate for internal change? At what point did you realize that he was Josh's source? How did that realization affect your feelings toward Cameron? At the end of the story, what were your final impressions of him, both as a business executive and as a man?

4. Cameron's decision to betray his company in order to save it is a profound one. The risks are monumental. If the lawsuit goes to trial, he will almost certainly be exposed. If the case destroys Presto, he will go down with it. If Josh fails to keep his identity secret, he will have to flee the country and live in exile or face massive fines and jail time. Cameron is a master strategist, but he isn't delusional. He knows there are variables beyond his control. What compels him to make such an extraordinary gamble? How much is his decision influenced by his ideals? By his guilt over Presto's complicity in the suffering of Sonia, Jashel, and Alya, among others? By his culpability in Olivia's death? By the connection he feels to his ancestor, Cornelius, and his failed quest for reparations? By his desire, as a son, to do something that would make his father proud?

5. In their independent investigations overseas, Cameron and Josh discover all manner of worker abuse, corporate complicity, and even criminal behavior within Presto's apparel supply chains. In Bangladesh, bottom-tier factories like Millennium are inherently dangerous to workers like Nasima and Sonia. In Malaysia, even in the best factories, some foreign workers like Jashel are hired under false pretenses and forced to work without pay for years. In the worst factories, workers are treated like beasts of burden. In Jordan, female garment workers like Alya are sexually abused by their supervisors. How do these discoveries make you feel about the clothes you are wearing right now? What do you think should be done to improve the rights and treatment of garment workers in the developing world? Should brands like Presto make more clothing in countries where legal protections for workers are stronger? What role should governments and labor unions play?

6. After the filing of the lawsuit and the dueling press conferences, Josh and friends from the *Washington Post* visit a Presto superstore in the rush before Black Friday. Josh interviews a diverse array of shoppers, all of whom have different opinions about the allegations and what relevance, if any, they have to the shoppers' buying decisions. What did you feel about these exchanges, particularly the final exchange between Alisa and Donna? Have you ever wondered whether the products you buy—clothing or otherwise—are ethically made? How does that concern affect your decisions as a consumer?

ABOUT THE AUTHOR

Photo by Micah Kandros

Corban Addison is the international bestselling author of *A Walk Across the Sun*, *The Garden of Burning Sand*, and *The Tears of Dark Water*, winner of the 2016 Wilbur Smith Adventure Writing Award. His work has been published in twenty countries. *A Harvest of Thorns* is his fourth novel. An attorney, activist, and world traveler, he is a supporter of human rights and social justice causes around the world. He lives with his wife and children in Virginia.

Visit the author's website at corbanaddison.com
Facebook: CorbanAddison
Twitter: @CorbanAddison